D0928931

Also by Anna Jacobs

THE ELLINDALE SAGA
One Quiet Woman

THE RIVENSHAW SAGA
A Time to Remember
A Time for Renewal
A Time to Rejoice
Gifts For Our Time

THE TRADERS
The Trader's Wife
The Trader's Sister
The Trader's Dream
The Trader's Gift
The Trader's Reward

THE SWAN RIVER SAGA
Farewell to Lancashire
Beyond the Sunset
Destiny's Path

THE GIBSON FAMILY
Salem Street
High Street
Ridge Hill
Hallam Square
Spinners Lake

THE IRISH SISTERS
A Pennyworth of Sunshine
Twopenny Rainbows
Threepenny Dreams

THE STALEYS
Down Weavers Lane
Calico Road

THE KERSHAW SISTERS
Our Lizzie
Our Polly
Our Eva
Our Mary Ann

THE SETTLERS
Lancashire Lass
Lancashire Legacy

THE PRESTON FAMILY
Pride of Lancashire
Star of the North
Bright Day Dawning
Heart of the Town

LADY BINGRAM'S
AIDES
Tomorrow's Promises
Yesterday's Girl

STANDALONE NOVELS
Jessie
Like No Other
Freedom's Land

ANNA JACOBS

One Kind Man

Ellindale Saga Book Two

HODDER

First published in Great Britain in 2018 by Hodder & Stoughton
An Hachette UK company

This paperback edition published in 2018

1

A CIP catalogue record for this title is available from the British Library

Paperback ISBN 978 1 473 63087 1

Typeset in Plantin Light by Palimpsest Book Production Limited,
Falkirk, Stirlingshire

Printed and bound in Great Britain by Clays Ltd, St Ives plc

Hodder & Stoughton policy is to use papers that are natural, renewable and
recyclable products and made from wood grown in sustainable forests. The logging
and manufacturing processes are expected to conform to the environmental
regulations of the country of origin.

Hodder & Stoughton Ltd
Carmelite House
50 Victoria Embankment
London EC4Y 0DZ

www.hodder.co.uk

Dear readers

I hope you enjoy my new series, set further up an imaginary Pennine valley from Rivenshaw in a tiny village I've called Ellindale. The stories are set during the early 1930s. How I enjoyed researching that era in more detail!

If you're interested in what England was really like in the 1930s, try reading J. B. Priestley's *English Journey*. He went round England and wrote about what he saw in a most entertaining manner, thus providing me with a great research resource. Thank you, Mr Priestley!

One of the things that inspired me to write historical novels in the first place was the sense of history I grew up with. There were a lot of older people in our family, since one grandma was one of twelve children, her husband one of seven and the other grandmother one of four. The tales they used to tell fascinated me. The final grandfather would never talk about his family and I don't remember meeting any of them. You have to wonder why!

I'm fortunate enough now to be custodian of the family photos and I knew most of the people in them, even though I might not have known them when they were young. I love to look at them, and study not only the costumes but the expressions on their faces.

I shan't share the photo of my great-grandfather with you (1860s) as he's one of the scariest looking men I've ever seen with a great big dark beard. He has such a fierce expression that as a child I didn't like the photo.

Later I found out that in those days you had to stay perfectly still for over a minute to be photographed.

Hard to do that and keep a pleasant expression on your face. Just try to smile happily at a camera for a minute and a half without moving and you'll see what I mean!

You might like to meet my great aunt and great-grandmother, though. The photo with the long dress and towering hairdo from the early 1900s is my Great Auntie Peg – my father's favourite aunt on his mother's side. She didn't have any children, but she was happily married and she certainly led an interesting and fashionable life. She remained lively right till she died in her early 80s. In her 70s she dyed her hair bright red for a couple of years for the fun of it. It looked awful, but she didn't care. She'd look at herself in the mirror and fall about laughing.

In great contrast is my great-grandmother, Ann Wild, my maternal grandfather's mother. He was one of her seven children. She was a quiet, gentle woman, rather like the heroine of the first Ellindale story. I still have her blouse from the late 19th century and it's incredibly intricate. No one would have the time to make such an elaborate blouse these days. It's one of my treasures.

I hope you enjoyed these tastes of 'real history' as well as my historical fiction that's based on such research. I'll end this letter by wishing you a happy visit to Ellindale. My great-grandmother and other Gibson ancestors are buried in a very similar village called Cross Stones near Todmorden. The little cemetery (not used now) lies above the village on the very edge of a windswept moor. It's a fascinating place to visit.

The characters in this story are as near to the Lancashire people in my family as I could manage in the way they face the ups and downs of life, and look after their family members. I hope you enjoy meeting them.

This story is for my wonderful husband.
Dave is one of the kindest people I've ever met and
that gave me the idea for the hero's character.
Thank you, Dave, for the many extremely happy years
and latterly, this story idea.

I

Lancashire: 1931

Alexander Finlay Carlisle, more often known as Finn these days, picked up the letter that had taken a while to catch up with him and cursed under his breath when he saw the address embossed on the back of the envelope. It showed a firm of lawyers, the ones who usually handled his family's affairs, the few there were these days because he came from the poorer side.

He wasn't sure he wanted to read it because there was only one close family member left who might want to contact him and he didn't want to deal with his cousin. He turned the envelope round and round in his fingers, looking at Sergeant Deemer, who had passed the letter on to him. 'I could wish you'd thrown this in the fire. Couldn't we . . . lose it?'

'I'm afraid not, Finn lad. The District Inspector forwarded it and asked me to make personally sure you received it. Took me a while to find you, though. What were you doing in Edinburgh of all places?'

'I was doing a small job for someone, finding a lost daughter.' Finn sighed as he looked at the letter again. He'd tried to leave his past behind him, and had managed to do that for a few years, but it seemed to be catching up with him again.

The only way to have completely avoided this would have been to emigrate, he supposed, but he could never have done that. He'd been born in Lancashire and kept wanting to come back here, even now. It was *home*: grey skies and rain, soft sweet drinking water, wind across the moors, drystone walls, small mill towns clinging to the sides of valleys and, above all, friendly people who weren't as afraid to chat to their so-called betters as some rather meeker folk he'd met on his travels in other parts of the country.

'Oh, well.' Taking a deep breath, he slit the envelope neatly along the top with his penknife. He didn't like doing things in messy, clumsy ways, but his fancy paperknife was stored in a friend's barn with the rest of the possessions from his previous life. He was only just beginning to think of retrieving them.

He folded the blade of the penknife back into its case, looking at it with fond approval. He'd used that clever little knife for many purposes while he tramped the roads of England, trying to walk himself into a new life but gradually realising that he'd been running away from the place where his sadness might heal more easily.

He'd stopped running now, so he'd better stop fiddling around and damned well deal with this letter. He pulled it out of the envelope. It was typed on the very best notepaper, which felt silky smooth beneath his fingertips and crackled faintly when he spread it out. It was dated nearly three months ago.

> *Linton and Galliford*
> *Drake Street*
> *Rochdale*

> *20th May, 1931*

Dear Mr Carlisle,
  We regret to inform you that your great-uncle, Oscar Dearden, has passed away. He appointed us as his lawyers and executors of his will many years ago.
  It's my pleasure to tell you that he has left all he owned

*to you, which includes a property near Rivenshaw. You are
the only nephew he recognises, since he disowned his half-
sister's son, Digby Mersham, many years ago.*

*We have had some difficulty finding you, and I'm afraid
the death occurred some months ago, on the 10th of August
last year to be precise, with the funeral two weeks later.*

*You were sighted in Rivenshaw recently and Inspector
Utting informs us that you have been returning to the area
intermittently to assist your former colleagues in the police
force, so we have some hope that this letter will reach you
sooner or later.*

*We respectfully request that you come to see us at our
rooms in Rochdale at your earliest convenience. We will then
give you full details of the bequest, arrange the transfer of
all necessary goods and chattels, and hand over the smaller
items, including keys, that were in your uncle's possession
when he died.*

Yours faithfully,
George Linton,
Senior Partner

Finn reread the letter, but it gave no details of what exactly
had been left to him. He vaguely remembered meeting his
father's elderly uncle a couple of times when he was a youngster, and remembered that Oscar Dearden owned a house
somewhere on the edge of the moors, but had no idea why
the man would leave anything to him.

And fancy Uncle Oscar living near Rivenshaw, of all places!
Finn had spent a few weeks there earlier in the year, doing
a job for the local police force. It was a nice little town at
the lower end of a long, narrow Pennine valley.

He turned to his companion. 'Do you know somewhere
called Heythorpe House, Sergeant Deemer? It's supposed to
be near Rivenshaw.'

'The name seems familiar, but I can't quite place it. I mustn't have had anything to do with its owner because once I've visited a place, I never forget it. It'll be out in the country somewhere.'

It was good that this hadn't happened until now, Finn thought. He was ready to settle down again, though he didn't intend to marry – not again, never ever again! But if his great-uncle had left him a little money, it'd come in handy in the peaceful life he was planning to lead.

There couldn't be very much involved in this bequest or his former father-in-law would have known about it. The man had been very skilled at sniffing out money and had been furious at his daughter for marrying a mere policeman who brought very little of it into the family.

But Ivy hadn't cared for that. She had fallen in love with Finn as quickly as he had with her.

Deemer cleared his throat and Finn looked up, swallowing the hard lump that came into his throat sometimes still when he thought of his late wife. 'Sorry. I was daydreaming. It seems I've been left a small inheritance.'

At his sigh, Deemer raised one eyebrow in the way he had when questioning something. 'That's good news, surely?'

'I suppose so. It's taken me by surprise. I'd forgotten my father's Uncle Oscar, because he was a recluse and I hadn't seen or heard about him since I was a child.'

'Well, it's good timing if you've just finished a job. This will give you something to move on to, lad.'

He liked the way Deemer called him 'lad' and acted half the time as if he was an honorary uncle. It was Deemer who had first offered him one of the little jobs that had helped him start to put a decent life together again and stop wandering aimlessly.

He studied the letterhead. 'I'd better go to the Post Office and telephone these lawyers, hadn't I?'

'Use the phone here. Inspector Utting can't object, because he was the one who forwarded the letter and asked me to deal with it.'

Finn took a deep breath and made the phone call. The clerk he spoke to said Mr Linton was with a client, but gave him an appointment for the following morning.

Well, he could wait another day to find out what his great-uncle had left him. He was tired after travelling back from Edinburgh and would go to bed early.

The following day, Finn made the journey by train, annoyed that he had to go into Manchester and out again to get there, since there was no direct branch line connecting Rivenshaw to Rochdale. Well, this was a small town and Rochdale was much larger.

It would have been much easier to get there by motor car. Once he had a job, he intended to save up and buy himself one, a second-hand Austin Swallow or something like that. Maybe, if he was lucky, his uncle would have left him enough to buy some modest vehicle.

Grey skies made Rochdale look bleak and it was chilly for August, so Finn walked briskly down towards the town centre from the station to warm himself up. It was easy to find the lawyers' rooms because Drake Street was on his way.

George Linton was grey-haired and plump. He greeted Finn briskly and wasted little time in civilities, so Finn decided it must be a small, unimportant bequest.

'Your uncle has left you a house,' the lawyer began.

Finn stared at him in shock. '*A house?* What sort of house?'

'Quite a large one, but it's been neglected for a good many years because he inherited it from an elderly cousin and never lived there. It's near Rivenshaw, as I said in my letter, but in fact he preferred to stay in his comfortable lodgings in Rochdale. He enjoyed reading, so visited the library frequently, and went to the theatre both in Rochdale and Manchester.'

'Was he married?'

'No. He preferred to remain a bachelor and indeed, his landlady told my clerk he never had a visitor in all the years he was with her. A very solitary type of gentleman, your late uncle.'

'Where exactly is the house? The police sergeant in Rivenshaw who passed on your letter hadn't heard of it.'

'It's not *in* Rivenshaw but near it. If I understand correctly, there's a long valley with the town at the lowest point, a large village called Birch End part way up the slope and a small village called Ellindale at the upper end, just about on the moors. Your house is in Ellindale and I gather there's only one other house further up the valley.'

'Good heavens! I spent some time in the district earlier this year, so I've already seen the house, though only in the distance as it's half-hidden from the road.'

'Well, that makes my job easier. I won't need to explain anything else about the location to you.'

Finn tried to pull himself together. The last thing he'd expected was to inherit a house, and for it to be in Ellindale made him feel good because he liked the village and its people. It was a rather special place.

'He has left you some money as well. It's invested and brings in enough to live on if you're careful.'

'Money too!' Finn shook his head, finding all this unreal, as if he was in a dream. 'I didn't know my great-uncle was well off.'

'In a modest way. You mustn't think you've inherited a large fortune.'

'I didn't expect to inherit anything. Is that all?'

'There are the contents of the house, of course. It's apparently fully furnished still, because when your great-uncle inherited it, he simply locked the house up and walked away.

He told me it could stay like that for all he cared, because he preferred to live in the lodgings where he was so comfortable. I believe he had some maintenance work done occasionally on the house to keep it weatherproof, but never went there himself.'

'Good heavens! My father said his Uncle Oscar was a strange fellow and always had been. It was known in the family that even as a child, he preferred to be on his own and hated to have his daily routines disturbed. They were relieved that his strangeness wasn't, um, troublesome to other people.'

'That fits with what his landlady told my clerk when he went to collect your uncle's personal belongings. An ideal tenant, she called him, no trouble, never made a noise.'

The lawyer pushed a leather satchel across his desk. 'These are the contents of his pockets and of the desk in his lodgings. We took it upon ourselves to return some library books, but there are quite a few other books and papers, which we have stored here in our cellar. We can send them on to you once you've settled in.'

'Thank you.'

'Do you have any questions?'

'No. Do you think there's anything else I need to know?'

Mr Linton steepled his hands together, wrinkling his brow. 'I can think of nothing else. We only saw your great-uncle twice, once when he came to make his will and once when he came to sign it and make a statutory declaration that nothing was to go to his other great-nephew. If you had died or weren't found after five years of searching, everything was to go to a children's charity of some sort.'

He pushed a folder of papers towards Finn. 'This contains a copy of the will and a list of what's in the satchel. If you wish to check it before you sign for it, my clerk will find you some desk space in the outer office.' He looked across at the elegant gilt clock on his mantelpiece. 'Unfortunately I have another appointment shortly.'

'No need to check it, I'm sure. Where do I sign?' He didn't really care what was in the satchel, after all.

'Here. Thank you.'

Finn scrawled his signature with the expensive modern fountain pen that was handed to him. He might buy himself one of those. It wrote beautifully.

'There's one more thing we need to do: get your uncle's bank account transferred to you. My chief clerk will take you to the bank now, if you like. It's not far from here.'

As he walked out, Finn felt literally heavier, as if he had entered the lawyer's rooms a free spirit and come out loaded with possessions and responsibilities. Which was foolish, really. Because he'd also come out with enough money to live on and a home to live in. It was very timely. Perhaps he felt strange because he wasn't used to being lucky.

But what sort of home would it be if it hadn't been lived in for years? From the way people in Ellindale had talked, the house was in a tumbledown state.

And how would he spend his time if he settled in a small village? The only thing he was certain of was that he didn't want to go back into the police force, even though he'd enjoyed helping out with one or two small jobs.

In fact, he had no idea what to do with the rest of his life, only that he wanted it to be worthwhile.

And he wasn't going to marry again. No one could replace Ivy.

The farm cart creaked its way slowly up the hill from Rivenshaw and the old man driving it glanced back over his shoulder to see whether the lass was still breathing. She'd been so weak when they laid her in his cart, poor thing, that he'd wondered how long she'd survive.

Yes, she was breathing. She was a fighter, Lily Pendle was. He'd known her since she was a little lass and she hadn't had an easy life.

When he got to the village of Ellindale he breathed a sigh of relief. No need to ask the way to the shop run by Nancy Buckley. It was such a small village there was only one shop and one pub too. He'd have a wet of ale at The Shepherd's Rest before he started back, while his old mare Betty had a good feed and a drink from the horse trough outside the pub.

He drew up just as a woman was about to go into the shop, so he left the reins lying. His horse was old, like him, and tired. She wouldn't budge for a good while. 'Excuse me, missus. Is this Mrs Buckley's shop? Good. Could you please ask her to come out and help me? Only I've brought her cousin's lass, who's sick, and I can't carry Lily in on my own.'

The woman nodded and went quickly inside.

'Nancy, there's an old man outside with a sick young woman on his cart and he says she's your cousin's lass.'

'*What?*'

Nancy was out from behind the counter in a flash, running out of the door.

The customer put her basket down, wedged the doorstop in place and went to see if she could help.

'Ah, there you are, Nancy. You never change,' the old man said. 'I've brought your cousin Roland's lass. Lily needs looking after. Her mother just died and the poor girl is as weak as a kitten.'

'Is it something catching? Only I've a shop to run.'

'No. The two of them have been trying to manage with nowt to eat but the odd piece of bread. What the government is doing letting decent people starve to death, I don't understand. Mean, that is. Does it think folk don't *want* to find work? They're as hungry for work as for food, poor souls, but there isn't much of either around these days.'

Nancy was already clambering up on to the back of the cart. 'She has a look of my cousin. Not many people have such silvery-blond hair.' She stroked it back gently. 'Well, let's get her inside.'

'You'll have to help me. I'm getting a bit old for carrying folk. Only no one else had the time to drive her all this way. I reckoned if she was left without help for another day or two, we'd have been too late to save her. You have to *tend* someone who's this weak, build up their strength again. So me and my old mare brought her to you.'

The customer joined them. 'Let me help carry her, Mr . . . ?' She looked at him enquiringly.

'Trutton. Sidney Trutton.'

The woman turned to the shopkeeper. 'Why don't you go and get ready for her, Nancy? Mr Trutton and I will carry her in.'

'Thanks, Leah. Don't try to take her upstairs. She'll have to lie on my couch, so that I can nip in and out of the shop to serve my customers as well as keep an eye on her.'

It wasn't until the young woman had been taken through to the back room that Nancy thought to ask, 'How did you come to be helping her, Mr Trutton?'

'I'm a neighbour of theirs in Martons End. It's only a little village so you won't know it but it's near Netherholme on the other side of Rivenshaw.'

'I do remember Martons End slightly, but I was only a child when I went there.'

'Well, then. You know how small the place is. Even I didn't know how bad things were for them. Mrs Pendle allus kept herself to herself after her husband went, you see. Our farm is outside the village. The farm belongs to my grandson now, because my son died at Ypres and *I* can't manage the heavy work, not at my age.'

'I'm grateful to you, Mr Trutton. Very grateful indeed. Did Lily's mother really die of starvation?'

'Yes, missus.'

'I'd have taken them food myself if I'd known.'

'So would other folk. But Mrs Pendle were too proud to ask for help, an' she starved her poor daughter along with herself. By the time Lily defied her and came to us for help, her mother were nobbut a skeleton and she died quick as that.'

He snapped his fingers to illustrate the point, then went on, 'False pride, I call that. As if folk wouldn't have spared the odd crust. Look how you're taking this lass in without hesitating.'

'These are hard times,' Nancy said with a sigh. 'I haven't seen my cousin for years. Roland should have come to me for help if he needed it. I suppose he died first. When was that?'

The old man sighed. 'He didn't *die*. Runned off, he did, a few years ago now, with a woman from the village.'

'Roland did? Good heavens. I'd never have thought it of him.'

'Well, his missus were a hard woman to live with, I'll grant him that, though you shouldn't speak ill of the dead. But he give her his promise in church and should have kept it.'

'Who was the woman he ran off with?'

'A neighbour. She left three little kids behind. Shame on the pair of them, I say. Selfish to the core. I heard tell they were going to Australia, but no one ever found out whether they got there or not. Lily had a live-in job as a maid when her father ran off and could send most of her wages home to her ma, but the family she worked for lost their money earlier this year and had to sack all their servants.'

He sighed. 'Mrs Pendle wasn't well by then an' she needed someone to look after her, so Lily came home. A nice lass, she is, pretty too when she has a bit of flesh on her bones.'

He lingered for a cup of tea and it was a while before Leah could get him on his way. He was still talking as he climbed up on to the cart.

'My grandson says he'll clear the house and put their things in our barn. Plenty of room there. Though there's not a lot left because they had to sell stuff to live.'

'That's very kind of you.'

'Don't lose my address now.'

'No, I won't.'

'Give the lass my best wishes.'

'I will.' Smiling, Leah watched him go. He'd probably be talking to himself all the way back to his family farm. Ah! Now, he'd stopped at The Shepherd's Rest. Well, who could blame him?

Nice old man, but did he ever stop talking?

She turned to Nancy. 'I hope Lily gets better soon. Now, I need to finish my shopping and get home. I haven't seen my little sister for ages, not to chat to. If I'm not busy, she's up in her room studying.'

'Your Rosa's a nice lass, quiet like you, but pleasant to everyone. You're doing a good job of mothering her.'

'I hope so. I've been looking after her since our mother died. Goodness, that was over eight years ago now. She's growing up so quickly.'

Lily Pendle opened her eyes and stared round, not recognising the room or the woman hovering nearby. 'Where am I? Who are you?'

'I'm your cousin Nancy and this is my house. Mr Trutton brought you to me in his cart. You were unconscious when we carried you in.'

It took a few moments for the words to make sense, then

Lily studied the woman. 'Are you really our Cousin Nancy? My father used to talk about you. You visited one another's families sometimes when you were children.'

'We did. We'll talk about our families later, though. I think the main thing is to get some food into you. Do you think you could start with a drink of milk?'

Lily could feel herself blushing in embarrassment at being so needy. She couldn't even take the glass herself because she was too weak to hold it safely.

'Let me help you with that, dear. Just sip the milk slowly. How long since you've eaten?'

'Two days, I think. Or was it three?'

'And before that?'

'I don't remember. We haven't been eating properly for a while. There was no money after I lost my job, you see, and my mother wouldn't accept charity. She was so fierce about it, so sure we could manage till I got another job. But how could I leave her? She was weaker than she would admit.'

She added bitterly, 'When my employer went bankrupt, he couldn't even give us servants the wages we were owed and you can't eat a character reference, can you? That was so unfair of him because he paid all the tradesmen. Why couldn't he have shared the money out among everyone he owed?'

She sipped again. 'My mother was so *stubborn*. There were no more small items left to sell or pawn, you see, and she had no way of taking the bigger pieces of furniture to the pawnshop without people seeing what was happening – as if they didn't know! – so she refused to do it.'

'Of all the stupid, false pride!' Nancy exclaimed involuntarily.

'I agree. I was going to have it out with her, only I found her dead in her bed that very morning. They took her body away and gave her a pauper's funeral. She'd have hated that but I didn't have any way of paying for a proper funeral.'

She paused, gathering the strength to finish her tale. 'I got soaked at her funeral and then had to walk two miles home. I fell ill and I don't remember much after that.' She paused again, weak from the effort of talking. 'I was feverish and calling out, I think. Someone must have heard me.'

The glass was empty now and her kind cousin patted her hand a couple of times as if offering comfort. And it was comforting.

A bell clanged and Lily turned her head slightly. 'What's that?'

'This is a shop and that's the doorbell. I have to go and serve a customer. I'll be back soon. It's not a busy time, so we can get you settled and find something for you to eat in a while. Why don't you have a little doze?'

She bustled out and Lily closed her eyes. There was the sound of voices in the next room, but she couldn't be bothered to listen. She was so very weary.

Her cousin was lovely, so kind.

Maybe I'm not going to die after all, she thought as she snuggled down.

When Nancy had finished serving two customers and went into the back room again, she found her young cousin sleeping, a little frown creasing Lily's forehead.

Roland Pendle, what were you thinking of to run away and leave them? She stared down at the gaunt young face and lank hair, with just a few short wisps showing its true colour. It sounded as if her cousin's wife died of starvation, and this poor girl might follow her mother if she couldn't regain her strength.

'Well, she's not going to die if I can help it,' Nancy muttered aloud.

What that lass needed to build up her strength was a good hearty broth. You couldn't beat it. She'd have to send down to Birch End for some stock bones and stewing beef, but there were always people around to run errands for a penny or two. She'd had the telephone put in, but telephones couldn't carry shopping back, could they?

She went and looked out of the shop door for someone just as Tom Dotton was slouching past. He hadn't had a job for a year or two, poor man, and had trouble filling the empty hours each day.

'Like to earn threepence?' she asked.

He brightened up immediately. 'You know I would, Nancy. Any time.'

'I'll pay you to walk into Birch End and get me something from the butcher's.'

It cheered her up to see how he straightened his shoulders at the prospect of earning even such a small amount.

'Come in and I'll get my purse. A shilling's worth of good beef stock bones is what I want, and half a pound of stewing beef. Here.' She took out a few broken biscuit pieces. 'To help you on your way.'

He sighed at needing her handout but took the biscuits. 'I'll pay you back one day for helping me, Nancy. Even a few pence can make a big difference to feeding the kids.'

'Get on with you. You're running an errand for me. That's not charity, but you doing a job in return for payment. My niece has just arrived to stay and she's been ill. She needs feeding up and the sooner the better, so come back as quickly as you can.'

She watched him take a bite of a biscuit as he set off down the hill and wished she could do more for him. But she didn't have much money to spare herself. If it hadn't been for the hikers who bought refreshments from her shop on fine weekends, she'd not have had any pennies to spare to pay people to run errands. Or to get the telephone put in. She was still unsure whether that was too extravagant, but she could always have it taken out again.

Eh, the folk in her village were having a hard time of it, they were that, and it was the same all over Lancashire, if the tales in the newspapers were true. Were it not for people round here helping one another whenever they could, even in small ways, some of them would be in the same state as that poor lass.

But they did help one another in Ellindale. It was a good place to live. You couldn't find a better village in the whole of Lancashire.

2

When he looked at the papers the lawyer had given him, Finn found a neat summary of his inheritance. He was astonished at how much money there was in Uncle Oscar's bank account. The lawyer might consider it an insignificant amount, but it seemed a very nice sum indeed to him.

Also, there was an income coming in every half-year from the investments, even now when times were hard, though not nearly as much as it would be in better times. How had his great-uncle accumulated and kept so much money? They weren't a rich family.

He couldn't speak for a moment or two as the realisation really sank in that he need never work again if he didn't want to. No one else in his immediate family had ever had enough to live on without working, not that he knew of anyway, though he was from decent stock.

The Carlisles were the sort of people whose breadwinner brought in enough money for food, clothes, one general maid perhaps, and the decencies of life, as long as they were careful. In the old days they'd not been 'carriage folk' and these days they didn't usually aspire to own a motor car, either.

Finn's own family was one of the poorer branches of the Dearden-Carlisle tree, so the money meant even more to him. His father had been old when he was born and as the years passed, he'd often struggled to carry on working. All Finn had wanted as he grew up was to go into the police force and help maintain law and order.

It was only later, after his parents died, that he'd realised how hard his mother had worked to keep the house nice, all on her own with only a weekly scrubbing woman. On top of that, his father had expected her to wait on him hand and foot when he came home from work as a clerk.

It had seemed such a worthwhile thing to do, going into the police force, but after the death of his young wife, together with the unborn infant she was carrying, nothing had seemed worthwhile. Finn had loved Ivy dearly and they'd been happy together in a quiet way.

After he'd buried them, he couldn't see the worth of bothering to get on in the world when everything you cared about could be taken away from you at the drop of a hat. Ivy had died because of a little-known complication of pregnancy. The child would have been a son they'd told him, but he cared far more about losing his wife. Dear, sweet Ivy.

He cut off those thoughts. He mustn't sink into misery again. His father had told him regularly that he was too soft. He didn't agree. He could stand up for himself when necessary but he didn't see the point of getting into fights and always wanting to outdo other people, like the cousin who hadn't inherited from Great-uncle Oscar.

Finn's mother had taught him to help people and he preferred her way of looking at the world to his father's, wished she was still alive to comfort him.

After the first shock of Ivy's death, he'd decided he needed time to get over the unfairness of it all, hence leaving the police force and going off on the tramp. It had taken a while for him to see the world without that haze of anger colouring everything. But gradually, as time passed, he'd adjusted to life on his own.

He shook off those sad thoughts and let the lawyer's clerk take him to the bank, where Finn arranged to transfer the money to an account in his own name and base it at the Rivenshaw branch, the nearest to his inheritance.

After that, the clerk went back to work and Finn bought a pie from a bakery, sitting at a little table in the corner of the shop, with a cup of tea to wash it down before starting his journey back.

As the train chugged along, stopping at every single village, it occurred to him that he could definitely afford to buy a motor car now. That lifted his spirits considerably, because it would make life a lot easier and anyway, he enjoyed driving, had been taught how in the police force.

He just missed a connection in Manchester, so didn't get back to Rivenshaw until teatime. By then he wasn't at all in the mood to walk several miles up the hill to Ellindale and look over the house. It might not be dark on the way there, but it would be dark inside the house and on the way back.

If he remembered correctly, the village had recently been connected to electricity and a telephone line. He'd have to arrange to have them put in at his house, at least he would if the place was at all suitable to live in. It might be derelict if his uncle had neglected its upkeep. You couldn't see the building from the road up the hill, only part of the roof.

What a day of surprises it had been! And what excellent news! He lay smiling in the darkness until he felt sleep stealing over him, then gave in to it willingly, eager for the morning to come.

Finn woke early, as he always did, and got up immediately the landlady at the small lodging house knocked on his bedroom door. He'd arranged for her to provide him with a simple breakfast at seven o'clock. He ate quickly then went out to catch the early bus she'd told him about that went right up the valley to the top end.

It brought back the schoolchildren from outlying areas to

the grammar schools in Rivenshaw, but there were only a few people riding right up to Ellindale with him at this time of day, most of them clearly hikers. Up on the moors, there were tracks open to everyone, while in the more settled lower areas landowners refused pedestrians access, to protect their young grouse ready for the shooting season.

There had been a lot of fuss about that lately. He'd read about it in the papers. Hikers were saying the countryside should be freely accessible to everyone and were causing trouble. If he'd still been in the police force he'd have hated having to arrest them, because he agreed with them. If you'd been toiling in the mills and workshops, you'd want to fill your lungs with fresh air at weekends.

When he got off the bus, he stood for a moment studying the village with new eyes. Last time he'd just been passing through the valley, doing a job, but now Ellindale was potentially his home.

There were about twenty houses, spaced unevenly along the main street or clinging to the slopes above it in a higgledy-piggledy fashion. In the open area at the centre was a small general store, run by a Mrs Buckley if he remembered correctly. Very useful that would be, if he settled here.

And on the other side of the open area there was a pub, The Shepherd's Rest. He wasn't a boozer, but it was good to have company sometimes and if they kept good beer, he'd enjoy the occasional glass there.

He started up the hill, striding quickly because he was eager to see his house properly. After leaving the village behind, he stopped at the wide gap in the drystone wall that edged the track. As he remembered, there were no gates, or even gate posts, nor was there a sign with a house name, but it could only be Heythorpe House. He knew from his previous visits to the area that there was only Spring Cottage beyond this one, then the moors took over from man.

Just inside the entrance there was a wide, level space about thirty yards in diameter. Weeds were growing there now, but they could soon be removed. It'd have been for horse-drawn vehicles in the old days, but now you could park your car there. If you had one. He beamed at the thought that he'd be able to afford one now. He might have a garage built to one side to put his car in.

He turned slowly on the spot to take it all in. The house and its grounds were below the level of the lane, occupying a piece of more or less level land, which looked as if the narrow valley had bulged out sideways when it was being formed. Beyond the garden on the upper side of the house was hilly ground, with small outcrops of rock near the top edge, millstone grit probably. After that the moors would no doubt take over again.

He couldn't remember seeing any buildings beyond Heythorpe House except Spring Cottage and its outbuildings. He'd call there later to tell Leah and Jonah his news. He'd met them earlier in the year when they'd been attacked by criminals and he'd been helping Sergeant Deemer keep order in the valley. He hoped it would be a peaceful place to live without those villains.

It'd be good to have the Willcoxes as his closest neighbours, and he hoped they'd become good friends. He'd try to make other friends round here, too. He wasn't like his great-uncle Oscar, wanting to live alone.

A footpath led down from the far side of the entrance area, twisting down the gentle slope and splitting to go round the sides of a two-storey building. He could only see the end wall of it from here, but it seemed much bigger than a cottage.

The path was made of crazy paving, but had dead grass and weeds jutting out from the cracks. It not only needed weeding, but he had to walk carefully to avoid tripping over uneven stones. He'd either repair the path himself or pay someone to do it, he decided.

He stopped moving to suck in a sharp breath as it occurred to him that this was the sort of odd job he'd done during his wandering years. How thankful he'd been for the chance to earn a little money. And now he could give employment to someone else in desperate need of work. How wonderful it would be to be able to do that!

Presumably the left path would lead to the front door because there were views down the valley to Rivenshaw from that side. The right path would go to the rear of the house. He turned left but stopped after a couple of steps because for the first time he could see how big the house was. He was surprised at that, shocked, too. How could a house this big belong to him?

The path to the front door was bordered by a tangled mixture of vegetation, both wild and garden plants, with new plants struggling to find a way through the tangles. These must have been flower gardens once. Some plants had still survived without any human help, though, so the soil couldn't be all that bad.

He could learn an important lesson from those gardens. You just had to carry on with what life dished out to you. There would be a lot to do to get things straight again and he'd welcome that. He closed his eyes briefly for a moment as the anguish of a sudden thought hit him: gardens like these would be a perfect place for children to play.

Oh, how the loss could pinch unexpectedly! He'd always liked children.

Taking a deep breath, he went up to the front door. The wood was faded from the weather beating against it, the varnish mainly stripped away. The knocker had been removed, presumably to show in the old-fashioned way that the owners were not in residence.

From what the lawyer had said, his great-uncle hadn't lived here at all after inheriting. Had Oscar even visited it or at least sent someone to check that the house was all right and still weatherproof? Who knew?

Finn took out the bundle of keys he'd been given and had to try three of the larger ones before he found the correct one for the front door. He pulled a neatly rolled length of thick string out of his pocket, took that key off the thin chain holding sixteen others (he'd counted them) and slipped it on to the string, fastening a loose bow to keep it in place. He'd put the keys to the outside doors on the string too for the time being, he decided, once he found out which they were.

He tried to push the front door open, but it was swollen and stiff, and he had to thump against it with his whole body several times to get in. Even then it stuck halfway, so he had to shove with all his might to get it fully open.

His first impression of his new home wasn't good, because it smelled musty and looked to be in a mess. He knew he was tidy to a fault, or so Ivy used to tease. He grimaced at the dust that lay everywhere, more than he'd ever seen in a house before. He left footprints in it as he walked across the parquet floor and avoided touching the cobweb-decked banisters that led upstairs on the right.

He didn't see the cobweb that hung down until it caught in his hair. 'Ugh!' Clawing it off, he wiped his hand on a dusty umbrella in the hallstand for lack of anything else. Nasty sticky things, cobwebs were! Seeing some walking sticks in the hallstand, he took one out and wielded it against stray cobwebs as he moved forward again.

There were doors on either side of the entrance. When he peeped into the room on the right he found heavy curtains drawn so tightly it was hard to see what the room itself was like. There was enough light from the hall to thread his way in and out of the furniture to the window. He drew one curtain back but when he tried to move the other one, it resisted, so he tugged harder. It promptly fell down on him, sending out a cloud of choking dust. He had to fight his way out of its heavy folds, coughing.

'What a welcome!' His voice echoed, sounding eerie.

But at least morning brightness was now flooding in through the window, though the sun wasn't shining directly in, so the front of the house must face west. The room was about six yards square with pieces of furniture dotted here and there, protected by canvas covers. He left them there. He'd bother about what the furniture was like when he knew the lay of the land and was ready to set things in order.

Across the hall was a similar sized room. He pulled the curtains back more carefully this time and though one of the rails sagged, they stayed up. Ah! This was a sort of library, with one wall covered in glass-fronted bookcases. He went across to read the titles, but the glass was dirty and the bookcases were locked.

Another room to look at in more detail later.

He followed the hall to the rear, where once again everything was only dimly lit. As he went round pulling back the curtains, he revealed a dining room, two smaller rooms, then a large kitchen, another room and several pantries and storerooms in a wing that stretched backwards.

Good heavens! Why would anyone need all these store-rooms? The items in them were covered in sheets of old, yellowed newspaper. Another set of things he was reluctant to disturb for the moment.

He peered down the cellar steps but didn't go there. That would be for next time, with a good hand torch or even an oil lamp to light his way. There were lamps in one of the storerooms, but where the oil for them was stored, he didn't know. Anyway, there might not be any left. He'd definitely ask to have the electricity connected.

Upstairs were six bedrooms but no bathrooms. He grimaced again. He'd definitely want bathrooms put in and two of the bedrooms had small dressing rooms attached to them that might serve the purpose.

When he next came to the house, he'd bring a notebook to list the jobs that needed doing. He should have thought of that before.

He debated for a moment or two, then gave in to curiosity and went up some more stairs to the attics. There was enough daylight coming in through the uncurtained dormer windows to find his way around and check for signs of leaks or weather damage. Thank goodness, there were none!

He sneezed violently several times. He needed to go outside and breathe some fresh air to get the dust out of his lungs, he decided.

Perhaps his great-uncle had sent someone to check the roof. Or else the house had been particularly well built. He couldn't see any signs of damage by winter storms, as he'd expected.

What he needed before anything else was an army of cleaners to go right through the house. He'd move in within a day or two if he could find a bed that wasn't damp and buy some provisions.

He'd be able to get more than enough help in the village. Leah Willcox had talked of helping her poorer neighbours in these hungry times. Well, he'd be able to do that too now. First they'd have to clean the house from top to bottom and make it habitable, then . . . then what would he do with his life?

One step at a time, he told himself. In such a large house, he'd still need help with the housekeeping, so that was at least an ongoing job for a cook-housekeeper and maid, and a gardener too.

It felt as if he'd been given a huge gift by fate. Not the money itself so much as what it could buy: a chance to do something worthwhile with his life by helping others. It had been so long since he'd had a real purpose in life.

He looked down at the bundle of keys. He had now found four to outside doors and transferred them to his piece of string. He jiggled it, making them clink, and laughed aloud for sheer happiness.

As he was locking the front door, there was the sound of breaking glass from the other side of the house and a voice crying out in pain. It sounded like a lad's voice.

Without hesitation he ran round to the back, hearing the sound of muffled sobbing from a shed. He went quietly across to see who was there.

The door of the shed was open and a lad was lying on the floor inside with blood pouring out of a bad cut on his upper leg. Glass from the broken window must have sliced right through his trousers.

At the sight of him, the lad let out a moan of sheer terror and cringed back.

'I'm not going to hurt you,' Finn told him. 'But we need to do something about that cut.' He fished out a handkerchief, which was a lot cleaner than the lad's skin, and tied it tightly round the wound on the thigh, then sat back. 'Who are you?'

The way the lad pressed his lips together said he didn't intend to reply.

'If you won't answer, I think you must be hiding from someone.'

'How did you—?' The lad pressed one hand to his mouth, struggling with tears, looking younger suddenly.

Perhaps he wasn't as old as Finn had first thought, a big lad of what, about eleven or twelve? 'I guessed. We'll leave names for the moment because we need to stop that bleeding. I've not moved into this house of mine yet so there's nothing to wash the cut with here except dusty cloths. I'll take you up the road to Spring Cottage. I know the people there and I'm sure they'll be happy to help.'

He studied the lad, frowning. 'Hmm. I don't think you should walk or you'll set the bleeding off again, so let's see if I can carry you. If not, I'll bring help back.'

'I don't want anyone to know I'm here. Please don't give me away, mister. My leg will be all right.'

Finn had enough experience of lads to know there would be no reasoning with this one unless he could be persuaded that he was safe here. 'Then tell me what you're doing in my garden.'

The lad stared at him, realised he wasn't going to back down, and said, 'When my dad died, they put me in the children's home, and the man there beats us nearly every day. He enjoys hurting people. So I ran away. I wasn't going to stay and be beaten. My dad never hit me like that, with a whip, never, only a quick slap if I was naughty. It's left marks on my back, and I won't go back to that place whatever you say.'

'Show me the marks.'

After a doubtful look, he let Finn uncover his back, which was both bruised and scarred from beatings. One cut was recent and oozing pus. The lad definitely wasn't telling lies. How could anyone whip a child so severely?

He helped the boy to fasten up the shirt. 'I promise I won't send you back to a place that does that sort of thing to children. Will you tell me your name now?'

'Reggie.' He looked at Finn apprehensively.

He didn't press for a surname. 'I'm Finn Carlisle. Now, first things first, let's get your leg properly cleaned and bandaged, then we'll work out what to do with you.' He held up one hand as the lad opened his mouth to speak. 'I promise faithfully I won't send you back.'

Reggie studied him, then nodded slowly, as if the man had passed some test.

Finn picked the lad up, expecting him to weigh a lot more than he did. He was all skin and bone and must have been going hungry for a while to get this thin, he thought angrily.

Finn was big and secretly proud of his strength, but he doubted he could carry the lad all the way to Spring Cottage, so he set him down on a bench and went to find a wheelbarrow. Luckily there was one in a shed, old but it seemed still to work.

'Here we are! Your carriage awaits!' he said cheerfully.

There was the faint hint of a smile in response. Good. Lads shouldn't look so downtrodden and despairing.

He lifted the boy into the barrow. 'Cheer up. I'll look after you.'

That got him a frown and an assessing stare. 'How?'

'I don't know yet, but I'll find a way.'

Another assessing look, followed by a nod, then the lad took hold of the sides of the wheelbarrow as it jolted along.

3

The squeaking of the wheelbarrow brought people out of Spring Cottage and the huge old barn nearby before Finn had done more than move past the neat blue and white sign on the perimeter wall saying *Ellindale Spring Mineral Waters*. That was new.

He wrestled the old wheelbarrow through the gateway and past another sign, this time on the end wall of the barn: *Ellindale Spring Youth Hostel.*

An older woman wrapped in a large, faded pinafore dress, came to the cottage door, wiping her hands on a small towel. Before he could go across to her for help, Leah Willcox, who was also wearing a large protective wrap-around pinafore, came out of the central doorway of the barn. She was accompanied by a man Finn didn't recognise, but as he was wearing a white overall, he was presumably working there.

There was an air of bustle and life about the place, so different from the slow-moving lethargy usually exhibited by people in depressed areas. Finn had known that Jonah's wife was going to manufacture and sell ginger beer, and was pleased to see signs of progress in that venture. He hoped it would be successful in creating jobs for the folk of Ellindale – his village now, he realised in mild surprise.

'Hello, Leah,' he called. 'Remember me?'

'Of course I do, Finn.'

'I found this injured lad down at Heythorpe House and

brought him here for help, since there was nothing there to dress his wound with.'

That brought her hurrying across to check the boy's leg. 'That's a bad cut. Bring him inside straight away. Mrs Dutton, could we have some boiled water, please?'

The other woman vanished into the house and Finn was about to wheel Reggie inside when Leah touched his arm and whispered, 'Jonah's been ill with a heavy cold. Try not to show your shock at how bad he looks. He's a lot better than he was.'

Her husband, who was one of those unfortunate men gassed in the war, was lying on a sofa in front of the fire looking like a pale ghost of himself. When he stood up to greet the visitors, he moved slowly, but he greeted them cheerfully.

Finn carried Reggie inside and explained the problem.

'Let's have a look.' Jonah bent over the leg to check the injury, seeming to know what he was doing. 'It's deep and needs stitching. You'll have to take him to the doctor's in Rivenshaw.'

Reggie sent Finn a look of frantic appeal.

'Do you think that's absolutely necessary? I don't have a car and the boy can't walk far.'

'It's necessary if you want the skin to heal properly. It must be stitched carefully into place because he's still growing and it might pull later. Leah can drive you down there in our car. All right, love?'

She nodded and went to call across the yard, 'Stan? Will you keep an eye on the brew and carry on cleaning the rest of the bottles? I'm sure I can trust you to get them perfectly clean. I don't know how long I'll be. We have to take this boy to the doctor.'

As she came inside and began to slip out of the damp pinafore and put on a hat and coat, Reggie sighed and closed his eyes, looking white and weary.

'What are you doing up at the top end of the valley, Finn?' Jonah asked. 'Another job for Sergeant Deemer?'

'Not this time. Um, actually, I've just inherited Heythorpe House.'

They all stared at him in surprise, then Leah said, 'Congratulations. We'll be very happy to have you as a neighbour. I'll just phone the doctor's.'

'You didn't say you had relatives in the valley,' Jonah said.

'I'd only met Uncle Oscar as a child and wasn't sure where he lived. He never actually lived here, just left the house empty when his relative died and he inherited it. The legacy came as a complete surprise to me. Today is the first time I've even seen the place.' He gestured to the lad. 'Good thing I was there to help poor Reggie.'

'What was he doing there on a weekday, playing hooky from school?'

Reggie sent another terrified look at Finn, who replied smoothly, 'He needed help quickly. His parents died a few months ago and when he heard I was coming here, he came to look for me. He, um, regards me as an honorary uncle.'

Leah rejoined them. 'I've just phoned Dr Mitchell. His wife says he's taking morning surgery and since it's an emergency, he'll look at Reggie's wound as soon as we arrive.'

By this time the lad was looking so panic-stricken Finn laid a hand on his shoulder, murmuring, 'It'll be all right.' After the lad's back, he definitely wasn't going to send a helpless orphaned child back to endure further brutal treatment. But what was he going to do with Reggie?

The answer seemed to float into Finn's mind. *He could take the lad in himself.*

The more he thought about it, the more he liked the idea. He'd already decided to use his newfound wealth to help others. As if to test his resolution, Fate had immediately tossed someone at him who was desperately in need of help.

His wife wouldn't have hesitated to take Reggie in, he knew, because Ivy had had the kindest heart of anyone he'd ever met. Finn wasn't going to hesitate either. Apart from anything else, the lad would be company for him.

'All right if I sit in the back of the car with Reggie?' he asked Leah. 'Only I need to discuss something important with him.'

'Of course it's all right.'

He edged into the corner of the back seat, holding Reggie's legs across his lap. 'Look, lad, this is a bit quick, but how would you like to come and live with me instead of going back to the orphanage?'

Reggie gaped at him, seeming too surprised to speak.

'My wife and child died a few years ago, and it'd be good to have some company. You're on your own too.'

The boy stared at him so incredulously that Finn carried on speaking to give him time to take in the offer. 'I've just inherited that big house and today was the first time I'd seen the place. It's in a bit of a mess at the moment so it won't be exactly comfortable to live in for a while.'

'You really mean it? You want me to live with you?'

'Yes. What do you think of the idea?'

'I think . . . I can't believe . . . oh, it'd be wonderful!' Reggie swallowed hard and tried to sniff back the tears as he added, 'I can't understand why you're offering, though. You don't even know me.'

'Well, why are you accepting my offer? You don't know me, either.'

'I trust you.'

Leah spoke from the front of the car. 'I can't help overhearing. Reggie, Mr Carlisle used to be a policeman. He's a good man and you're right to trust him. I'm sure he'll be kind to you.'

'Thank you, Leah.' Finn turned back to the boy. 'Well?'

The words came out in a rush. 'I'd love to live with you. Thank you, Mr Carlisle. I'll, um, try to be good.'

The last sentence didn't sound hugely confident and Finn had to stop himself smiling. No normal lad was good all the time. 'I'm glad, Reggie. I'm sure we'll do well together.'

He felt happy about the decision, very happy indeed. The sound of his own voice echoing in the big, empty house had upset him. He could understand why Uncle Oscar, a confirmed bachelor with a comfortable life in Rochdale, had chosen to stay where he was. But Finn wanted to live out in Ellindale, had fallen in love with the moors.

Leah stopped outside the doctor's house in Rivenshaw and helped get Reggie out of the car.

When Finn would have picked up the boy, she laid one hand on his arm. 'I'm interfering again, but it might be a good idea if Reggie calls you Uncle Finn, don't you think? People are bound to ask questions about why you're giving him a home.'

'Good idea. Did you hear that, young fellow?'

'Yes, sir. I mean, Uncle Finn.'

As he carried Reggie inside the surgery at the side of the house, Finn heard him mutter it two or three times under his breath as if impressing it on himself. The lad turned his head slightly and their eyes met.

'I think we'll do all right together, don't you?' Finn asked quietly.

He got another nod for that and saw the lad's eyes brighten with unshed tears.

The long narrow hall was full of people waiting to see the doctor, sitting on benches along one wall. It was a common system. Every time a patient went in to see the doctor, the whole line moved up.

A woman with a nurse's winged hat and starched white apron came to the door of a small side room, looked at Reggie and asked, 'Mr Carlisle?'

'Yes.'

'Come in here and show me the wound.'

She needed only a quick look to say, 'It definitely needs stitching. The doctor won't be long.'

When Dr Mitchell showed a patient out, he took a quick look at the cut and whistled softly. It was so deep at one end, it was still oozing blood. He apologised to those waiting in the hall in a voice with a slight Irish accent, before beckoning Finn and Reggie into his surgery. The nurse followed them. 'My wife will help.'

Mrs Mitchell laid out implements and got a bowl of water ready. 'My goodness, Reggie, you certainly don't do things by half.' She watched her husband clean the wound carefully, mopping blood away for him as he stitched the edges of the cut together and bandaged it.

As he moved, the doctor limped slightly. It couldn't be a war wound because he was too young, Finn decided. Whatever it was, it seemed part of him, as if he didn't even know he was limping.

Reggie's knuckles were white from clenching his fists as this was being done, but he didn't cry out or pull away.

'How did you cut yourself so badly, young fellow?' the doctor asked.

'He was climbing a wall and fell against the window of a shed,' Finn put in quickly. 'Unfortunately, the glass was already cracked and it gave way.'

The doctor rolled his eyes. 'Lads! I've stitched up half the lads in Birch End from one reckless act or another.'

When he'd finished, he told Reggie he was a brave lad, then turned to Finn. 'Keep the wound clean and bring him back in two days for Mrs Mitchell to check that the leg is healing properly. If it is, there will be no need to see me till I take the stitches out in ten days' time.'

Finn had taken a liking to the busy doctor and decided to

ask his help. 'There's another thing I'd like you to look at. Someone's been beating Reggie.' The lad looked frightened again, so he took Reggie's arm and said soothingly, 'We need the doctor's help if we're to keep you safe. It'll be all right, I promise you.'

Reggie flushed in humiliation, but let them take off his shirt and the rather ragged undervest and examine his back.

Dr Mitchell whistled softly in shock. 'Some of these marks have been made quite recently. Who did this? Whoever it was deserves flogging himself.'

'The man who runs the orphanage, apparently. When Reggie's parents died, he was taken there. I was away at the time, but I was a friend of his father and when Reggie heard I was back, he escaped and came to me for help. He's always known me as "Uncle Finn".'

'What are you going to do about him? You can't send him back there to a place where children are ill-treated. In fact, it needs looking into for the sake of the others who've nowhere else to go. Which orphanage was it?'

Finn nudged Reggie.

'Wemsworth.'

'I'm not going to send him back, doctor. He's coming to live with me, as his parents would have wanted. But if the man at the orphanage causes any trouble . . .' He let the words trail away and looked enquiringly at the doctor.

'I'd be happy to bear witness that he'd been beaten viciously and unreasonably.'

'Thank you.'

'My wife will put some salve on the latest cuts on his back.' Then, with a distracted look at the clock on his mantelpiece, Dr Mitchell called in the next patient.

'There's always a queue to see him.' Mrs Mitchell led them back into her own treatment room and opened a cupboard door. As she took out a pot of salve, she said in a brisk tone, 'We don't charge the poorer patients for this sort of thing, but I capture the richer ones here before they can escape without paying.' She smiled as she added, 'You don't look like a poor man, Mr Carlisle.'

He smiled back. 'I'm not and I'm happy to pay.'

'Good. First we'll see to this young man, then I'll take your money.'

She spread the salve over the lad's back, put a cap on the pot and handed it to Finn.

He pulled out his coin purse and gave her the money, then picked Reggie up and left.

To his surprise, when he got outside he saw a tear sliding down the young lad's cheek. 'What's wrong? Is your leg hurting?'

'Not much. I don't know why I'm crying, when I'm so happy, sir.'

'Relief, I expect. And I'm Uncle Finn, remember?'

'Yes. Sorry. *Uncle* Finn. Am I really coming to live with you?'

'Didn't I just tell you so? But you'll have to muck in and help me set the old place to rights. It hasn't been lived in for years.'

'I could see that when I looked through the windows. I thought if no one was living there I'd be safe in the shed for a couple of nights, just till I could work out what to do next.'

'Well, now you'll be sleeping in a proper bed and you'll have me to help you work out what you do with your life. First things first, though. I daresay you're hungry. I know I am.'

'I'm always hungry, Uncle Finn. But I'll try not to eat too much.'

He chuckled. 'Eat as much as you like. Growing lads need

their food and it looks as if you're going to be quite tall. How old are you?'

'Eleven.'

Leah was waiting for them near the car, chatting to another woman.

When she'd said goodbye to her friend, Finn explained about showing the doctor the beatings.

She frowned. 'A quick slap's one thing, but whipping children is shameful. And they'll be doing the same thing to other children in that place. I can't bear to think about it.'

'Mr Buddle likes beating people.'

Reggie had said that before, Finn thought, and seemed very sure of it.

'Well, he's not going to touch you again,' Leah said. 'I have a young sister myself and if anyone tried to whip her, I'd go after them with a big stick.'

She didn't start the car, but turned round in the driving seat to ask, 'Would it be worth putting this matter into Deemer's hands, do you think?'

Reggie began to look anxious.

'If you can spare the time, yes. Reggie and I are both hungry, so we'll buy something to eat. Is there anywhere that will make us all a quick sandwich, my treat? And I need to find somewhere for the lad for tonight, so would you mind calling on my landlady as well, to see if she can fit him in? I'm sorry to trouble you, but I don't want Reggie walking about on that leg.'

'Of course not. Anything else while we're in town?'

'Well . . . I need several people to clean my house from top to bottom. Are there any women in Ellindale who'll do it, or should I ask here in Rivenshaw?'

'Half the people in the village are out of work, so you'll easily find as many as you need close by. I've been here long

enough to know all the families. Would you like me to help
you find a strong man and a couple of women and send
them to see you at Heythorpe tomorrow? You're going to be
inundated with people wanting work and I know most of the
people in the village.'

'I won't have the equipment to clean it by then.'

'Well, if your uncle left the furniture in the house, there
will probably also be mops and brushes. Um, I hope you
don't mind me saying, but Mrs Buckley in the village shop
would be glad of your custom for the soap and polish, and
other bits and pieces. She stocks a little of everything.'

'Thank you. I'll call on her later. I'd prefer to shop locally.'
He turned to Reggie, who was looking sleepy now. 'If I find
you somewhere to lie down, will you wait there for me till
the house is ready?'

'Could I come with you, s— I mean, Uncle Finn? They'll
be looking for me and I'll feel safer with you.'

'All right. Don't forget to call me uncle and don't mention
the orphanage to anyone except Mr and Mrs Willcox.'

'I won't . . . Uncle Finn. You're sure Mr Buddle won't be
able to take me away from you?'

'He definitely won't. That's why we're going to see Sergeant
Deemer.'

Reggie jerked away from him. '*Sergeant* Deemer! A
policeman! No! He'll lock me up and force me to go back
to the orphanage like the policeman did last time I ran away.'
He began scrabbling at the car door, trying to get out, looking
panic-stricken.

Finn grabbed his arm. 'How many times do I have to say
it before you'll believe me? I promise I won't let them take
you back.'

'Yes, but they—'

'Orphanages are always glad to find homes for their children so why would they even try to stop you finding a home?'

But Reggie was weeping. 'Mr Buddle said he'd never let me go to anyone, never, to pay me back for fighting when he hit me.'

Leah joined in. 'There's another thing to remember, Reggie. When you live in Ellindale, everyone in the village will keep an eye on you, I promise. We look after one another.'

'But they won't be able to do that if I'm at school in Rivenshaw and if *he* comes after me, the teacher will believe him, not me.'

He was a sharp-witted lad, Finn thought. 'We'll not send you to school till it's all settled. It's only a few weeks to the summer holidays anyway.'

Reggie had stopped struggling to get out, but he still looked hunched up and unhappy.

'And if Finn has to go somewhere, we live just up the road,' Leah added, 'so you can run to us for help if necessary. There's always someone at Spring Cottage now we've started brewing our ginger beer, and we'll be making dandelion and burdock soon, too.'

'There you are. You'll soon feel at home.' Finn risked putting his arm round the boy's thin shoulders.

Although Reggie stiffened for a moment, he let out a weary sigh and laid his head against Finn's chest. 'I want to stay with you, I do. But Mr Buddle is a terrible man. He'll find a way to get back at me.'

'And we'll find a way to keep you safe, I promise.' Whatever he had to do, Finn added mentally. He solemnly made the sign. 'Cross my heart and hope to die if I don't.'

And Reggie nodded, seeming more reassured by that small ritual.

4

Sergeant Deemer listened to Finn, frowning. 'Come through to my office and we'll get all that down.'

He questioned Reggie shrewdly, insisting on getting the lad's real surname. 'Barston, eh? How do you spell that?'

He wrote some more notes on the case, then said, 'You'd be best getting a lawyer behind you on this, Finn. Mr Lloyd has offices on the town square and I'm sure he'll be happy to help you. He's a kind fellow and a good lawyer.'

'You haven't heard anything about that particular home for boys?' Finn asked when the questions came to an end and the sergeant began to gather his papers together.

'There have been one or two rumours, but nothing definite. I'm going to ask around quietly, though. And look, I'll wait till tomorrow to tell the inspector about young Reggie, which will give you time to get Mr Lloyd on your side.'

They had to wait half an hour to see Mr Lloyd, so Finn took them for a cup of tea and a buttered teacake at the bakery, which had a small table to one side. The owner looked happy to have an unexpected customer. 'New to the town, sir?'

'I've visited Rivenshaw before. It's a friendly place.'

'It is indeed. You come back any time, sir. You won't find better baked goods anywhere.'

Reggie's currant teacake vanished down his throat before Finn was even halfway through his, so he ordered another one for his protégé.

'Are you sure? I can manage without.' But the lad licked his lips as he looked at the food and beamed when another teacake was placed in front of him. 'Thank you, Uncle Finn.'

'You're welcome.' He winked at Leah, who was eating her own teacake slowly and daintily.

She winked back and he thought yet again what a lovely woman she was and how lucky Jonah was to have a wife like her.

She stopped outside the bakery. 'I'll do some bits and pieces of shopping and meet you back at the lawyer's. And I want to call in and see my brother-in-law.'

The lawyer was a frail-looking man who must have been nearing sixty. He listened to Finn's tale, then asked if he could see the boy's injuries, tutting softly as he stared at the boy's back.

'Give me the details, and allow me to contact the chairman of the orphanage committee. He worships at the same church as I do. I don't know Buddle, but I've seen the injuries with my own eyes and no decent human being can ignore this sort of treatment.'

'I think we should do something official about me getting guardianship of Reggie, so perhaps you could contact them on my behalf and do whatever is necessary to get them to release him from the orphanage?'

'Yes, of course. It's not going to be complicated. And there shouldn't be any trouble. Orphanages are always glad to place a child whatever that man may have told this lad.'

'I'll leave it in your hands, then,' Finn said. 'If we may, we'll wait here for my neighbour to pick us up. Reggie can't walk more than a few steps on that injured leg.'

Leah went along to Charlie's pawnshop, the bigger of the two he owned. She'd decided to ask his help about getting a van to deliver the drinks, because they had a few orders already and had made enough bottles of ginger beer to cover more orders. They were starting in a small way, but she hoped to find more customers all across the district before she was through.

She'd woken at night a couple of times worrying about how much money this was costing her husband, but he insisted he could afford it. And she did so enjoy organising and planning her little business making ginger beer and other fizzy drinks, though most of all she enjoyed helping the people who worked for her.

Jonah had told her *she* should discuss the van with Charlie, to make it clear to her brother-in-law that it was *her* running the business. She smiled wryly. She might be the one in charge but behind the scenes she often asked Jonah's advice, and took it too, and couldn't have done it without his money. He was not only a wise man but a good financial manager.

It amused her that Charlie's wife, Marion, who was expecting a baby in a couple of months, had designed the labels for Spring Cottage. They'd all been surprised by that, since Marion had never flaunted her artistic talent. And it was a talent. Leah was as delighted with her sister-in-law's work as Marion was to have something 'real' to do with her skill.

Charlie was in his office at the back of the pawnshop.

Leah got straight to the point. 'I need a van for the business, for deliveries and picking up ingredients. Jonah thought you'd know how to find one.'

'I guessed you would and I've been keeping my eyes open for you.' He paused, then added. 'Actually, I'm thinking of starting up a business selling second-hand cars so you needing a van is just up my street.'

'I'm sure it'll make you money, Charlie.'

He grinned. 'Your faith in me is touching.'

'For obvious reasons. You've done well even in these troubled times. What you'd have done if business was flourishing, I don't know. Become a millionaire, perhaps.'

'I still might. Now, what sort of van?'

She shook her head ruefully. 'I don't know much about them. Do you?'

'As it happens, I've heard a whisper of one going cheaply. Will you leave it to me to find out if it's a good runner? We don't have a lot of choice if we're to get you something quickly. It takes months to order a new one.'

'Gladly.'

'Who are you getting to drive it for you?'

'Nancy suggests Peter Cotman.'

'Do I know him? Oh yes. Used to work for Pearson's. Nice chap, but with too many kids to get on in the world.'

'Maybe he likes kids better than money.'

Charlie shrugged.

'Are you looking forward to becoming a father?'

He shrugged. 'It's Marion who'll be looking after the children. No sign of you having one yet?' He patted his stomach suggestively.

Tears welled in her eyes before she could stop them. It hurt even to think about her lack of a child.

'Sorry, love.'

She nodded, blew her nose and changed the subject. 'I'll go and see Peter after I get back, offer him the job.'

'I'll go after the van for you. If it's any good, you'll have it in a couple of days.'

She went back to the car and picked up Finn and Reggie from the lawyer's. 'Anything else or shall we get you home now?'

'I saw my landlady walking past and ran out to speak to her. She said she could find Reggie a bed if he didn't mind

the box room, which he doesn't. So we're all set. I do appreciate you giving us a lift today. I really must get a car.'

She laughed. 'Then we'd better go back to Charlie's shop.
He's going into business selling second-hand cars.'

Charlie hurried out to the shop when he was told Leah
was back. 'Is something wrong?'

'No. I just brought you another customer, though perhaps
you ought to discuss what he needs in your back room. I'll
take Reggie back to the car and wait for you there, Mr
Carlisle.'

Charlie listened to what Finn wanted and beamed at him.
'My new partner Todd will find you something, I'm sure.'

'The quicker the better. As long as it's reliable, I don't care
what sort of car I get.'

'Todd's a whizz with motors. He'll find you something
good.'

'Fancy you inheriting Heythorpe House,' Charlie said as
he showed Finn out.

'Came as a surprise to me, I can tell you.'

'Nice surprise, I'm sure.'

'I'm getting used to it.'

The two men shook hands and Finn got back into the car.
'Done,' he said. 'I'll call for a taxi when we're ready to go
home again.'

'You can use our phone.'

'Thank you.'

It made Leah feel very happy to be able to offer Peter Cotman
a job. He was the father of six and seemed a very practical
and capable man. Everyone said how well he was coping
with being out of work, considering, but she was sure he was
just putting the best face he could on the situation and using
his skills with his hands to make things last.

The dole money was never enough to feed a family properly, she was sure, even though many prices had fallen during these hard times, and some men were able to bag the occasional rabbit to help with food.

The trouble was, she couldn't afford to pay Peter a generous wage, though she intended to pay him more than he got on the dole. One day, though, she'd pay more generously.

She stopped her car near a lad lounging around near Nancy's shop and sent him to fetch Peter, then took Finn and Reggie home.

She was surprised at how quickly Peter arrived at Spring Cottage.

'I came straight away. I thought you might have an errand I could run for you and heaven knows, my wife needs every extra penny I can get.'

'I do want to offer you a job.'

'I'd be glad of a day's work, Mrs Willcox.'

'Not a day's work, a regular job.'

Peter stared at her as if she'd spoken a foreign language, his mouth slightly open, shock on his face. Then he clapped one hand to his mouth for a moment, as if to hold in an emotional reaction. 'A job,' he said at last, in a voice that shook slightly. 'A real job?'

'Yes.'

'I'll take it and thank you with all my heart.'

'You haven't asked me what it is.'

'It doesn't matter what it is, I'll take it. Anyone in my position would.'

'I need a driver and delivery man, but also someone who'll do any little job that's needed, not just making mineral water but in the youth hostel, be it scrubbing floors or whatever.'

'I'm happy to do anything.'

But he was frowning slightly so she asked, 'Is something troubling you?'

'I was just wondering why you offered the job to me? There are half a dozen men in Ellindale who're seeking work.'

'Nancy said you were a steady fellow and cheerful with it. I need someone who knows how to drive but he must also be cheerful with customers and with other workers. I know that sounds a foolish reason, but I want those who work with me to get on with one another.'

She remembered only too well her father's tales of miniature feuds in the laundry, especially when Mr Harris's horrible ex-wife had started poking her nose in. It was her fault the machinery hadn't been kept safe and Leah's father had been killed. It was a good thing, in her opinion, that he'd found his wife with her lover and been able to start divorce proceedings. She realised Peter was speaking and pushed her memories aside.

'Well, I'm a hard chap to quarrel with.'

'That's what I heard.'

'I have good references from Pearson's. I was happy there and they were happy with my work, only they had to dismiss me when their younger son lost his job. You can't blame them for that. Family should always come first. The thing that upset me was that he doesn't like doing deliveries, because he was working in an office before. But beggars can't be choosers so he's doing it now, not me.'

'No need for references. My husband speaks well of you, too.'

'When do you want me to start?'

'Tomorrow. You'll need to tell the people at the Labour Exchange about it, I think.'

'Yes. I'll do that this very afternoon. Nancy will let me phone up from the shop.'

'Let's hope my venture works out.'

'Nancy says your ginger beer is the best she's ever tasted.'

'Oh. That's nice. It's definitely the best I know how to

make. I'll have to ask you not to tell anyone exactly how we make it. We're trying to tempt the sort of people who want fancier products. I don't expect we'll ever become a big business like Schweppes and other producers of mineral waters, but I hope we can make something special.' She was working on a recipe for a new sort of lemonade, which she thought of as 'tangy lemon'.

'What time do I start work?'

'Eight o'clock till six, with an hour for dinner around midday. I'll provide dinner. It'll only be sandwiches, mind, and making them might be one of your jobs.'

'I'll be there.'

As he turned to leave, she called him back. 'You better have my phone number in case someone from the Labour Exchange wishes to contact me about employing you.'

'Oh. Yes. Thank you.' He gave her a rueful grin. 'It hasn't sunk in yet. I don't know whether I'm on my head or my heels.'

He went off looking bemused, a man whose body seemed designed to be sturdy but was too thin, and whose face was drawn and haggard beneath its kindly expression.

She hadn't told him, but Nancy had thought hard then said, 'You need someone who's good with customers, someone people will like to deal with. That's partly why I suggested Peter.'

Leah could see why she'd said that. There was something innately kind and likeable about Peter Cotman.

Hiring him was another step along the way. She prayed it would all work out, that she really would create jobs for a few people and that it wouldn't end in disaster.

5

Lily woke with a start, uncertain where she was, then smiled and snuggled down again in the narrow bed as she remembered what had happened. She was with her cousin and she was sleeping in the attic, because Nancy used the second bedroom to store her stock for the shop. This made for a lot of running up and down the stairs, but the roof of the outhouse leaked and the landlord wouldn't repair it, said it'd cost too much, so nothing could be stored there, and they were using the other room on the ground floor, which opened off the side of the shop, as a sort of café with little tables for people to sit at on rainy days.

When she heard her cousin stirring, Lily got up and had a quick wash in cold water, then dressed and went slowly down the narrow stairs on wobbly legs, determined not to be a burden any longer.

Nancy was using the poker on the coal slack she'd used to damp down the fire overnight. It had slowly fused into a crust and she needed to break that up to get the fire burning up again to boil her kettle.

Gas, electricity and the phone had only just been brought out to Ellindale by men working on relief schemes, and Nancy was hesitating about spending money on getting electricity connected to the whole house on top of the phone, which she'd considered more important. With it, she could place orders with the wholesaler in Rivenshaw by phone, a godsend to a woman working on her own.

In the meantime Lily was remembering how to cook on a coal-fired stove, which seemed so old-fashioned after the gas cooker at her former employer's. Her mother hadn't cooked much in the few months she'd spent back at home, because they couldn't afford to buy much food.

Nancy turned and jumped in shock at the sight of Lily standing at the foot of the stairs. 'Eh, I didn't hear you come down, love. You'd better sit on the sofa. You still look a bit wobbly.'

Lily obeyed because there wasn't much room to move around the cluttered room, where items from the shop mingled with private bits and pieces. 'I'm feeling a lot better today.'

Nancy studied her. 'You are getting a touch of pink in your cheeks. You were chalk white when you arrived. I was that worried about you.'

'I don't remember the first day very clearly, but after several days of being cosseted, I do feel a lot better. I'm so grateful you took me in.'

'I wasn't going to turn a relative away, now was I?'

'I'm not used to sitting idle, though. Surely there's something I can do to help you today?'

'We'll think about that later. Let's get some breakfast into you first. Porridge, eh?'

There was a knock on the shop door just then and Nancy sighed. 'Some of them can't plan ahead for more than the next meal.' She wiped her hands quickly on the dishcloth before going through into the shop.

When she saw who it was, she sighed and muttered, 'Oh, no! It's Madge Judson again!'

The woman at the door looked at her pleadingly. 'I'm sorry to trouble you so early, Nancy love, but do you have a stale loaf from yesterday?'

'If you have the money to buy it.'

There was silence then, 'Barry gets the dole money on Fridays. I can pay you then.'

'I'm sorry, love. You know I can't afford to give credit.'

'Please, Nancy. The kids are crying from hunger.'

'I saw your husband going into The Shepherd's Rest last night. He should have spent his money on bread for his children, not beer.'

'He only had half a pint.'

'Well, that twopence halfpenny would have paid for a stale loaf. Sorry.' Nancy hardened her heart and closed the door, hearing Madge sobbing loudly.

That was for effect, she knew, an attempt to soften her heart, because Madge would be far more worried about her husband getting angry at having no food than about her children going hungry. Everyone in the village knew what the Judsons were like. They'd pinch a biscuit from a baby, they would. She felt sorry for their three children, and it looked as if the youngest was developing rickets, poor thing.

As she returned to the back room, she wiped away a tear with the back of her hand and when Lily looked at her anxiously, explained, 'I hate to say no when children are going hungry, but if I gave credit to one customer, I'd have to give it to another, and I simply can't afford it.'

'You can't afford to feed me for long, either.'

'I can do it for a good while yet. You're already wanting to help but the Judsons are lazy scroungers. He spends half his dole money on beer and she has no idea how to be careful with what money he does give her.'

Lily wasn't going to take no for an answer. 'Well, I may be family, but I'll feel better if I'm helping you, Nancy. You're on the go from dawn till dusk.'

'You can help me when you get stronger.'

'Please let me start now.'

Nancy had a think and snapped her fingers as a solution

came to her. 'I know. You can brew pots of tea and make sandwiches for the hikers, and you can rest in between. There are always a few passing through at weekends at this time of year. I'll knock up some scones after breakfast and show you how to serve the tea. They're a godsend to me, those hikers are. But you must tell me if it's too much for you at the moment, mind.'

'I'm sure I'll be able to cope with that.'

'I'm glad I turned that front room into a tea room. I never really used it anyway. Now people can come inside for a snack on rainy days, and they often buy something they'd not have bought otherwise.'

'You're a hard worker, Nancy, and clever with it.'

'I've had to be since my husband died. Eh, it's over ten years ago now, but I still miss him, miss the companionship.' She took a deep breath and said in another tone of voice, 'There's a youth hostel opening soon up at Spring Cottage, just up the hill from the village, and that may bring me some more customers. You and I will have a stroll up there one evening when you're a bit stronger and I'll show it to you.'

'I don't know what a youth hostel is.'

'It's a new thing. They're setting up places where young folk from the towns can get a bed for the night cheaply so that they can enjoy a walking holiday in the country. When Leah Willcox heard of it, she decided to set one up in Ellindale because they had a big barn standing doing nothing. She's making ginger beer and other fizzy drinks in another part of the barn. Eh, that woman is full of good ideas.'

'Who is she?'

'She grew up in Birch End. Her mother died when she was fourteen so she raised her sister, and did a good job of it, too. Last year she married Jonah Willcox and moved up here. His mother's family have owned Spring Cottage since before my grandmother's time, and the land round it as well.

She's given work to a few people from the village. Eh, I bless the day she and Jonah came to live here, I do that. And I'm not the only one.' She smiled. 'They have rules for these hostels, which sounds a good idea to me.'

'Rules? Like at school?'

'Yes. I read about it in the paper. It costs a shilling a night for a bed, and there's no smoking, gambling or boozing allowed. They put the lights out at ten thirty and after that there's no talking allowed. So those who stay there won't disturb folk nearby, will they? Was that all it said? Oh no, they also have to share the chores.'

'Which is fair enough,' said Lily. 'A shilling a night won't buy you hotel service, will it? You must have a good memory to remember all that.'

'I have to remember details when I'm running a shop. Eh, I'd have enjoyed a walking holiday when I was younger,' Nancy added wistfully.

Just then there was a hammering at the door and a man shouted, 'Open that damned shop, Nancy Buckley, and let us have a loaf! My kids are faint with hunger.'

'Oh, heavens! It's Barry Judson. He's a terror when he gets angry, lashes out at people, causes damage. They should lock up men like him and throw away the key.'

The thumping went on. 'Open up! O-p-en up! Or I'll damned well open up for you.'

Nancy picked up a poker. 'I hope someone will hear him and come to our aid.'

'Can't you phone for the police?'

'The police station's down in Rivenshaw and we only have one constable in Birch End. By the time he gets here, my shop could be smashed up.' She cast an anxious look towards the window. 'Some of the men from our village usually deal with him.'

There was a thump and the door rattled.

Nancy gasped. 'Judson's getting worse. I've never seen him this bad before. If he damages my shop, I don't know how I'll afford the repairs. He broke the catch on the door once. You'd better take the small poker, in case we have to defend ourselves.'

Startled, Lily did as she was told and followed her cousin into the shop.

'Go away, Barry!' Nancy yelled.

'Open that bloody door, you fool of a woman!' the man outside roared.

Lily's heart began to thump as she looked through the glass panes of the shop door. Judson was not only big but looked like a wild animal, eyes staring, mouth open in a snarl. How could two women fight someone like him off?

Then they heard footsteps.

'I hope that's help. Oh, thank goodness!' Nancy exclaimed as one man came running down the street and a second one appeared from behind The Shepherd's Rest. They both stopped short outside the shop when Judson swung round to face them, fists clenched.

'What are you doing, Barry lad,' one man said in a coaxing tone of voice. 'You don't want to hurt Nancy.'

'That's Don from The Shepherd's Rest,' Nancy whispered.

'Come on, Barry,' the other man said. 'You can't take Nancy's food without paying for it. She barely makes ends meet as it is.'

'She could have let us have one lousy stale loaf. That wouldn't break the bank. I've children who need feeding.'

Don scowled at him. 'You were drinking in my pub last night. Two pints you bought, said you'd found a little job. You were lying, weren't you, spending the housekeeping money again? You should have thought of your children before paying out ten pence for beer.'

'A man needs a wet now and then, else what's the world coming to?'

'If he can't feed his children, he shouldn't be buying any beer, so I won't have you drinking in my pub from now on. You can save your money for your children or walk down into Birch End for your drinks.'

'You can't stop me coming in. It's a public house.'

'I have the right to refuse to serve anyone causing a nuisance.'

For a moment Judson stared at him in disbelief, then he yelled, 'You wouldn't dare do that, Don Dewey!'

'Oh, wouldn't I? Just try coming in and you'll soon find out what I dare do under my own roof,' Don retorted.

'This is all *her* fault, that bitch in the shop!' Judson bent and snatched up a big stone from the side of the road, turning to hurl it at the shop window. He only just missed, hitting the house wall next to it instead and sending a few chips of stone flying. Cursing, he began searching for another stone to throw.

Nancy squeaked in fear and clutched her young cousin's arm even more tightly. 'He'll break my shop window, I know he will.'

'I can see someone else coming up the street,' Lily said.

Nancy stood on tiptoe to peer over the piles of tins and packets in the shop window. 'Thank goodness! Barry's not usually this bad but when he gets into a rage, it takes more than two men to stop him.'

Three more men joined the first arrivals and after a few low-voiced words, they spread out and approached Judson from all sides. At Don's signal they rushed at the red-faced brute, knocked another stone from his hand and wrestled him to the ground.

One of the latecomers produced some rope and they dragged the struggling, yelling man to a stone post that must have been set up in the old days for tethering horses, and tied him to it, hands behind him.

It looked to Lily as if they'd had to do this before.

'You can stay there till you've calmed down,' Don said. 'And remember, from now on you're not welcome in my pub.'

Shouting and swearing, Judson tried to pull free, but they'd tied him carefully and after a while he stopped struggling. He leaned his back against the post, closed his eyes and continued muttering to himself.

Don came towards the shop. 'You all right, Nancy love?'

'I am now. It was a close call, though. What am I going to do, Don? He only just missed with that stone and I can't afford to have my shop window broken. *He* wouldn't be able to pay for a new one.'

'Well, we'll do our best to keep him away from you.' Don looked at the shop thoughtfully. 'I've got an old bell in my shed. How about I fix it to your upstairs wall and you can ring it if you need help?'

'Oh, would you, Don? I'd be ever so grateful.' She saw him looking curiously at Lily. 'Have you met my cousin's lass? Lily's mum died and she's come to stay with me for a while. Lily, this is Don, who runs The Shepherd's Rest.'

Three of the men had walked away, but one was still lingering. 'And this is Tom Dotton, who lives at the top end of the village and helps me out from time to time.'

The two men nodded and smiled at Lily, then the women went back into the shop.

'Might as well leave the door on the latch,' Nancy said. 'It's a bit early to be opening but I'm wide awake now.'

'What about that man out there, Judson? Will anyone be calling the police?'

'No. They'll just leave him to calm down, and eventually they'll untie him. His rages never last more than an hour or two, then he goes and sleeps it off. I pity his wife tonight, though. He's bound to thump her if he can't go to the pub.'

'He might come back here. You should report him to the police.'

'I would if we had a policeman here, but we haven't and Judson would really go mad if I reported him. Constable Peters is supposed to keep an eye on Ellindale, but he lives the other side of Birch End, and he only has his bicycle so it takes him a while to get here. No, it's better for us to continue sorting out any problems in the village ourselves.'

Lily followed her into the back room. 'It was kind of those men to come and help you.'

'We've been neighbours for a long time and they've watched out for me ever since I opened the shop. It's a good place to live, Ellindale is.'

Nancy turned to the fire where the kettle was starting to send out steam. 'Oh well, worrying about what might happen won't help. I shall be glad of a nice cup of tea, I shall that.'

'I'm making it, remember.'

Her cousin gave a tired nod and moved towards the front room again. 'Thanks, Lily. Call me when it's ready. I'll just set things up in the shop. They'll be delivering the milk churn soon. Can you bring the ladle through to measure out the milk?'

Finn and Reggie caught the early morning bus up to Ellindale. The landlady had found a crutch for Reggie, to help him take the weight off his injured leg, and he'd assured Finn that he'd be all right.

They both stopped in surprise to see a glowering man tied to a post in the open space just past the final bus stop. He had a bruise on one cheek and was scowling at the world.

When he saw them he yelled, 'What are you staring at?'

Another man walking past called, 'Ignore him. That sod's not worth a second look. He'll have been attacking Nancy at the shop. They leave him there to cool down.'

'Goodness! Have you called the police?'

'No. We have to look after ourselves up this end of the valley.' With a cheery wave he continued on his way.

The man at the post sent a string of curses after him.

Finn clapped Reggie on the shoulder. 'We'll ignore him, then. Let's go into the shop before we go up to the house. I need to buy food and cleaning supplies and order a lot of other stuff.' He pushed open the door and Reggie limped in after him.

'Dear me! Whatever have you done to yourself?' Nancy exclaimed. 'Sit down there, lad, while I serve your dad.'

'I'm not his dad; I'm his uncle and guardian,' Finn said. 'My name's Finn Carlisle and I've just come to live at Heythorpe House.'

'Ah. I heard they'd found the heir. Welcome to Ellindale, Mr Carlisle. How can I help you?'

He pulled a crumpled list out of his pocket. 'The house hasn't been occupied for a long time and we're going to need everything: food, cleaning supplies, you name it. Mrs Willcox at Spring Cottage said you'd be the person to get the things for me. I made a list as best I could, but tell me if I've missed anything.'

Nancy stared at him and swallowed hard. 'You need everything?'

'Yes, please. You can probably order in the things you haven't got in stock.'

'Oh, I can. I definitely can, Mr Carlisle.' She held out a hand that trembled slightly and took the list. 'Let's have a cup of tea and go through this together.'

'Good idea. And Reggie would no doubt like something to eat and drink. It's nearly two hours since he had his breakfast.' He looked across at a sign. 'How about a glass of ginger beer? Is it Leah's own brew?'

'It is and you won't find better anywhere.'

As Reggie beamed at the prospect, she chuckled. 'He's at the age where they grow like weeds, isn't he? How about a cheese sandwich with it, young fellow?'

'Yes please, Mrs . . . um?'

'Mrs Buckley. Now, you sit down and I'll ask Lily to get us some refreshments, then you and I will go through that list in detail, Mr Carlisle.'

'And don't hesitate to tell me if I've forgotten something.'

Her voice became faint and choked-sounding for a moment. 'No. No, I won't.'

A few moments later she said, 'You might need paraffin for your lamps. There's no gas or electricity there.'

He nodded vigorously. 'You're right.'

'I've got some. I'll have to find something to put it in.'

'If you've got a whole new tin of it, I'll take that. It's a big house.'

'Certainly.' She pinched herself to make sure she wasn't dreaming then got back to work.

6

Mr Carlisle didn't leave until an hour later and when the shop door had shut behind him, Nancy went into the back room, dropped some pieces of paper on the table and burst into loud tears, covering her face with both hands.

Lily rushed to put an arm round her. 'What's wrong?'

A loud gulp was her first answer, then, 'Wrong? Nothing's *wrong*, love. It's the best day I've had since I opened the shop, and why I'm crying about it, I can't think. Only, it's a long time since I've been so h-happy.' More sobs followed.

'Oh. Right.' Lily took a step back, puzzled by what her cousin had said and uncertain what to do next.

Nancy blew her nose loudly, then grabbed Lily and danced her round the kitchen, into the shop and back again, picking up the pieces of paper as they passed the table and waving them about. 'These are all one order, just – one – order. It'll bring me in as much money as three months' sales in the shop. I shall even be able to put a bit of money aside for a rainy day. Just from this one order, Lily.'

'That's wonderful.'

'And Mr Carlisle is coming to live nearby, so there'll be other orders to come if I do this one right.' Another tear trickled down her cheek and she wiped it away impatiently, staring at the papers then smacking a big kiss on them.

'That's wonderful.'

'And he came to me for these, not to someone in Rivenshaw. To my little shop! He's going to be a godsend to this village, that man is, an absolute godsend. Just as she is. Eh, lass, a few kind people can make a big difference in this world, they can that.'

Then she wiped her eyes determinedly, nipped into the shop to serve a customer, before starting to make proper lists depending on which supplier she would be buying from. She was interrupted from time to time by other customers and once by four brawny young men on a hiking holiday, who wanted sandwiches and tea.

'Oh, it's such a good day,' she whispered to Lily who was making sandwiches for them.

When she'd finished sorting out her lists, Nancy went to the shop door and beckoned a gangly youth across. 'A biscuit for you if you find Tom Dotton and send him to me.'

'If you want someone to run an errand, I could do it.'

'Not this time, love. Now hurry up!' She thrust some broken biscuit pieces from the bottom of the broken bits tin in the shop into the youth's hand.

Tom arrived a few minutes later, breathless from running. 'Is there an errand?'

'Yes. Several. And money to be earned. Come inside and I'll go through them with you.'

'You could phone the orders through to the wholesaler.'

Nancy looked down at her lists, then slowly shook her head. 'No. There are too many things on my lists and anyway, I want Mr Carlisle to have some of them today, if possible. Can you borrow Jim Thorneycroft's bicycle and the little trailer he made for it? Tell him I'll pay him sixpence. Ride down into Rivenshaw to the wholesaler and bring back the things I've marked with a cross. I think you'll be able to carry them all.'

He nodded. 'From Pearson's, those are?'

'Yes. Ask him to deliver the rest as quickly as he can. We need to *prove* ourselves to Mr Carlisle. Then give Sammy

Binns the other list and tell him we'd appreciate it if he sent the things up as soon as possible, and he'll see the benefit in the future with this new customer.'

She paused to study one of the lists. 'Mr Carlisle's forgotten something. Rags. You need a lot of rags when you're doing a big clean-up. Go to the market and buy a sack of rags from the old woman with the stall in the corner. You know the one?'

He nodded, muttering, 'Yes. Sack of rags.'

'It won't be too much for you to bring on the bike, Tom?'

'No, of course not.'

Tom held up one hand. 'Wait a minute. You need to make another list before you go any further.'

She broke off and frowned. 'Why?'

'For me. So that I can check everything off. I don't want to forget anything.'

'Good thinking, lad. I'll pay you a full day's wages for this afternoon and another for helping me tomorrow, when I'll need your help carrying the stuff Henry delivers up to the back bedroom.'

His smile faded and he frowned. 'I'll have to tell the Means Test Man about it, or I'll lose my dole completely, because someone in Rivenshaw is bound to see me and dob me in. I don't think anyone would from our village, but them in the town's not as caring. The old Means Test Man would have allowed a day's work and just deducted a day's dole payment, but I don't know this new one. And the damned government keeps changing the payment rules on us and calling things by different names. A plain man can't keep up with 'em.'

'Send the Means Test Man to me. I'll explain that we're just starting up and you're only working a day now and then, and declaring them honestly. I'm sure I read somewhere in the newspaper that they can allow part-time work if you declare it, especially if there's a chance of more work in the future.'

'I hope you're right, especially about finding work.' He sighed. 'It's been two years now since I had any sort of proper job, Nancy. And that was just labouring. Two years! It's hard to fill the time. You could make things, but you can't afford the materials. And I'm one of the lucky ones. There are chaps who've been out of work for far longer than that.'

Her voice grew gentler. 'I know, lad. But Mr Carlisle is going to need all sorts of things from me, isn't he? And help in getting Heythorpe House put right. So there may well be more chances of work for a few people. But we have to do it right this time and show him we in the village can give good service.'

He nodded. 'I'll get back as quick as I can, Nancy, I promise you.' At the door, he hesitated, then said, 'Watch out for yourself when they turn Barry loose. He can be a mean devil.'

He was whistling cheerfully as he rode off. She hadn't heard Tom whistle like that for ages. Well, she felt like singing herself today.

Mr Carlisle's custom would make such a difference to them all.

When Finn and Reggie left the shop, he was pushing a handcart on which there were several canvas shopping bags Nancy had lent them, loaded with food and cleaning supplies. Reggie was riding on it, keeping the tin of paraffin steady.

As Finn walked up the hill to Heythorpe House, he tried to feel as if he was coming home, but he couldn't. Perhaps the house would grow on him? He'd not even spent a night there yet, after all.

Two women were waiting near the gate and they ran across to Finn the minute they saw him.

One grabbed his arm, her fingers digging in, and he had to set down the handles of the cart for a moment to deal with her.

'I heard there might be cleaning work going here, Mr Carlisle. I'm desperate to feed my kids, desperate. My husband went off looking for work a year ago and he hasn't sent any money back for months. Nothing *I* do brings in enough to feed them properly and the relief money isn't enough, because they're always growing out of their clothes.'

His heart sank. She had a thin face and looked hungry, and if what she said was true, she obviously deserved a chance of the work – but so did others. How was he to know who would be reliable or not, let alone who was the most deserving?

Leah had hinted that it would be hard to choose who to employ, and now the dilemma was facing him before he'd even finished exploring the inside of his new home.

'There will be jobs going, but Mrs Willcox is going to help me find people, and I don't need anyone today. Why don't you give her your names?'

He hoped Leah would understand and not mind him sending women to her. He had planned to start looking for help tomorrow, when he'd decided which rooms he wanted to use.

But something about the way the woman's shoulders sagged for a moment before she took a deep breath and squared them again, tugged at his heart. The other woman just looked at him pleadingly, with hunger in her eyes as clearly as if the word was written there.

Before he knew what he was doing, he said, 'Look, I'll give you both one day's work today and nothing further promised.'

Reggie was watching all this, wide-eyed.

Then Finn realised there was another problem. 'I don't even know how much it would be fair to pay you.'

'They usually pay five shillings for a day's cleaning and a meal found,' the first one said.

'We could manage without the meal today if you've no food here yet, as long as you pay us straight away,' the smaller woman offered.

She didn't look strong enough to do hard physical labour, let alone do it on an empty stomach, but he couldn't turn her away if he was taking on her taller, fiercer companion. He just couldn't do it.

'No need for that. We have some food. Come inside.' He helped Reggie down from the handcart, gave him the crutch and picked up two of the bags. As he unlocked the front door, the fierce one picked up the tin of paraffin and followed him and Reggie inside, which showed she could think for herself at least.

'What a mess!' She stared round at the dust and cobwebs and mouse droppings.

'Yes. I, um, suppose the kitchen would be a good place for you to start.'

She nodded and followed him across the hall and into the big, dark kitchen at the rear. Setting down the can, she rolled up her sleeves. 'Where did they keep the cleaning things?'

'I don't even know that. I've hardly explored the house, let alone gone through the cupboards. There's some scrubbing soap and polish in the bag Reggie was carrying, as well as odds and ends, but I've only been inside the house once before today.'

To his surprise it was the gentler woman who suggested, 'In that case, we could all search this part of the house to see what cleaning things we can find, then decide what to do first. They won't have left cleaning materials in the main rooms, but they haven't taken the furniture from the ones we passed, so I doubt they'll have taken the brushes and dustpans.' She flushed. 'Well, that seems likely, don't you think?'

'Yes. But before we do anything, tell me your names.' He looked at them expectantly.

Naturally the fierce one spoke first. 'I'm Beth Rawton. Mrs.'

He looked at the other woman.

'I'm Dilys Jarratt. And you might as well know that my Norman was killed before we could get married, so I have a daughter born out of wedlock. She's going on fourteen now, nearly old enough to find a job herself. But she was born from love, Mr Carlisle, and I'm glad I've got her, because she's all I have left of Norman. We live with my mother and Gillian's the joy of her life too.'

She held her head up and looked him straight in the face. 'If you'd rather not employ me because of that, just say so now and I'll leave.'

'Your private life is your own business, Dilys. I judge people I employ by how hard they work and how honest they are.'

She closed her eyes, swaying slightly. 'Thank you. You won't regret it.'

Beth was standing with her arms folded across her chest and for all their physical differences, both of them had two things in common: they were extremely thin and looked hungry.

He couldn't bear to see that. 'How about a slice of bread and butter before you start work?' he suggested. 'It'll give you some energy.'

Both of them stared at him as if they couldn't believe what they were hearing, then Dilys whispered, 'Butter?' in a tone of disbelief.

'What's so strange about that?'

'People like us live on bread and margarine, Mr Carlisle,' Beth said. 'It's cheaper. Butter would be a real treat.' She licked her lips, probably wasn't even aware she was doing it.

He looked at the dusty tabletop with marks of mice or maybe even rats tracking across it. 'We'll need to clean that table before we get out the food. I think Mrs Buckley at the shop put some rags in the bag.'

'I'll go through the kitchen cupboards,' Beth said. 'You go through the scullery, Dilys.'

'It's that door there.' Finn pointed then tipped out the cleaning things he'd bought from Nancy on to the wooden draining board as Beth started opening and shutting the cupboard doors.

'There's a broom cupboard in here,' Dilys called. 'There are all sorts of brushes, but they're as dusty as everything else. Ugh!'

'What is it?'

'There's a dead rat.'

Finn went to investigate. It was a desiccated thing, long dead. He found a dustpan and scooped the body up. 'I'll throw it outside for the moment.'

'Thank you.' She took a deep breath and began to sort out some brushes.

'I could light the fire for you, Uncle Finn,' Reggie called. 'We can boil a kettle and make a pot of tea then. I can sit on a chair to do it, so it won't hurt my leg.'

'Good idea.'

'There's still kindling and wood in the basket. They must have just walked out and left *everything*.' Reggie's eyes were gleaming. 'It's like a story in the *Boys' Own Paper*, isn't it? What fun we're going to have exploring the house!'

Dilys smiled at the youngster's enthusiasm as she came back with some dusters and started cleaning the kitchen chairs, while Beth swept the table and began washing it down. 'Cold water's better than nothing,' she said, then stopped. 'There's a drawer here, sir. It was hidden by the chairs before.'

'Open it. Don't hesitate to look into cupboards and drawers.'

'Goodness. It's full of tablecloths. They've gone all yellow on the creases, but I bet the ones underneath will be all right to use.' Her eyes betrayed her as she glanced towards the bag of food.

'Get one out that looks clean, then. Reggie and I have just

eaten, but you two can have a slice of bread and butter now, then I'll leave you to work on the kitchen in any way you see fit.'

He saw Beth blink in surprise and added, 'I'm not an expert on cleaning houses, so I'll trust you two to do it properly. We'll eat again at about one o'clock. I wonder . . .' He walked across to the clock on the mantelpiece and wound it up, setting the correct time. A quiet tick rewarded him. And for the first time, he felt at home.

The two women didn't take their eyes off him as he cut slices of bread and buttered them, then nudged them to the edge of the piece of paper that had wrapped the loaf.

Dilys closed her eyes and swallowed hard, then took a hesitant bite, chewing slowly. Beth was already swallowing her first mouthful, a blissful look on her face.

He couldn't bear to watch the poor things eat. He'd always got upset at the hunger he'd seen on his travels, because he'd experienced hunger too at first, till he'd learned how to use his status as a former policeman to find odd jobs. He'd been able to give Sergeant Deemer as a reference and a phone number, which had often made all the difference.

'There's only water to drink till we get the fire burning properly,' he said. 'We'll brew a pot of tea as soon as the kettle boils.'

It was strange, he thought as he surreptitiously watched the two women, how Beth changed towards Dilys once he'd accepted the younger woman's services, seeming to grow more friendly. Maybe she'd been afraid he'd scorn her for associating with an unmarried mother. Some people could be very cruel about that sort of thing, as if a woman had created a child all on her own.

He shook his head. He'd better get on with things. 'Reggie and I will go exploring and leave you two to the cleaning,' he said abruptly. 'Well, we will if your leg isn't hurting, Reggie.'

'I'm all right if I go slowly and use the crutch.'

'Don't you want to tell us what to do first, even?' Beth asked.

'No. I want you to decide for yourselves how best to clean the kitchen area. My main purpose here today is to get a proper understanding of the layout inside the house while it's still light.'

'Those women were very hungry, weren't they?' Reggie whispered as he followed Finn into the front of the house. 'Not peckish like I am, but really, really hungry.'

'Yes. Half-starved.'

Reggie stared at him solemnly. 'Even at the orphanage we had something to eat. It didn't taste very nice, and it wasn't always enough, but it put something in your belly. Those two would have worked without food.'

'Yes, but I'd have felt guilty if they'd had to do that.'

'You're a very kind man, Uncle Finn. I want to be just like you when I grow up.'

It wasn't always comfortable being kind, Finn thought. He wanted to help all the hungry people he met, and that wasn't possible. He couldn't even help all those in Ellindale.

And he still wasn't used to knowing he owned this house. Apart from that fleeting moment in the kitchen when it felt like home, he still felt as if he was an intruder here.

What was he going to do with the place? How ridiculous, one man having such a huge house to live in!

He could understand why Uncle Oscar hadn't moved in. But Finn wasn't going to leave the place to rot. Or to stand empty and useless. He'd find something worthwhile to do with it.

What, though?

7

Adam Harris walked slowly along the two streets that took him from home to the laundry he owned in Birch End. He lifted his face to the sun, enjoying the promise of warm weather.

Then suddenly a woman in the distance reminded him of his ex-wife and he stopped dead, thinking for one terrible moment that Ethel had returned. Then the woman turned towards him and he saw that it wasn't her. Oh, thank goodness!

Ethel still owned property here, he knew, various terraced houses that were rented out, so it was entirely possible that she might come back to the village one day. He prayed not, or at least not until his divorce was final.

Rumour said that she'd sold all her properties in the valley, but Adam's lawyer had found out this wasn't true, like so many of the tales she'd told. A new fellow was now collecting the rents for her and had been seen to deposit the money in the bank she'd used. He'd gone in carrying a bag heavy with coins and come out swinging it cheerfully to and fro. That gave no clue to which other branch the bank was sending it, though.

For the umpteenth time, Adam wondered where Ethel was living now. A long way from Rivenshaw, he hoped. She'd not been sharing a house with him even before she left town on that dreadful night her lover had been killed while attacking Leah at Spring Cottage.

When the police made inquiries they found that a few people had seen Ethel driving her car away from the town on the Manchester road well before the incident took place up in Ellindale. Two of them had noticed her because she was driving so erratically. She was a terrible driver.

As she couldn't have been involved in the events that led to Sam Griggs's death, the police hadn't pursued her. She had been in such a hurry she hadn't taken most of her possessions with her. Adam had arranged for them to be packed and put into storage, getting rid of every single tiny item that had reminded him of her. The lawyers had sorted that out and the boxes had been taken away.

He had never understood what attracted Ethel to a violent man like Sam, except that she seemed to crave excitement. Adam didn't. All he wanted was a quiet life filled with simple daily pleasures, a family of his own (if there was still time, he would turn thirty-eight in November) and a few good friends. He shouldn't have married Ethel in the first place, but she'd fooled him into believing they wanted the same things out of life. And she'd been very pretty – no, not pretty exactly, but striking. Yes, that was the word.

Well, he knew now how horrible she was under that attractive exterior. He had started divorce proceedings and gained his decree nisi because he'd caught her in bed with Sam Griggs, with witnesses to help him prove her adultery. She hadn't even attempted to defend the court case, and her lawyer had produced a doctor's note from somewhere in London to say she was too ill to attend the hearing.

The judge, a local man sympathetic to Adam, had granted him a divorce without any further fuss, which was the main thing that mattered.

What a stupid process getting divorced was, though. Why couldn't people just agree to end a marriage and register that with the authorities? Even now, Adam still had to wait six months for the decree absolute, which would finally and completely dissolve his unhappy marriage and leave him free to marry again. And if anything cropped up to put the divorce in question, it could be even longer because the legal system was set up to keep married couples together.

By late afternoon he'd had enough of the laundry with its steamy air and clanking machines and felt like a breath of fresh air. He asked his foreman to close up today and planned to go up to Ellindale later to visit his friend Nancy after her shop shut.

It was always pleasant to chat to her and he also wanted to see if she had any bottles of ginger beer for sale. He didn't drink alcohol, not after years of living with a drunken wife, but he was very partial to Leah Willcox's ginger beer. He always bought it from Nancy's shop in the next village to give her a little profit and to give him an excuse to visit her.

When a car pulled up behind the shop that evening, just before closing time, Lily was surprised to see Nancy become a little flustered and rush to the mirror to check that her hair was tidy.

If Nancy had been younger, Lily would have thought she was expecting a young man to come courting, but her cousin was in her late thirties and surely past that sort of thing. She'd been a widow for a good many years, ever since her husband had come home from the Great War so badly injured that not even the most careful nursing could do more than ease his last couple of years. People had told her about Nancy's devotion to him.

'It's Mr Harris,' Nancy explained when she saw Lily looking at her. She blushed slightly as she added, 'He was a friend of my husband's and he drops in to see me sometimes to, um, buy Mrs Willcox's ginger beer.'

Lily didn't allow herself to smile at such an obvious excuse for a man to call on a woman. 'That's nice. I'll go and keep an eye on the shop, shall I?'

The blush deepened. 'Well, um, yes. Thank you. But stay to meet him first.'

The man who knocked on the back door was tall, with greying hair and a slight limp, no, not a limp, more a halting way of walking, Lily decided. He had kind eyes and when they settled on Nancy, the corners of them crinkled in an almost-smile.

'I hope you don't mind me calling, but I've run out of ginger beer.'

'You're welcome any time. This is my cousin's daughter, Lily, who's come to stay with me.' Nancy didn't look at Lily as she said that; she was too busy studying Adam, as if to make sure he was all right.

He gave Lily a quick nod but he didn't really look at her either.

'I was just going to have a cup of tea. Would you like to join me, Adam?'

'I was hoping you'd offer. You make the best tea of anyone I know.'

Lily noticed that Nancy got the fancy tea caddy out of the cupboard, the one with the special tea leaves in it that they only used on Sundays as a treat. This was definitely a favoured visitor, then.

She picked up a book and went to sit in the refreshment area of the shop, not expecting any more customers. The others didn't seem to notice her departure, because they were laughing about something that had happened years ago.

To her surprise a man came into the shop. He was a bit older than Lily but not much, she judged, with a kind expression. 'Can I help you, sir?'

'I'm from Spring Cottage.' He held out a slip of paper.

'Mrs Willcox asked me to drop off her groceries order. And I'd like a quarter of a pound of humbugs for myself, please.'

'I'll give the order to Nancy. She's busy at the moment but I can weigh you some humbugs.' She had watched it done enough times.

'I'm Ben Lonsdale. You must be her cousin Lily. Leah said you'd been ill.'

'I'm a lot better now. I'd been going a bit short of food, that was all.'

He gave her an understanding nod. 'I had a patch of that myself last year. Not pleasant, is it?'

'No. Do you work at Spring Cottage?'

'I'm working there at the moment, finishing off some renovations to their old barn. I'm a stonemason.'

'Oh yes. Nancy mentioned the changes they're making.' But Lily had thought the stonemason must be an older man, not someone as young and good-looking as this.

He paid for the humbugs and turned towards the door. 'I'd better get a move on. I'm on my way to visit a man in Birch End who wants a small job doing. They're mostly repair jobs these days, but I'm just starting up in business so I welcome anything.'

Lily left the shopping list on the counter and went to stand behind the shop door, looking out through the glass panes. Not to watch him stride off down the hill, certainly not! But she couldn't help noticing how strong and fit he looked. There weren't a lot of people with that look of good health these days. He must be eating well.

She glanced back towards the room behind the shop. She could hear their voices, still low and confidential. With a smile, she left them to it and went to stand outside in the shop doorway, enjoying some mild sunshine on her face.

She was sorry when another customer arrived and disturbed her quiet moment.

She had to disturb Nancy too, because Lily didn't know all the prices yet.

Shortly after Adam left, half an hour later, taking with him the rest of Nancy's bottles of ginger beer, two men sauntered up the hill, chatting. They stopped outside the shop and one came in to buy a packet of five cigarettes. She rarely sold more than a small packet like that, and also sold cigarettes one at a time, making a farthing profit on each one.

The stranger tried to chat to Nancy about the newcomer at Heythorpe House, but she wasn't going to gossip about her best customer. Anyway, she didn't like the look of this fellow and the fact that he was with Judson only intensified her feeling of dislike. At least Judson had had more sense than to come into her shop, because she'd let it be known that she'd not serve him again, whether he had money or not.

When she gave the stranger his change, she discouraged any chatting by thanking him curtly for his custom and turning back to Lily. She was showing her young cousin how to weigh dry goods and fold the tops into neat packets, the pointed final flap stuck down with a dab of glue.

As the door had closed behind the man, she said, 'Just a minute, love!' and went to stand to one side of the shop window to watch what he did.

'What's he doing hobnobbing with that Barry Judson?' she wondered aloud. 'Yes, and now he's offering Judson a cigarette, so they're definitely on friendly terms.' Only she'd never seen the stranger before and Judson rarely left the valley, so how could they be friends? What was going on? Nothing good, if Judson was involved.

She watched the two of them walk up the hill and out of sight, then returned to her task. 'Sorry, love. I don't know why I feel suspicious of that fellow, but I do.'

'I didn't like the look of him, either, and did you see the

way he stared at me?' Lily tossed her head. 'I hate it when men look at my figure. It's so rude.'

'You're getting pretty now you're eating properly, but they still shouldn't be so rude, I agree. Let's shut up and lock the door. I'm tired.'

Lily could tell that the encounter continued to worry Nancy because she came back to it several times during the evening.

'Where do you suppose they were going? There's only Heythorpe House or Spring Cottage up that way, and I'm sure men like them aren't going to call on that nice Finn Carlisle or the Willcoxes.'

'I'll sit and read my library book and keep an eye out for them coming back.'

'You do that, Lily. We can't be too careful out here in Ellindale. If there's any trouble, my shop could get damaged and then what would I do?'

Barry saved the cigarette the stranger had given him for later, slipping it into his pocket with a nod of thanks. He walked up the slope beside his new friend, wishing he'd go more slowly and puffing slightly even after such a short walk. He was losing his strength, that's what, going so short of food. His wife was a poor manager.

He stopped at the gateway to point. 'There you are. That's the place the fellow you were talking about inherited. There's a lad living with him, too.' He sniggered. 'You have to wonder what's going on there.'

His companion didn't answer, just stood staring thoughtfully down the slope at the roof of the old house. 'Looks like a big place.'

'It is. But they say it's nearly a ruin because no one's lived there since I were a little 'un. The new chap is still staying in lodgings in Rivenshaw but someone told me he's planning to move in, the lucky sod.'

'I'd make it worth your while to keep an eye on the house and see if you can find out what's going on there. You could let me know when they move in, for instance. I'll give you a couple of stamped postcards to send to me.'

Barry seized the opportunity. 'Hard to keep an eye on things when I've no money to go into the pub. That's where you hear the most gossip.' He didn't mention that he wasn't welcome there. Surely Don would let him buy a beer if he apologised?

The man pulled out a florin and tossed it at Barry, who caught it adroitly. 'See what you can find out at the pub, then. I'll be back in a couple of days. I might come into the pub with you then. You could introduce me as your cousin.'

'If you like. You'll have to tell folk you're Jimmy's lad. He's the only one of my dad's brothers who went away and never came back. Dad allus thought he must have died, but no one knows for certain.'

'I'll be Jimmy's lad, then.' He turned and started walking back to the village, parting company there with a wave of the hand and a loud call of, 'Glad to have found you again, Cousin Barry.'

Which made old Simeon who was sitting in the sun in front of his house sit up and take notice. 'Cousin Barry?' he muttered. '*Cousin?* That one isn't a Judson. They've allus got big, lumpy noses, them Judsons have, every last one of them.'

Simeon shared his thoughts with the landlord of the pub that evening, earning himself a second half pint, because Don encouraged folk to keep him up to date with all the latest gossip and rumours.

When Barry came into the pub later on everyone fell silent, looking from Don to the man hesitating in the doorway, waiting to see what would happen.

Don said loudly, 'I thought I told you to stay out of my pub, Judson.'

'Aw, don't be heartless. I'm sorry if I caused trouble before. I really did earn some money today down in Rivenshaw, though, an' I've give Madge enough to buy a loaf *and* some margarine. What's more, I'm only wanting half a pint of beer. I've turned over a new leaf, I have. Give us a chance.'

Don, remembering what old Simeon had told him, chewed the corner of his mouth thoughtfully, then said, 'Only a half pint then. And no trouble.'

The other men turned back to their beer, but no one made room at their table for Barry or even spoke to him. After a moment's hesitation, he went to stand at the corner of the bar, scowling into his beer until someone he knew came in and stood with him.

'That sod's up to something,' Don told Izzy after they'd closed up that night.

She yawned. 'What sod?'

'Judson.'

'Oh, him. Perhaps he's learned his lesson. Perhaps he'll treat his family better from now on.'

'And pigs will fly to the moon!' Don scoffed. 'He's up to something, that's what. I just know it.'

'Well, if he is, it'll be his wife who suffers, not us. Mrs Potter said she saw Madge buying a loaf and a packet of margarine today, so he wasn't lying to you tonight. How Madge puts up with him, I don't know. I'd keep the poker under the bed if I had a husband who slapped me around.'

He grinned at her and spread his arms wide. 'You won't need a poker with me, love. You can have your way with me any time you like.'

She rolled her eyes. 'Get on with you. You'll be asleep before I am.'

But he wasn't.

Finn and Reggie spent the rest of the morning exploring the house from the attics to the cellar, drawing a rough map of each floor as they went. They could hear the two women cleaning downstairs, but Finn kept out of the kitchen. If people could work without constant supervision, they were likely to make good servants.

'This place isn't as big as the orphanage, but it's still big,' Reggie commented. 'I didn't know people with families lived in houses so grand.'

'Well, you'd better get used to it, because it's where you'll be living from now on.'

The boy beamed at him.

Finn was pleased to find that everywhere was dry, even if dirty. The house had clearly been well built and had no leaks. The cellars were smaller than he'd expected and hadn't got much in them.

Reggie was disappointed by that. 'You'd think we'd find something interesting down here,' he complained as they finished their tour of the big, dark space. 'Secret passages or ghosts. Not just dust and dirt.'

'Well, there isn't anything and modern families don't use cellars half as much as they needed to when they had to produce and store a lot of their own food, so I doubt we'll be putting much down here either. I'm just glad it's not damp.' He pulled out his pocket watch. 'One o'clock. Time for something to eat, don't you think?'

Reggie brightened up at once, forgetting his disappointment and trying to race up the cellar steps ahead of his companion. But he had to slow down almost immediately because his leg hurt, even though he'd sat down to rest it several times while helping his new uncle to explore.

The kitchen floor was still damp in places and had obviously had a good scrubbing because the flagstones paving it were several shades lighter in colour.

When Beth looked across at him challengingly, as if to ask whether he was satisfied, he said, 'This looks a lot better. You two must have worked hard.'

'We did.'

'Ready for something else to eat?'

For the first time she gave him a real smile. 'Always.'

'There's only bread and cheese.'

'Only?' Dilys whispered. 'I haven't had cheese for months.'

He couldn't think what to say to that, so got out the loaf in silence and passed it to Beth. It had only had a small part cut off, the two slices the women had eaten before starting work, so they hadn't tried to sneak an extra piece. Good. 'Cut us two slices each and let's see what's left to put on them.'

While Beth did this, he got out the neat little parcel of butter, wrapped in greaseproof paper, and divided it into four.

Without being told, Dilys found them plates and when the food was placed on them, she bent her head and tried in vain to stem the tears.

Beth came round to pat her on the shoulder. 'She'll be all right in a minute. We appreciate your generosity, Mr Carlisle, we really do. Especially considering how we pushed ourselves on you today.'

'You were both desperate.'

'Yes. Very. It's hard to see your children going hungry.'

'It must be. Let's begin eating, eh?'

But both women sat staring at the food on their plates for a few moments longer before they followed his example. Then each cut the sandwich carefully into four and began to eat slowly. By the time they started, Reggie had finished half his food.

After two of the four pieces of her sandwich had gone, Beth gave him a pleading look. 'I can't fit any more food into my belly, Mr Carlisle. Would it be all right if I saved this for my tea?'

He guessed she was keeping it for her children, but didn't

let on. As far as he was concerned it was hers to do as she wanted with, as long as she ate enough to fuel her body for the cleaning work. He didn't like the thought of kids going hungry.

That incident helped make another decision for him: he couldn't refuse to give these two women further work.

'Shall we start next on the other rooms you'll be using?' Beth asked as Dilys made them all a pot of tea. 'Which rooms will you want scrubbing out first? A sitting room and a bedroom?'

He nodded. 'I'm thinking that if we can get a bedroom cleaned and ready to sleep in, Reggie and I can move out here permanently, then we won't have to be bound by the bus timetables. We can use that little room at the back for sitting in. I think they'd have called it the breakfast parlour.'

'All right. You could ring for a taxi from Nancy Buckley's shop if you wanted to stay later than the last bus, mind. She lets people phone from her shop, not that I've ever had the need, but she only charges twopence. You can't help knowing what's going on in such a small village.'

'Have you always lived in Ellindale?'

She shook her head. 'No. I moved here when I married Neil. He'd been brought up here by his aunt and she let us live with her. She died a couple of years ago, though, and he lost his job soon afterwards, but the farmer let us stay on in her house if we paid him something now and then. When my husband couldn't find work round here, he went off on the tramp, leaving me and the kids behind.'

From the scowl on her face, Finn guessed she hadn't wanted her husband to go. He waited and more words poured out, as if she needed to tell someone.

'It's a godsend the owner of our cottage is a farmer who has no need for it at present, Mr Carlisle, an absolute godsend. Well, Mr Unwin's the owner of Dilys's cottage too. They're only small places, no good for big families, and he's not employing as many men these days anyway, so he's let us all stay on there or we'd be in the workhouse. I promised to pay him what I could, so I'll have to give him sixpence from the money you pay me and if they find out I'm earning anything, the dole people will take it out of my payments.'

She sighed and fell silent, staring into space. 'It's one step forward and two steps back.'

'And how's your husband going?'

'I don't know. He sent money back at first, enough for us to manage on if I did odd jobs here and there, but he hasn't sent anything or even written us a postcard for over six months now. I had to apply for relief and go before the Committee to plead my case. They keep changing what they call it but it's still charity and it's not enough to keep body and soul together, let alone buy clothes for growing children.'

He heard the bitterness in her voice and couldn't blame her for feeling upset. What the hell was her husband playing at? Had the fellow abandoned his wife and children? Finn had heard of that happening. It was surprising Beth had managed to cope this long.

'Where was your husband when you last heard?'

'Chester. Working for a minister, would you believe, helping him renovate the churchyard and Sunday school. Neil's good with his hands . . . when he wants to bother. The church was called St Crispin's, he told me, so I wrote to him there. I thought the postman would have known the church even though I didn't have the full address, but I never got a reply. I wrote again but nothing happened. Nothing.' She made a helpless movement with her shoulders and stared blindly into space for a moment.

'That must be hard.'

She gave him a quick glance as if wondering whether he

meant it, then forced a smile and changed the subject. 'Thank you for listening, sir. Now, which bedroom do you want us to get ready for you?'

'Let's have one at the front, Uncle Finn,' Reggie said eagerly. 'The ones at the back only look on to the hillside.'

Finn had no particular preferences, but that seemed an obvious choice. 'All right. If you'll clear up the kitchen, Dilys, the rest of us will go and choose a bedroom.'

'Don't forget to fill the kettle again,' Beth called over her shoulder before following Finn out.

To his amusement, Beth took charge when he couldn't make up his mind which bedroom to take because all the front ones had the lovely view.

She grew visibly impatient with his dithering, then burst out with, 'If you're both going to share, why not take the corner room? It's the biggest. Then, if you want Reggie to have his own room later, you can stay there, sir.' She led the way back along to that bedroom without waiting for him to agree, so he followed, hiding a smile.

For a moment she stood by the window and said in a tone of wonderment, 'Just look at those views. It lifts your spirits not to be hemmed in.'

He was looking at her, not the views. The more he got to know her, the more he liked her. Beneath that sharp tongue was a good brain, and she seemed a sensible woman struggling against huge odds. No wonder she'd been desperate enough to accost him at the gate this morning if she had two small children to feed.

'Who's looking after your children today?'

'Dilys's mother. We live next door. She likes children and earns a penny or two caring for them when people find a bit of work.'

So Beth would have to pay her something too. Today's five shillings wouldn't last long at this rate.

'We can bring in a single bed for Reggie, sir. There's plenty of room.'

When he didn't reply immediately, she suddenly seemed to realise she was ordering him around and looked at him anxiously, pressing her lips together as if to hold back more words. 'Sorry. My husband used to say I was too bossy.'

'I don't mind you suggesting things, but I've come to the conclusion that I'd rather not share a bedroom with Reggie. He snores.'

'I do not!' Then the boy looked at him anxiously and added, 'Do I?'

'No. I was just teasing. But I would prefer a room of my own. You can have that small one near the other end of this corridor.'

Which had Reggie limping along to check it and sending out a loud hurrah when he saw that it too looked to the front. As if he wouldn't let the lad have a view over the valley when there were six bedrooms to choose from, Finn thought.

'He's a nice lad,' Beth said softly. 'He's lucky you took him in.'

'I'm lucky I found him. I didn't realise how lonely I was.'

'It bites sometimes, doesn't it?' From her expression she'd been lonely too. 'Anyway, do you know where the sheets are, sir? You should get them washed before you use them. If you take them to the laundry early tomorrow morning before you come up here, they'll do a quick job for you and if you pay a bit extra, they'll deliver them here by teatime. Mr Harris might even bring them to you in his car. He's very obliging. Nothing too much trouble for his customers.'

'Good idea.'

By the time they'd sorted out all the details, Finn was tired. He could see that the two women were exhausted, though they were trying to hide it. Well, they would be tired if they'd been half starving, wouldn't they? But they'd not stinted on the work and both of them had saved some of their midday meal for their children. That said something about their nature, didn't it?

'That's enough for today. About tomorrow . . . could you come for another day's work?'

Dilys burst into tears and it was left to Beth to answer for them both.

'Thank you very much, sir. We'll be happy to do that. What time do you want us?'

He didn't think he'd ever heard anyone sound more truly thankful. 'Reggie and I will catch the second bus up from Rivenshaw, so that we can go and show his leg to the nurse first. When you see the bus arrive, come and meet us at the house.' He gave each of them five shillings and walked with them to the back door, locking it after them.

When he returned to the kitchen, he found Reggie sitting drooping at the table. It had been an eventful day in many small ways, but Finn was hungry and tired now, and he bet the lad would be too. 'Come on, young fellow. I know you're tired but I want to see Mrs Willcox before we go back, and then if she'll let us use her telephone to call the taxi from her house, we'll not have to walk into Ellindale and wait for the last bus. I'm exhausted. Aren't you?'

'I'm all right, Uncle Finn. Just a bit of an ache in my leg.'

It was clearly more than a bit of an ache and Finn felt guilty for letting the boy do so much with an injury, but how could he have stopped him? He definitely had to find himself a car as soon as possible.

He locked the house carefully, checking each external door, and walked slowly up the hill. Reggie was limping badly now. He'd sat down without being told for much of the latter part of the afternoon, too. But each time he'd found a place to sit near where Finn was working, a fact the man was well aware of, and found touching.

It seemed a long time since someone had cared so much about being with him.

8

Leah heard a motor vehicle draw up in the yard of Spring Cottage and went out to see who it was. A small van painted a dull grey was standing in front of her house and when Charlie got out of it, beaming triumphantly, she began to hope it was the vehicle he'd found for her deliveries.

The van had been driven by a man she didn't recognise, nor could she tell much about him from his general appearance. He was neatly dressed but he had a pirate's face, with a confidence to the way he looked at the world that you didn't often see.

He got out and stretched his tall body slightly, then noticed her watching him from the doorway and stopped to study her openly in return.

Charlie came across and tugged her hand. 'I found you a van, Leah. Come and look at it. See what you think. Sit in it. Come *on*!'

She hid a smile. Her brother-in-law often got excited and enthusiastic about what he was doing. It cheered people up as well as making them feel more confident about dealing with him. She heard footsteps behind her and Jonah came out to join them.

'Ha! You're looking better today, my lad,' Charlie said at once to his brother.

She didn't think Jonah was looking better but at least he wasn't looking any worse.

Charlie gestured to the stranger. 'This is Todd Selby. I

served with him in the war. He's a wizard with motor vehicles. He's recently come back from travelling the world. Just imagine. He's been everywhere you can think of – New York, Canada, Australia. But now he's home and we're going to set up in business together.'

The stranger nodded but didn't add a smile to the salutation. Then he cocked his head on one side, studying Jonah now as if wondering where he'd seen him before.

Jonah was giving him the same slightly puzzled look, then said suddenly, 'Verdun, 1916. You were helping a friend and I . . . was being loaded on to a stretcher.'

'Ah, that's it! We met in hell, didn't we?'

'Yes. Then you visited your friend in hospital and he was in the next bed to me. They moved me out a few days later. How did he go on?'

'He didn't make it. It's good to see you did, though, Jonah. You look to be doing well, considering how badly you were affected by the gas.'

Leah gasped to hear this said so openly, but Jonah merely laughed. 'You haven't changed. Still as blunt as ever. One of the nurses said you were the rudest officer she'd ever met, but at least you were honest. And yes, I have done well, considering, and I'm not on death's doorstep yet, either.'

'Good. I shall look forward to catching up with you now that I'll be living nearby.'

'We three chaps will have a meal together at the Green Man one night,' Charlie declared, grinning at Leah and adding, 'Ex-soldiers getting together and reminiscing. Always a good night, and good to get the memories out of your system.' He paused and said more quietly than usual, 'I haven't done that in a long time. You wouldn't mind Jonah joining us, would you, Leah?'

'Of course I wouldn't.'

'I'd definitely enjoy that,' Jonah said.

When she glanced quickly at him, she thought his expression was happier than she'd seen for a while, so she mentally forgave the stranger for his bluntness. Anything that cheered Jonah up was all right by her.

'Let's look at that van, then.'

'Tell her the details, Todd,' Charlie said.

'Doesn't your brother want to know the details, too?' his friend teased.

'Yes, of course, but the business is Leah's.'

There was a moment's silence, then Jonah defused the awkwardness. 'I do the accounts for Charlie and my wife. I'm the book man. But I do drive and know something about cars, so of course Leah and I will be choosing a van together.'

'Ah. I see. Well, this is an Austin, as you can tell. It has a commercial chassis and the body can be changed to suit your needs, if necessary, but I should think the hinged side panels will be helpful when lifting crates of fizzy drinks in and out of it.'

They checked out the body of the vehicle, then he said, 'Why don't you have a drive, try it out?'

Leah looked at Jonah, who gestured to the van, as if to tell her to do that.

She gave in to temptation. 'I'm cooking tea, so I've only time for a quick drive into Ellindale and back. Wait a minute. I'll just get my glasses.' She glanced at Todd. 'I need them for long distance vision.'

She put them on and got in, letting Mr Selby show her the controls. She drove it out of the yard and down towards the village and back, turning at the wider space in front of the entrance to Heythorpe House, then testing out the reverse gears by manoeuvring round the yard between Spring Cottage and the huge old barn.

By the time she got out, she was satisfied it would do what they needed and that it was quite easy to drive. 'I have to look at my cooking now.' She went inside, passing Jonah, who had come to the door to watch her reverse.

'Why don't you come in for a few moments, Mr Selby?' he asked. 'I don't know about you but I'm dying for a cup of tea.'

Mr Selby's expression softened. 'I know I'm back in Britain when people offer me a cup of tea. I missed good tea while I was travelling. The Americans are not usually good at making it and I drank some rather strong brews in Australia.'

'I met some great chaps from down under during the war. What did they call themselves?' Jonah frowned, tapping his forehead as if to knock the word out.

Todd provided it. 'Anzacs. Which is short for Australia and New Zealand Army Corps, if I remember correctly, Jonah – or do you want me to call you "Mr Willcox"?'

'Jonah is fine. Ah yes. That's what it's short for.'

'A lot of fellows from the colonies fought for the motherland and paid the price. I had some good chats with ones who'd got back to Australia safely. We owe our colonies a lot. They didn't hesitate to come to our aid when war started and they lost a lot of men.'

Leah had come back to join them and judged it time to add a more cheerful note. 'What adventures you must have had! How many years did it take you to go round the world, Mr Selby?'

'Just call me Todd.'

'And please call me Leah.'

He gave her another of those penetrating looks and nodded. 'I set off just after the war. I wanted to get away from England with its grey skies and battle-weary men. I didn't come back till a few months ago and I've been travelling round Britain ever since, catching up. So, it took me about thirteen years, give or take.'

That seemed a long time to be away. Not only away, but lacking real roots. Leah wouldn't like to be homeless for so long. Her home mattered a great deal to her.

'I've always wanted to visit Australia,' Jonah said wistfully. 'I hear they're having some hard times there too, but at least they get the sunny weather.'

'Yes, very hard times, but I still managed to earn my way most of the time, because chaps who understand car engines are always in demand. Took me two years to work my way from one side of Australia to the other, starting in Sydney, finishing in Perth. It's just under two and a half thousand miles from east to west, but I went the long way, via Melbourne and Adelaide. I bought an old car and drove, taking my time. I loved the big, open spaces, and I found the peace and quiet outside towns very soothing.'

He fell silent, staring at his memories, she guessed.

After a moment or two Charlie clapped his friend on the shoulder in that friendly way he had. 'Todd was thinking of settling out there but luckily for me, he changed his mind and came back.'

'What made you do that, Mr Selby?' Leah could hear how cool her voice sounded but something about the stranger, perhaps that bold, assessing stare of his, made her want to keep him at a distance.

'I found myself getting homesick for all this.' He gestured round them. 'The north of England and the moors, hard times and rainy weather notwithstanding. The sun down under . . . well, it can be too hot. I found myself longing for crisp, frosty mornings. And the rolling slopes of the moors.' He glanced towards them as he spoke.

'I doubt there's anywhere in the world perfect,' she said. 'It's the people who matter most to me, though I love living in Ellindale.' She loved it in spite of the violence she'd faced here in the past. But then, there was violence everywhere underneath the surface. It was law and order that held it back, most of the time anyway.

'Yes. If you have people you care about. But I don't have any close relatives left so I indulged myself and set out to see the world.'

'You were never tempted to marry and settle down?' Charlie asked.

'No. I came near to it a couple of times, but I lay down in a darkened room till the urge passed.'

Was he joking? she wondered. Or did he really think of marriage in such a negative way?

'It can be wonderful to have a companion in life.' Jonah put his arm round Leah. 'Maybe we can find someone here that you'll want to settle down with. You must come round to tea one day and tell Leah and me more about your travels. She'll be interested as well. She loves learning about the world. How I envy you those travels!'

Leah hadn't realised her husband had longed to travel. Presumably this was another of the things prevented by his poor state of health. He never complained about his limitations or dwelled on them, but she wished he'd share more of his deeper feelings and regrets with her. At times she had to guess what he wanted as she did her best to make him happy.

She was fond of him but she never fooled herself about their relationship: it hadn't been a love match. And even if she'd fallen madly in love with him, Jonah never let her or anyone else, not even his brother, come too close. She and her husband were good friends, though, and he did his best to make her happy.

Most people would consider it a really good marriage. Well, she did too, but like every other young woman she'd once dreamed of falling in love. And she had only just turned twenty-two, after all, though she felt years older, so she was entitled to a few daydreams, even if they were a long way out of reach now. She'd never do anything to hurt Jonah.

She suppressed a sigh. She never told anyone how she felt. The only person she'd been able to talk to freely in her whole life had been her father. Her little sister said the same thing. You could have told their dad anything, sure he'd never scorn you or make you feel silly. Her mother had often been too busy to chat, though a loving woman in her own way, but her father had been . . . special, very special. She and Rosa had both been devastated when he was killed in the accident at the laundry.

She realised she was standing staring into space and the three men were waiting for her to move out of the doorway. 'Sorry. I was remembering my father. I still miss him. Oh, look! Here come Finn and Reggie. That poor boy looks absolutely exhausted. I'd better drive them back to Rivenshaw afterwards. Reggie shouldn't be walking about on that injured leg.'

'We can take them back with us and save you the trouble,' Charlie said. 'If you like the van, Todd here will give it a good going over before you take it away. Hoy, Finn! Come and meet my old friend Todd.'

'You must join us for a cup of tea.' Leah saw the boy's face brighten at that and smiled at his eager face. Lads that age seemed to be permanently hungry.

Finn kept his hand on Reggie's shoulder as he moved forward. 'If Mrs Willcox doesn't mind, a cup of tea would be lovely. And after that I'd like to pick everyone's brains.'

He exchanged glances with Leah and jerked his head slightly towards Reggie, trying to indicate the bad leg. He then watched in admiration as she quickly realised what he wanted and got the boy seated with his foot up. He was grateful when she gently persuaded him that resting it regularly was the quickest way to heal it.

'What did you want to pick our brains about?' she asked as she turned back to her tea making.

'What sort of second-hand car to buy.'

Charlie let out a crow of laughter. 'You're looking at the best man to deal with right this minute, Finn.'

'The best men,' the stranger corrected. He held out one hand. 'Todd Selby.'

'Finn Carlisle.'

The two men shook hands.

'Charlie and I are going into business together, selling second-hand cars. I enjoy tinkering around with motors and can tell a good vehicle from a bad, while he enjoys the selling. You'll have to tell us what sort of car you're looking for.'

Jonah shot his brother a worried glance. 'Surely this is the worst time to start another business?'

'Depends how much it costs you to start up and how long you can afford to wait to make decent money,' Charlie said. 'Bad time to borrow money, yes, but we've enough between us to make a start. People told me it was a bad time when I opened my second pawnshop in Rivenshaw, but I've proved them wrong.' He tapped the side of his nose. 'Trust me, I've got a feel for business.'

Todd joined in. 'It'd not be a good time to sell new cars, mind. There are so few being made at the moment and there are long waits for delivery. But we're not thinking of going down that path. We'll only be selling second-hand vehicles. Sadly, some people are forced to sell them because they can't afford to run them.'

It was out before Leah could stop herself. 'And you'll be taking advantage of their troubles.'

'We'll be paying fair prices, unlike some dealers,' he snapped, glaring at her.

She glared right back.

Charlie intervened hastily. 'I own a plot of land just outside

Rivenshaw and it's sitting there doing nothing. It's got an old house on it, bit of a ruin, but I thought Ben might make a couple of rooms habitable for Todd to live in and we can put up a shed to house the cars and stand them outside at the front during the day. People will come to have a look, if nothing else.'

He spread his arms wide. 'So there you are. Willcox and Selby Motors.'

'You could shorten that to Will Sell Motors,' Reggie said suddenly, then flushed as everyone turned to stare at him.

'Good idea. Why not?' Charlie cocked one eyebrow at Todd, who nodded.

'There you are, lad, you've just given our new business a name.'

Reggie's smile was about a yard wide, Leah thought. How different that boy looked when he was happy. She carefully kept from meeting the eyes of Charlie's new partner. She shouldn't have spoken out like that, couldn't understand why she'd done it. Men didn't want women's opinions about business matters, even women who had started up their own businesses.

Once they were settled with cups of tea, Todd asked again, 'What sort of car are you looking for, Finn?'

'Any small to medium car that'll get me about. I care more about it being reliable and reasonably comfortable than anything else.'

'Price?'

'Whatever is reasonable. I, um, inherited a little money so I can afford something decent, but not a luxury car, of course.'

'Give me a couple of days. I know some people in the Manchester car trade. I'll see if any of them can find you something.'

Leah listened to the men talking while she checked the stew and put some potatoes on to simmer on the cooler part of the cooker top. The timescale outlined by Mr Selby was rather ambitious, considering the man had only just come to the area. He seemed to be as optimistic and pushy as Charlie, but would he be as lucky? So many people couldn't make a go of it in times like these, however hard they worked and then they took others down with them.

And the dratted man was staring at her again. She wished he wouldn't do that. It made her feel uncomfortable, that stare did.

Charlie put his empty teacup down. 'You should have a proper drive in the van, Leah.'

'We-ell, I've got the cooking to a stage where I can leave it for a while, so why not?'

But it was Todd who showed her all its technical capacities, and she had to admit that he seemed to know what he was talking about.

This time she drove it right into Birch End with Todd by her side. She continued to feel slightly uncomfortable, especially now she was alone with him but tried not to show it, just concentrated on the driving because the van wasn't as easy to handle as their car. She was grateful when Todd gave her a few pointers.

'You'd make a good driving teacher,' she said without thinking.

'I may add that to selling cars. I haven't decided all the details of my new life yet, but I like to keep busy.'

'Let's call on my delivery driver so that he can have a go at driving it. No use buying it if he doesn't like driving it. Peter lives in the village so it's on our way.'

'Have you employed someone who isn't a skilled driver?' Todd asked with a frown.

'He seems a very steady and capable driver to me.'

To her relief Peter coped easily with the van, better than she had, in fact.

'He's a good man,' Todd admitted on the way back to Spring Cottage.

She nodded, but didn't try to speak because she was once again concentrating on the driving. She didn't want to make any mistakes in front of *him*.

When they got back, Jonah and Charlie were sitting with Finn, a small glass of ginger beer in front of each man, while Reggie was asleep in the armchair, looking white, exhausted and much younger.

'You're just in time for a glass of Leah's home brew, Todd,' Charlie said cheerfully. 'How did you go with the van? You were away long enough to give it a good testing.'

'We let Peter have a drive as well.'

'And what was the verdict?' He cocked his head to one side, waiting.

'He thinks it's a good one and he's already working out how to stack the crates for delivery.'

'Good. We'll drink to that.' He poured another glass for Todd and looked at her questioningly. She shook her head. She got enough tastes as they were making the ginger beer. That was the only down side. She could no longer drink it for pleasure.

Todd tasted the pale, slightly cloudy liquid and swallowed it slowly.

She tensed, waiting for his verdict, guessing he'd say so if he didn't like it.

It seemed ages till he said, 'Mmm. That's very good.'

She realised she'd been holding her breath and tried to let it out without anyone noticing, but from his quick half-smile, Todd had noticed, she was sure. And Jonah had too. She didn't know which of them noticed more about the people they dealt with.

Strange that the two men should be so alike in that, because they weren't alike in much else. Todd was bursting with health and vitality, and didn't hesitate to question people's capacities, while her poor Jonah had difficulty sometimes coping with physical activity, but was tactful and kind to everyone.

Ah, life could be cruel sometimes. But it did no good to let things get you down. Her father had always told her to save her worries for things she could change, advice she found very comforting at times.

She was glad when Charlie decided it was time to leave, and took Todd away with him, as well as Finn and Reggie.

She and Jonah had the kitchen to themselves for one of their quiet evenings, because her younger sister Rosa spent a lot of time up in her bedroom with her books and had gone straight back there after tea.

'I like him. Don't you?' Jonah said.

'Who do you mean? Finn or Mr Selby?'

'Todd of course. We've already agreed that we like Finn. Though I like him even more for taking that poor lad in.'

'Yes. So do I.'

'So, do you like Todd?'

'Mr Selby seems very capable, but he's a bit too blunt for me.'

'It's just his way. And didn't you hear him tell us to call him Todd? And you said to call you Leah.'

'Yes, but I don't usually go to first-name terms with a man I'm not related to straight away, so I'm not used to it yet.'

'Well, he's going to be almost part of the family, isn't he, if he's going into partnership with Charlie?' Jonah frowned. 'I hope they know what they're doing.'

'They'll be all right. Your brother's lucky in business. He seems to have the golden touch.'

'But this is the first time he's gone into a business with someone else. What if Todd isn't as lucky as he is or doesn't pull his weight?'

She couldn't help smiling. 'When I'm with Charlie, he

worries about you. And now you're starting to worry about him.'

He smiled back. 'He's my only brother. You worry about Rosa in just the same way.'

'Not so much since I married you, Jonah. You've become her brother too these days, and you've provided us both with a good home and security.'

'My pleasure. I like Rosa and I admire the way she works so hard at her studies. No wonder she won the Esherwood Bequest to pay all her school fees. The Esher family have helped a lot of poor children get schooling over the years with that award. But if I can help in any other way with her years at grammar school, I'll be only too happy to do it. The bequest might pay for her tuition and books, but there are bound to be other things she needs.'

He yawned suddenly and pushed his chair back. 'I've had enough for today. Are you coming to bed?'

'Yes. I'm tired too.'

But she wasn't too tired to wait till he'd gone upstairs and stand for a moment enjoying her clean, tidy kitchen. She loved living here at Spring Cottage and found her new business venture very exciting.

If only she could have a child! Things would be perfect then. Well, as perfect as she could expect, given the circumstances.

But her husband would be asleep within seconds of his head touching the pillow. He seemed to tire more quickly these days and that was starting to worry her. She didn't dare talk to anyone about it, either. If she told Charlie, he'd make a fuss and try to drag his brother to the doctor's. Jonah would hate that. He usually refused to discuss his health with her, just told her he was doing fine, considering. It was that word that always worried her. *Considering*.

But from what she'd read and heard, the doctors couldn't

do anything to help her husband. His lungs had been seriously damaged when he was gassed and you couldn't grow new ones!

So she did her best to look after him unobtrusively, and caught him sometimes smiling tolerantly at her as if he knew perfectly well what she was doing.

Beth had collected some sheets and suggested Finn take them to the laundry. She'd hung some blankets outside on a line to air. She was an amazing woman, good at thinking ahead.

Once he'd left Reggie at their lodgings to rest his leg, he took the bundle to the laundry, paying extra to have them washed quickly the following day and delivered to Heythorpe House with the afternoon deliveries up the valley.

He then called at the doctor's surgery and Mrs Mitchell had agreed to look at the boy's leg before breakfast.

'It won't take a minute to check that leg,' she said cheerfully. 'I'm up anyway by that time.'

So the following morning they walked to the doctor's. And indeed it didn't take long. But even that short walk had Reggie limping more noticeably and looking as if the leg hurt him.

'It's healing well,' she said. 'But the boy's too thin. I hope you're feeding him up.'

'I'm having trouble filling him up. He has hollow legs,' Finn assured her and she smiled at the old joke.

'Come back in a week's time to let the doctor take the stitches out.'

'We'll do that. Look, if I pay for the call, could I phone for a taxi from here. There isn't a phone at our lodgings. I don't want Reggie walking about too much on that leg.'

'Threepence.'

As they waited outside the doctor's house for the taxi, Reggie said mutinously, 'Do I really have to keep the stitches in that long?'

'You'll do as the doctor tells you.'

That was met by one of his loud, aggrieved sighs.

Finn couldn't help ruffling the boy's hair and suddenly Reggie looked up and smiled in a different way, looking shy and yet happy.

'I like living with you,' he said simply.

'I like having you live with me.'

'You do? Really?'

'Yes, lad. Really.' He gave Reggie a quick hug. He was smiling and so was the boy.

The moment gladdened Finn's heart, made the future seem brighter.

9

Beth got up as soon as it was light, giving her children a piece of bread each with a scraping of margarine. She'd been able to give them a quarter of a cheese sandwich the previous night, as well as a slice of bread, which had pleased her. Cheese was good for growing children.

She'd also bought some wrinkled apples cheaply from Nancy's shop, so now gave them half an apple each to finish off their breakfast, seeing their eyes light up. At five, Daisy was old enough to understand that you had to make the food last, but three-year-old Kit cried sometimes, desperate for more. Then all Beth could do was kiss and hug him, and pray for better times.

She wasn't even sure whether she wanted her husband to come back or not. A poor sort of provider Neil had turned out to be, and greedy with the food, taking more than his share when it was scarce.

She prepared another slice of bread and marg for the children's midday meal and added another apple, before taking them next door to Dilys's mother. Mrs Jarratt was happy to earn sixpence for looking after them all day. It ought to be more, but who knew whether there would be any work after today?

If she ever did start earning regular money, Beth vowed to make sure her friends were all right. You didn't forget people who'd helped you through the hard times.

Dilys came to answer the door, beaming at her. 'You'll never guess what?'

From the look on her face it was good news. 'No. Tell me.'

'It's our Gillian. She's got a part-time job at The Shepherd's Rest doing the cleaning on Friday and Saturday mornings. And they're going to give her a midday meal each day too. Isn't that wonderful? Izzy's not stingy, so it'll be a good meal, I'm sure.'

'Things seem to be going a little better for us all at the moment. I hope it continues.'

'So do I. I like working for Mr Carlisle, don't you?'

'Yes. He's a very kind man. Reggie is lucky to have him.'

'Reggie's a nice lad.'

Beth didn't say it, but Dilys always saw the best in people. She was a good-hearted woman, just like her mother.

They walked to a wall where they could sit and watch for the second bus to arrive from Rivenshaw.

'What do you think he'll give us to eat today?' Dilys wondered.

That set Beth's stomach rumbling. She hadn't eaten that morning, hoping Mr Carlisle would give them a snack before they started work. She was guessing he would. But if he didn't, well, she'd gone hungry before.

Finn and Reggie arrived in Ellindale by taxi before the second bus got there. The taxi driver stopped in front of the shop, as instructed, and Finn beckoned to the two women waiting for them. Both of them looked relieved to see him and that made him realise yet again what power he had to make people's lives easier.

He waited for them to walk across. 'I'm just going to buy a few things to eat from the shop. You two go ahead to the house.' He waited to watch them set off, then went back to the shop, leaving Reggie sitting in the taxi.

Nancy beamed at the sight of him and he decided on frankness. 'I need some food for my two helpers to start the day's work on. I doubt they've had much to eat at home. Can you put me something together?'

'Yes, of course, Mr Carlisle. I've got yesterday's scones. They could toast them and put butter on.'

'Good. So I'll need some butter as well. And how about a couple of pounds of those apples? Later on, can you send round some food for a midday meal for four? How about some corned beef sandwiches?'

'Easy. Beth and Dilys will love that. I doubt these two see any meat from one week to the other. And an apple pie?'

'Home-made?'

'Yes. My cousin Lily is learning to cook, so it may not look as nice as it should, but it'll taste good.'

'Excellent.'

After he'd paid, he was aware of Nancy watching him go from the shop doorway, looking very happy, no doubt because he was once again spending money. It made him feel humble to think what a difference these small amounts of money made to people's lives.

As the taxi drove up to his house, he realised he was smiling too. He hadn't felt this contented for a long time – not since his wife died. Ivy would have been the last person to expect him to mourn for ever. Actually, she'd told him once that if anything happened to her, he was to get married again and have a good life.

He remembered with a pang how he'd laughed at her and told her he wouldn't let anything happen to her. That had been stupid of him. As if you could stop blind chance hurting you and those you loved!

Reggie nudged him. 'We're here, Uncle Finn.'

He realised the taxi had stopped, shook his head to clear those unhappy thoughts and looked down the sloping path at the two women waiting for him at the corner of the house. 'You go on ahead, Reggie. I'll bring the bags.'

As the boy got close to the house, however, he stopped dead and turned to bar the way to the two women, yelling, 'Don't go past me! Uncle Finn, come and look at this!'

The two women stopped, looking at him in puzzlement, and Finn hurriedly paid the taxi driver, grabbed the bags of food and hurried down to join them. 'What's wrong?'

'Stop there, Uncle! Be careful where you put your feet. Someone's been here while we were away. Look at those footprints.' He pointed to the side of the path away from the house. 'They're not ours. And there was a heavy shower after we left last night so these must have been made since then or they'd have been washed away.'

Treading carefully, Finn moved past the women and joined the boy. Together they studied the piece of ground Reggie was pointing to. 'You're right. Probably just some tramp passing through, though. He'd have been knocking at the door asking for a handout.'

But Reggie shook his head. 'My friends and me learned about tracking from one of the old boys' comics at the orphanage. You have to look at the details really carefully. Those footprints don't go right up to the door; they go past it, so he couldn't have knocked. And they've been made by new shoes. Look how regular the edges of the soles are, with no worn bits at the back of the heels from walking on them, like mine are.' He held out his own foot to show the sole.

Beth moved forward to stand beside them. 'He's right, you know, Mr Carlisle. But I reckon those prints are from boots, not shoes. I can always tell the difference because I was the one who had to clean the family's shoes when I was a lass, and after I got wed I did the same job for my husband. He always wore boots and my father wore shoes, you see. People usually put hobnails in boots to make the soles last longer.'

'Hmm. I'd better let you three in through the kitchen door, then I'll walk round the house and check where the footprints go.' He led the way, making sure not to tread on any further footprints. And there were some here and there.

'Can I come with you?' Reggie begged. 'After all, I'm the one who noticed them.'

'Let me go round first, then if it looks suspicious, I'll come back for you and we'll study everything in detail together.'

'Aaaw.'

Beth caught hold of the boy's arm. 'Come inside, Reggie, and let Mr Carlisle get on with it. You don't want two more sets of footprints messing up the evidence, now do you?'

The boy gave a loud sigh and hurried across to the kitchen window, where he stood watching his new guardian.

Beth and Dilys exchanged amused glances and got on with their work, lighting the fire, filling kettles, setting out cups and saucers for their employer and his nephew.

'It'll just be a tramp, like Mr Carlisle says,' Dilys whispered.

But would it? Beth wondered. After what Reggie had said, she'd studied the footprints more carefully, and he was right. They hadn't been made by worn boots but by quite new ones. Not a penniless tramp, then.

Finn walked slowly and carefully round the house, staying clear of the footprints, which showed up clearly wherever the tangle of vegetation gave way to bare earth. Whoever it was had done a complete circuit of the building, not caring where he'd walked. Must be a town dweller, not used to reading the land beneath his feet.

Trampled patches showed where the intruder had stopped now and then. He seemed to have moved about on the spot in those places. Had that happened while he had paused to study something more carefully? Possibly. But what?

There was no damage to the house, no signs of a forced entry, just the tracks of one person making a careful circuit of the building and outhouses. Who the hell could it be? And why had he done it? Finn couldn't work it out and in the end went into the house to report his findings to the eager lad.

'Someone must have been doing a reconnaissance,' Reggie said at once. 'I reckon he'll come back and break in another time.'

Finn pictured this happening and gave a wry smile. 'Well, good luck to him if he does because all he'll find is old furniture, cobwebs and dust.'

'There are some pieces of silverware, too,' Beth commented. 'I saw them in a cupboard yesterday.'

That made Finn stop and think. He was astonished to think he owned silverware. He realised Reggie was tugging at his sleeve.

'Can I go outside and take a good look round now? Can I, Uncle Finn? Please?'

'Oh, very well. But you're to be back in half an hour at most to rest that injured leg, and you're not to climb walls or do anything rough. We want that cut to heal quickly. I'll send Dilys or Beth to call you when your time's up, so stay within hearing.'

The lad hurried off as fast as he could limp.

As Finn watched him go, he thought again about someone going round the outside of his house, peering in through the windows, and found he didn't like the idea of that at all. Even less did he like the idea of anyone breaking into his home and stealing things.

Hmm. There was only one way to prevent that. He went to find Beth. 'The sheets will be delivered from the laundry later this afternoon. Can you and Dilys get a bedroom ready for Reggie and me to occupy tonight? I'm not having my house broken into.'

'Yes, of course, sir. I'd come and protect the place too, if I had a real home.'

Her words touched him. 'Real home' she'd said. She mustn't feel at home where she was living, and how could she when the farmer might throw her and her children out at any time? What was that husband of hers doing, leaving his family to fend for themselves? Fancy leaving them with no settled home!

He had no patience with people who shirked their responsibilities.

Just before midday, Finn walked down to the village shop and asked to speak to Nancy privately. He'd taken a liking to the shopkeeper and was sure he could trust her completely.

She left her niece in charge and took him through to her back room, listening in silence as he explained what had happened.

'That's in confidence, Nancy. Don't share the information with anyone else from the village. I'm going to move into the house today, then if anyone tries to break in tonight, they'll get a big shock. But that means Reggie and I will need something to eat.'

'Food for your tea and breakfast. What do you want? I don't keep big stocks. I get some items in specially for Mrs Willcox – no one else can afford them – and when I know what you like, I can do the same for you.'

'Anything will do for tonight. I'm not fussy and Reggie definitely isn't.'

She smiled. 'My brother was the same. Mam used to say he'd eat his belt if you put jam on it.'

'I'll leave that up to you. I hadn't planned to stay here tonight, so I'll have to go back to Rivenshaw this afternoon to collect our things. Perhaps you know the times of the buses from Birch End? I know there aren't any that come right up to Ellindale at this time of day.'

'If you don't mind me saying so, why not call the taxi

again? Robert will be glad of the money and he'll be able to collect you from Heythorpe House and wait for you wherever you need to go in Rivenshaw, so that you can bring back all your things at once.'

'I haven't got used to the idea yet that I can afford to take taxis. This inheritance came as a surprise.'

'Well, I'm sure you'll put it to good use, and your living here will help people.'

'Yes. I hope so.'

'Now, let's get you that taxi.' She picked up the phone and waited to be connected, then spoke to Robert and handed over the telephone to Finn. He arranged for the taxi driver to come up to Heythorpe House at three o'clock to take him down into Rivenshaw, then wait and bring him back as soon as he'd packed.

As Finn turned to leave, it occurred to him that he'd be leaving two women and an injured lad on their own, so he turned back to Nancy. 'Is there a man who'd come up and keep an eye on things while I'm away. I don't know why and it defies logic, but I have a bad feeling about this intruder.' It had saved him from harm once or twice when he was a policeman, that sort of feeling had, so he always paid heed to it.

'Beth and Dilys will still be up there working and I don't want them or the lad put in danger.'

'I can find you someone. If Daniel delivers the food for your meals, no one will wonder at him going up to your house. And if he doesn't come back straight away, they'll assume he's doing a job for you, which he will be.'

'Good idea. You're a sensible woman, Nancy, and you've been a big help to me. Tell the person you send to wait there till I get back. I'll pay him for his trouble.'

She stood near the shop window and watched Mr Carlisle stride back up the hill, then said to Lily, 'It was a good day for Ellindale when that man inherited the old house. The money he spends isn't enough to matter to him, but it's going to make a big difference to me, and other people too.'

'He has such a kind face.'

'Yes, he does. You can tell a lot about people from their faces.' She gave her cousin a sudden hug. 'It's a good thing you came to live here as well, because I'm going to need a bit of help in the shop. You *are* staying on with me, aren't you?'

Lily blinked her eyes rapidly. 'Yes. Oh, yes, Nancy. It's as if I've come home, being with you. They treated us as if we were dirt in the big house, as if we had no feelings. After Dad died, my mother needed the money desperately or I'd have left. I'm never going into service again if I can help it.'

'A pretty girl like you will get married.'

Lily shook her head. 'I don't want to get married. I want to run a shop like you do. You're in charge of what you do and how you do it. That must be wonderful. We had to do jobs in such silly ways sometimes at the big house. It made a lot of extra work.'

'Well, if you think of better ways to do things here, don't hesitate to tell me.'

At three o'clock promptly a taxi arrived at Heythorpe House and Reggie yelled to announce its arrival. He walked out to it with Finn, who looked down at him. 'I can pack your things for you, Reggie.'

'I'd rather go with you.'

'You should be having a rest.'

Reggie stared down at the ground, drawing patterns with the toe of his bad leg. 'I don't want to be on my own here. What if Mr Buddle comes after me?'

Finn couldn't say no to that plea, even though a gentle giant called Daniel Pollard had brought up two bags of food from the shop and was staying on to protect the house and help the two women with any heavy lifting. 'Get in, then.'

Beth hurried out with another pile of sheets. 'Since you're going by taxi, you can take the other sheets to be washed, sir.' Without waiting for an answer, she turned to the taxi driver. 'Robert, while Mr Carlisle is packing, you can take these to the laundry for him. They all smell musty from lying around in cupboards for years, but they're not worn.'

'All right, love.'

Finn waited till she'd handed over the sheets, then said, 'You're in charge while I'm away, Beth. I trust you to organise everything.'

She nodded. 'Yes, sir.'

She looked pleased. He was finding her a very capable woman, much more intelligent than Dilys and sensible with it. She was a few years younger than him, but seemed older than her years, presumably from having to cope with a difficult situation in her own life.

Many folk were in the same boat these days. It surprised him that so many of the locals were still mainly cheerful about life. People in the south hadn't been as cheerful, well, not the ones he'd met on his wanderings, anyway.

When they arrived at their lodgings, Finn told the landlady only that he'd taken a sudden fancy to move into his new home. 'It'll save all the travelling to and fro.'

'Well, I shall miss you, Mr Carlisle, I shall that.'

He paid her for that night, even though he'd not now be staying, then he and Reggie went upstairs to pack.

He was ready within minutes, which made him realise how few personal possessions he had nowadays. And the boy had even fewer. Finn had some things in storage and would have to get them back. He could face seeing the furnishings Ivy had chosen now that he'd got used to her being dead.

He walked out with Reggie. 'We'll have to get you some more clothes, my lad. Something smart for going to church on Sundays.'

'New clothes, do you mean?'

'Yes.'

'Brand new?'

'Yes.'

'I've not had any decent clothes since I was put in the orphanage. They took my best things away from me when I got there.'

'And what did they do with them?'

Reggie shrugged. 'One of the other children whispered that Mr Buddle sold the things he took away from us.'

Anger made Finn draw a sudden deep breath. Wasn't it enough that the children in the orphanage had lost their families? Did that man have to take everything away from them? And beat them too? It was disgusting behaviour morally, as well as theft. 'Well, no one will ever do that to you again, Reggie, I promise.'

The landlady farewelled them at the door. 'If you ever need somewhere to stay again, Mr Carlisle, don't hesitate to come back. You've been a very pleasant lodger, very pleasant indeed.'

Her words left a warm glow. Indeed, it was as if the world he lived in was warming up in many ways these days. He'd been out in the cold for a long time, but Sergeant Deemer had started the changes by offering him occasional jobs, and then he'd inherited Heythorpe House, which meant he had a home again. He was starting to feel like his old self. Well, almost like his old self.

He might not have a wife and family now but he could still live a fulfilling life and make a difference to his corner of the world, as a decent man should. And raise this boy with love, as a child should be raised.

He looked out through the windscreen as the taxi chugged back up the long, gently sloping valley to Ellindale. He was glad to be moving into the house today, whatever had caused the sudden change in plan. Each day he spent there made it feel a little more like a real home to him.

Reggie didn't say anything and when he looked sideways, he saw that the lad was asleep. He smoothed a stray lock off the young, unlined forehead. It had only been a few days, but already he cared greatly for this young fellow, as if he really were a nephew.

10

When the taxi drove into Ellindale and on to Heythorpe House, there was no one out and about in the village. They hadn't passed any vehicle or pedestrian for the last few hundred yards, now Finn came to think of it, except for a car parked in a lane at the lower side of the village. He wasn't sure who that belonged to because he hadn't seen it before.

'It's very quiet in the village today,' Robert commented.

'Too quiet. Drive slowly.' Finn turned his head from side to side. The children would all be home from school now, but there wasn't a single one playing out in the street. Strange, that, at this time of day.

'Uncle Finn—'

'Shh, Reggie. Let me just watch and listen.'

Old Simeon wasn't there, either, which was even stranger. When the weather was fine, he usually sat on the bench outside his house for most of the day watching for people to chat to. And the weather was lovely today, the sort of day that usually sent children out to chase their friends and adults out to sit in the shade and chat.

Something was definitely wrong in the village. Finn wondered whether to ask Robert to turn back and call in at Nancy's shop. If anyone knew what was going on, it'd be her.

But they were at the entrance to his home now so he didn't say anything.

When he saw the front door of his house gaping wide open

with no one standing there, he became extremely wary. 'Reggie, stay in the car till I find out what's wrong,' he ordered sharply.

He moved towards the door and realised why no one had come to greet them: people were screaming and shouting inside.

Thinking like the policeman he had once been, he didn't rush inside blindly but stood quietly near the doorway, just out of sight from inside.

'Where is he?' a man's deep voice yelled.

'He isn't here. I *told* you. Let go of my arm. You're hurting me.'

That was Beth's voice. The taxi driver had got out of the car, so Finn gestured to Robert to stay by it. He moved to where he could see inside the house. If there was one thing he'd learned in the past few years, it was not to rush into sorting out trouble till you had some idea of what was really going on.

There were two burly men in his hall, strangers to him. The rougher looking one was struggling with Daniel and the nearer one, who was much better dressed, was shaking Beth as if she was a rat. Since he was a big man, she was unable to free herself.

There was no sign of Dilys, but as Finn began edging forward, she came tiptoeing out of the kitchen area brandishing a saucepan. The combatants didn't notice her and she didn't see Finn because her eyes were on the nearest intruder, the one struggling with Daniel. She darted forward and hit the man with the pan before he had noticed her.

That allowed Finn to turn his attention to the more urgent problem of the better-dressed man, who had just twisted Beth's arm behind her, making her cry out in pain. The fellow had his back half-turned to the front door and hadn't seen Finn come in.

Beth saw him, but though her eyes widened in relief, she had the sense not to cry out or give any sign of his approach and continued to struggle.

When Finn suddenly dragged the man off her, she took advantage of her attacker's shock to kick a very tender part of his anatomy as he struggled against Finn's hold. He yelled out in pain and tried to clutch himself with his free hand.

Finn seized the opportunity to swing him round far enough to punch him in the face. 'Fight someone your own size, you coward!'

The man's head jerked back with the blow, then he shook his head, as if to clear it, moving into a better position to fight off the newcomer.

'What the hell are you doing in my house?' Finn shouted at the top of his voice.

The man froze for a moment, looking shocked, then stepped back, unclenching his fists with an obvious effort. He stretched out his hands, palms flat against an invisible wall, as a signal that he didn't wish to continue the fight.

Finn waited but remained at the ready to defend himself. 'Well? What are you doing here? Damn well answer me.'

'I came to retrieve some lost property, sir. Larry, stop that!'

This shouted command caused his companion to step back, but Daniel seized the opportunity to punch him on the jaw and the two of them started fighting again. There was such fury on Daniel's face that Finn didn't intervene and when Daniel knocked the stranger to the ground, Finn nodded approval before signalling him to move away now that honour was satisfied.

'You should have followed my example and stopped your man continuing the fight,' the stranger snapped.

'*Your* man shouldn't have started it in the first place. Mine obviously felt he had a score to settle, so who am I to stop that when I didn't see how it started? Now, are you going to tell me who you are or not?'

The man drew himself up. 'I, sir, am Lemuel Buddle, Director of the Wemsworth District Orphanage.'

Reggie had been right. Buddle had pursued the poor lad. 'And that fellow is . . . ?'

'My manservant.'

'Does he have a name apart from Larry?' He watched, seeing Buddle hesitating, or was he imagining it?

'Larry . . . um, Smith.'

'Then kindly tell Mr *um, Smith* to leave my house this instant.'

Again there was a moment's hesitation before Buddle said, 'Wait for me outside, Larry. Within hearing.' He turned back.

Finn looked at Beth. 'Did you let these fellows in?'

'No, sir. When I opened the front door to see who was knocking, they pushed their way inside.'

So he turned back to Buddle. 'I'm still waiting for you to explain why you've committed an act of trespass.'

The man drew himself up and said in a booming voice, far too loud for normal use. 'I'm seeking justice.'

Was he a bit deaf or trying to verbally bludgeon those listening? Finn deliberately responded more quietly. 'Oh? Since when has justice been served by someone forcing entry into a private residence? You're obviously not a policeman so have no right to do that.'

'Your servants refused to let us enter to make a lawful search for a fugitive who has absconded from the orphanage. They even refused to answer my questions about this matter. You, sir, are extremely ill served.'

Finn could see why Reggie was afraid of the fellow. Any lad would be. But he wasn't a lad and he loathed bullies, especially ones who seemed to consider themselves entitled to do and say what they pleased. He had not forgotten the scars on Reggie's back.

'On the contrary, I think I'm extremely well served.' He inclined his head towards the two women and Daniel, now standing quietly at the back of the hall listening. 'Tell me about your fugitive, Mr Buddle. Is he a murderer that makes it necessary for you to attack my servants?'

'Of course not. But he's an extremely violent lad by the name of Reginald Barston, who's been getting into trouble.'

Dilys had gasped at the sound of Reggie's name, and though Beth dug her in the ribs in an attempt to quieten her, it was too late.

Buddle swung round. 'It seems your maid knows the name, so I was clearly right to attempt to find that boy here. He needs be taken back to the orphanage and taught a sharp lesson to prevent him from falling into criminal ways. We traced him to your house and now we've proved he's here. He must have broken in.'

Now who could have given Reggie away? Finn wondered. It had to be someone from the village.

When Finn didn't speak, Buddle took a step forward, thrusting his face too close to Finn's. 'I am the boy's guardian and am exercising my *legal right* to take him back where he belongs and make sure he can't cause further trouble.'

Finn had had enough of this ridiculous posturing and attempted bullying, so thrust out his hand and shoved the man away. There was another brief standoff as his unwelcome guest almost retaliated but thought better of it.

'I can relieve you of your problem, Mr Buddle. The lad has caused us no trouble and anyway, I know him well because I'm a long-time friend of his family. I absolutely refute your claims that Reggie is dangerous.'

'But he—'

Finn raised his voice and continued, 'I was unfortunately

away in Scotland when his parents died and have only just
returned to the area or I'd have taken him into my home
straight away. It was agreed between his father and myself
that if anything happened to them, I'd become his son's
guardian.'

A moment's silence, then, 'Alas. If it were any other youth,
I'd be delighted for him to find a home, but with this one,
you are better leaving him to my care. I have considerable
experience in recognising wayward youths and bringing them
into line.'

So Reggie had been right about Buddle refusing to let him
get out of the orphanage. 'As to that, I take my promises
seriously so there is no need for you to be further involved.
I've already set in train the necessary steps to establish myself
as his legal guardian.'

'I'm afraid the courts won't support you in that claim once
I reveal his character and misdemeanours to them.'

Finn hoped he'd hidden his astonishment at such a statement. 'Well, let's wait and see what happens in the courts.
In the meantime, if you try to force your way in here again,
I'll have you arrested for breaking and entering. And now,
since I'm a busy man, I'll ask you to leave my property and
let me get on with my day.' He gestured towards the open
door.

'You will be hearing from our lawyer, Mr Carlisle.'

'He can deal with my lawyer, Mr Lloyd of Rivenshaw, who
is already aware of the situation.'

Buddle's expression said he didn't like the sound of this.

Suddenly a voice from outside yelled, 'Sir! He's out here!'

Buddle was out of the door more quickly than anyone
would have believed possible for so plump a man. Finn
followed him, calling, 'Daniel, with me!'

They found the taxi driver struggling with Smith while
Reggie cowered in the car. Even as they watched, Smith

knocked the driver to the ground and dragged him away from the car.

With a growl of anger, Buddle went straight to the car door, trying to open it while Reggie clung to the handle from inside to prevent him.

Finn yelled, 'Stop that!' and grabbed Buddle's collar, jerking him away. Within seconds he was involved in a fight in which dirty tricks were immediately employed by his opponent, who was suddenly cursing in a not-so-genteel voice, quite different from the way he'd spoken previously.

Daniel was fully occupied dealing with Smith, who was an equally dirty fighter, because Robert was leaning against the front of the car, looking dazed.

It was Beth who broke up the fight with Buddle by using the saucepan on the back of his head. He howled in anger and would have turned on her had Finn not shoved him away and yelled once again, 'If you don't stop this, it's you who will be arrested for violence. And I have plenty of witnesses to it.'

After a moment's hesitation, Buddle stepped back again, but the look on his face said they weren't done with him yet.

'Leave him, Larry. *For the moment.* We'll bring in the orphanage's lawyer.' He cast a threatening look at Reggie, still huddling in the car looking terrified, and called out slowly and with menace, 'You're going to be really sorry, boy, and wish you'd been more obedient to my wishes from the start. I'll give you one last chance. Come with me and take your medicine like a man.'

Finn intervened. 'Bring in as many lawyers as you want, Buddle. I'll make sure you don't take Reggie back to that place under any circumstances.'

'*That place* is an orphanage, where children in need are given safe housing and taught useful skills. Any court would give us custody of a known delinquent, rather than you.'

'No, sir. Any court would prefer the boy to go to a good home, where he will be schooled gently and with affection. Now, *get – off – my – land*. And don't come back.'

The two men eyed one another and after a moment, Buddle muttered something under his breath and beckoned to his assistant.

He turned at the gateway to yell, 'We will be back and we'll be bringing the police with us next time.'

'I'll look forward to seeing them.'

Once the two bullies were out of sight, he turned to the car. 'You can come out now, Reggie.'

The boy nearly fell out and clutched him with both hands. 'You should have told him *you* used to be a policeman, then he wouldn't dare come back.'

'I think he would come back, whatever. He is, as you warned me he might be, intent on vengeance against you, for whatever reason he imagines it necessary.'

'But if you—'

'It's never good to play all your cards at once, my lad: in other words never tell an opponent everything. Trust me on that. I'll telephone Sergeant Deemer and my lawyer tomorrow and tell them about this incursion into my house. I'll also make sure we get a phone line run out here as quickly as possible, whatever it costs, so that any of us can call for help if necessary.'

Reggie stepped back but Finn saw that the boy was still looking doubtful so gave him a quick hug. 'I won't let them take you, I promise.'

For a moment the boy clung to him like a much smaller child would, then straightened himself and said, 'Thank you!' in a husky voice.

Finn turned to Robert to thank him for his help and ask him to unload their things. Then he paid him for the taxi ride and a bit extra for his help, before watching him drive off.

Beth was also standing with her hands on her hips staring thoughtfully in the direction the taxi had taken. Finn moved across to her and said quietly, 'Thank you for helping us.'

'They were fighting dirty, Mr Carlisle. I can't abide that. And I was mad at them for pushing their way in when I told them you weren't home. That fat one shoved me out of the doorway so hard I'd have fallen over if I hadn't bumped into the hallstand and grabbed hold of it. The cheek of it! Just walking into your house!'

She stared at him, biting her lip and her expression changed, but after half-opening her mouth, she snapped it shut again. She'd looked as if she wanted to ask him something and he could easily guess what it was. She must be worrying that he'd blame them for letting Buddle in and not offer them more work.

'Could you and Dilys come in again tomorrow to help out, do you think?'

Beth's sigh of relief was very audible and both women beamed at Finn.

He had a quiet word with Daniel as well, giving him a bonus for his help in the fight and asking him to return the following day. 'Could you spread the word in the village tonight to watch out for those men, do you think? I'd appreciate people letting me know if they're seen around.'

He hesitated, then added, 'Someone must have let them know where Reggie was. If you get any hint who it might be, please let me know that as well.'

'I'll keep my eyes and ears open, Mr Carlisle, but I've seen that Larry before. He's known in the area for a troublemaker and his name isn't Smith, it's Clapton. I could spread the word that he's causing trouble again and to let you know if he's seen with any strangers. The best way for me to do that is in the pub, because chaps come in from the farms sometimes of an evening. They may see things we in the village don't.'

He hesitated and flushed a little as he added, 'Only I'd have to ask for some extra beer money, just enough for half a pint and I'd make it last all night, I promise you, because my wife needs today's money for food. Growing children get hungry.'

'Good idea.' Finn fished out another florin. 'No, keep the change.' A shilling or so meant nothing to him these days, though it had once meant the difference between eating and going hungry, but it'd make a considerable difference to Daniel's family, and he'd bet the man really did make half a pint last and gave the rest to his wife.

It was wonderful to be able to help people like this, though he tried to do it in small ways, to which they couldn't take exception. People had their pride, even when their bellies were empty.

Daniel couldn't stop grinning as he pocketed the money. 'First time I've ever been paid to go to the pub, Mr Carlisle, but I'm happy to do anything I can to help, as I hope you know.'

Finn watched him walk up to the road and smiled to hear him whistling cheerfully. He wondered what Daniel's wife would say about the big bruise on his face. The extra money would no doubt soften her annoyance at that. And he wondered if Daniel would make a good general helper, working mainly outdoors.

It was strange. The last thing he'd expected when he came to live in a peaceful English village, where he'd thought all the villains had been rounded up previously, was to need to defend himself and those he employed against an openly waged attack. Perhaps Buddle thought law and order didn't stretch this far, and that orphans didn't matter to people.

Well, he was wrong. Finn believed passionately in right and wrong, and wouldn't let anyone bully him or those he cared about.

But why was Buddle so confident he was going to win the legal battle? There had to be some reason for that. Perhaps he was bribing some official.

Finn was definitely going to let Sergeant Deemer know about the situation. He'd have to warn Jonah and Leah about Buddle and his bullies, too, and the sooner the better, since the Willcoxes were his nearest neighbours and could help keep an eye on things.

'I'd better go and let Mr Willcox know what's going on,' he said abruptly. 'Beth and Dilys, I'm sure it'll be safe for you to walk home now. I'll lock up after you. Reggie? Are you coming with me?'

As if he needed to ask. Reggie might have to limp there slowly, but he'd stay with Finn and it'd be good for the lad to get to know the neighbours better.

11

Jonah opened the door, took one look at Finn's expression and gestured to him to come in. He stared in shock at his visitor's bruised knuckles. 'Whatever happened to you?'

'I have a bit of a problem and I think you should know about it.'

Leah was cooking tea, from the smell of it a lamb stew or hotpot, but she stopped to listen to Finn's story after slipping the ever-hungry Reggie a crust of bread with a smear of butter on it.

When Finn had finished speaking, Jonah looked at him with anger sparkling in his eyes. 'I detest the idea of that man taking advantage of orphans. I saw what he did to Reggie before. If you're not going to look into it, I will.'

'Don't worry. I'm going down to Rivenshaw tomorrow to speak to Sergeant Deemer.'

Just then the telephone tinkled, so Leah went into the back hall to answer it. She came back a minute later. 'It's Charlie on the phone. He wanted me to give you a message, Finn, but you might as well speak to him yourself.' She gestured to the door at the rear of the big room and he followed her through.

When he rejoined them, Reggie was setting two more places at the table under her direction. She smiled at Finn. 'You will stay to tea, won't you?'

'I don't want to inconvenience you. I'm sure you weren't planning for guests.'

'I can stretch the meal with some bread and finish it with

a cake. I haven't even cut into the cake yet, so there's plenty. And good neighbours aren't "guests" in that sense.'

'Well, thank you, Leah. I'm grateful and Reggie's probably even more grateful because I'm not the world's best cook and the food smells delicious.'

Reggie let out a cheer.

'What did Charlie want?' Jonah asked.

'To say he'd found a car that might suit me. It'll give me a good excuse for going down to Rivenshaw tomorrow. If I could beg a further favour, I'll phone Robert from here and arrange for him to collect me in his taxi in the morning. I should have booked him before he left, but I was still too angry to think clearly.'

Reggie immediately looked anxious.

'Daniel, Beth and Dilys will be there to keep an eye on you,' Finn said gently.

But Reggie still looked at him pleadingly.

'Why don't you come here while your uncle's away?' Jonah offered. 'You can keep me company. I'll teach you to play chess.'

'I can play it already . . . but not very well. I'd only just got started when my father died.'

'Then I'll improve your understanding of the game. It's a good way of training the mind.'

Reggie blinked away tears, saying nothing but a quiet thank you, clearly relieved to have somewhere to come that he felt safe.

'Finn, you've just got time to telephone Robert before I serve tea,' Leah said briskly, tactfully taking the attention away from Reggie.

Once again, he went through into the rear hall to make his call. When he came back, he said grimly, 'I hope you don't mind, but I locked your back door. While there's trouble around, you'd be best keeping it locked all the time, even when you're at home, because anyone could get in that way without you knowing and sneak upstairs.'

After a moment's shocked silence, Leah nodded slowly. 'I never thought of needing to be that careful again. I hate having to lock my doors as if I don't trust my neighbours, but you're right. That man got into our back garden by coming across the moors last time. Better safe than sorry.'

She shivered at the memory of the night she'd been attacked by a madman intent on killing her.

It was Finn's turn to change the subject because he'd been involved in the previous troubles and understood her feelings. Indeed, that was what had made Deemer bring him to the valley the first time, to help deal with the problem. 'While I'm away tomorrow, Daniel will be able to keep an eye on Heythorpe House and the maids, and I'll make sure they keep our outer doors locked too.'

'How are they working out as maids?' Leah asked as she began to serve the stew.

'Really well. Beth is a capable woman and she's organising Dilys's work for me, as well as making some useful suggestions as to how to do things. If Beth wasn't married, I'd be offering her the housekeeper's job.'

'She might be married but no one's seen her husband for months. He could be dead for all we know.'

'Do you think that's likely?'

'Who knows? Neil isn't a bad man, though he's weak and easily led. He did send money fairly regularly at first, though, so why did he stop sending it and not even let her know where he was? That's a bit worrying, don't you think?'

Jonah took his seat and gestured to their guests to sit down. After that he changed the subject firmly to something more cheerful, Charlie's new business venture selling second-hand cars.

Finn took the hint and they had a peaceful meal discussing cars and the improvements in modern motoring since the early days.

Ben walked back to Heythorpe House with them and waited until they'd checked that nothing had been disturbed in the garden, before waving cheerfully and heading on down the hill to The Shepherd's Rest for a convivial hour with friends.

He seemed a cheerful young fellow, newly qualified as a stonemason and managing to scrape a living with Leah and Jonah's help as he acquired the tools necessary to set up fully in business.

The following day Finn saw Reggie off to Spring House and left the maids to their work, with Daniel in the garden to check anyone who approached the house.

He'd booked the taxi the previous day and it arrived on time, so he felt things were starting well, at least. When Robert dropped him at the pawnshop, he went to find Charlie, feeling excited about buying a car.

Charlie took him out to the backyard, talking exuberantly as usual. 'We've found two cars for you to look at, actually. Todd has some good contacts in Manchester. He says they're both good runners, but as you can see, one's a lot smaller.' He frowned at it. 'It looks too small to be safe, to me.'

Finn smiled. 'I've driven a Chummy before. They're good little cars but I agree, they're far too small for my needs. Though I do like other Austins. Goodness, how we used to cram five people into a Chummy, I can't think.'

Charlie let out a crack of laughter. 'I told Todd you'd not want it. It looks more like a toy car to me.'

'Don't let the size fool you. It's a real car with a four-cylinder engine and four-wheel brakes. You can't fault it there.' Finn gestured to himself. 'But I'm a bit tall for it and Reggie seems to be growing taller by the week.' But he went across to give the car a pat and remembered the bright-eyed young woman who'd once driven him and a group of friends around in one. Till he met Ivy and settled down.

The other car was a bull-nosed Morris and a much better size for his purpose, though still not a large vehicle. The body-work seemed to be in very good condition. 'Does it run well?'

'Why don't you try it out?' Charlie suggested. 'Todd looked the engine over and says it's fine. Well, it can't have been used much because there isn't a lot of mileage showing.

'I'll give it a drive, then.' Finn got in, pleased when Charlie stepped back and waved to him to carry on.

The car started the first time. He set off, going slowly at first until he got used to how the vehicle handled. By the time he'd driven round the square in the centre of Rivenshaw a couple of times, and tried reversing the car on one of the back streets, he'd decided to buy it.

After a few minutes' haggling with Charlie, he went to the bank to get out some money, then came back and paid for the car with eighteen crisp, white, five-pound notes. He checked the paperwork quickly, but decided to do any neces-sary form filling later.

The government had clamped down on car owners in the last few years, and that meant not just paying for a licence for a motor vehicle, but also following the newly issued Highway Code when you drove. He'd have to pick up a copy of that to be sure he knew all the latest rules. He smiled. A penny a copy was cheap enough for just about anyone to afford, even these days.

More important for the moment was to go and bring Sergeant Deemer up to date with what had happened at Heythorpe House and Buddle's threats. His happy mood faded. No one was going to hurt his lad!

At the police station a young constable was manning the front desk and he obligingly went to speak to his sergeant then showed Finn through.

Deemer grinned as he indicated a chair. 'Nice to see you

again, lad. I hear you've been causing trouble up in Ellindale.'

Finn stared at him in surprise. '*I've* been causing trouble!'

'I had a phone call half an hour ago from a colleague in the Wemsworth Area Office, making a complaint about you obstructing the director of the orphanage, who was chasing a vicious fugitive. Apparently you attacked Buddle and his assistant.' He leaned back and grinned even more broadly at his visitor.

'*What?* But I was only—' Finn took a deep breath to calm himself down. A second glance showed that Deemer was still looking amused, so presumably he hadn't taken the complaint seriously. He explained quickly what had really happened, but it was hard not to get angry all over again at the lies that had been told about him.

'I know you too well to believe you'd have started any trouble. One thing puzzles me: when my colleague spoke to me, he didn't seem to realise you were an ex-policeman.'

'No. It wasn't any of Buddle's business, so I didn't tell him.'

'Whoever trained you as a policeman did well by you.'

'I've always thought so. He always said to play your cards carefully. He died, poor chap, just keeled over one day. Only fifty as well. Goodness, that seems so long ago. To get back to this spurious complaint . . .'

'It may be a pack of lies but it must be answered officially. Justice has to be seen to be done. And since I saw the lad's back well before this happened, I know who has been attacking whom.' He shook his head sadly. 'I can't abide folk who beat children so severely. A good clout around the ears is one thing, whipping a child till blood flows is the act of a vicious brute.'

'I agree. Did you tell your colleague that?'

'No. Like you, I believe it's always good to hold a card or

two in reserve and Taylor was so vehement in urging me to collar the boy and charge you with an offence that I smelled a rat. But we need proof before we can put a stop to Buddle's antics, so we'll have to give the fellow more rope and let him hang himself. It won't reflect well on my colleague, either, but then, I never did think he was clever enough for a sergeant's job.'

He gave Finn a solemn look and added, 'But just to be safe, *you* should go and see your lawyer again. Tell him what's happened. He can phone me to check the details any time he likes, and our local taxi driver has a good reputation, so he'll make an excellent witness to them attacking you – and him. In fact, he should come and make a complaint about it to me.'

'I'll tell him.'

'In the meantime, I'll also have a word with an old friend of mine. Miss Peters' brother was a lawyer, damned good one, too. He's just been made up to judge and he's a decent, honest sort of chap. Any advice he gives will be worthwhile listening to.'

'Thank you.'

Deemer gave him a serious look, all traces of amusement gone. 'Like you, I believe very firmly in justice, but occasionally administration of the law falls into the hands of warped individuals, so I keep light on my feet and watch out for such problems. I give you my word, Finn, that even if the worst comes to the worst, and the villains gain the upper hand for a time, I won't let anyone send me or my constables to take the lad back without warning you in advance. I'll also warn you if I hear of anyone coming at him in other supposedly legal ways.'

He sighed and shook his head sadly. 'No area of life is free of villains and chicanery, unfortunately.'

Finn nodded agreement. He trusted the wise old sergeant

absolutely, but he would also take some precautions of his own to protect Reggie.

Deemer gave him a moment or two to think things through. 'All right. Now, how about a cup of tea and you can tell me about that car you drove up in? New, is it?'

'New to me, anyway. It's a fairly ordinary vehicle but it drives solidly. Come and have a look at it. In fact, how about I drive you round the streets and you can see how it feels? I know you're a good driver, but I need to get to know it myself before I feel safe to let anyone else get behind the wheel.'

'Very sensible of you. I shall enjoy a little drive round town and you see more of what's going on by getting out and about than by sitting in the office, especially on such a fine day.'

After he'd dropped Deemer back at the police station, Finn went to see his lawyer.

Henry Lloyd fitted him in for a short emergency consultation and listened intently to what he said about the encounter with Buddle – and the complaint that had been made about Finn, based on lies.

'I didn't get a chance to speak to my friend at church about the orphanage, Mr Carlisle, as I promised, because he was ill last week. However, I'll have a quiet word with him as soon as I can. In the meantime, you should refer any legal queries to me, and give me the names of your witnesses to the incident.'

He sat with his head slightly to one side as they finished the discussion, sunshine shining on his sparse silver hair and glinting off his spectacles. 'Ah, our taxi driver. An honest fellow who will make a credible witness. And I'm glad you're keeping Deemer involved. He's a good man to protect your back.'

He paused and had a think. 'I might also ask another friend of mine about the sergeant at Wemsworth. I'd have heard if there was a new fellow, so I know a little about this one already and haven't found Taylor particularly helpful.'

He tapped his forefinger against the side of his nose as if to indicate he could say more but wouldn't at this stage. 'Leave it to me, Mr Carlisle. And in the meantime, I'll try to hurry the adoption procedures.'

'Adoption?'

'I thought that was what you wanted.'

'Um, I was thinking of becoming his guardian, but . . . well, why not go the whole hog and adopt him? He's a grand lad.'

'Good. In the meantime don't let him out of your sight.'

Finn didn't need telling. He had an uneasy feeling about the situation. Very uneasy.

12

The afternoon sun was shining brightly and Lily hummed as she watched over the shop while Nancy attended to her baking. She stood near the house door and watched her cousin pull a batch of scones out of the oven and replace it with a new batch of small buns. Lily was going to ice these for her later.

Nancy's scones were very popular with hikers and with one or two of the people in the district who did have wages coming into the household, and she took every opportunity to earn an extra penny or two. Lily admired that.

As she looked round, she noticed that a stray sunbeam was showing up some dust on one or two upper shelves, as if Nancy had been interrupted by a customer when she was in the middle of her daily dusting. Lily decided to wipe them down and make sure the items displayed in the window looked neat and tidy, too. She liked to keep busy now she was feeling so much better and she wanted to earn her way at her cousin's house.

The shop door opened and a man came in. His behaviour was polite enough at first but his eyes soon betrayed his thoughts, lingering on her breasts and then rising to her face.

When he saw that she'd noticed what he was doing, he said in a husky voice, 'Can't blame a chap for looking.'

'Decent men don't look at women like that,' she snapped. She didn't care if he was a customer. She wasn't putting up with such rudeness without a protest.

He sucked in a breath as if her sharp reply had surprised him. 'You should be flattered by my attention, girl.'

'Well, I'm not.'

He opened his mouth and his expression seemed so threatening suddenly that she retreated a step, letting out a yelp of shock as she bumped into Nancy, who must have come to the doorway that led to the house.

'I'll serve this customer, dear.' The older woman's hand tugged the back of her skirt, pulling her out of the shop and Lily obeyed that secret command willingly.

Once out of sight, she put her hands to her cheeks, which felt burning hot with embarrassment. One of the few good things about being in service had been that you were mostly sheltered from men with that horrible way of looking at women or worse, giving them sly touches on the body when they thought no one would see.

She stayed where she was in case Nancy needed help, listening to the conversation. Not for the first time she marvelled at how chill and disapproving her cousin could sound if a customer behaved in anything but a polite way.

'What can I get you, sir?' Nancy waited, but the man was still staring across her shoulder to where Lily had gone.

'What's she called?' he asked.

'I beg your pardon?'

'That lass. What's her name?'

'My cousin, do you mean?'

He grinned. 'Ah. I see. A relative. Guarding her closely, are you? I'm not surprised. She's quite the beauty with that glorious blond hair. Any man would be tempted.'

'She's a good girl, so I'll thank you to keep your thoughts and your looks respectful in her presence . . . and mine.'

'Ah, I meant no harm, missus. I'd like a packet of cigarettes, please. Twenty. I'm not short of money.'

She took a packet from under the counter. 'I only have this brand in twenties, sir. Not many people in our village buy that many at a time these days.'

'That'll do. And a quarter of wine gums to sweeten my breath.'

Nancy could see he'd not stop his innuendoes so weighed out the quarter pound of sweets as quickly as she could and passed them to him. To her astonishment he took hold of her hand as well as the white paper bag with its twisted corners.

'Wouldn't you like to earn some extra money?' He gestured round them with his free hand. 'This shop can't be bringing in much.'

She tried to pull away from his hand but he wouldn't let go, and he had a strong grip, so she stopped struggling. Presumably he meant to offer her money for access to Lily and she wasn't having that. 'No, thank you. This shop puts bread on my table and pays the rent, and does that *honestly*, which is the main thing for me and my young cousin.'

But his response surprised her.

'Suppose you were to give me some information about the new gentleman living at Heythorpe House, such as what he does, where he goes and who visits him. I could slip you five shillings here and there, and that's not breaking the law, is it? That's *honest* enough, surely?'

She managed to get her hand away from his in a sudden jerk, hoping she'd hidden her revulsion at the touch of his dry skin. Too warm that hand was, like his words. As if he had a fever. And his skin had a scaly feel to it. Ugh. 'I don't gossip. Now, is that all . . . sir?'

'I'll give you ten shillings for each piece of information, then.'

What did he think she was? 'As I just said, I don't gossip and certainly not about my customers.'

'Think about it. I'll be back.' He pulled some money out of his pocket, threw it carelessly down on the counter and turned to leave.

'Your change, sir.'

'Keep it.'

'No, thank you.'

He turned and shouted at her, 'Keep it, damn you.'

But she threw it right at him. 'No.'

He didn't pick it up but he scowled at her and said softly, 'You might regret angering me.'

His tone was so vicious she didn't dare answer him back again and after staring at her for another moment or two as if daring her to say anything else, he left at last.

Once the door had closed behind him, she blew out her breath in a whoosh of relief, staring down at the new coins lying on the floor near the entrance, catching the sunlight and glinting as if to taunt her.

Well, she couldn't leave them lying there, so she went out from behind the counter to pick them up. As she glanced through the big shop window, she saw that Barry Judson had joined the stranger further down the street. Two bad ones together, those, she thought.

Beyond them she saw old Simeon get up and hurry into his house, shutting the door behind him. In fact, the village street was bare of folk, except for those two men.

What was going on? Who was that man? *She* didn't recognise him, but some people must have done to have got out of his way so quickly.

She hoped he wouldn't come into her shop again, whoever he was, because she didn't want his money. She stared down at the seven shillings in her palm: two shiny, new half-crown pieces and an equally shiny florin. They seemed to be mocking her. She wasn't keeping them. She'd give them to some of the poorer people in town and maybe that'd get rid of the dirty feeling she'd got from touching him and his money.

She looked out again at Judson and amended mentally: she'd give it to the *honest poor*, not to such as him.

That fellow must be where Barry Judson was getting his money from lately. She'd been wondering. She'd keep her eyes open. People didn't realise how much you saw from inside a shop. And she'd ask Simeon later who the stranger was. Maybe she'd tell Adam Harris about the incident too and Mr Carlisle. Yes, of course. He'd been a policeman once. He might know if she should do anything about today's incident, if it was all right to give the money away.

Did bad people think if they came up to Ellindale no one would see what they were doing? The opposite was true. In such a small place little went unnoticed. She'd been into Manchester a few times and had felt herself to be invisible there. Even at the quiet times, people there walked past others in the street without really looking at them, let alone nodding or saying a polite good morning.

Oh, no! Here came Madge Judson. Well, if she wanted credit, she'd go away empty-handed. Nancy went back behind the counter, put the offending coins in a jar and waited, arms folded over her pinafore.

Madge came in, smiling brightly. 'I'd like a loaf and two of your scones, please. Buttered.'

'Do you have the money?'

Madge scowled and slapped two sixpences down on the counter. 'Yes, I do.'

More of those shining new coins, and for the second time that day. Easy to guess where they came from. Grimly, Nancy buttered two scones, wrapped them up in greaseproof paper and handed them over. She put the coins in her cash drawer, giving out the change.

Once her customer had left, she went to stand behind a

tower of tins and boxes in the window, watching Madge saunter along the street. The woman was already biting into one of the scones. The Judson children wouldn't get a treat like that, Nancy was sure.

Peter Cotman arrived early for work that day, thrilled at the prospect of making his first trip in the new Spring Cottage delivery van. Once he'd transported the bottles of ginger beer, lemonade, and dandelion and burdock, he was to leave the van with the sign painter in Rivenshaw and take the bus back. Stan Gordon had agreed to put neat signs on each side panel, on the rear doors and on a metal plate over the windscreen.

Peter felt like a king as he took to the road, enjoying the freedom of driving out on his own. He'd never been able to afford a personal car, or even the cheaper alternative of a motorcycle and sidecar, but had learned to drive in the Army when he'd been conscripted just before the end of the war. He was lucky. He'd never had to go to the Front because the war had ended just after he finished his training, thank goodness.

He'd had a job as a van driver for a short time in the early twenties and had enjoyed it, but then the company's sales had started to decline, however hard their employees worked and they'd all known what was going to happen.

It wasn't the only firm to close down. Some had shut completely, some smaller ones had gone back to bicycle deliveries, and jobs of any sort had become increasingly scarce. He'd found work now and then, but only temporary. Such jobs never lasted and didn't pay nearly as much as his driving job had. Most had been downright drudgery but when you had a family to feed, you did what you had to.

Then Leah Willcox had given him a job as general helper in her new business, so that he could come off the dole. He didn't care what he did there as long as he took home a wage packet every week. But the work was quite interesting and she treated her employees well.

He had another chance to make a decent life for his family now and he blessed the day Leah Willcox had started her small business. It wouldn't be his fault if things didn't go well for her. He'd work his fingers to the bone to help keep the business running.

One thing he might be able to do was find her some new customers while he was out. She hadn't thought of that and had listened to his suggestion with interest. She'd even offered to pay him a bonus for each customer who started buying Spring Cottage Mineral Waters regularly. Not many employers would do that.

He had also suggested putting some spare bottles of fizzy drinks on board, which he could sell one at a time for people to try out, and one bottle of each type that he could open to give people tastes. She hadn't thought of that either, so he was proud of doing it.

In fact, he was a very happy man that day, singing cheerfully as he jolted along the road, heading down towards Rivenshaw and out to various other nearby villages.

The first stop was at the pawnshop in Birch End, where Charlie Willcox had put in an order.

Vi, who managed the shop for Charlie, shook her head in amusement when he delivered the bottles. 'Mr Willcox loves ginger beer. He's working mainly in the Rivenshaw shop now, so can you deliver it there next time, so there will be a stock in each place?'

'Yes, of course. And I like this ginger beer myself. It's the best I ever tasted.'

'Better sell me a bottle as well. I'm having my sister to tea on Sunday.'

And if that extra sale at his first stop wasn't a good sign, Peter had never seen one.

13

A few days later someone knocked on the kitchen door and when Dilys went to open it she found her mother standing there, with Beth's two small children pressed against her sides. Daisy was holding her big brother Felix's hand and both looked white and anxious, in the way children had when they knew something bad was happening, but weren't sure what.

From her reddened eyes, her mother must have been crying. Dilys flung her arms round her. 'What's wrong, Mum?'

'Everything.' Mary Jarratt gulped back a sob. 'Mr Unwin came round to see us. He gave me this, but you know I'm not very good at reading long words, so I asked him to tell me what was in it.' She held out an envelope. 'He says we've to get out of the cottage within the week. And there's a letter for Beth too, saying the same thing.' She pulled a second crumpled envelope out of her pocket.

'Oh, Mum, no! Come in, all of you and sit down at the table. Don't touch anything, you two. I'll go and find Beth. She'll know what to do.' Surely her friend would, if anyone did? They relied on her for that, she was such a clever woman.

Dilys ran upstairs to where she'd left Beth checking the bedrooms to decide which one to clean next, but there was no sign of her friend, so she clattered downstairs again and stood in the hall, listening.

Following the faint sound of voices, she found herself outside the small room at the far side of the house from the road, where Mr Carlisle sat during the day. She'd seen him staring out across the gardens down into the valley sometimes, but other times he was bent over doing paperwork on his big desk with its brass drawer handles that she was itching to polish.

She could never quite figure out what 'paperwork' meant. Accounts meant sums she supposed. Her mum couldn't read very well and Dilys was no good at big sums, though both of them were experts at making a penny do the work of two at the shop.

Reggie usually sat in a corner of the room with a book while Mr Carlisle was working there. The poor boy never felt safe unless he was near his guardian.

Well, no use hesitating about whether to interrupt them. This was too important. Dilys knocked on the closed door.

Beth opened it and Dilys forgot about Mr Carlisle, saw only her friend and couldn't hold back tears any longer. 'Mr Unwin is throwing us all out of our cottages! Oh, Beth love, what are we going to *do*? They'll put us in the workhouse, I know they will.'

Mr Carlisle said, 'Bring her in, Beth. Now sit down, Dilys, and start your tale at the beginning.'

She explained all she knew, which wasn't much, then realised something. 'Oh, I've forgotten to bring the letters. I'll go and get them. Mum and your kids are sitting in the kitchen, Beth. I hope you don't mind, sir. Mum's that upset. She's been crying and she never usually cries.'

Finn took charge. Someone had to because even Beth was looking shell-shocked and hadn't issued any of her crisp orders. 'No, of course I don't mind. In fact, why don't we all go to the kitchen and share a pot of tea while we work out what to do?' He led the way out briskly, Dilys followed him, and Beth and Reggie followed her.

Mrs Jarratt jumped to her feet when he entered the kitchen.

'I'm sorry to intrude, Mr Carlisle. I haven't got my Dilys in trouble by coming here, have I?'

'No, of course she's not in trouble. Why don't you introduce me to your children, Beth?'

She went to stand behind them, laying a hand on each little shoulder in turn. 'This is Felix, my clever little boy who's just turned three. And this is Daisy, my big helper, who's nearly six now.'

Gravely he shook hands with each child in turn, watching the three women calm down a little, seeing the fond looks they all gave the children. They were almost like a family, and yet when he first met them, Beth had stayed aloof from Dilys, presumably in case *he* scorned her friend's unmarried state and wouldn't employ someone who befriended her. Beth would do almost anything to protect her children and put food on the table, he guessed. Well, who wouldn't? If his child had lived – no, better not think of that.

By the time he'd calmed them all down and cheered up the two children with a couple of biscuits, Beth had prepared the tea.

'Are there any other cottages standing empty in the village?' he asked once they'd taken a few sips. He could pay the rent for them as a temporary measure.

Beth's reply was bald, her voice bleak. 'No. And if there were, they'd not let us have them because we're not in steady work and we don't have men to take care of us. Even if we did have regular jobs, we wouldn't earn as much as a man would, so we couldn't afford to pay the rent as well as put food on the table. Those cottages of ours are in a bad state, I know, but they've been a lifesaver to us.'

'We managed all right until my father died,' Dilys added, 'though because I'm not married some people haven't spoken to me for years, even though I only went with the man I was going to marry. But lately, it's been – well, hard.'

His heart went out to her. She wasn't as clever as Beth, but she was a nice lass and a hard worker, and he respected that.

'It'll be the workhouse!' Mrs Jarratt burst into tears again and the two children started wailing in sympathy.

'None of that!' Beth told them sharply. 'Crying doesn't help and you don't want to annoy Mr Carlisle.'

They gulped into silence and she dabbed at the children's eyes with her handkerchief.

As she put it away again, Finn caught her gaze and hoped she'd realised that he wasn't upset by the crying so much as the reason for it.

'Our landlord's been as kind to us as he could. Mr Unwin wouldn't have turned us out if there hadn't been a good reason. Did he say why, Mary?'

Mrs Jarratt shook her head. 'I was too upset to ask him, couldn't stop sobbing, and he got all embarrassed and left.'

Finn hated to see that beaten look on Beth's face and the words were out before he could think twice about the idea. 'There's only one thing for it, then. You'll all have to move in here.'

The three women gaped at him as if he'd suddenly grown horns, then Beth asked cautiously, 'How do you mean, exactly?'

The expression on her face wasn't flattering to him. 'I mean, there are attics for the servants. You're working as my maids, so why not sleep up there in the servants' quarters? There's room for your families and I'm sure Mrs Jarratt will help out around the place too when she can, so she'll be paying her way.'

But even the older woman was looking at him suspiciously, so he said it bluntly, 'I'm not asking any of you to move into my bed. I'm not like that, as you ought to damned well know by now. You'll all be sleeping together in the attics. Reggie and I will stay on the first floor.'

Beth sagged and for the first time tears welled in her eyes. She was such a brave woman, had had to endure so much, and had done it so bravely that tears from her touched him to the core.

She blinked hard and only a couple more tears slid down her cheeks before she blew her nose and said in a husky voice, 'You're the kindest man I've ever met, Mr Carlisle.'

'I'm not! I'm just being . . . well, neighbourly.'

'I don't know many people who'd take neighbourliness that far.' She took a deep breath and said, 'We accept gratefully. Only . . . can we bring our furniture, please? It's not much but it's all we've got and there's plenty of room for it in the attic. We'll find someone to fetch it here.'

'I can bring some of it in the car.'

Her voice was just a whisper. 'You'd even do that?'

He nodded, feeling even more embarrassed. 'I've had bad times myself and people have helped me. I try to do the same to others and I'm sure you will too once you're in a better position yourselves.'

She swallowed hard and nodded.

He waited, noticing yet again the way the Jarratts turned to Beth for guidance. If he was kind, what was she? Capable and brave, that's what, caring too, for all her brisk, no-nonsense ways. If he'd been married to a woman like that, he'd not have gone off and left her without help. What was that husband of hers thinking about? Himself, that's what, not his family.

'There's Dilys's daughter as well, Mr Carlisle. Gillian, she's called. She's almost fourteen and she helps out at The Shepherd's Rest sometimes, but she'll be happy to do some work here for her keep.'

'Of course she can come. I haven't even got as far as thinking of wages, so we'll discuss that side of things later. The first thing is to put a roof over your heads, make you feel safe.

She looked at him gratefully. 'Thank you.' Then she turned to the others. 'That's settled. And we'll work very hard for Mr Carlisle, won't we?'

They all nodded vigorously.

Mrs Jarratt, who must have been old enough to be his mother, let out a sigh of relief and gave him a shy, grateful smile.

He drove Beth and Dilys back to the cottages to assess how many of their smaller belongings he could move for them in his car.

The bigger pieces wouldn't fit into the vehicle, or even on the car's rear luggage rack, and to his eyes their furniture was falling to pieces – like the cottages.

As he looked round, he saw Beth flush, then put up her chin defiantly as if to say she was doing her best. There was a battered bucket in one corner of her cottage under a stain that showed the roof leaked there. Could the landlord not have mended that, at least?

Finn heard footsteps outside and turned round as a man walked in. He'd seen him in the pub, an older man wearing comfortable though well-worn clothes, but hadn't spoken to him.

As they eyed one another, Beth stepped into the breach. 'This is Mr Carlisle and this is Mr Unwin, our landlord.'

The two men shook hands, then the older man turned to Beth. 'I'm sorry to turn you out, lass, but I've family who've lost their jobs and have nowhere to live so I have to put them first.'

She didn't smile, just said coolly, 'We've found somewhere else to live, thank you. Mr Carlisle needs servants and has plenty of room for us all in his attics.'

'Well, I'm thankful to hear that.'

Beth folded her arms, not giving even a hint of her mood softening.

'We're deciding how to get their things across to Heythorpe House,' Finn said.

'Well, that's one thing I can help you with, at least,' Mr Unwin offered at once. 'It'll only take two trips across with my cart to carry all your bits and bobs, I reckon. My sons will help lift and carry.'

Now her smile fluttered to life, making her face look soft and pretty for a few moments. 'Oh. Thank you ever so much, Mr Unwin.'

'If you take the rest of the day off to pack, we could move you tomorrow,' Finn suggested.

She gave him a wry smile. 'It'll take me an hour to pack if that, sir, so I can do it tonight. We've not much left now because I've pawned everything I could. So I'd rather go on working and earn my day's pay, if you don't mind.'

'We'll do the move tomorrow morning, then. Early, if that's alright, Beth lass,' Mr Unwin said.

'As early as is convenient for Mr Carlisle.'

Finn decided it'd be best to get on with it. 'Or how about we move them and their things today? If your sons are free, that is, Mr Unwin? Get it over and done with. The day's already been broken into. What do you think, Beth?'

'We'll do whatever is most convenient for you, sir,' she repeated.

Dilys looked from one to the other. 'What about Mum and the kids? And our Gillian?'

'I'll drive back and fetch them, or if you can manage their packing, I'll just tell them what's happening. Perhaps your mother could sort out the attic bedrooms at my house, Dilys?'

'Oh, yes.'

Beth looked thoughtful. 'She can scrub out two rooms while she's waiting.'

'Two? You'll need more than two, surely?'

'I didn't want to presume.'

'There are plenty because they're only small. Dilys, how do you want to sleep? There are a lot of small rooms in the attics. You could each have your own, if you wanted.'

'Eh, I'd be scared to sleep on my own. I've never done that in my life. Me and Mum and Gillian always sleep together.'

'I'd like my own room if you don't mind,' Beth said. 'If I want to read in bed at night, I won't wake Felix and Daisy then. But I'd like them to be next to me.'

'Fine. I'll start Mrs Jarratt on the cleaning after she and I have sorted out which ones to use. It's very dusty up there.'

He left them to it and Mr Unwin walked out with him, stopping at the car, to say, 'I didn't like having to turn them out, Mr Carlisle. I'd have let them sleep in the barn till they found somewhere, if necessary. You'll . . . treat them gently?'

'I will. I need servants to help me set the house to rights. And I can guess what you're worrying about, but they'll have nothing to fear from me.'

'Good. That all works out well, then. I'll see you later when we bring the cart across.'

Finn found Daniel clearing out one of the garden sheds, with rusty rakes and hoes propped against its outside wall, and a miscellany of other small items spread out for inspection.

'Where's Reggie?'

'Still up at Spring Cottage with Mr Jonah.'

'That's good. He'll be safe there. No trouble here?'

'No sign of anyone, sir, except a couple of hikers going up towards the moors.'

'Good.' He explained what was happening and went to find Mrs Jarratt.

She was just finishing mopping the library floor, chatting to the children, who were sitting in a corner of it, waiting for her. 'I thought I'd make myself useful, Mr Carlisle. I don't like to sit and do nothing.'

'That's very good of you.'

When he explained what was going to happen, she accepted it placidly. 'I knew Beth would work things out for us. She's a clever lass, that one. Our Dilys can easily pack my things, as well as hers and Gillian's. She knows what's what.'

'Then you and I should choose some rooms and you can scrub them out, ready. We haven't even started clearing out the attics and it's still very dusty up there. But today's fine and warm, so the floors will soon dry.'

'I'll enjoy that. I like making things look nice.' She told the children to sit in the kitchen till she'd looked round the attics. He suggested giving them a glass of milk and a piece of bread and butter, and saw their eyes brighten at that.

As she followed him up to the attics, Mrs Jarratt oohed and aahed at the size of the house. Then she surprised him by choosing their bedrooms shrewdly, with an eye to which might be warmest in winter, something that would never have occurred to him. 'Just in case we stay here, sir.' She stole a quick glance sideways and added, 'You won't get more willing servants anywhere, I promise you.'

'I'm sure I won't. I'll just get some extra food sent up from Mrs Buckley's and then go back to help the others move. Can you put the food away, or cover it up, whatever it needs?'

'I'm happy to. Eh, we're that grateful to you, sir.'

'Well, I'm grateful for your help.'

The look she gave him said she didn't quite believe that, but she didn't voice her doubts.

He was thoughtful as he drove to the village shop. Life here in Ellindale seemed to have gathered a momentum of its own and was sweeping him along willy-nilly. But he wasn't sorry he was doing this, bringing them all to live at Heythorpe House.

He stopped walking for a moment and smiled as an image of Beth came into his mind, her head up as if challenging the world. No. He wasn't sorry, not at all. He was glad to be able to help her. And the others, of course.

And he was also glad to have people round him. Life was getting back to normal again now, well, better than normal with his inheritance. That felt so good, like coming into the warm, bright sunshine after being in the shadows for a long time.

Two days later, Mary Jarratt suggested to Beth that she take over the cooking and buying of food for the inhabitants of Heythorpe House.

'You've already done that, Mrs Jarratt. I didn't know you could cook so well.'

'I've not had proper food to cook with for a long time. So, you'll speak to Mr Carlisle about it?'

'I think you should do that.'

'Oh, I can't. I'll go all nervous and my voice will wobble.'

'You were joking with him only last night.'

But Mary shook her head. 'He made me laugh. This is too important and I can't say it like you would.'

So after the evening meal, which Mr Carlisle insisted they all eat together, Mary took the children upstairs to get them ready for bed. Dilys took Reggie into the scullery to help her wash up and Beth was left with Finn.

He looked across at her and raised one eyebrow. 'Is there a reason everyone has left us alone?'

'I need to ask you something.'

He leaned back in his chair, smiling so encouragingly she lost a lot of her nervousness.

'We wondered if Mrs Jarratt could be put in charge of cooking and shopping.'

'Sounds like a good idea to me, if the meals of the past two days are anything to judge by.'

Beth had let out a relieved breath before she could stop herself.

She was surprised when Finn took her hand. 'You shouldn't be frightened of asking me such things, lass. To all intents and purposes you've become the housekeeper here, after all.'

'Me? But I just—'

'—organise us all extremely efficiently.'

She knew she ought to pull her hand away but didn't like to make a fuss about it because he didn't seem aware of what he was doing. And actually, she didn't want to pull away. It was a long time since anyone had offered her such a comforting gesture. Certainly not her husband, who was only interested in bedding her whenever he could and having someone to look after his home. Neil had disappointed her in quite a few ways.

Mr Carlisle let go and she clasped her hands together in her lap, hoping she hadn't given away her reaction to his touch. 'I hope I haven't been too bossy, sir. Neil always said I drove him mad, bossing him around.'

'Maybe he needed it.'

'He did. But he'd never listen to me, so I was wasting my breath most of the time.'

'I listen to you because you're so capable. If you think Mrs Jarratt should be cook and quartermaster, then she shall be. I'll set up an account at the shop for her.'

'Um, it'd be better to put some money in a jar. She's no good with paperwork and figures. She can hardly read, but she's good at handling the money itself, even in small amounts, and doesn't get that wrong.'

'Fine. We'll do that. Um, about the reading. Do you think she needs glasses to help her see better?'

Beth looked at him in surprise. 'I never thought of that.'

'We'll get her to the optician and have her eyes tested once things settle down a bit with Reggie.'

'Mrs Jarratt will need better clothes to go there or she'll feel shamed. It's one thing for her neighbours to know she's short of money and clothes, because most of them are too. But down in Rivenshaw, it'd be strangers who'd see it.'

'Are there any old clothes in the attic which she could use?'

'No. I had a look round. I hope you don't mind. There are only a few things stored up there.'

'Then we'll ask Vi to find her – no, find you *all* some clothes from Charlie's pawnshops.'

She flushed scarlet. 'I wasn't asking you to do that.'

'You didn't ask. I offered. And I'm not offering new clothes, just second-hand ones. I prefer to have my servants – and their children – decently dressed.' He waited a moment or two and added, 'Please accept this gift. It really won't cost me a lot.'

Her shoulders sagged and she said in a half-whisper, 'Very well. And I am truly grateful.'

'Only it's hard for you to accept charity.'

She nodded.

'I had to accept help after my wife died. I went on the tramp for a couple of years, left the police force, couldn't come to terms with her death, and the unborn child's.'

It was her turn to fleetingly touch his hand.

'It was Sergeant Deemer who helped me, even when I didn't want to be helped.'

'He's well thought of – except by thieves and villains.'

'And rightly so. I'll phone Vi about clothes for you all tomorrow, then. Oh, and I'd like to officially offer you the job of housekeeper.'

She gaped at him. 'Me?'

'Yes.'

'But I'm a married woman. When my husband comes back I'll have to leave and keep house for him.'

He heard the sigh that followed. It was sad that she never

spoke positively about her husband. She didn't sound to have been at all happy with him. Finn had been happy with Ivy. Very happy. He realised Beth was looking at him questioningly.

'You can be the temporary housekeeper then. Until your circumstances change.'

'I shall enjoy that. Thank you.'

14

The youth hostel at Spring Cottage had already opened without fuss or fanfare, except for a neat sign on the wall outside saying Ellindale Youth Hostel. Leah had also registered it with the recently formed Youth Hostels Association and it would be listed in their quarterly journal.

For the moment she found herself getting clients by word of mouth because there was some open moorland here for hikers from Manchester, whereas many areas were barred to them by landowners in order to protect the young grouse.

'How ridiculous!' she'd raged to Jonah one day after reading an article about it in the newspaper. 'Protecting grouse so that men can shoot and kill hundreds, if not thousands of them. I never heard of anything so arrogant.'

'The time of arrogant landowners is limited,' he said in his mild way. 'There's a movement to open public rights of way again to anyone wanting to walk across the countryside. I'd join in if I were fitter, but can you see me protesting and marching up to the moors?'

His sigh told her this was another of the things that limited his life and upset him. She gave his hand a little squeeze to show her sympathy, but what could you do? The damage had been done.

Small groups of people had stayed at the new hostel for one or two nights and Mrs Dutton's eldest daughter had been employed to clean it after they'd gone. At the regulation one shilling charge per night, Leah wasn't making much of a profit yet, but you had to start somewhere and at least it gave some occasional employment to another of the villagers.

When Charlie phoned one day to say he was coming to see them with an idea for both a grand opening of the hostel and a way of improving sales, Leah started to protest that it was open already. But he'd already put down his phone, so she went to share the news with her husband.

'I never met anyone like your brother for making an extra shilling here and there. But this seems like bolting the stable door after the horse has galloped off across the moors. Still, I suppose it'll mean more work for Mrs Dutton's daughter.'

'You always think of others first,' Jonah commented. 'It'll mean extra money for you, too. Well, eventually.'

'I suppose so. If it does improve sales. Though I don't have to scrabble for every penny when I have a breadwinner like you because you're good at making money yourself.'

'I do my humble best.'

He gave her one of his warm smiles, but she couldn't help thinking that like many men he kept the details of his finances to himself, not even telling his brother. She didn't think Charlie realised how comfortably circumstanced Jonah was, but her husband must be doing well because there always seemed to be money available when she needed it.

She could see that her compliment had pleased Jonah, though, which was something.

An hour later there was the sound of an engine chugging up the hill and Leah went to look out of the window. 'A car's just turned into the yard. Oh, look! It's your brother who's driving it!'

'Charlie driving!' Jonah hurried across the room to join her at the window. 'He's doing it under Todd's watchful eye, thank goodness. I'm not sure my brother will make a good driver, even with the spectacles. He's too impulsive and you should have seen how badly he used to play cricket. He has terrible coordination, can't catch a ball unless it falls into his hands.'

He strolled out to greet the new arrivals, but before he could open his mouth, Charlie snapped, 'Don't say anything about my driving! We didn't all get the chance to learn during the war and I don't welcome any comments on my progress, thank you very much.'

Todd got out of the car just then, rolling his eyes as if to say that Charlie wasn't making a good start.

'I'm sure you'll soon get the hang of it with practice,' Jonah said tactfully. 'Nice car. Is it yours?'

Charlie patted the steering wheel. 'Yes. I just bought it.'

'I'd have thought a Hillman Straight Eight was a bit big for you.'

'Well, it isn't, whatever anyone says about smaller cars being easier to drive. If I'm having a car, I'm having one which has comfortable seats and doesn't look like it's been thrown together in some backyard shed.'

'I like the look of it. I'd love to have a drive,' Jonah said.

'Any time you like.'

'I'll have a tootle round Rivenshaw one of the mornings I come into the office, then.'

'Fine.' But Charlie heaved a sigh and still didn't look his usual happy self.

'Is something the matter?'

'This driving's opened up a damned can of worms at home and Marion is insisting on learning to drive as well. As if she won't have enough to do looking after a new baby, let alone the problems of fitting behind a steering wheel with that great big belly. I've told her she should wait.'

Jonah grinned openly. 'And what did she say to that?'

'What do you think? You know what she's like. She said if

I won't help her get lessons, she'll find someone else who will.'

'I've got to give it to your Marion: if she decides to do something, she doesn't let anyone or anything stand in her way.'

Charlie made a faint huffing sound as if venting his annoyance. 'You don't have to tell me that. She never goes against me in business matters, thank goodness, but in everything else she can be very, um, determined.'

'What's the problem about Marion getting driving lessons? Everyone who can afford it is getting a car these days. You're going to make a fortune out of selling them.'

'The problem is, she wants a car of her own. I told her my money's busy at the moment but she's got some cash tucked away that she inherited from her grandmother so she said she'd dip into that. And to crown it all, she's fallen in love with that little car Todd showed you, that Chummy. So she's decided to buy it. Just like that!' He snapped his fingers to illustrate this. 'Before she even knows how to drive it.'

Jonah was glad when Leah came out of the house and strolled across towards them.

Unfortunately Charlie hadn't seen her and turned to say to Todd, 'I wish you'd never got hold of the damned Chummy. You know what bad drivers women make and—'

As his brother said this, and Leah's expression changed from a smile to a glare, Jonah said hastily, 'That's not true. My wife is a particularly *good* driver, better than most men.'

Todd dug an elbow in his friend's side as Charlie opened his mouth again. 'Women are as varied as men about driving: some good, some bad. You shouldn't make outrageous statements like that, old man.' He jerked his head to the side and Charlie noticed his sister-in-law standing there, hands on hips, a challenging look on her face.

'Oh, er, present company excepted,' he said hastily.

'Not just present company,' she said sharply. 'I hope you don't make a habit of saying such rude things about women, because it'll upset me every single time, whoever you're referring to.'

'Ah. Sorry. Wasn't thinking.'

'Well in future, think first, speak second. Especially when you're talking about women, because the world's full of them. We lost so many men during the war that women outnumber you!'

Jonah only just managed to hold back a chuckle at his brother's expression.

Though she felt annoyed by Charlie's comments, Leah let the matter drop. After all, not only Jonah but also their visitor had done some of her protesting for her. She'd have expected such support from her husband, but not from Todd and it raised him in her estimation.

She'd only met the man a few times, but she couldn't figure him out, never quite knew what to expect from him. He'd given her a quick grin today as if he knew what he was about to say would surprise her. Which it had.

Charlie threw up his hands. 'Sorry. Didn't mean to upset you, Leah. I was just feeling a bit miffed about, um, about things. Anyway, what I came to tell you was that I'm getting the Mayor of Rivenshaw to come and open your youth hostel for you in a fancy ceremony.' He gestured to the old barn.

'It's just a small business using a barn that was already built,' Leah protested. 'And people have already stayed there, so what's to open?'

'It's a new business in an area short of jobs and that's a good thing to make a fuss about in times like these. It cheers people up when they read about it in the papers.'

'But even so, why would the mayor take the trouble to do a fancy opening?'

Charlie gave her a smug look. 'Because he owes me a favour.'

'Shouldn't you save your favour for something more important?'

'This fizzy drink business *is* important. Not only because of Jonah and you, but because if I'm part of a business, I want to make as much money as possible from it, otherwise why bother to take a share? Think about it: a fancy opening complete with mayor will be reported in the *Rivenshaw Gazette*, and they'll mention the mineral waters you make right next door to the hostel. And *that* will help our sales. If you have something to sell, you have to let people know about it.'

'But we aren't trying to develop a huge business.'

'Oh, aren't we?'

Jonah put an arm round her shoulders. 'You've let the genie out of the bottle, my dear. Don't be surprised when it starts waving its magic wand.'

Charlie bowed to her, flourishing one hand like a stage magician. 'Abracadabra! You just make sure you have plenty of fizzy drinks waiting to be sold, Leah, and of course we'll offer them round at the opening, with a few fancy cakes. You'll need to invite some people from the village as well to give us a nice crowd.'

'But—'

He put one finger on her lips. 'Let me do the selling, you start making extra fizzies.'

'I can make more bottles, of course I can, but—'

'You might as well do as he says,' Jonah put in quietly. 'My brother's as stubborn as his wife and if I know him, he'll enjoy following a new business direction.'

Charlie nodded vigorously. 'Exactly! I now have two new businesses, actually: selling cars and fizzies, as well as my two pawnshops.'

She hadn't been able to stop him calling her drinks fizzies, though she preferred the term *mineral waters*. 'Well, I want to make one thing clear right from the start: I'm not changing my delivery driver, not for anything.'

'You won't need to. Peter's a good man. With a few hints from me, he'll do a great job of making extra sales for us.'

'How can you be sure of that?'

'He was delivering a couple of bottles to that little grocery shop across the road from our shop, so I sent Vi out to ask him if he was carrying any extra bottles and he not only sold her two – two, mind you, not one, and this is Vi we're talking about and she's no pushover! He has a nice way with him, Peter does — and Vi enjoyed it so much she was happy to place a regular order.'

Since Charlie had joined them, Leah sometimes felt as if she was driving down a hill without brakes. She didn't think her brother-in-law would cheat anyone, let alone a relative. He was very well thought of in the town. But he certainly dived into things. She liked to work more quietly and steadily.

As she went back into the house, she had a thought that made her smile: if Charlie and Peter did increase sales, she would be able to increase the number of people she hired. Which was one of the main points of setting up the business, after all.

Well, that and giving her something to do with her time now she had help with the housework. Jonah still had a rest most days, and he still read voraciously, not even hearing what anyone said to him when he was engrossed in a book.

It was a strange sort of marriage. Not unhappy, but not what she'd once hoped for. Her hand went up to her stomach and a sad sigh escaped her. Not at all what she'd hoped for.

By the time Charlie left, he had walked round the youth hostel and the small drink factory, muttering to himself.

On the way out Todd lingered beside her for a moment. 'He's like a whirlwind, isn't he? But he's right about getting your new business known.'

'He might have asked me what I wanted before he spoke to the mayor.'

Todd chuckled. 'That's not how he operates. He's always sure of his ideas, so he dives in to set things up. And he does have a knack for making money. He'll be a millionaire before he's through.'

She was startled, because the family joked about that, but they didn't really believe it. 'Do you think so?'

'Oh, yes. If I didn't have faith in him, I'd not have gone into business with him. I've a lot to learn from him.' He winked and added, 'And from you. You're a clever woman, too, with a knack for getting people on your side. That's your strength, I think, that and your recipes.'

She couldn't think what to say to that so didn't say anything but waited to wave them goodbye. It was only as she turned to go back into the house that it sank in what Charlie had done: got her to agree to organise the details of the grand opening. Which would take a lot of fiddling around.

She went to collapse in a chair opposite Jonah, who was looking tired now. 'Your brother!' she exclaimed. 'Whatever will he do next?'

He chuckled. 'Who knows? He certainly doesn't.'

There was silence for a few moments, then he said, 'What about the catering for this grand opening? How about asking Don and Izzy from The Shepherd's Rest to do it? I can ferry the food from their place to here in my car.'

'Good idea. That'll bring in some extra money for them.'

'And we'll invite some of the locals to the opening, those two included.'

'We can't invite everyone in the village, so how do we choose?'

He thought for a moment or two. 'I know! We pull the names out of a hat.'

'I'm only doing that if I can check whose name goes into the hat. There are some people in the village that I won't have in my house. The Judsons come to mind.'

'The opening will be in the youth hostel itself, surely?'

'You've no need to take me literally, Jonah Willcox. But we must make sure Nancy gets an invitation. Only how are we to do that?'

'When I was teasing Charlie about him saying *Abracadabra*, he told me Todd used to do little magic tricks. We'll invite him to put the names into the hat and then pull them out again.'

She didn't like to protest, but it seemed to her that Todd was worming his way into their family. Did she want to be closely associated with him? Did she have any choice, given that he was now Charlie's partner?

The trouble was, Todd still made her feel uneasy, which was strange when he was very nice to everyone. He was a little cheeky. But then, she doubted Charlie would have taken on a partner if he wasn't a bit . . . adventurous.

Oh, why was she thinking about Todd Selby when she had a dozen things that needed doing in the old barn, or the 'fizzery factory' as Jonah and Rosa were both now calling it?

When someone knocked on the front door, Finn went to open it himself. Until he was sure that Buddle had stopped chasing them, he'd told the women to leave answering the door to him or if he was out, Daniel.

It was Vi with a bundle of clothes and behind her he could see Charlie's new car.

'Did you drive up here yourself?' he asked in surprise.

'Yes. Don't look so surprised. Like a lot of other women of my age I learned to drive during the war, helping run a canteen for the soldiers stationed in that little camp beyond Rivenshaw. Charlie was going to drive me up here today so that he could get more practice, but something came up.'

'It wouldn't take much to put him off driving, I should think.'

She smiled tolerantly. 'He's good at so many other things, we can forgive him his clumsiness with cars, surely? Anyway, I have several bundles of clothes for your maids and their families to try on.'

'I'll help you carry them in. It'd be so much easier if people delivering things could drive round to the back of the house.' On that thought he stopped to study the lie of the land. 'Perhaps I'll hire some men in to dig out a track. It'd fit into the side of the hill there, don't you think?'

She studied it for a moment. 'Yes. You'd have to shore up the edge of the track carefully, though, because if there are winter storms it could give way suddenly.'

'Yes, that's what I've been told. But the job would be worthwhile in more ways than one. It'd provide work for a few men for weeks, wouldn't it?'

'And you could maybe get one of those government grants to provide employment for men who've been out of work a long time.'

'Good idea!'

He took her and the bundles into the house the front way and as he was closing the door behind them, he saw a movement from the corner of his eye and swung round quickly. But he could see nothing out of place. Probably just the wind blowing one of the bushes along the edge of the car parking area.

Only he didn't usually imagine seeing things as he had excellent eyesight, so once inside he dropped the bundles. 'Wait a minute. I thought I saw something.' He nipped into the front parlour, a room they didn't use and peered round the edge of the dusty curtain, trying not to move it more than a fraction.

As he scanned the entrance area, he saw a man move out from behind the clump of bushes to one side of the entrance. 'Come here quickly, Vi.'

She was already standing beside him.

'Do you recognise that man?'

In silence they watched the stranger check the road, presumably to make sure no one was around. Then he went out but stopped to stare at the house, as if he'd just been walking past.

'Hmm. I've seen him somewhere, Finn, but I can't remember where. I don't really *know* him.'

'I wonder what he's doing here.'

'Looking for Reggie, do you think?' she suggested.

'Must be. But he's not the man who came here with Buddle. Who else could be interested in Heythorpe House, though?'

'I don't know. You'd better make sure Reggie doesn't go wandering around on his own.'

'He'd never do that. He's too scared of Buddle. Hmm. I'll have to see if I can find out more about that chap. Anyway, let's show these clothes to my staff.'

'You'd better leave that to me, Mr Carlisle.'

'Call me Finn. You did before I inherited.'

'I didn't want to offend you. Some people don't like ordinary people or employees being over-familiar.'

'I'm not "some people", Vi. And to be frank, I'm still not used to having a big house and all that goes with it.' He waved one hand around. 'This makes me feel . . . well, guilty, somehow.'

'No need for that. You should be grateful. Now, leave these women to me. I'll make sure they have decent clothes to wear.'

'Dress Beth for the housekeeper's role, if you don't mind.'

'So Charlie said. Does she know enough about that job?'

'She can learn. She's a very capable and clever woman and manages the other servants without upsetting them. And Mary Jarratt is going to be my new cook and will do the shopping. Dilys will act as general maid, helping out where necessary. And there are still plenty of other little jobs to do, because the place hasn't been touched for decades, so we'll hire people as needed.'

He'd noticed her staring round as they moved towards the kitchen. 'You're welcome to have a look at the house, if you want. Get Beth to show you round once you've sorted out the clothes.'

'Are you sure you don't mind?'

'Not at all.'

He went to study the books in the library, but couldn't help overhearing the excited voices and laughter coming from the kitchen. It made him feel lonely.

He couldn't settle to reading and thought about the man who'd been hiding and watching them. Who else would be taking an interest in Heythorpe House? There was only one possibility: his cousin Digby. Who knew? He might have been furious when Finn inherited. No, surely not? Digby's side of the family weren't poor, so he couldn't be desperate for this run-down old place.

Could he?

No. There was no need to see enemies everywhere you turned. Buddle was enough to deal with at the moment. Finn turned his attention back to planning what to do next with the house. Perhaps he should get some gates fitted to the entrance, for safety?

Only if he did that it'd make it hard to turn a car into the parking area and he'd have to get out to open the gates every time he drove back home. No, he'd think about that some more.

But a means of access to the rear of the house was a necessity if the place was going to be used. The grounds of this place were very inconveniently set out. Could he get a government grant to help with that? Not for him, but for the local men.

Who would know about building roads over moorland terrain? He thought about the people he'd met since coming to the valley, and of course, he thought about Ben. Did he have enough experience to do a job like that?

There was a knock on the library door and he turned to see Vi waiting there.

'All finished now?' he asked.

'Yes. But if it's all right with you, we need to get them some underwear. They won't want other women's knickers, but I know someone at the markets who can supply you with them at a very reasonable cost.'

'Good. Do that.'

She waited and he wondered why.

'Don't you even want to ask about cost, Finn?'

'I don't know what women's knickers cost, but it can't be hugely expensive. I'm assuming you won't be buying them silk and satin!'

'No. Plain and practical cotton.'

'Good. Do it. And Vi . . .'

'Yes?'

'I'm very grateful for your help. Go and have a look round the house now. I know you're dying to.'

He saw Beth taking her up the stairs and the sight stopped him in his tracks.

Beth looked very different in the nicer clothes. Not like a maid at all. He felt a stirring of attraction at the sight of her and had to take a few deep breaths to calm himself down.

Wasn't it typical of fate that he should be attracted to a woman for the first time since his wife had died, only the woman was already married? What's more, Beth was a decent person, not the sort to play around, any more than he was.

He grimaced. He was a very stodgy, old-fashioned sort of man, the type who wanted to marry and have children, not the type to have affairs.

But he couldn't help being attracted to Beth. The more he was with her, the more he liked her, and her two wide-eyed children who were no longer afraid of him and would stop to talk to him sometimes.

She was married, though. He had to keep that in mind.

Finn woke early the next morning and decided there was no use lying in bed, even though he felt tired after a restless night.

He'd told his maids when they moved in that he'd go down for his own shaving water every morning and that he'd wash in the cold water taken to his room the previous evening. At this time of year, who needed warm water bringing up to wash in? That was a waste of his servants' time.

Anyway, he still wasn't used to the idea of them waiting on him physically, and since he preferred to sleep naked in the warmer weather, he'd told them as they moved in that he'd come down to the kitchen for his morning cup of tea and collect his shaving water at the same time.

All three women were in the kitchen when he got up, with cups of tea in front of them. He smiled at them and sat down beside Dilys. 'I hope there's some left in the pot.'

Beth broke the silence. 'Yes, of course, Mr Carlisle. And we were just about to toast some bread. Do you want your breakfast yet? We'll learn your ways quickly, I promise you.'

'No, thank you. I'm never hungry first thing in the morning, but a cup of tea would be very welcome.' He stared down at the delicate china cup she'd set before him and pushed it back towards her. 'I prefer a big mug for my tea.'

She took it away. 'Very well. You have only to say when we do things wrongly. You'll find us quick to learn your ways.'

'I'm sure I shall.' But he could see that his presence put them on edge and when he looked across at Beth it was clear that she understood what was going on, because she looked at him ruefully. Was it his imagination or was she more at ease with him than the others? He hoped so.

When he came downstairs again after shaving, she met him in the hall. 'Could I talk to you, sir?'

'Yes, of course.'

She led him into a small room he'd not paid much attention to before. 'If we clear this out, perhaps you could have your meals here.'

'I upset them when I sit with them, don't I? Reggie doesn't, though.'

'Well, employers don't usually eat with the staff. We all know that, at least. And he's still a child.'

He nodded reluctantly. 'It's going to be lonely being master here.'

'Um, I could bring my cup of tea in when you have yours and we can discuss what you want us to do during the day. If you like.'

'I'd like that very much. Can you clear out this room, then?'

'Yes, of course. And what about Reggie? Like many lads he needs turning out of his bed in the morning. Do you want me to do that?'

'No. I'll do it, but only after I've had a peaceful first cup of tea. He can be a bit grumpy in the mornings.' He paused, then said it, 'I'm glad you accosted me about a job that first day, Beth.'

'Oh?'

She sounded wary. 'Yes, because you're perfect for this job and you've saved me the trouble of looking for help in the house. Where are your children?'

'Gillian is going to see to getting them up and dressed for me in the mornings. They'll be no trouble to you.'

'Don't think you have to keep them silent all the time. I like to hear the sound of children laughing and playing. I always wanted to have a big family.'

Her voice became sharp and what she said was unguarded for once. 'It's all right to have big families if you can afford to feed them. I can't bear to see children going hungry. And when it was my own two, I'd have done almost anything to put food on the table.' She gave him a shamefaced smile. 'Anything short of murder, that is.'

'Tell me what you think of this idea then: I thought of buying milk from a farmer and giving all the village children a drink of it every day.'

For a moment or two she just stared at him, then she smiled. 'It's a *wonderful* idea. Another of your kind acts. But you'd better not give the milk to the parents because some of them would drink it. The children should have to turn up somewhere and drink it there and then.'

'I'd come to that conclusion myself. Where could they do that, do you think? It's too far for the little ones to walk out here.'

'There's a back room at The Shepherd's Rest that isn't used for anything except storage. I'm sure Don and Izzy will be happy to clear a space and let you use that. You might give them a few shillings a week to keep it clean and wash the cups, though. And you'll have to buy some cups.'

'Good thinking. You're always full of ideas, Beth. I like that. Never hesitate to suggest something. I can only say no, after all.'

She nodded, then gave him a worried look and said quietly, 'I'd better go and join the others now.'

He'd made her uncomfortable, which upset him. Though actually, it was this feeling of connection between them that was making them both a little uneasy at times. You didn't have to *do* anything specific to feel an attraction towards someone.

It would pass as they got used to living in the same house. Wouldn't it?

And he'd better get Reggie up. They needed to drive down to Rivenshaw later and get those stitches taken out.

15

Leah picked up the telephone and was surprised to hear Sergeant Deemer at the other end.

'Could you give Finn a message for me, please, Mrs Willcox?'

'Of course.'

'If you could just let him know from me that the parcel he's worried about will be picked up later this morning.'

She was puzzled by this, then heard a faint sound in the background. She'd heard it before and it usually meant that someone at the telephone exchange was listening in to the call.

They all knew this happened and it was infuriating because though you could never prove that anyone was listening in, you never dared discuss anything important or highly private. And there were very few automatic telephone exchanges out in the country, though the big towns all seemed to have them now.

'Did you cough just then?' he asked.

'No.'

'I didn't, either.'

Which was his way of warning her that someone was eavesdropping. 'I'll pass on your message straight away. I have to go into the village.'

'That would be very kind of you. Goodbye.'

The phone connection went dead and she hurried into the living room, unfastening her pinafore as she went.

'Who was that?' Jonah asked.

She stopped to study his face because he was looking tired

this morning. He did sometimes, but never complained or disturbed her if he was wakeful during the night. 'It was Sergeant Deemer with a strange message for Finn. And someone was listening in again. I think he wants me to deliver the message straight away.'

'Be careful.'

'I will.' She flung the pinafore over the back of a chair, crammed the first hat she picked up from the hallstand on her head and didn't bother to put a shawl round her shoulders because it was a beautiful June day.

Jonah went to the door to watch her hurry down the hill. He had an uneasy feeling, for no reason he could work out. On a sudden impulse he kicked off his carpet slippers and put on his outdoor shoes, then went out to the car to follow her and make sure she stayed safe.

So anxious was he that he flooded the motor and it was a minute or two before he could get the engine running.

When he got to the lane, he saw Leah stop a lad and speak to him. She slipped him a coin and the lad nodded then she went on into the village shop. The lad climbed over the wall and down to the rear of Heythorpe House.

Jonah frowned when he saw a car came up the hill from the village, a police car by the looks of it, but not Sergeant Deemer's vehicle. It turned slightly to the left and parked in the gateway of Heythorpe House, blocking his way in. He stopped where he could see what was going on, wondering whether to go and check that Leah had arrived safely.

A constable got out of the police car, stumbling on the rough ground, and came towards him.

'Were you intending to go to Heythorpe House, sir?'

'Yes. Why else would I have stopped to turn off here? If you'd ask your driver to move further into the parking area, I'll get off the road.'

'It'd be better if you came back later, sir.'

'I'm here to pick up my wife. Is something wrong? Because if so, I'll need to make sure she's safe.'

'But sir—'

'Let me past.'

The constable stepped back, still protesting, but no one made any attempt to move the car.

Who was this young fellow? Not one of the valley's two policemen. Highly suspicious now, Jonah made sure his own car was parked in such a way as to prevent the police car from leaving and took his ignition key with him, locking the car door as well, so that no one else could push the vehicle out of the way without his permission.

'Sir, can you please—'

He ignored the man. Whatever was going on, he didn't like the look of this. When he stared down towards the entrance, he saw a man he knew slightly by sight, Sergeant Taylor from Wemsworth, striding towards the front door flanked by two burly policemen. What the hell was that fellow doing in Sergeant Deemer's jurisdiction?

He moved quickly down the slope towards the house, with the constable trailing behind, still bleating at him to stop. If someone from Wemsworth was involved, this could only mean they were here for Reggie.

Damn! He had no one to send with a message.

Daniel burst into the kitchen of Heythorpe House and locked the back door behind him, something unusual enough to make the maids stop work in surprise.

'Where's the master? There's a police car come to the house but it's not our sergeant or constables in it.'

'Mr Carlisle's in his office.'

'And Reggie? I reckon it'll be best if he hides till we know what they want.'

'I'll see to Reggie,' Beth said. 'You go and let Mr Carlisle know, Daniel. Dilys, don't open the back door unless I tell you to. In fact, you and your mother should hide in the scullery so if anyone looks through the window, they'll think no one's around.'

The other two women didn't hesitate to do as she said.

Beth ran up the back stairs, knowing Reggie was up in the attic, going through a pile of old children's books he'd found carelessly tossed into a corner. That lad loved his reading.

He'd be upset about this visit. He was terrified of being sent back to the orphanage and the brute who'd hurt him so badly.

Finn was lost in thought and jumped in shock when Daniel burst into his office.

'Some police have arrived in a car, sir, four of them, and they're not *our* police from the valley, neither.'

'What? Oh, hell. I should have noticed their arrival. Where's Reggie?'

'Beth's gone to find him, to tell him to hide.'

'Good.'

Someone hammered at the front door and when Finn hurried out across the hall he saw the door handle turning as if they were trying to open it. Furious at this and knowing he and Daniel were outnumbered if there were four of them, he went into the front parlour and opened the window slightly to call out, 'What do you want?'

'Police business, as you can see for yourself,' the sergeant said. 'Kindly let us in, Mr Carlisle. We have a warrant to detain the dangerous youth who's been hiding here.'

'There's no dangerous person here. Who are you talking about?'

'He's called Reginald Barston.'

'Then you're mistaken. Reggie is my ward and he's only eleven. He isn't dangerous in any way.'

'That'll be for the courts to decide. Now, let us in or we'll have to break the door down.'

Another voice yelled from further up the slope, 'What's going on here?'

The sergeant swung round.

Finn raised his voice. 'Jonah. I'm glad to see you. I need a witness to this because these people are threatening to break down my door.'

'Break down the door? Who's in charge here?'

The sergeant turned round. 'I am. As you can see.' He tapped the stripes on his arm.

'And your name is?'

He hesitated for a moment, then said, 'Sergeant Edward Taylor of Wemsworth District.' He brandished a piece of paper. 'This is from our local magistrate's court, giving me the authority to seize a dangerous youth.'

'He means Reggie,' Finn called through the window.

'Our Reggie? You've been misinformed, sergeant. He isn't at all dangerous.'

'I'm afraid you must leave that judgement to those who know him better, sir. May I ask who you are?'

'Jonah Willcox and you have a poor memory if you don't remember me because we've met before. I own the next property to this. And I'm well acquainted with Reggie because he and I play chess together.'

'From what I've been told by a gentleman I trust, the lad can barely read, and I doubt he can play a game like chess.'

'Then you've been told wrongly about that as well. Not only has he learned to play chess, but I've lent him a couple of books and discussed them with him after he'd read them. I find him both intelligent and polite.'

There was the sound of another car chugging up the hill and stopping in the lane outside. A man called, 'Am I at the right place? Is this Heythorpe House?'

Finn felt a surge of relief. 'You are indeed, Mr Lloyd, and in the nick of time, too. Perhaps you can help us find out what this is all about? For a start, I don't know why the police from Wemsworth should be dealing with something in our valley.'

'Nor do I.' The newcomer walked down the slope to stand right beside the police officers. 'I'm Henry Lloyd, Mr Carlisle's lawyer. And you are?'

The sergeant sighed but introduced himself again.

Mr Lloyd pulled out a notebook and propelling pencil and wrote down the man's name. He looked at the three other officers, clearly waiting for their names.

'Is this necessary, Mr Lloyd?' Taylor asked.

'I believe so. Are you refusing to give me your men's names?'

The sergeant waved one hand. 'Tell him.'

Mr Lloyd wrote them down then asked, 'And why exactly are you here, again?'

'To take a dangerous youth into custody in case he attacks people again,' the sergeant said stiffly.

'Who are you talking about?' Mr Lloyd asked.

'Reginald Barston.'

'Rubbish. I've met him and he's not dangerous in any way. In fact, he's a rather quiet, nervous lad who has been badly treated.'

'You don't want to listen to what he's telling you. No one's treated him badly.'

'I saw the evidence of ill treatment with my own eyes. Now, where is your warrant?'

Breathing deeply and looking furious the sergeant pulled out a folded paper that crackled and held it just out of reach of the lawyer.

Mr Lloyd smiled and waited for him to move closer.

Breathing deeply, Taylor waited as well, then as the seconds ticked slowly past, he gave in and passed it over.

The lawyer read the document carefully, taking his time. 'This only requires the lad to appear in a local court next week. It says nothing about you taking him away and detaining him. Or forcing entry into my client's house.'

'It was thought best to make sure of him till the hearing, so that he can't run away or cause any more harm in the meantime.'

'Then whoever told you that should think again. I will personally guarantee to produce the boy on the required date, if you'll give me my client's copy of this warrant.'

The sergeant hesitated. 'This is the only copy I have, sir.'

'Well, you either give us a copy or we won't recognise the warrant. Without an official document, I shall advise my client to ignore your instructions from now on.'

Finn moved from the window, smiling as he crossed the hall, but the smile vanished as he opened the front door and Taylor swung round as if to push his way in.

'Do not try to enter without the owner's permission.' The lawyer moved up the steps and entered, and the sergeant tried to follow.

'Stay back!' Finn snapped. 'I have no intention of letting you or your men into my home. Is your man going to move and allow my neighbour to pass? Or do you intend to play games?'

'This is not a game. We're concerned to apprehend a dangerous person. I shall report your refusal to cooperate to my area inspector,' Taylor said.

Mr Lloyd laid his arm on Finn's and answered for him. 'Do so. I shall be doing exactly the same thing with him. Did you inform the local sergeant of your presence in his juris-diction today, by the way?'

'I saw no need to do that. The lad comes from Wemsworth.'

'The lad has been living here for a few weeks, as I under-stand it, and intends to make it his permanent home once

Mr Carlisle's adoption of him goes through. And in any case, courtesy is a wonderful tool for helping society to run more efficiently, don't you think?'

As the lawyer turned away and Jonah joined them inside, Finn closed the front door and bolted it. 'We can watch them leave from the window.' The four men went into the next room and stood watching in silence.

The lawyer made a tutting noise. 'Oh dear! My car is blocking the way.' But he made no attempt to go out and move it, and was smiling broadly.

'Mine's in the way too,' Jonah murmured.

The group of policemen moved up the hill, only to find two cars blocking their way completely. They all turned as one to scowl at the house then the sergeant stabbed a finger towards the nearest man and said something.

Scowling, the fellow clumped down the slope to the front door again.

'Do you want me to move your car for you, Jonah?' Finn asked.

His neighbour chuckled. 'No. I walk quite slowly up hills. I'll move it once they've asked. Then I'll nip back home in it and phone Deemer, let him know what happened.'

'I walk rather slowly too,' the lawyer said. 'But don't do anything till they've asked. Angry men can sometimes let information fall.'

Finn looked at him. 'I presume it was Deemer who warned you what was happening?'

'Yes. We're just round the corner from the police station.'

'How did he know?'

'Someone tipped him the word.'

'He has a lot of useful friends.'

'He's been sergeant here for quite some time and has helped a lot of people.'

When the police car had eventually been allowed to drive

away, Finn offered the lawyer a cup of tea and Daniel went back to his work outside.

'I'd better see the lad first, so that I can attest to his state of mind,' Mr Lloyd said.

Finn went to yell up the back stairs, 'All clear, Reggie. They've gone.'

Reggie peered over the banisters, then came quickly down, moving silently in his stockinged feet, with his shoes in his hands.

'Where did you hide?'

'In the—'

'No. Don't tell me. If they come again I can say with perfect honesty that I don't know where you are.' Though he had a fair idea and intended to make the hiding place even more secure if he could. Just in case.

Mr Lloyd looked at Reggie who stared back nervously. 'Is there a reason for the stockinged feet?'

'So that I could move quietly.'

'Good idea. Could you hear what the men wanted?'

Reggie shook his head.

'Well, let's sit down and I'll go over it while someone makes us a cup of tea. I'm parched.'

When Finn and the lawyer had explained why the police had come to the house, Reggie blurted out, 'If I go to court, they'll take me away, I know they will.'

'There will be a magistrate and—'

'Mr Morris. He's a friend of Mr Buddle from church. He'll not believe a word I say. He didn't last time.'

'That explains why Buddle was so confident of winning custody,' Finn said thoughtfully. 'Whether a magistrate decrees it or not, I shan't let them take you, Reggie, even if I have to come and rescue you from the orphanage and run away to Australia.'

'They send bad boys to a correction centre and it's got high walls with barbed wire on the top,' Reggie said gloomily. 'You can't escape from there, so I'll have to run away before the hearing.'

'No, don't do that, lad.' Mr Lloyd's voice was surprisingly gentle. 'I have a friend whose brother is an experienced judge. I'll go and have a little chat with Miss Peters.'

Reggie looked from one man to another, clearly not convinced.

'I give you my word I won't let them lock you away, Reggie,' Finn said. 'But it'll be best to do this the legal way if you want me to adopt you and bring you up here.'

The lad pressed one hand to his mouth, then swallowed hard. 'You promise!'

'Yes.'

'I don't really want to run away.'

'And I don't want you to go.'

Mr Lloyd nodded and smiled gently at them. 'I'll call at my friend's house on the way back. Miss Peters lives in Rivenshaw. Do you have any idea when you'll be getting a telephone connection here, Mr Carlisle? It'd make things a lot easier if I needed some information in a hurry.'

'Any day now. I'll see if I can hurry them up.'

He turned to Reggie. 'Come on. We still have to get those stitches removed. No time like the present.'

When the lawyer had left, Finn walked up to Spring Cottage and asked to use their phone, calling the local telephone exchange to which he'd applied for connection.

To his surprise the man at the other end gasped and exclaimed, 'But you rang up and cancelled the order for a connection only yesterday.'

'There must be some mistake. I definitely didn't do that. Someone has played a malicious trick on me. Can you please reinstate my request for a telephone connection and mark it urgent? I've a sick lad here and I need the phone connecting as soon as possible in case we have to call in the doctor.'

He winked at Reggie as he spoke and the lad relaxed enough to wink back. Since he had been fed regularly, Reggie had grown rosy and looked to be bursting with health.

'I'm so very sorry, sir. I don't know how the mistake occurred. The request should have been made in writing and there's no sign of a letter from you. I'll see if we can put in your connection tomorrow because we have men going up the valley to another house.'

'Thank you. And can I give you, and only you, a password in case the person tries it again? You can give the other people instructions to contact you if they have any queries.'

'A password! Do you think that's necessary, sir?'

'I do. I used to be a policeman and I can assure you that villains are prepared to go to any length to get what they want.' He gave the man a long, invented nonsense word that no one could have known and put the phone down.

Who had done this? Buddle? It didn't seem an action that would help the man regain control of Reggie.

But Finn still found it hard to believe that a distant cousin was trying to harm him, or indeed anyone from his past. He'd left his old life behind and started a new one here in the valley. What's more, he'd trust the few friends he'd made here with his life.

He woke in the middle of the night, staring into the moonlit darkness because he'd been dreaming of his boyhood and his family, such a small family and so divided.

His father had hated his half-brother with a passion, so Finn had never played with his cousin, or done more than face his second cousin Digby across his great-aunt's sitting room. Digby. What a stupid name for a lad! It had been his mother's name apparently.

Now why had all this come back to him in a dream? He frowned into the patchy darkness. It had happened before. He'd dreamed of something as a warning.

Was this a warning? Who knew? He certainly didn't.

But . . . There was always a but. He was probably being stupid, but it wouldn't hurt to see if he could trace his cousin, see what Digby was doing. See whether he resented Finn inheriting from Uncle Oscar.

That side of the family were far wealthier than Finn's side so Yardley couldn't be short of money, surely?

It was a long time before Finn got to sleep again and he hadn't changed his mind about checking into Digby's life.

In the meantime, Reggie's safety must be his first concern.

16

It was a sunny afternoon and Peter Cotman whistled cheerfully as he drove the van slowly along the narrow, twisting road that was the only way into a small village near Wemsworth. This was on the other side of Rivenshaw from Ellindale, in flatter country, and it was the first time he'd come here. But they'd had an order by telephone, so here he was.

He enjoyed his job, loved driving and meeting people, even enjoyed the challenge of selling extra bottles of Spring Cottage Mineral Waters to chance customers. Mr Charlie Willcox had given him some good hints about how best to approach people.

He stamped on the brakes abruptly as a man jumped out into the road, his face covered by a knitted balaclava cap, which was pulled right down to hide all but his eyes.

It was as if Peter had been catapulted back into the war. It had been over a decade but his instincts took over before his brain had consciously registered that he was being attacked. The back doors of the van and the other door in the driving cabin were already locked, so he locked his own door with a quick flick of the hand.

Only just in time! He let out an angry yell as another masked man leaped out of the bushes and tried to open it.

As he put the van into reverse to try to get clear of them, the man in front of him raised a rock and hurled it at the windscreen.

Only the fact that Peter was already accelerating backwards

saved the windscreen from being smashed. The rock bounced off the front bonnet of the van, causing a dent.

'Damn you!' he yelled.

The man at the side had jumped on to the running board and he too was carrying a rock, so Peter slammed on the brakes, then accelerated then braked again.

'Got you!' he yelled as the man fell off.

He continued to reverse back along the lane, tooting the horn loudly, thankful for his experience as a driver in the Army. But however good you were, you couldn't reverse as quickly along a twisting narrow lane as you could travel forward.

The man who'd jumped on the running board had got quickly to his feet and started chasing after the van, followed closely by the other fellow. Another rock narrowly missed the windscreen, but Peter could only continue reversing at a safe speed.

When he saw a car in his rear-view mirror, he braked, praying that this wasn't part of the trap. He saw a middle-aged woman dressed in a tweed jacket peering through her windscreen, mouth open in shock, and sagged against the steering wheel in relief. She was either a brilliant actress or she wasn't part of the trap.

She surprised him by flinging open her car door and putting two fingers in her mouth to whistle shrilly as she jumped out. A huge dog leaped out after her, teeth bared, uttering a series of loud, challenging barks.

For a moment everyone seemed to freeze, staring at one another, then Peter's attackers turned tail and hared off down the lane again.

The dog twitched visibly. 'Stay, Benny!' the woman shouted and the animal stopped where he was, looking longingly after the two men.

She leaned into the luxurious car and came out with a

rifle, holding it at the ready before moving cautiously up to the van. 'What's going on?'

'Them two jumped out at me, missus, and one tossed a rock at the windscreen.' He gestured to the dent in the bonnet. 'If I hadn't put the van into reverse, he'd have smashed it. The other man jumped on the running board and tried to open my door, but I'd locked it.'

'They tried to rob you in broad daylight! Where do they think they are? This is Britain, dammit, not the wilds of Africa.'

'I'm glad you turned up, missus, you and this young fellow here.' He bent to offer his hand to the dog to sniff and then rubbed it under the animal's chin. 'I used to have a dog when I was a lad. Can't afford one for my own children though.'

She was studying the van. 'Spring Cottage Mineral Waters. Never heard of them, I'm afraid.'

'It's a new company. My employer is making ginger beer, dandelion and burdock and lemonade. Superior products for the discerning palate.' He nearly smiled at the way the words Charlie Willcox had suggested rolled automatically off his tongue. 'She's creating jobs for some of us in the village, bless her.'

He shook his head, feeling a bit shaky now that the crisis was past. 'I wonder if they were trying to put her out of business by attacking the van? It's the only one we've got. I can't work out why they'd want to do that, though. It's not as if we're a big company, or there are any others like us operating nearby.' He heard his voice wobble and felt annoyed with himself.

She looked at his face. 'You all right?'

'Well, I'm feeling a bit upset, I must admit. You don't expect that sort of attack in England. I've got out of the habit of fighting these days.'

'Serve in the armed forces, did you?'

'Yes, ma'am. In the Army. I was a driver.'

'Good for you. Look, I live just down the lane. You'd better come home with me and have a shot of whisky to steady your nerves. It'd upset anyone to be attacked like that. I'll buy a couple of your bottles while I'm at it. I hope they're as good as you say.'

That steadied him more than whisky ever could. 'I can give you a taste before you buy.'

'We'll do that. Now, let's get going. I can just squeeze my car past you, then you can follow me home. I'll keep my rifle handy and if we see any sign of an attack, I'll fire first and ask questions later. I'm a pretty good shot.'

Peter was astonished to find that her 'home' was a huge old house, a country mansion if he was any judge. He'd never been inside a place like that before.

When a groom came out of the stables cum garage, he shocked Peter again by addressing her as 'my lady'. Peter hoped his shocked gulp hadn't been overheard.

'Paxley, this chap has just been attacked by two hoodlums. Could you please check his van out and see if anything else has been hit besides the dent they made in his bonnet. They had the nerve to attack him on my land, so get the chaps to ask around. Someone must have seen them. I'll have those villains' hides pinned to my front door if I catch them.'

She turned back to Peter. 'This way. What's your name, by the way? And who's your employer?'

She strode into the house, firing questions at him, and Peter followed, stunned by this development but relieved to have a breather before he continued working.

'What do you think they were after? Money?'

'I've no idea. If so, they'd have been disappointed. I'm only just starting my day's deliveries. All I have is some small change in case I make extra sales, and bottles of ginger beer aren't exactly valuable, are they? So I can't see why anyone would bother to steal them.'

He tried to picture the scene again. 'Now I think about it, they seemed more concerned to pelt the van with rocks and damage it than try to get my money.'

'Strange. Here. Get this down you.'

He accepted one small whisky to steady his nerves but refused a second one. 'It's not good to get drunk when you're driving, ma'am, I mean your ladyship. But it's excellent whisky, that. Been a long time since I've tasted any. This is the first real job I've had for years, you see.'

Then he realised he was neglecting his duty. 'Can I offer you a bottle of ginger beer as an expression of my gratitude and that of my employer, or would you prefer dandelion and burdock? You won't find any better, I promise you.'

She leaned back, grinning. 'Ginger beer. I'll get Mavis to bring us something to eat and some glasses. We'll broach the bottle now.'

So there he was, sipping ginger beer with a titled lady who reminded him of one of the good officers he'd served under rather than a snobby rich person.

'You seem to know about cars, your ladyship.'

'I did a fair bit of driving myself during the war, ferrying bigwigs round London.' She stared blindly into the distance. 'We lost some fine people, my brothers included.'

'We did indeed.' He raised his glass in a silent toast to friends long gone and was only mildly surprised when she reached across to clink hers against his and do the same as if she recognised the meaning of the gesture.

A little later he noticed the time and was shocked. 'I'm afraid I'll have to go now, your ladyship. I still have my deliveries to make.'

'I'll come over and visit your employer one of these days.

I'd love to see a ginger beer factory in operation. And you'd better put me on your delivery list for a dozen bottles of ginger beer a month. You're right. It is good, best I've tasted.'

She frowned, then added, 'I'll get Paxley to drive along the lane behind you, just in case.'

'I'd be grateful for that, your ladyship.'

Leah stared at Peter in amazement when he explained why he was late back. 'You were attacked?'

'Yes, Mrs Willcox. I can only suppose they must have been trying to steal the van.'

'You aren't hurt, though?'

'No, ma'am. Not at all. Thanks to Lady Terryng.'

'The name sounds vaguely familiar, but I can't quite place it.'

Jonah chimed in. 'I've read about the family. The Terryngs are an old Lancashire family. They've lived near Rivenshaw for generations, and are known for living quietly and keeping themselves to themselves. If I remember correctly, this woman must be the last of them. Two sons, her brothers that'd be, were killed in the war.'

'You're a mine of information,' Leah said.

'Most of it fairly useless.'

She exchanged quick glances with Peter. Jonah had been upset by the police trying to take Reggie away and had been a bit down ever since.

'Don't risk yourself defending our van, Peter,' Jonah said. 'Nothing is worth a man's life.'

'I was thinking about that on the way back. Mrs Clements out at Heytop Farm has an idiot son. He's very big and strong. If I took him with me when I deliver, he'd look frightening, even though he'd never hurt a fly. She'd be glad of a rest from looking after him, poor soul. She's getting a bit old now to run round after him. And if we could just feed Sammy the odd meal, they'd be relieved. It's his only fault, that. He does like his grub and sometimes snatches food from children if you don't watch him.'

'Wouldn't he get in the way of the deliveries?'

'No, sir. Sammy knows me and does what I tell him.'

Jonah looked questioningly at his wife and Leah said at once, 'Then do it, Peter. We'll supply the lad with a good, hearty meal every day. I just want you to be safe.'

'He's more than a lad in years, but still a child in mind. He must be well over thirty.'

When Peter had gone home, she came to sit with Jonah. 'Why? Why would anyone attack our van? If they stole it, the sign on the side would give them away till they could paint over it, and someone would be sure to notice them as they drove it away.'

'You've got me there. It could be meant as a warning, but about what?'

She frowned. 'Perhaps they want me to pay protection money, like that Sam Griggs tried to do in Rivenshaw last year, but if they think a woman is a soft touch, they can just think again.'

'Or perhaps they're warning us to stay away from Reggie.'

They stared at one another as this suggestion sank in.

'This situation is getting out of hand. I think we should go to that hearing as well, in case Finn is attacked once he's out of our valley.'

'Yes. Good idea.'

They found out the following afternoon that the attack was indeed a warning when a letter was delivered by second post, addressed to Jonah. The message inside was printed using a child's wax crayon and said simply:

STAY AWAY FROM THAT BOY
IF YOU WANT TO KEEP YOUR VAN SAFE

Jonah swore and tossed the sheet of cheap paper across the table to Leah. 'Look at that!'

She stared at the message angrily. 'I never did give in to bullies.'

'Yes, but you'd better be careful with this lot. They're far beyond bullying; they're criminals. You'd better warn Peter when he comes back.'

'It won't make any difference. I'm not giving in to such threats.'

'I agree. I'll phone Sergeant Deemer, just to let him know about the threat. In the meantime, Peter's bringing Sammy Clements to meet us this morning.'

'Talk of the devil.'

Peter was waiting by the van, talking earnestly to a plump man, who had a child's wondering gaze in his doughy face.

Peter gestured as Leah came out to join them. 'This is Mrs Willcox. Say Mrs Willcox for me, Sammy.'

'Mississ Will-cox.'

'Now say hello to her.'

'Hello, Mississ Willcox.'

'Hello, Sammy. Are you going to help Peter?' she asked.

He nodded several times. 'Help Peter. Sit in the van.'

'We'll see you again at lunchtime, Peter. We'll have some food ready for you both.'

'There's no need to feed me!' Peter said quickly.

'You can hardly be expected to sit and watch your assistant eat. Mrs Dutton will have the meal ready for you both.'

Later that afternoon Leah was taking a break with her husband, sitting on kitchen chairs in a sunny patch of the yard when a woman and a man came strolling across the nearby moors on the hikers' path that took a roundabout way to Ellindale from Birch End. They were followed by a huge dog, but at a word from the woman, it stayed behind them.

'Lovely day, isn't it?' the woman called.

'Beautiful weather. I hope it's going to last.'

'Do you sell your drinks to passers-by?'

'I'm afraid not, but Mrs Buckley at the village shop sells refreshments, including our drinks.'

'We'll call in there on the way down the hill, then.'

'Have you come far?'

'No, not far, just up from Birch End, following the path across the lower end of the moors.' She looked at a fob watch pinned to her jacket. 'Better get going again.'

She nodded and set off.

'That woman has sadness deep in her eyes,' Jonah said. 'She's dressed like a woman of means, but money can't help you avoid some unhappiness in this life, can it?'

In the village, the two hikers stopped at Nancy's shop for refreshments and she sent Lily for a bowl of water for the dog.

'We passed the factory that makes fizzy drinks. Do you serve their drinks?'

'Oh, yes. They're very popular.'

'Two large ginger beers, then.'

'And would you like a scone or an iced bun with it? They're freshly baked.'

'Good idea. I've certainly worked up an appetite. We'll both have a scone.'

The man hardly said a word but the woman chatted happily to Nancy, asking about the village and the people who lived there.

'I feel as if I've seen her before,' Lily said after they left.

'She didn't look familiar to me. Perhaps she lives near your old home?'

'Ah. That could be it. But I still can't think of her name, Nancy. Well, I was away in service for years and then tied to the house with my mother.'

'Stop trying and her name will come to you.' She cleared the table and glanced happily at the cash drawer. She still had to live carefully but she was making a reasonable living these days, what with the new people up the hill, the hikers coming in for refreshments and the occasional folk from the youth hostel.

Lily was proving a big help, too, quick to pick up how to do things. She hadn't asked for a wage and Nancy couldn't afford to give her one yet, but the girl was earning her keep and was good company too.

Once the engineers had left, Finn smiled at his brand new telephone, which the man in charge had called a 'Number 232'. It was so different from a candlestick phone, and its handpiece sat across the top of a small stand that had a dial in the front part. A much neater apparatus and not as easy to knock over as the candlestick style. That was progress for you.

He decided to ring all his friends and let them know his new number.

Reggie, who'd been hovering nearby since the men left, watched carefully as Finn made the first call.

'Can I do the next one?'

'Yes, of course. We'll phone Leah and Jonah, shall we?'

So Reggie, beaming, placed the call and told Jonah about their brand-new telephone and its number.

When Jonah asked to speak to Finn, the lad stayed beside his guardian, easily able to overhear what was said. His smile vanished as he realised he'd been the reason for the attack on the delivery van.

When Finn put the phone down, Reggie said, 'I'd better not go up to Spring Cottage any more.'

'On the contrary. You'll go just the same, but someone will watch you going and coming back. Oh, and make sure you have something to defend yourself with even when you're out in our own garden, just in case they dare to come up here. I don't think they will, though. I doubt they'll do anything till after the hearing.'

'I can't bear it if the magistrate sends me back.'

'He won't. Stop worrying.'

'He's a friend of Mr Buddle so he might.'

'In that case, I'll spirit you away.'

But the boy's shoulders were drooping and fear was there in his face. Finn hated to see that.

'Let's go and see them hand out the milk for the first time, eh? The children will be home from school now.'

'All right.'

The old storeroom at the back of The Shepherd's Rest had been cleared out and a trestle table set up.

A milk churn stood next to it with its lid off and the ladle hanging over the edge by its curved tip. Beside it, one hand on the table which contained rows of glasses and the other on a jug of milk, Gillian stood ready to act, proud to be entrusted with this job.

She heard footsteps and a little boy peeped through the doorway. Another, smaller boy held on to his shirt, one thumb in his mouth. 'Would you like a drink of milk?' she asked.

Two heads nodded but the older boy held the other back. 'Mam says to make sure it's free, because she's no pennies left.'

'Absolutely free. Mr Carlisle is giving the milk to all the children. If you come every day at this time, I'll give you each a glass.'

Other children were hanging back, then suddenly a bigger girl pushed through to the front and dragged two smaller girls with her. She got as far as the table and looked at the churn, then at Gillian, not sure what to say or do next.

'Get a glass and I'll fill it.'

'My sisters are too little to hold a glass without spilling. Mam says I've to see they get theirs first.'

'Why don't they sit down over there against the wall and you can carry their glasses across to them?'

She nodded and took her sisters to sit down, then came back for the milk.

'How about I give you half a glass each for them, then it'll be easier to hold. You can come back when they've finished that and get the other half.'

The girl held her head on one side, considering this, then nodded. She couldn't have been more than six, Gillian reckoned, but already she had the weight of responsibility for the smaller ones on her shoulders, like so many children.

When all three were served, Gillian turned to the others, a trio of little boys.

Two bigger boys came running along the path and pushed to the front, shoving the smaller ones out of the way.

'No pushing to the front!' she ordered. 'Go and join the end of the queue.'

One of them licked his lips. 'What if the milk runs out?'

'It won't.'

'Promise you'll save some for us?' his companion begged. 'You won't give it all away?'

'I told you, there's plenty.'

One by one the children drank the milk and left, some with a milky moustache to bear witness to their treat, all of them beaming. The first girl helped her little sisters to stand up, now they'd had all their milk, and said a polite thank you.

Finn went inside as Gillian was taking the last empty glass back. 'Everything go all right?'

'Yes, sir. What do I do with the milk that's left?'

'I'll drink it for you,' a bigger boy standing near the door volunteered.

'You only get one glass a day. But you'll get another tomorrow. Go on, now. Home with you!' She turned to wait for Finn's instructions.

'Give anything left to Izzy. She'll know which families to pass it on to.'

'They'll be that grateful, sir.'

He and Reggie turned to leave and saw Izzy watching them with a smile.

'I kept my eye on things,' she said cheerfully. 'Gillian made sure the kids behaved themselves. She's good with kids. Wanted to be a teacher but there was no chance of that because they couldn't afford the training.'

He filed the information away in case he could help the girl achieve her ambition. 'Can you share out any milk that's left every day, Izzy? I buy it by the churn so the quantity isn't exact.'

'Of course I can. Eh, Mr Carlisle, you're a kind man to do this. It'll make a big difference to some of those little 'uns, stop them getting rickets, I shouldn't wonder.'

He shrugged, always uncomfortable with compliments. 'I like to help people. But they need to play out in the sun as well to stop rickets.'

'They'll have more energy to do that now. We're all grateful to you. People love their kids.'

He tipped his cap to her and left. When folk gave him compliments like that, he never knew what to reply. Anyway, those who had a bit to spare should help their neighbours. Jonah and Leah did as well.

It was good that today had gone well and the system for

giving out the milk had worked. The doctor had told him it would make a big difference to the children's health and it'd help the farmer too. One churn a day didn't cost very much, not compared to children's health.

He hoped Uncle Oscar would have been pleased with how he was using the money, but doubted it. What little he'd heard about the old man had suggested he was a selfish recluse.

Finn's cousin probably wouldn't have spent the money on helping people, either. His father had refused to discuss why they didn't get on, just said that some selfish sods were not worth knowing.

17

Adam Harris watched the last of his employees walk quickly down the street and carefully locked up the laundry before strolling home. It had been a busy day but things had gone smoothly. They mostly did now that his ex-wife wasn't here to interfere.

He was looking forward to visiting Nancy Buckley after tea, ostensibly to buy some more bottles of ginger beer from her shop, but in reality to spend time with her.

There were two letters waiting for him on the hall table, one a bill he'd expected and the other . . . 'Oh, no!' The mere sight of the handwriting wiped away his happy smile before he'd even read the words inside.

'Is something wrong, sir?' his senior maid asked.

'What? I was just, um, surprised by this letter, Minnie. I'd better go and change my clothes.'

He made a habit of changing out of his suit as soon as he got home. This action normally marked the transition from work to leisure, and it made him feel pleasantly relaxed to don a pair of casual slacks and a soft-collared shirt that didn't need a damned tie. Now, changing would give him an excuse to read the letter in private.

As he walked away he saw Minnie's worried expression reflected in the hall mirror and he knew she'd have recognised her former mistress's handwriting on the envelope. But she was tactful enough not to comment.

In his bedroom he briefly considered burning the letter

unread in the fireplace, but abandoned that idea with a sigh. Better to know what his ex-wife wanted than to lie awake worrying in case Ethel was up to more of her nasty tricks.

The letter contained an abject apology, not specifying what for, and a plea to be given a second chance in their marriage. He closed his eyes but the message seemed imprinted on his mind.

Why was Ethel doing this? He loathed the mere sight of her now and she definitely didn't want to return to him. It had only taken a few months of marriage for her to tell him he was a bore, but he'd been so naive it had taken him much longer to realise that she was seeking the thrills she craved with other men.

What did she want now? Whatever it was, he was giving her nothing. He didn't feel he owed her a penny because she had plenty of money of her own. She still owned various terraced houses, which she rented out through a different but just as nasty rent collector as the one who'd been killed.

She hadn't married Adam for his money, but for his position in Rivenshaw as a member of a family accepted by other more affluent citizens. Only they'd never really accepted her. They'd seen her for what she was, a whore at heart!

She'd fled from Rivenshaw on the day her lover had started his violent rampage. The police had found that she'd taken a train to Manchester, but no one knew where she had gone after that. As she couldn't be proved to have committed any crime beyond that of being a terrible landlord and the mistress of a man willing to commit murder, they didn't bother to look for her. She wasn't important enough to waste time and money on.

He wondered yet again what she was doing, where she'd gone. Her lawyer must know of course. He was a youngish fellow more interested in money than justice. Adam hoped she was living at the other end of the country and would stay there for good. He'd hate her to return to Rivenshaw.

He studied the letter again. What possible reason could she have for coming back to him? Why would she even pretend to want it? He wasn't even going to reply.

He changed his clothes and when he felt calmer, went down to ask Minnie to send her sister out for their tea, a simple meal of fish and chips from the local shop. He ate his in the dining room and the two maids ate theirs in the kitchen. He could hear them laughing and chattering and often wished he had someone to share his meal with. His life now might be peaceful but it was lonely too.

They all dined on fish and chips twice a week because he loved it and anyway, he felt the maids didn't have the time to do much cooking on top of everything else they did for him. He didn't want to employ more staff and had no desire to lead an active social life, so it suited him just fine to live simply.

His main sadness was not the breakdown of his marriage, but the fact that he had no children. But there you were. In this life you were never guaranteed that all your dreams would come true.

Thank goodness for friends. He still had a few he'd kept in touch with in spite of Ethel. But Nancy . . . Ah, she was special. Once he got his decree nisi and his divorce was final, he intended to ask her to marry him and he felt sure she'd say yes.

He prayed it wouldn't be too late for them to have children and he was finding the waiting frustrating because he had a man's normal needs. Not a need for immoral women like his ex-wife, however glamorous, but for wholesome women like Nancy, with their clean, shining faces, tidy hair and warm smiles.

After his meal he drove up the hill to Ellindale and went to visit Nancy. There was usually someone within earshot when he went there, to act as a sort of chaperone: her niece Lily or her next-door neighbour. But that meant he and Nancy could never do more than exchange a chaste kiss in farewell.

This time, however, there was no sign of anyone else in the house.

He was so surprised, he asked, 'Are you all alone tonight?'

'Yes.' But she was studying him with eyes narrowed in that way she had, seeming to sense that something had unsettled him. 'What's wrong, Adam? Tell me.'

'I heard from Ethel today. A letter.'

'Ah. What does she want this time?'

'For me to take her back.'

Nancy stiffened, but didn't ask the obvious question.

'I would never do that. Never. You know that I—' He broke off and looked round. 'Where's Lily? Is she sitting in the shop?'

'No. I sent her out for a stroll with a friend of her own age. She won't be back for a while. And I didn't ask Mrs Cording next door to come in, either, because I'm tired of not daring to show our feelings and . . . and needs.' She broke off for a moment, then took a deep breath and added, 'It's more than time we did grow closer, don't you think, Adam love?'

'You must know that I want to marry you.'

'Of course I do. But we're neither of us getting any younger and I'm so tired of waiting. I want to have children if . . . while I can, and I think you want them too.'

'Yes. Very much indeed.'

'I went to speak to the doctor's wife about it and she said once a woman is in her mid-thirties it gets harder each year to conceive a child. And I just turned thirty-seven! I'm in my *late* thirties now, Adam. Mrs Mitchell's a nurse. She knows things like that.'

'The years pass so quickly. I'm feeling the same about my

age.' He put one arm round her shoulders, leaned his head against hers and quoted one of his favourite poets, '"At my back I always hear Time's winged chariot hurrying near".'

'Exactly. And I've been hearing it for a while now. Talking to Mrs Mitchell made me think good and hard about what I want most in life. I want you and I want children.'

She flushed, hesitated, then said, 'I used to enjoy being married, Adam love. I'm not an inexperienced girl. Me and my Stanley were happy that way . . . in bed.'

He was just about to respond when she said it for him. 'We should do something about it or we may lose our chance of children.'

'Do you mean what I think?'

'Yes. Oh, Adam love, I'm that desperate to have a child! Every time I see a new mother pushing a pram, I could weep for the pain of never having had a baby of my own to cuddle. So many young men were killed during the war that there are a lot of women of my age who'll never know that joy. But I have you, so I made up my mind to talk to you about it and to *do* something before it's too late.'

He stared at her in shock. 'I can't ask that of you, Nancy love. If anything goes wrong, prevents my divorce being finalised, and you're expecting a child, people will shun you.'

'I don't care, not if I can have *your* child. And I don't think people would shun me. Not the people round here in Ellindale, anyway.'

For a few breaths, he didn't dare move, then he gave in to temptation and cradled her head gently in his hands, kissing each soft cheek tenderly. She had been brave enough to broach this subject, far braver than him. His voice came out husky. 'Are you sure, my darling girl?'

'Very sure, Adam.'

'I want you too; have done for a long time. And I too long for children.' He took her in his arms then and kissed her with all the love a heart could hold. And this embrace was so different from the scrambling, mindless activity he'd indulged in with his ex-wife, he could have wept for the slow, tender beauty of it.

When they drew apart, she raised his hand to her lips. Then, with a brilliant smile, she led the way upstairs.

Lily and her friend Hope came back from their stroll and stayed in the square chatting. They sat on the stone bench near the horse trough, a favourite place for younger folk to gather, enjoying the last of the evening sunlight.

Ben came out of The Shepherd's Rest and Hope waved to him.

'Do you know him?' Lily whispered.

'He came a few times to repair and finish off our wall and chatted to my mother and me. He's a nice young man, but I'm walking out already with my Dennis, as you know. Besides,' she nudged Lily, 'it's you Ben's looking at, not me.'

He strolled across and stopped in front of them. 'Good evening, Hope, Lily. Mind if I join you for a few minutes? It's such a lovely evening, too nice to go indoors yet.'

The young women moved up along the stone bench to make room for him.

'Been drinking, have you?' Hope asked.

'Just a pint of beer. There's a lot of dust when you're working with stone, and your throat gets dry. I only ever have one pint, though, even after a hot day. I'm not a boozer and I've no money to waste on drinking with a business to set up.'

'Dad says you're good at working with stone and will do well,' Hope told him.

'Thank you.'

Silence fell and Lily couldn't think what to say.

'Did I interrupt something? Would you two lasses rather be private?'

Hope laughed. 'Dear me, no. We've been talking about the free milk. Everyone's so pleased the children are to get a glass every day. It's bound to do them good. Isn't Mr Carlisle kind to pay for it? My aunt's got two little 'uns and they go for their milk every afternoon now.'

'It's a grand thing for him to do. I hate to see children going hungry. I've had experience of clemming myself when my master died and his son threw me out. It was Mr and Mrs Willcox who helped me and first gave me work in Ellindale.'

'Do you like living here?' Lily managed.

'Very much. Nice people.'

'I've not been here long, either, but I feel the same,' Lily said. 'People have been so kind to me. I—'

They all stopped talking to stare at two men who were walking through the village. They had packs on their back, as most hikers did, only they didn't look like hikers. Their boots were wrong and they didn't have the thick socks to cushion their feet when walking. They didn't even look very clean. For some reason hikers usually looked healthy and clean.

'Stay with us till they've passed, Ben,' Lily whispered. 'I don't like the way they're staring.'

'I don't like the looks of them, either.' Hope edged closer to her friend.

The men made a comment about pretty, curvy lasses, which had both young women flushing and Ben stiffening in shock at such open rudeness.

When the strangers had continued up the hill, he stood up. 'If you'll be all right now, I'll follow those two back to Spring Cottage, in case there's trouble. They're not hikers, so why are they here?'

The others watched him go then Hope said abruptly, 'We'll be better off at home with those two men on the loose. See you tomorrow, Lily love.' She didn't wait for agreement but ran off along the narrow lane that led diagonally up the hillside to her family's home.

Since she too felt uneasy about the strangers, Lily hurried round to the back door of the shop. She was surprised to see Mr Harris's car still there. He'd stayed longer than usual tonight.

Inside the house there was no sign of Nancy or her visitor. That was even stranger. She heard something from upstairs and it sounded like – it *was* a bed creaking. When she worked as a maid, the master's bed would creak like that sometimes and one of the older maids had explained why.

She smiled. About time too. Any fool could have seen how fond Nancy and Mr Harris were of one another. They deserved some happiness.

She went to sit in the little refreshment room that opened off the side of the shop. Getting out her library book, she sat near the narrow window to read it, but spent more time daydreaming than following the story. She did hope she'd meet a young man she could love one day.

There were a lot of couples who were going through long courtships because they couldn't afford to marry. Still, at least they had hope for the future.

An image of Ben Lonsdale came into her mind. He was nice. But he couldn't afford to marry at this stage in his life, either.

When Ben got to the gate of Spring Cottage, he saw Leah standing at the door facing the two men. Her arms were folded and she looked angry. He stopped, listening, not wanting to interrupt unless he was needed.

'I'm afraid we're closed for the night.'

'We don't need anything but a bed, missus. You can't be full at this time of year.'

'We're closed. You'll have to find somewhere else.' She tried to shut the door, but one man put a hand on it and held it open.

'We've the money to pay for a night's rest. You've no right to refuse us lodgings.'

Her voice was as quiet as ever. 'I have every right. How many times do I have to tell you that the hostel is closed. And it's a youth hostel, not for men of your age. What's more I wouldn't take in anyone who shouted at me like you're doing. You'll have to find somewhere else to stay. Now, please take your hand off the door.'

The man shoved the door back suddenly and it flew open, banging against the wall. Taken by surprise, Leah stumbled backwards.

Ben moved forward, trying to keep his voice mild. 'We're still doing renovations. I was working on the old barn all day and I've not cleaned it up yet.'

'We don't mind a bit of dust,' the less talkative one said.

Jonah appeared behind Leah, moving forward to stand between the men and his wife. 'I'm sorry but you'll have to go elsewhere.'

They stared from him to Ben and all hung in the balance.

Leah moved quickly across to the fireplace, picked up her poker and rattled it against the stand. Then she moved back to stand beside Jonah, staring out at the strangers and holding the poker ready to defend herself with.

'Ah, the place has probably got fleas,' one said loudly. Turning, they walked slowly out of the yard, pausing at the gate to scowl back at the three people in the doorway, then walked off down the hill.

'Should I have given them a bed for the night, do you think?' Leah asked Ben in a low voice. 'Only I didn't like the look of them.'

'No. Definitely not. I didn't take to them either. And with

the threats you've had lately, you can't be too careful. I'm going to follow them and watch what they do.'

'I'll keep the poker handy.'

He grinned. 'Did you see the surprise on their faces when you brandished it? You looked furious. I'd not like to face you if you got that angry at me.'

She looked down at the poker. 'Would you really say I *brandished* it?'

'Definitely. You're a quiet sort of person till your temper's roused, then watch out.' Jonah put an arm round her.

Filled with admiration for her courage, Ben moved across the yard and stood pressed against the gatepost in a patch of shadow. He saw the men slow down at the entrance to Heythorpe House, looking up and down the road. But they didn't see him.

One of them slipped inside the entrance, taking advantage of some bushes and Ben stiffened. Were they going to try to break into the big house? Was that why they'd asked for a bed at the hostel, so that they could keep watch on it and sneak out once everyone was asleep?

He ran back to Spring Cottage, explaining quickly what was going on. He asked Jonah to phone Finn and let him know he had an intruder, then he went back to keep watch on the man standing waiting on the dirt road near the entrance.

People lived quietly out at Ellindale, but anyone hoping for an easy conquest would find the locals hard to best because they always stuck together, well, most of them did. There were one or two who didn't fit in.

He'd spread the word about these two strangers and he was sure people would keep an eye out for trouble at Heythorpe House.

Who the hell were these men? Had they been sent by Buddle to try to frighten off those associated with Reggie?

That didn't make sense either. Why would Buddle go to such lengths about one boy? Orphanages were usually glad to find homes for their inmates.

There must be some other reason for this incursion. But what?

Finn put down the phone and switched on the new electric lights he'd just had fitted to the outside of the house. Some might have considered that an extravagance, but there were no street lights this far out of town, no neighbours within shouting distance even, and as a former policeman he always had an eye to security. It was well known that thieves were more likely to avoid well-lit areas.

He opened an upstairs window quietly and set Beth to watch out in case anyone came round the back. Next he went into a front bedroom and did the same, standing back out of sight but able to see the front of the house clearly. Then he waited.

His patience was rewarded when he saw a man stand at the top of the path that led down to the house, hesitate and stare at the outside lights. He nodded in satisfaction as the intruder moved back into the shadows and made no attempt to walk down the slope.

Though it was darker up on the road, Finn thought he saw the outline of a second man up there.

He stayed where he was for about ten minutes but nothing else happened. He thought he saw the bushes move a couple of times but couldn't be sure.

Just as he was about to turn away, he saw another figure approaching the house. This person was making no attempt to hide and Finn wasn't surprised when the man came straight into the lighted area.

It was Ben. He ran down to open the front door.

'They've gone off towards Ellindale, Finn. I watched them

go through the village, then I came back to make sure you were all right.'

'Yes. They didn't even try to get into the house, so I think the outside lights deterred them. I wonder who they were and what they were looking for.'

'They were two so-called hikers who turned up late asking for a bed. Leah didn't like the look of them so refused them. They were starting to get rather nasty about it when I turned up.'

'Someone is keeping an eye on things around here, sending men to stir things up and make us feel uneasy. It's most likely to be Buddle, I suppose, though there is . . .' His voice trailed away and he didn't finish his sentence.

'Is there someone else with a grudge against you? If so, you should tell folk who to watch out for.'

'I'm not sure. Probably just imagining things.'

'And?'

'There's a second cousin, the only other relative I know about. Digby didn't inherit this house and might be unhappy about that. My side of the family has never got on with his, so I've only met him a couple of times. Even when we were kids, I didn't take to him. But I can't believe he'd try to kill me for the inheritance.'

After a pause, he added, 'He wouldn't get it, though. I've made a will leaving everything to Reggie for the time being, and Jonah's agreed to act as his guardian if anything should happen to me.'

'You're looking on the dark side.'

'I'm just taking precautions. People can die young . . . like my wife did.'

'Ah. Yes. I'm sorry about that. But I'll bear in mind that your cousin might be a possibility.'

'I don't see why. Apart from anything else, his side of the family have plenty of money, unlike mine.'

After a pause, he added, 'No, it can't be Digby. We haven't seen one another for years. I don't even know where he lives these days.'

'But if he expected to inherit, he'll know where you live now.'

Finn sighed. That had occurred to him too. He shook his head. No, he was looking for trouble where there was none. It must be Buddle.

Well, whatever the court said, no one was going to lock Reggie away. That lad had had a bad time of it and would always bear the marks of Buddle's cruelty on his back.

'Well, thank you for your help, Ben. I think we can probably both go to bed now.'

'I'd feel happier about leaving you here if you had a big dog to give you warning.'

'Perhaps I should look for one. We'll see.' He waved to Ben and closed the window, but stood watching as the younger man walked up to the road and turned left towards Spring Cottage.

Then he went to tell Beth she could go back to bed now and he did the same.

But he slept lightly and woke several times during the night, thinking he'd heard something.

This was all getting ridiculous, he decided in the morning, like one of those foolish gothic tales. All they needed now was a castle and a few ghosts floating around terrifying people!

18

The hearing was to be held at eleven o'clock in the morning in Wemsworth. 'It's a good thing we have a car,' Finn said to Reggie. 'It's not a very convenient time to be travelling cross-country beyond Rivenshaw. You'd better go to bed early and get a good night's sleep. Oh, and wash your hair while you're having your bath. We want you looking your best tomorrow.'

'I don't think I'll be able to sleep, Uncle Finn.'

'Well, do your best, lad. And trust me, I won't let them take you away.'

Reggie stared down at his feet. 'How can you stop them if that's what the judge says?'

'It's not a judge; it's a magistrate. And you know Mr Lloyd is coming with us. He's a well-respected lawyer and it'll be he who stops anyone taking you away from me. He'll know the best legal way to do it.'

'There was a lawyer on Mr Buddle's side last time. What if his lawyer is cleverer than Mr Lloyd?'

'They won't be able to ignore the fact that you have a good home now. I'll repeat it as many times as necessary. I promise I won't let them take you away from me.'

Reggie suddenly flung himself at Finn, giving him a big hug, then clattered off up the stairs.

Finn turned to see Beth watching them. She gave him a little nod, as if approving of his promise to his ward.

'Everything all right?' he asked.

'Me and the others are a bit on edge about poor Reggie. He has no faith in the courts and neither do I. It's rich people who do well in them, not poorer folk. It's a good thing Reggie's got you on his side.'

'I'm not rich!'

She smiled tolerantly. 'You always say that but you're what I'd call rich. I can't imagine how it would feel to have as much money as you do. Eh, imagine not worrying about putting a meal on the table or being able to buy new shoes when yours wear out.'

She indicated her feet, clad in the neat shoes Vi had provided. 'These are the best shoes I've ever had and I'm more grateful for my clothes and everything than you'll ever understand.'

'It was my pleasure. After all, you're walking around in them to serve me all day, every day.'

'Well, all I can say is: to be able to help people, the way you do, must be lovely!'

'It does feel good to help others, I will admit. Sergeant Deemer helped me a lot and gave me a shining example of how to treat others.'

'He's a good man. And so are you.'

She vanished into the kitchen area and Finn was sorry to see her go. He always enjoyed talking to her. She had such a sensible view of the world. She had lost that gaunt, haggard look now and he was surprised at how pretty she was.

Since he didn't feel like sitting on his own, he wandered out into the garden. Twilight had softened everything, casting faint shadows across the paths and the roof of his car, not the black shadows of daytime, but softer grey ones.

He strolled up to his car. He'd checked the tyres and filled it up with petrol this afternoon, so it was all ready to go. He hadn't told Beth but he was wondering whether to sleep in or near it because it had occurred to him that those two men might have been reconnoitring in order to come back later and damage the car.

Daniel came strolling up the slope to join him. 'I think I'd better keep watch over your car tonight, sir. We don't want anyone sabotaging it.'

'Actually, I was just wondering about sleeping in it, for the same reason.'

'You need your sleep. You'll want to have all your wits about you at the hearing. Let me do it.'

'Well, that's very kind of you. Be sure to keep a big stick handy. Just in case. And yell if you need help. I'm a light sleeper.'

'I will, sir.'

But when Finn looked out of his bedroom window an hour later, he saw three other men standing talking to Daniel near the car, men from the village. He went to find out what was going on.

They fell silent and turned to watch him approach.

'Is something wrong?'

One of them nudged Daniel.

'Two strangers have been seen talking to Barry Judson, sir. We thought we ought to make sure there were enough people here to protect your property.'

'Then you must let me pay you for your trouble,' Finn said at once. He knew these men were all out of work and would have spent the day tramping up and down the valley looking for work or any odd job. And on Wednesday they had to queue up and sign on for the dole – a waste of shoe leather, because everyone knew there were few jobs to be found. He felt touched that they were intending to give up their night's sleep for him.

'No need for any payment this time, sir. You're buying milk for our kids. We can do this for you in return.'

What could he say but, 'Thank you. Much appreciated.'

'You get a good night's sleep, Mr Carlisle, and look after that nice lad tomorrow.'

'I will sleep well now you're here.'

He felt a lump in his throat as he walked back to the front door.

Beth was waiting for him in the hall. 'Is there trouble?'

'No.' He explained.

'Well, we can all sleep soundly now.'

For a moment their eyes met, then she whirled round and just about fled up the stairs.

He followed more slowly, sure he'd not sleep, but to his amazement, he did. In fact he was sleeping better these days than he had for a long time.

Leah woke up early. She was alone in the bed but she could hear someone moving about in the kitchen. She went down to find Jonah preparing breakfast and Rosa sitting at the table, fully dressed.

She was surprised to see her sister. 'It's the school holidays. What are you doing up so early, Rosa?'

'I want to come to the hearing with you and Jonah. I've never seen a court in action and I think it'd be interesting.'

'I'm not even sure *I* should go,' Leah said. 'They won't bother to ask a woman about anything when there are men to question.'

'We'll all go,' Jonah said. 'Finn and Reggie will feel better for having some support. I've already arranged with Ben to keep an eye on things here and others will be watching Finn's house.'

'I'd better go and put something smart on, then.'

'Sunday best,' Rosa agreed, indicating her own clothes. 'And Finn phoned to say they're setting off a bit earlier than planned.'

When they drove down the lane they could see Finn's car standing waiting, looking well polished. Two men were nearby, cradling mugs of tea in their hands.

Jonah stopped and got out of the car to chat to them. 'Any trouble?'

'Suspicious persons were seen in the vicinity,' one said, managing a fair imitation of Sergeant Deemer.

Everyone grinned.

'They were chased away, but unfortunately, Clumpy Joe here tripped and got in our way, so we didn't manage to catch any of them.'

'I allus were clumsy,' Joe agreed.

'They were prowling round your place too, Mr Willcox, but Ben had sorted out someone to keep an eye on your car with him.'

'Had he now? He didn't mention intruders. I must thank him. Who was helping him?'

They shrugged. 'Someone who owed you a favour. Ah, here they come. Look nicely turned out, don't they?'

They turned to watch Finn and Reggie come up from the house to join them, also dressed in their Sunday best, which for Reggie meant a whole new set of clothes.

Finn was looking angry. 'They were trying to play another dirty trick on us. But they haven't succeeded. It's good to have friends.' He pulled out his pocket watch. 'I'll tell you about it later. We have to get going.'

He had already received a report on the night's doings from Daniel, so called out to his guards, 'Thank you. I'm grateful for your help.'

Reggie didn't speak. Finn cast him a quick glance. The poor lad was looking pale and hadn't eaten much breakfast.

'Let's get going, then.'

The car started first time, which seemed like an omen and they were soon on the road, followed by Jonah's car.

Margot Terryng got up early, as usual, though she sometimes wondered why she bothered. There would be no one with her at the breakfast table whatever time she rose.

She had half a mind to go to the hearing today. No, why bother? She liked to keep an eye on what her poorer neighbours were up to, but Councillor Withnall often upset her when he took over as a magistrate, because he was so brutal in the penalties he imposed on the lower classes, whom he seemed to loathe.

It was strange, though, that she hadn't been asked to preside over this case, because she was the local magistrate here in Netherholme. What's more the authorities usually preferred her to deal with any cases involving children and she was senior to Withnall by several years. He'd slid into the magistracy at the end of the war, when they were short of men. He'd not have got a place on the bench otherwise.

She strolled out to the stables with her cup of tea and leaned against the wall, sipping it and enjoying the early morning sunlight on her face.

Her chauffeur cum general helper came out of his room over the stables that were now half garage, whistling softly. He stopped when he saw her. 'Ah. You're up early, my lady. Is it still all right if I take the car this morning? Only I have to go to the hearing to act as clerk because Mrs Unsworth is ill and though they tried to get Michael Dean, he's away from home visiting his mother.'

'Strange to have them all away at once.'

'Yes. Councillor Withnall was apparently very annoyed when the regional clerk told him he'd have to use my services.'

She wasn't surprised. Withnall didn't like having anything to do with her or people she knew.

'Anyway, I'll need to get off earlier than usual as I'll be the only one there to prepare the room. They sent word last night that they're starting the hearing at nine o'clock.'

'Oh? That was late notice. Is there some reason for the sudden change? They normally start at eleven o'clock.'

He shrugged. 'Only Councillor Withnall can tell you that. He's the one who set the time. I'd have thought they'd have started it later, actually, with folk having to come all the way from Ellindale.'

The uneasy feeling that had been floating in and out of her mind suddenly became stronger. Something was definitely going on. 'I think I'll come with you and attend the hearing as a spectator, Falding. I like to keep an eye on what's happening to the children in this district. And besides, what you've told me about the arrangements is not making sense. I'll go and get ready straight away.'

She didn't move straight away, though, but said, 'Could you phone Mr Carlisle at Heythorpe House to check that he's heard about the earlier start? The operator will know his number.'

'Yes, of course. You'll have to wait around for me to clear up after the hearing, I'm afraid, my lady.'

'Doesn't matter. I'll take a book to read.'

When she got back, he was looking angry.

'No one had told them about the earlier start, my lady. But now they know, they'll still be able to make it. It's a good job you thought to warn them.'

'Isn't it?'

There was no one in the parish hall where the local hearings were always held and there was more than half an hour to go before they started, so Margot found herself a quiet, sheltered corner in the nearby churchyard, got out her book and left Falding to set things up.

She heard other cars pull up but didn't go back to the hall till nearer the time. To her surprise she found a group of people arguing with a burly man standing in front of the door. She recognised him: Hubert Trumpson. She'd sentenced him to six months in jail a year or two ago for assault. He was noted for violence and had been warned about it several times. He was a strange choice to have working for the magistrate's court.

'You have no right to keep us out!' an older man said.

'Magistrate's orders. Only those involved in the hearing to come in.'

'But I'm Mr Finn's lawyer. I'm definitely involved in the hearing.'

She recognised him, though he didn't usually deal with cases in this district, but kept to Rivenshaw. What was he called? Yes, Lloyd. That was it. He had a good reputation, if she remembered correctly.

'I'm not taking Reggie in without a lawyer to represent us,' a tall man said.

'You have no choice about it, sir. It's a court order and the boy will be held in contempt of court if he doesn't attend.'

This was not according to any rules Margot had read about hearings dealing with minors. She was about to intervene when she caught sight of the lad who must be at the centre of this case. Her breath caught in her throat and for a moment the world spun round her.

It was him! It had to be, the resemblance was so strong.

Finn couldn't believe it when everyone was told to stay outside the court except for himself and Reggie. Not even his lawyer was to be allowed inside. And if he hadn't phoned Mr Lloyd, his lawyer wouldn't even be here.

Something was very wrong indeed and the magistrate himself must be involved in it for them to do this. Was this Withnall manipulating the hearing to help Buddle? Were the two of them in cahoots? Surely they couldn't get away with it?

Well, Finn wasn't moving away from his lawyer and the other witnesses, not if he had to return home with the boy who was trembling visibly next to him. 'Chin up, Reggie,' he whispered. 'I'll keep my word.'

'This is totally against procedure,' Mr Lloyd insisted yet again. 'Stand aside, fellow. You must have misunderstood your orders.'

The man's politeness slipped visibly. 'I haven't misunderstood anything. I was told what to do by the magistrate himself.'

'Well, I'd like to hear it from him as well.'

'He's busy. I've been told to keep order out here until it's time to start. Then we'll lock the doors.'

Jonah moved to stand beside Finn and say in a low voice, 'Don't go inside without support. They can do and say anything if you have no witnesses to the hearing.'

'Exactly what I was thinking.'

The man at the door was about to speak again when they all heard a woman's voice, one with a commanding, upper-class accent.

Margot pushed forward, saying it again, even more loudly, 'Let me through at once. I'm one of the local magistrates.'

Those waiting to go in moved aside, staring at her curiously. The man guarding the door was looking aghast.

'Move out of my way, Trumpson.'

'Your ladyship, I've been told not to let anyone in. There's an important case to be heard.'

'Why is it being heard *in camera*?'

He stared at her, brow wrinkled, obviously not understanding the Latin phrase.

She said it again in plain English. 'Why is it being held in secret?'

'They're, um, protecting a child.'

'Oh? And how are they doing that?'

'The lad gets violent. He plays up even more when he has an audience.'

Finn had his arm firmly round Reggie's shoulders. 'This boy is in no way violent. It's a pack of lies. And we don't usually do secret trials in England.'

She turned to study the boy again, as if she hadn't already memorised his features. He was well turned out and looked afraid, not belligerent.

'We definitely don't do secret trials, Mr . . . ?'

'Carlisle. I'm acting as Reggie's guardian unofficially till the courts make it legal.'

'I'm Margot Terryng.' She turned back to the man on guard. 'Let me in at once, Trumpson. And let these other people in too. They have every right to attend this hearing. There is no such thing as an *in camera* hearing until the magistrate has given a very strong reason and posted public notices to that effect.'

He was sweating now, looking more and more uncomfortable, but angry with it. He always seemed to be angry about something. He pointed to a small piece of paper tacked to one side of the door. 'There's the notice.'

She moved closer to read it. Long words that no one but a lawyer would understand and no reason given for the unusual procedures. She turned to the people involved. 'Have you been notified previously of this, Mr Carlisle?'

It was the lawyer who answered. 'No, your ladyship. Neither myself nor my client has been notified or I'd have protested officially. Nor were we notified officially of that earlier start.'

She turned back to Trumpson. 'Move out of the way. I need to come in and sort this out.'

'I'm sorry, my lady. I'll go and ask Councillor Withnall if I can let *you* in, but my orders are that no one but the lad and the fellow who calls himself his guardian are to be there for the hearing.'

As he opened the door, she saw her chauffeur at the far side of the room at the clerk's table and called out, 'Falding! Come and let me in!'

Trumpson hastily barred her way and pulled the door till it was almost shut. As he did so she heard the sound of a scuffle inside. She started to push it open, her eyes daring Trumpson to try to stop her physically, but someone slammed it shut from the inside.

She heard a loud voice yell even through the closed door, 'Touch me and you'll be under arrest for assault.' She recognised that foghorn voice. Buddle, from the orphanage. He had no power to arrest anyone. Was he yelling at her chauffeur?

Furious herself now, Margot turned and saw a few of her tenants standing gaping at a distance as well as the group near her. 'Will one of you fetch the constable, please? As quickly as possible. Tell him the law is being broken and I'm being threatened.'

'I'll go, your ladyship.' A young man ran off down the street towards the policeman's house.

She moved forward again, wondering if Trumpson would dare to lay hands on her. His hand half came up to push her back then fell again.

'You'd better not touch me or I'll have you arrested for assault,' she said firmly.

As she touched the door handle, however, he said, 'No!' and pushed her hand away. 'You'd better not try to interfere, your ladyship. Mr Buddle won't let no one defy him, 'specially not one of them orphans. That lad is in serious trouble an' you'll only make it worse.'

'Mr Buddle is about to learn that he does not have the power to administer or change the law, whatever the pretext. Move away!'

'I daren't let you in.' Trumpson shoved her away hard enough to hurt her shoulder.

'Ow! That's definitely assault.' And it was also the final straw. She had no intention of firing it but she pulled out

the small revolver she'd kept in her handbag ever since some
poachers had threatened her and said conversationally, 'Get
out of my way. You can tell them I pulled a gun on you and
I'll tell them why. I know who they'll believe.'

He lost all attempt at being conciliatory and raised one
fist. 'Following orders isn't assault. You wouldn't dare. You
can just stay back, ladyship or not. You're just doing this to
get me in trouble again.'

Suppressed violence was quivering in every line of his
body. She'd seen men get to this state in wartime and a few
times in court. Knowing Trumpson, she was beginning to
worry about the safety of the people around her.

He caught her by surprise with another shove that sent
her stumbling backwards away from the door and kept his
great meaty fist raised as if ready to punch her.

Someone muttered behind her and she ordered, 'Stay back.'
Aiming the gun at him, she said slowly and clearly, 'If you
lay hands on me again, I'll use this. I care very much about
upholding the law and I won't let a thug like you help pervert
the course of justice and attack innocent people. You've been
warned before and it'll be a longer stint in prison if you
assault me or anyone else.'

Trumpson shook his head, like a dog coming out of the
water. 'Damned well get back, then, woman! It's the magistrate's orders.' Grinning, he pulled his right fist back, slowly,
seeming to enjoy the prospect of punching her.

She'd seen men in that state of mindless violence before
and knew they could not be reasoned with. As his fist began
to move towards her, she shot him in the upper left arm.

But she'd left it too late to stop him assaulting her. His
fist hit her on the chin and she went flying sideways at the
same time as Trumpson roared in agony and staggered back
under the impact of the bullet.

Someone prevented her from falling and supported her as

she tried to keep her balance. The blow had knocked her dizzy for a moment or two so she could only cling to the person till her head started to clear.

As the doorkeeper seemed to move beyond words to physical violence, Finn shoved Reggie into Jonah's care and stepped forward, calling, 'Stop this at once.'

But he was too late and so wild did the man look that he wasn't surprised when the lady fired at him as he attacked her.

Unfortunately Trumpson's fist connected with her face before Finn could intervene, but he was in time to catch her and prevent her from falling, while people from the crowd ran to stand between them and the man.

Finn called out, 'Don't let him move away! I'm a former policeman and I'm taking charge here. Someone pick that gun up and give it to Mr Lloyd.'

As the woman stirred against him, he looked down and asked, 'Are you all right?'

'Yes. I didn't think I'd have to fire, not until I thought he was about to kill me.'

'I think he must have run mad. I need to stop him.' He raised his voice, 'Can someone help her ladyship? She's hurt.'

Mrs Willcox came forward and he turned to the man leaning against the wall, but Trumpson put up a bloodstained hand in a gesture of surrender and then clapped it against the wound, which was bleeding copiously. He leaned back for a moment then slid down the wall suddenly into a sitting position, as if the strength had left his legs.

'Thanks,' Finn said to the two young men standing there. 'Don't let him get up.'

'We won't, sir!'

They looked as if they were enjoying the excitement. Well, he wasn't. Not at all. Someone else was going to get hurt at this rate. Where the hell was the local police constable?

19

Margot saw the door to the hall open a crack and someone peep through it. 'I need to get inside.' She started moving forward, feeling rather wobbly, and found a woman by her side.

'Can I steady you, my lady?'

She'd last seen this woman on the edge of the moors. 'Thank you, Mrs Willcox. I am still a bit dizzy.'

'You're welcome. I don't like the look of what's happening here.'

They reached the door and Margot said, 'Will you help me push the door open?'

'Of course.'

They got the door open a little but whoever was behind it managed to shut it again.

She glanced quickly sideways at Trumpson but he was making no attempt to get up from the floor. She must have wounded him more deeply than she'd intended; she'd only meant to wing him. Well, it jolly well served him right!

Mr Carlisle had come to join her. He gestured to the door and mimed shoving it.

'Shall I help you get in?'

'Yes, please. And quickly.'

They all three flung themselves at the door and this time it flew open, sending the man on the other side staggering backwards.

She banged her arm on the doorframe but got through into the hall at last. Her companions stayed close to her.

The man who'd been trying to hold the door shut took one look at her and got up hastily from the floor.

'Good morning, Patterson,' she called to him. 'You'd better make yourself scarce unless you want to be hauled before me again for obstructing the course of justice.'

He turned and fled.

'Isn't he worth arresting?' Finn asked.

'No. He's small fry, a pair of fists for hire, usually. Those two by the table are the ones organising this, I'm sure, but I doubt we'll be able to charge them with anything. That's Councillor Withnall, the magistrate, and I believe you've met Buddle.'

'Yes. Who's the man they're holding back?'

'My chauffeur, who is also acting as clerk today. Luckily Falding isn't stupid enough to give a magistrate the chance to charge him with assault.'

Buddle was scowling at them and she saw the exact moment he caught sight of her bruised face, which was throbbing now. It felt swollen, too.

For a moment he stared in shock, then he began scrabbling together the papers scattered across the table. How a man as vicious as him could have been put in charge of children, she had never understood.

She called out, 'You're blocking the clerk's way, Mr Withnall. Could you let him past, please? I need him by my side in case I'm attacked again. I'm still feeling dizzy from Trumpson's assault.'

'What happened, my lady?' Falding shoved the councillor sideways before Withnall could say or do anything and hurried over to her.

He whistled softly at the sight of her face, so it must look as bad as it felt.

'Who did this to you, my lady?'

'Trumpson.'

'I hope someone's arrested him, and given him some of his own medicine.'

'No need to thump him. I had to shoot him to stop him pounding me to a pulp and that stopped him running away.'

She looked across at the two older men who had made no attempt to come near her but were listening to every word.

'You'll have to stop this hearing,' she said.

Withnall drew himself very upright. 'Madam, this hearing is in my jurisdiction. You have no right to interfere. I must ask you to leave and you should—'

She raised her voice, cutting him short. 'Let everyone present take note. As senior magistrate in this district, I declare this hearing to be invalid and therefore it will be postponed.'

'You can't do that!' Withnall protested.

'Oh, I think I can. Read the rules of procedure. It's about time you did. What's more, I shall be laying a serious complaint before Judge Peters about the way you've conducted things today. Keeping the boy's lawyer out, indeed! Hiring a known thug to attack people. Changing the time of the hearing without informing the participants. You're a disgrace to the magistrature and should be removed from the bench.'

Withnall glanced at Buddle as if for help and his fellow conspirator stepped forward, pointing one finger in Reggie's direction. 'You'll find yourself looking a fool, madam, if you try to prevent this court from dealing with a violent youth like that one. He belongs in a correction centre and that's where he's going.'

'Sentenced before he's even been questioned?' she asked. 'I'm glad I've got reputable witnesses to what you've just said.'

He was about to speak again when Reggie suddenly shouted back at his tormenter from the doorway, where he was standing next to Mr Lloyd. 'I'm not violent and I never have been, except when I was trying to stop you whipping me.

You're the violent one who whips people till they bleed, not me.'

'Hold your tongue before you get yourself into even deeper trouble, you stupid boy!'

Buddle turned back to Lady Terryng and gave her a triumphant smile. 'If the hearing is to be adjourned, then the boy must come back to the orphanage with me until another can be scheduled. That man he's with, who claims he used to be a policeman, isn't a relative. And who knows why Carlisle has taken up with a lad of such tender years? He has no right to have Reginald Barston in his care without it being made official, which it never will be. My testimony about the lad's incorrigible misbehaviour will ensure that.'

There was silence, then Margot turned to Finn. 'He's right about one thing, I'm afraid, Mr Carlisle. Reggie can't stay with you. But there's an easy solution to that.' She turned to the terrified boy. 'Would you feel safe with me, Reggie?'

He looked at her pleadingly. 'I feel safest of all with Uncle Finn.'

'We can't give the authorities cause to complain, so I think it will be best for you to be in the care of a relative.'

'But I haven't got any relatives, missus. That's why I was put in the orphanage.'

'You have at least one relative that I know of and—' She broke off as there was a murmuring at the door and another voice made itself heard.

'Your ladyship, I came as quickly as I could.'

'Sergeant Deemer, I'm delighted to see you.'

'What on earth's been happening here? That man outside says you shot him.'

'Indeed I did. In self-defence.' She turned the injured side of her face towards him. 'As you can see, he was attacking me and I feared for my life. I shall be happy to hand over the management of all this to you from now on, sergeant.'

Finn joined in. 'I saw that fellow attack her. He went mad; was so enraged that he was beyond reason. You've no doubt seen it happen occasionally.'

'I have. And I know Trumpson. He has a long record of violence. He seems to be getting worse as he gets older. If he was in one of his furies, we're lucky he didn't kill someone. Just a moment. Let's make him safe.' Deemer went back out to click handcuffs on the man still sitting on the ground just outside the door before Trumpson realised what he was doing.

The prisoner roared in anger, but when he tried to lunge at Deemer, he yelled in pain and stopped trying to use his injured arm.

'Take him in charge,' Deemer told the constable who was with him.

Margot watched in approval. 'I have just cancelled the hearing, sergeant, and would be obliged if you'll see that no one tries to continue it. I shall be informing Judge Peters of my reasons.'

Deemer nodded, then looked round. 'Where's the local constable? He should be dealing with any disturbances.'

'Her ladyship sent me to fetch him but he refused to come out, sir,' a young man who'd been watching avidly from one side of the doorway volunteered. 'Said he wasn't well.'

'Oh, did he? I think you've disturbed a nest of vipers here, your ladyship.' Deemer's eyes narrowed as he studied her. 'You're looking pale.'

'Well, it's no fun being punched.'

'You could return home and with your permission, I'll come there to take your statement about this incident – *after* you've been seen by a doctor.'

'I don't need a doctor.'

'You might need his expert opinion on your injury if there is an inquiry into the shooting. If I'm not mistaken, you're still feeling dizzy, aren't you? Best to have yourself checked by a doctor.'

'I suppose you're right.' She raised her voice again. 'I'd like to invite everyone involved in this affair to my house. We'll all be more comfortable there.' Her eyes lingered on Reggie again.

The boy was staring at her, too. 'You said I had a relative.'

'Yes. I'll explain about that at my house, Reggie.'

She turned on an afterthought to call out, 'I'm *not* inviting Withnall and Buddle, sergeant. I'd be grateful if you'd take their statements elsewhere – and with a big pinch of salt.'

He grinned as he nodded.

Only then did she lean on her chauffeur's arm and allow him to install her in the rear seat of the car, sitting with her head back and her eyes closed, the bruising showing clearly against her pallor.

'She's a valiant woman, that one,' Deemer said quietly. 'Pity she's the last of the Terryngs.'

When they got to the house, Margot allowed Falding to help her inside, ignoring the shocked gasp of the maid who'd opened the door.

Two other cars drew up behind hers. 'Show everyone into the drawing room, Lizzie, and send Carrie to my bedroom. See that my guests are given refreshments and apologise for me not being able to welcome them. I'd better see the doctor before I do anything else. Could someone send for him, please?'

Her maid was already hurrying across the hall looking shocked. 'What on earth's been happening to you, my lady?'

'I was attacked, Carrie. I just need a few minutes' peace.'

'I should think so,' her maid said. 'I'll fetch some ice from that American contraption of yours in the kitchen to put on the bruising.'

When they got to her bedroom, Margot let Carrie fuss over her and explained what had happened.

The doctor came from the village within a few minutes. He pulled a face at her injuries. 'Been fighting dragons again, Margot?'

'Just one dragon, Neville.'

'Better lie down and rest for a few hours.'

Margot had known the doctor since they were both children playing together while their mothers gossiped over the teacups. 'I don't need to lie down. I only sent for you to bear witness to the extent of my injury if there's an inquiry. I had to shoot the man who was attacking me, you see.'

'May one ask why he was attacking you?'

'Trying to stop me preventing a gross injustice.'

He gave her a wry smile. 'No one should tangle with you when you're trying to right a wrong. From the look of your face, he deserved shooting if that was the only way to stop him doing worse. I hope you didn't kill him, though.'

'I'm not such a bad shot as that. I just hit him in the upper arm.'

He held her head gently as he continued to check the injury. 'Just the one blow? Well, it must have been a vicious one, but I agree, I doubt it's caused any permanent damage. If you start falling asleep for no reason, though, call me back.'

'I haven't got concussion.'

He stood up. 'I'd better get off to the police station. They called me in to attend to a man who'd been shot. Your attacker, I suppose. Who was it?'

'Trumpson.'

'What? That man again. He's becoming a danger to the community.'

'He was working for Buddle and Withnall.'

'Ah. Maybe we can use this incident to get rid of a few

other nuisances at the same time. Those children at the orphanage seem to suffer a surprising number of accidents, and I'd be happy to bear witness to that as well.'

'I'll do my best to get it sorted out. And Neville, I think I've found Arthur's son.'

He stopped moving towards the door and came to give her a hug. 'That's wonderful news, absolutely wonderful. You must tell me all about it when we're both a little less busy.'

After he'd gone, she refused another cup of tea, told Carrie to stop fussing and changed her rumpled, blood-smeared clothes before making her way downstairs.

She went first to the library and knew exactly where to find the family photograph album, because she often glanced through it.

She prayed as she went on to join her guests in the drawing room that she'd do this right. It was so very important not to upset the boy.

Those gathered in the drawing room stopped talking and turned round as she went in.

As she hesitated in the doorway, Mrs Willcox came across to her. 'Are you all right, my lady? You're still very pale.'

'I've seen the doctor and I've to take it easy.'

'This isn't exactly taking it easy.'

Margot gave her a mischievous grin, wincing as it tugged at the swollen part of her face. 'As easy as I can, given the circumstances.'

'Then come and sit down. I think you have something to tell Reggie. Do you want the rest of us to leave you alone with him?'

'No, no. You all seem to have been caught up in this series of events, not just today, and it'll save me repeating my tale ad nauseam.' She sat on the sofa and looked across at the boy. Oh, he was so like his father! So very like.

'Will you come and sit beside me, Reggie? I have something to show you as well as things to tell you.' She held up the old photograph album and then gestured towards the other half of the sofa.

The boy came and sat down. 'I'm sorry for calling you missus earlier. I didn't know you were a ladyship.'

'That's all right. You're not afraid of me, are you, Reggie?'

His gaze was clear, still more that of a child than the man he would gradually become. 'No, I'm not afraid of you, your ladyship, and I'm sorry that man hurt you.'

'It'll heal.' She glanced round and saw that everyone was sitting quietly waiting, so turned back towards the one who mattered most. 'I've been looking for you for a long time, Reggie.'

'You have? Why?'

'Because you're the son of my brother, who was killed just before the end of the war. I have a photo of him. See.' She opened the album and showed him.

Reggie gasped and called across to Finn, 'He looks just like me.'

'Yes. There is no doubt in my mind that you're Arthur's son. See, here's another photo of him and his brother, who would have been your uncle, had he lived. They were both killed in the war. So long ago, and yet sometimes it seems like yesterday.'

'That's why I never saw my real father, then. He didn't abandon me like Mr Buddle said.'

'You shouldn't believe anything that wicked man says.'

'When I was ten my parents, the ones who brought me up that is, told me I was adopted. They said my parents were dead, which is why I'd been given to them. But then they got killed too.' He sniffed and wiped the back of his hand across his eyes. 'Sorry. I don't usually blub.'

'Anyone would in your circumstances. You've had some

hard times, poor boy.' She patted his hand, then dared to take hold of it.

He didn't pull away, but looked down at her hand with its family signet ring curiously.

'This is the Terryng family ring. It'll be yours one day.'

'Why?'

'Because you're the last Terryng left.'

'But my name's Barston, not Terryng.'

'It can be changed to your real father's name. His name was Arthur, by the way. We'll talk about doing that another time.' She waited but though he frowned slightly, Reggie didn't comment on that. And his hand was still clasping hers. That made her want to weep for joy and tug him into her arms.

'Anyway, to continue my tale: the war was a very sad time for me and my family. I'm the oldest child of three and I lost both my brothers, as well as the man I was going to marry. When Arthur was killed, a friend of his sent me a letter he'd written, telling me about you, or rather about your mother and the fact that she was expecting his child.'

'What was she called?'

'Penelope Goodkin.'

The boy mouthed the name then nodded, so she took it as a sign to continue. 'Arthur said he was going to marry Penelope on his next leave, but was writing the letter in case he was killed, as many soldiers did. If the worst happened, he hoped I'd help her and bring you both to live at Netherholme. If he hadn't written that letter, I'd not even have known about your existence.'

She sighed. 'I looked for you everywhere but there was no sign of you or your mother. I didn't realise she'd died in childbirth, poor girl. She'd left Rivenshaw to go and live with an aunt, neighbours told me, but her parents moved away from their old home and no one knew where they'd gone.

In those days young women often went to live with a relative when they were expecting a baby and didn't have a husband.'

She paused, trying to gauge how he was taking it all. 'You were told you'd been adopted, but did Mr and Mrs Barston know anything about your mother?'

'Not much. But they gave me some of her things, some photos of her family they said. There wasn't a photo of my father, though. And that horrible Buddle took the photos away from me. When I asked what he'd done with them, he said he'd burned them. You can't burn silver photo frames, though, can you?'

She looked at him in shock, then at Finn and Sergeant Deemer.

'We've got to find what he did with the lad's things,' the sergeant murmured.

Reggie leaned forward. 'He took other people's things too and sold them in his shop. We weren't supposed to know about that, but one of the boys who'd left the orphanage found out and sent a message back to his friend.'

'Did the boy say anything about where the shop was?'

'No. But someone else told me it was a pawnshop somewhere in Manchester. I don't know where exactly.'

'May I use your phone, your ladyship?' Deemer asked. 'I think time is of the essence if we're to retrieve anything that might help you and the lad before Buddle gets to it. It'll also help with the other things I need to do to set certain matters straight.'

He didn't need to specify exactly what these matters were. To treat orphans so badly disgusted them all.

Margot waved her hand towards the door. 'The phone's on the hall table.'

'Could you wait to tell the rest of the story till I've made this call, your ladyship?'

'Yes, of course.' As he went out, she turned a page in the

album and showed Reggie a photo of three children. 'That's me, in between my little brothers. I was the tallest then, but when they grew up they were both taller than me. Ah, they were such fine young men.'

More pages were turned and she showed him a photo of herself with two men in uniform. 'That one's Arthur, your father, and that one's Clarence, your uncle.'

Reggie stretched out his fingertip to touch the face of his father.

Her voice was thick with tears as she added, 'That's what you'll look like when you grow up, Reggie, but I pray you won't have to face a war.'

Sergeant Deemer came back. 'I've got someone looking into it, told them to see if your brother had any idea where Buddle's shop was, Mr Willcox.'

Jonah nodded. 'If anyone knows, it'll be Charlie. He's in the same trade, after all.'

They all turned expectantly towards Margot again.

She continued in a more formal tone of voice. 'I'm convinced that Reggie is my dead brother's son. I have Arthur's letter about his coming child in my bedroom. When is your birthday, Reggie dear?'

'July. I was born in 1918, and I turn twelve this summer.'

'Aha! That fits with what Arthur said.' She gave him a long, loving look. Her face was bruised and swollen where the man had punched her, but she was glowing with happiness.

'May I see the photos, your ladyship?' Finn asked.

'Yes, of course. What am I thinking about? Perhaps we should all sit at the table in the window so that we can pass them round. The pages of the album unclip.'

As they walked across to it, Finn put one arm round Reggie and gave him a quick hug. 'How lovely that you've found a relative.'

Reggie leaned closer to whisper, 'She's very nice, but I don't need anyone when I've got you.'

'We all need as many friends as we can find. Let's listen carefully to what her ladyship has to tell us, eh?'

'I'm not coming here to live with her. You promised you wouldn't send me away.'

Finn caught her ladyship's eyes on them and prayed she'd be understanding about the lad clinging to the only person who'd been kind to him since his parents died.

She gave him a little nod as if to reassure him and indicated the two chairs next to hers. 'Why don't you sit between us, Reggie? And don't worry. I won't try to separate you from your adopted uncle.'

'Thank you, my ladyship.'

'You could call me Aunt Margot if you liked.'

He tried it out. 'Aunt Margot.'

She fiddled with the photo album, unclipping it and taking a page from it. She slid it along the table to Finn, who stared at the photo of Arthur at the same age as Reggie, startled by how close the likeness was. It could have been Reggie.

'There can't be any doubt of the relationship,' he said quietly, 'none at all.' He passed the photo round the table and there were murmurs of agreement.

When it got back to Reggie, the lad stared at his father's photo and again touched the figure in it.

Finn looked at her ladyship and decided to tackle his main worry. 'Is it true that Reggie won't be allowed to live with me?'

'I'm afraid it is. And we don't want to go against the law and give that horrible man an opening to take my nephew into his care again.' She turned to Reggie. 'You could move in here with me and your uncle would be welcome to come too.'

Finn was torn about that. 'I have a house to protect, because there's been some trouble at the top of the valley. It could have been caused by Buddle, but I'm not sure. There is another possibility. I wonder . . .'

'Wonder what?' she prompted.

'If it's not too presumptuous, I wonder if you could move temporarily to Heythorpe House? Apart from any other considerations, I think Reggie would be safer up in Ellindale at the moment than here. The people in the village will keep an eye out for strangers. You seem to be on your own here. Am I right?' At her nod, he continued, 'I have enough spare bedrooms. You could bring your maid and chauffeur, any other staff you liked.'

Into the silence, Reggie said, 'You look very sad, Aunt Margot. I was sad too till I went to live with Uncle Finn. Maybe you'll be happier there, like I am.'

She stared at the boy in surprise, then looked thoughtful. After a few moments, she said, 'You're right, Reggie. I've been very lonely here since the war and yes, very sad indeed. The estate will run perfectly well without me for a while.'

He went back to staring at the photos of his father.

She turned to Finn. 'I hope Reggie will come to live here eventually, because he'll be the heir. But why don't I join you until he's used to me and we've sorted out the legalities? What do you think about that as a solution, Sergeant Deemer?'

'I think it's a good idea. Might be as well to consult Judge Peters about it before you do anything. In fact, you might tell him about what's happened today.'

'Yes. I suppose I'd better. I intend to make a formal complaint to him about Withnall. I'll telephone the judge after we've had some luncheon. There's no time to waste.'

Reggie brightened immediately at the mention of food.

'Be warned. Your nephew has a fine appetite, your ladyship,' Finn said. 'He'll eat you out of house and home.'

'So did his father.' Her eyes dwelled fondly for a moment on Reggie, then she began organising her staff for the move.

Jonah took his leave of Lady Terryng and drove his wife and young sister-in-law back to Ellindale.

As they passed through Rivenshaw, Leah said suddenly, 'I wasn't thinking! I should have thanked her ladyship for helping Peter when the van was attacked a while ago.'

'She'll be living just down the road. You'll have plenty of chances to thank her then.'

'Yes, of course. I like her, don't you?'

'Very much. Let's hope Reggie can take the sad look out of her eyes.'

'And let's hope her face heals quickly. That was a vicious blow. Trumpson is a dangerous man.'

The minute Sergeant Deemer had finished questioning them, Buddle and Withnall got into their own cars and drove off hastily to hold a private discussion in the big office at the orphanage, where no one would dare to interrupt them.

'They'll not be able to prove that boy's her relative,' Buddle said. 'Photos aren't proof. And her brother wasn't married, so at best that damned boy will be a bastard. They can't usually inherit.'

'But still, you'd better leave him alone from now on.'

'For the moment. In the meantime, you need to phone Judge Peters and lay a complaint against *her*.'

'I don't think I should do that. Not with him.'

'Why not? He's your superior in legal matters, isn't he?'

'Yes, but I don't get on well with him and he'd be sure to take her side. Trumpson was a fool to punch her like that.'

'And she was a fool to shoot him. Who's going to believe the other witnesses if you insist she was in no real danger and deliberately chose to hurt him? None of those people make nearly as credible a witness as a magistrate like you. And does she have a licence for that gun? You should check that. Details can be important.'

As Withnall still shook his head, Buddle added, 'You had better do what I ask . . . unless you want certain information to be revealed.'

'You wouldn't dare. I know plenty about you as well now.'

'If you say one word about me, it'll be your death warrant.'

His companion looked at him in shock, opened his mouth to protest, then closed it again.'

'That's right. You'll be wise to keep your mouth shut. You'll soon see what I dare do. *I* wasn't a war profiteer like you were. Your credibility as a magistrate would be totally destroyed if it were found out you'd been breaking the law all through the war.'

Withnall breathed deeply and said nothing.

'In the meantime, I'm going to go through any of that boy's possessions that remain among my special stores and see if there's any proof of who he is among them. I don't think we've sold the picture frame, for a start. If there's any evidence about who he really is, then it's even more important that I have him back in my power.'

'Why bother? You'd be better letting him go and getting on with your other plans.'

'I don't let children get the better of me under any circumstances, whoever they might or might not be related to. And especially one who might be the heir to Netherholme.'

20

Later that afternoon two cars wound their way up the hill towards Ellindale. Finn turned his vehicle into the parking area first, followed by her ladyship's nine horse power Riley, driven by her chauffeur and general factotum, Falding.

She and her maid were sitting in the back seat on top of a pile of neatly folded bedding because Carrie didn't trust houses run by men without wives to provide proper, well-aired bed linen for her mistress, especially when that particular man had only recently moved into the house.

'Well, at least it's a gentleman's residence,' the maid admitted grudgingly as she got out and stared down the slope. 'I just hope the mattresses aren't damp.'

'We can always send for some of our own feather mattresses if they are,' Margot said mildly. A sniff was her maid's only answer.

Carrie had once been her nanny and had worked by her side during the war, so was far more than just a lady's maid, just as Falding was far more than a chauffeur. He had been Clarence Terryng's batman during the war and still bore the scars on his body from the bomb that had killed her brother.

She'd had no hesitation in bringing these two with her, because apart from the fact that they were more family than servants now, both were sensible people prepared to turn their hands to anything, even though Carrie might, and usually did, grumble about it.

Finn sent Reggie ahead of them into the house to warn Beth and the others that he'd brought home visitors to stay a few nights. 'Come straight out again to welcome your aunt to the house when she arrives, Reggie. Don't go gossiping to the maids about her.'

'Well, I don't know much about her yet to gossip about, do I?'

'Precisely. So don't go guessing, either. You can show your aunt round and introduce her to everyone while I help Falding to unload the car and carry their things down to the house. I really must do something about making a road to the rear entrance. It's so inconvenient to have to haul heavier things round to the back on foot. Ask Beth to help them choose bedrooms.'

He bent closer to whisper, 'And don't say anything but I think your aunt is more tired than she'll admit, and her face must be hurting, so if you can show her the ground-floor rooms, then persuade her to sit down and rest, it'd be a good thing.'

'I'll try.' Reggie hesitated, then added, 'She's nice, isn't she?'

'Very nice. You're a lucky boy.'

'I'm most lucky of all to have met you, Finn, because you saved me from that horrible man.'

Sometimes, Reggie's remarks were very touching. Finn hoped the boy would have some happy childhood years before he had to grow up.

Finn liked Lady Terryng, too. She reminded him of an older version of one of his own aunts, a lively young woman who had married a soldier from Australia at the end of the war and gone off with him to the other side of the world.

He had meant to keep in touch with her, but when Ivy died, he'd been in too deep despair. He hoped there was still time to contact his aunt again. He probably had quite a few young cousins in Australia by now.

When the car turned into their parking area shortly afterwards, Reggie rushed through the house to the kitchen. As he skidded to a halt, everyone turned round to see what was the matter and he gasped out an explanation of his haste. 'Uncle Finn's brought some visitors to stay and one of them's Lady Terryng, the others are her servants. I have to get back and show her in.'

'What exactly happened at the hearing? Did you—' Beth began, but he had already dashed out again.

Mrs Jarratt stared at Beth in consternation. 'Did he say *Lady* Terryng? I don't know how to talk to a ladyship.'

'Just the same way as you'd talk to any other visitor, politely and doing your best to help her.'

Beth spoke briskly but she too was feeling somewhat nervous at the thought of looking after posh visitors, let alone one who was *Lady* something or other. 'We'll go and watch them come in and see if they need help carrying anything. Shove the kettle over the heat first, Dilys love. Children, stay where you are.'

The two little ones looked at her and nodded, and she gave them a fond smile before turning to lead the others to the rear of the hall. There she stood with her hands clasped over her apron, to keep herself from fiddling, relieved that she was now decently dressed. She was conscious that the others were staying further back and was just about to tell them to move forward and stand next to her when Reggie came back into the house.

The lady with him looked to be in her forties, Beth would guess. She had an air of authority and confidence that the younger woman envied. Easy to be confident when you had money *and* education, but still the woman had a nice smile.

By the time Reggie had given his aunt a quick tour of the

front parlour, library and dining room, Beth had decided the other maids would be better occupied making sure the fancy tea set was clean and setting things out on the trolley Finn had once told her should be used to wheel snacks into the drawing room.

When he'd finished helping unload the car, Finn went back to resume his duties as host. He heard Reggie's voice in the dining room, so walked across to join Beth. 'Did Reggie introduce you to our visitors?'

'No, sir. But the lady smiled across at us anyway.'

'Then let me have that pleasure when they come out of the dining room.'

'Can I ask? How did the hearing go?'

'It never took place. Lady Terryng stopped it. Ah, here she comes. My lady, may I introduce Beth, our housekeeper.'

Beth nodded a greeting, not sure whether to curtsey. 'I'm pleased to meet you, your ladyship, and if you need anything, just ask.'

Finn nodded as if approving what Beth had said and carried on.

'This is Carrie, her ladyship's maid, and Falding, her ladyship's chauffeur and manservant. Do I have that right, your ladyship, to describe how Falding helps you?'

'Yes. And since we have Reggie in common, why don't *you* call me Margot from now on?'

'Thank you. I'm usually called Finn by my friends.'

'Did Beth come here with you from your previous home?'

'No. I'd been, um, travelling and doing occasional jobs for the police when I inherited this house. Beth was living in the village. The house hadn't been occupied for about thirty years, so please don't blame her and her staff for any of its shortcomings. They've done a heroic amount of mopping, cleaning and sorting things out.'

Beth was relieved to see her ladyship's maid looking a little less disapproving after this explanation. It could be very useful to get on with this older woman, who would be joining them in the servants' quarters and who could probably teach them a lot about how to do their jobs better. Well, she might if they could get on the right side of her from the start.

'Beth has been living in Ellindale since she married but her husband has been away for several months looking for work, so when their cottages were taken away from them to house the farmer's family, she and her neighbours came to live here and help me. You'll no doubt meet Beth's children later, but they're only little and rather shy with strangers so they're probably hiding in the kitchen.'

Reggie was fidgeting from foot to foot, seeming unsure what to do next.

Beth was in a similar situation but had been reminded by the pile of bedding in the hall of one thing that couldn't wait. 'Please sir, I think we ought to air the beds for our visitors straight away.' She turned to the lady. 'We'd have got it ready if we'd known you were coming, my lady.'

'That's my fault. I should have phoned. I'm still getting used to everything.' Finn gestured helplessly round.

'I don't expect miracles of anyone, Beth. Carrie and Falding will no doubt help you with the extra work we cause. In the meantime, I must admit I'd like to sit down and perhaps someone could make me a cup of tea?'

'The other maids are seeing to that at this moment, my lady.'

'Oh, excellent! Bring it into the front sitting room, please, Beth.' She walked off with Reggie.

Finn had noticed Beth stealing glances at the badly bruised face of their visitor, so whispered, 'Her ladyship was attacked and injured earlier today, as you can see, and she needs to rest.'

As he followed Reggie and Lady Terryng, Beth turned to the two visiting servants. 'The kitchen is this way. I need to check how the tea's coming on. I dare say you'd like a cup, too.'

The manservant moved forward. 'I'd love one. Afterwards I'll help you start airing the mattresses. Perhaps we could light fires in the bedrooms to save lugging them up and down stairs. I could do that for you.'

'I'd be grateful for some help, I must admit.'

As they followed her into the kitchen Beth decided to be absolutely open about her ignorance. 'I'm not really a housekeeper, though I'm good at organising things, which is why I've taken charge. If I do anything wrong or there's a better way, I'd be grateful if you'd tell me. I'm a quick learner.'

Carrie gave her an approving look. 'Well, I'm glad you said that. I can't abide people who pretend to be what they're not. We'll all work together to make her ladyship comfortable here and to keep an eye on that boy.'

She exchanged glances with Falding and added, 'It's common knowledge now, so I'll tell you that Master Reggie seems to be her ladyship's brother's child and she's been looking for him ever since Mr Arthur was killed in the war.'

Beth felt greatly relieved because this explanation seemed to indicate that she'd been accepted by the older maid, who'd looked at her so scornfully when she first arrived. 'How exciting! It'll be wonderful for Reggie to have family of his own. He's had such a hard time lately. But I don't know what Mr Carlisle will do without him. He's grown very fond of the boy.'

'I could see that.' Carrie took a seat in the kitchen. 'I don't bite, lass, and I'd love a cup of tea too. We've been running round like chickens with their heads cut off since her ladyship came back from court and told us about Master Reggie being her nephew. Some people still seem to want to harm him, which is why we've come to stay here, to keep him safe.'

By the time Beth got her children to bed that night she was so exhausted with helping the visitors settle in she went to bed early herself. Her head was spinning with Carrie's instructions about how things should be done, and she was still trying to work out what they would do about feeding the visitors. *They* wouldn't be satisfied with bread and jam for breakfast, that was sure!

Mr Carlisle had found time to come and seek her out before he too followed his visitors' example and went to bed early. 'How did things go in the kitchen? I hope Carrie and Falding weren't too stiff and starchy.'

'They were very helpful. She's a bit fussy about how things are done, but she's all right. It's nice of her ladyship to come here for a while, isn't it? Reggie's still all of a twitter underneath, worrying about how things will work out in the end.'

'I know. We'll make sure they work out in his best interest. How are your children coping with the visitors?'

She smiled. 'They've won Carrie over. Who'd have thought she loved young children so much? Daisy fell asleep on her lap.'

A yawn caught him unawares. 'I'm ready for sleep myself. What a day it's been! Is the back of the house all locked up?'

'Yes. And Daniel's got men from the village patrolling the grounds. Fancy having to do that in Ellindale of all places! It's like one of those films at the cinema, with villains firing guns and galloping around on horses. Neil used to take me to the cinema in Rivenshaw when we were courting. I loved it.'

'You must miss him very much.'

She hesitated then shook her head. That was another

thing she wasn't going to pretend about, not after being abandoned for so long. 'I don't miss him at all. I can't lie about it to you, not when you've been so kind to me. Neil grew a bit rough with me because being out of work really got him down. In the end I had to get a big stick and hit him back.'

He was staring at her in amazement, but she wasn't going to pretend. 'He stopped hitting me, but we still quarrelled a lot. What upset me most was that he was so changeable with the kids. Sometimes he used to shout at them and make them cry; other times he'd play with them and give them rides on his shoulders. Most of all I miss the money coming in regular. I'm a good manager.'

She stared into the distance for a moment. 'I'm dreading Neil coming back, to tell you the truth, Mr Carlisle. I'm really enjoying working here. It's interesting and I'm learning so much. I don't get a lot of spare time, but being able to borrow your books and have a read now and then is wonderful, too.'

'You're doing an amazing job for someone who knew nothing about the job of housekeeper before.'

'Did you know anything about being a gentleman before you inherited?' she asked with a cheeky smile.

He chuckled. 'No. I was merely an ordinary policeman who'd been lucky enough to get a bit more education than usual.'

'Well, you're doing an amazing job, too.'

They stared at one another and the silence went on for too long. Neither dared speak certain thoughts aloud and in the end Finn said abruptly, 'We should go to bed now. We'll both have a busy day tomorrow, I'm sure.'

At the door he turned and stared at her again. 'Good night, Beth.'

'Good night, sir.'

You shouldn't talk so freely to him, she told herself later

as she snuggled down in bed. You keep forgetting he's your employer, not a friend. He can't be interested in your problems.

But Finn had seemed interested and he was so easy to talk to she couldn't help chatting openly to him. He was good looking as well in a quiet way and an affectionate man. Look at how he treated that boy. If he ever got married again, his wife would be a very lucky person indeed.

And when, or *if* Neil came home, it'd be the hardest thing she'd ever had to do, going to live with him again.

Why wasn't he sending any money? How did he think she'd feed and clothe their children without something coming in?

Where was he now? Had something happened to him? It was hard not to have the faintest clue about that.

At Spring Cottage Leah got up the next morning feeling as if they'd achieved something important the previous day by helping save Reggie. How strangely that had turned out. Fancy him being related to Lady Terryng!

She'd better get on with her fizzy drink business now, though. Peter was doing better than she'd expected at bringing in orders, so she'd had to set off extra batches of ginger beer, which was selling more than the other drinks. She needed to test that new batch of ginger beer today and see if it was ready for bottling.

Then there was Charlie. He'd rung yesterday to say they'd have to postpone the official opening of the youth hostel, because the mayor wasn't well. But he wanted to chat about some ideas he had for the future of the business.

She was a bit worried about that, if truth be told. She enjoyed making fizzy drinks and had an idea for a new sort, a bit different from others being sold. She was also enjoying the personal contact with those working for her and the messages Peter brought back from people who were delighted with her ginger beer brought a warm glow to her. But she didn't want to get buried in paperwork and spend all her time organising the business details.

She remembered her father talking about Mr Harris and how he seemed to spend most of his time in the office dealing with the paperwork. She wasn't cut out to sit in an office and stare at pieces of paper. But she couldn't ask Jonah to do that for her, because he had as much on his plate as he could cope with. He usually took the time to rest at some point in the day, still wheezed and fought for breath at times.

Rosa came down and hovered near her.

'Out with it. What's wrong?'

'There's nothing wrong exactly, but Leah, we need to buy my uniform for when school starts and we'll have to go into Rivenshaw for that. Is it . . . all right? We do have enough money for it, don't we?'

'Yes, love, we do. I should have done that sooner. You've got an Esherwood Bequest that pays all your fees and buys your schoolbooks but I can pay for your uniform.'

'They'll pay for a uniform too if I need it. You have to make a special causes application. I hope you don't mind, but I reread the letters they sent when I won the scholarship, just to be sure of what we had to do.'

'I can well afford it. No need for that.'

Rosa let out a huge sigh of relief and Leah had to give her a quick hug.

Helping her sister get ready to start at the girls' grammar school would be much more fun than doing her accounts, Leah thought, then felt guilty. How could she be thinking about what she did and didn't like? She was one of the lucky ones.

Agitation about the Means Test was sweeping the country. Men who'd been without work for years and were desperate about the cuts in the dole that had been proposed were marching on London to protest, coming from all over the place. And the newspapers said some of them were behaving violently.

Jonah said the newspapers were on the government's side and didn't always tell the truth. He didn't think most of the men would have turned violent unless provoked. He'd been frowning a lot at recent articles.

That had made her wonder who was right, so she encouraged him to discuss it with her. 'How can you be so sure?'

'Well, there are bound to be some bad eggs among so many people, but most of the ordinary chaps I fought with and commanded during the war were decent, caring only about providing for their families and protecting their country. And look at the chaps round here. They're not violent revolutionaries, are they? And some of them have been out of work for a long time.'

He smiled reminiscently. 'The ordinary chaps I've known have usually been more interested in horse racing and football than in trade unions, though they aren't saints by any means.'

His smile faded. 'I don't know how men have managed to cope with year after year of unemployment. I admire their stoic endurance greatly, and I also admire what you're doing with the fizzy drinks. It matters, even if you only provide jobs for one or two people. If more people made an effort like that, they'd make a bigger difference.'

He was lost in thought for a moment or two, then she cleared her throat to gain his attention. 'Can I borrow the car to take Rosa shopping for her uniform?'

'Yes, of course. I'll come home early today and you can have it this afternoon. You don't want to be lugging brown paper parcels home on the bus.'

'We'll call in on Auntie Hilda while we're there. I haven't

seen her for ages. I miss living near her. She was a wonderful neighbour to me after my mother died.

'She's got a new lodger, I think. I hope he's a nice, quiet man. She works far too hard for a woman of her age.'

When Leah and Rosa had left, Jonah had a sudden fit of coughing. It seemed to go on for longer than usual and when he looked down at his handkerchief, the stuff he'd coughed up was streaked with red.

His heart sank. It wasn't the first time this had happened, but lately it had been happening more frequently. He picked up the phone and dialled with a hand that shook slightly. 'Mrs Mitchell? I'd like to make an appointment to see the doctor. No, it's not urgent. How about Thursday morning?'

Having made sure the appointment was for one of the mornings he worked at the pawnshop, he tried to put what had happened out of his mind. He didn't want to worry Leah yet. After all, it was just a smear of blood now and then.

But he'd also been getting tired more quickly, too.

He went slowly and wearily upstairs to the bedroom to get ready for work and stood staring down the valley for a long time. Life could be so unfair. He'd hoped for longer with Leah before he got to this stage, which he'd been warned about.

Perhaps Dr Mitchell would tell him he was worrying about nothing. But the spark of hope was very faint. He knew only too well how badly he'd been affected by that damned gas and had seen how it affected others.

If only he'd been able to father a child. It was hard to know you weren't leaving anything of yourself behind.

21

Finn let his lawyer contact Judge Peters and when Mr Lloyd rang up to say the judge wanted to see them all informally, he agreed to take Reggie into Manchester in two days' time.

He didn't tell the lad about it till the following evening.

'A judge!' Reggie exclaimed. 'He'll send me back to the orphanage.'

'I'm sure he won't. This is only to find the facts. And this judge is an honest man, I promise you, very well respected and liked.'

'Do we have to go? Couldn't we just . . . stay here quietly and not upset anyone?'

'Of course we have to go. We need to sort everything out legally, not only for you and me, but also for your aunt. In fact, I think we'd better take her ladyship with us and the photos of your father.'

Margot was in agreement with that and had a further thought. 'We'll call at my home on the way and collect the rest of the photographs. The one I gave Reggie isn't the only photo I have. The judge can't fail to recognise the resemblance.'

They set off early on the day of the meeting, with Falding driving them in her ladyship's Riley, which was bigger than Finn's car.

They arrived at Terryng Hall before nine o'clock, shocked to find a police car standing outside and the front door wide open. A maid peered out, saw who it was and came running across to the car.

'Oh, my lady, I'm so glad you're here. We tried to telephone you but they said you were on your way.'

'What's happened?' Margot got out of the car without waiting for anyone else.

'We've had a burglary. They got into the house while we were all in bed and no one heard a thing. Oh, I'll never sleep soundly again.'

'What's been taken?'

'Nothing of value, just those old photograph albums.'

'*What?*' Margot rushed inside but it was as her maid had said. The photograph albums were all that had been taken. And it couldn't have been a mistake because every single one had gone.

Finn told Reggie to stay in the car with Falding and joined her, agreeing with her conclusion.

'It has to be Buddle. I'd hoped he'd leave Reggie alone now, but it seems he's still hell bent on getting his hands on the boy.'

She looked at him grimly. 'Well, he's not going to. Luckily, I had a few other photos with me in and Reggie's got the ones I gave him. We'd better phone your home and tell them to watch out for burglars.'

'The poor boy will be even more upset.'

She sniffed and blew her nose angrily, wincing as she bumped the bruise. 'I'm upset too. They've stolen my family memories. What's the betting that they've burned them?'

He sighed, unable to disagree with that.

When they went outside, Reggie was as upset as they'd expected, looking round in terror as if he expected Buddle's men to jump out of the bushes at him.

'It's a good thing we had some of the photos with us,' Margot told him bracingly. 'We still have proof.'

'Will they be enough?'

'I think so.' She brightened. 'And I have friends and relatives with copies of family photos. We'll get some of the others back. If it is Buddle behind this, he's not a very clever plotter.'

'I should think he relies on brute force rather than clever planning. I can't think why he believes he'll get away with it, though.'

'No, Finn. Neither can I.'

As they set off, Reggie sat in the back with her. After a while he said in a tight voice, 'It's horrid to have taken your photos. Now I'll never know what my father was like as he was growing up.'

'It is horrid, Reggie, but we'll come through it.' She put her arm round him and he didn't try to shake it off.

Judge Peters, a thin man in his fifties with silver hair at his temples giving him a distinguished look, was waiting for them in his office. It was a comfortable place with a big desk and several big leather armchairs.

Margot explained about her long search for her brother's child, then told him what had happened during the night.

'Are the police in your area capable?' Then he frowned. 'Taylor is the area sergeant, isn't he? How do you feel about him?'

She hesitated. 'I've had some doubts recently.'

'Sergeant Deemer has similar concerns. He's in charge of looking into matters. I'll ask him to contact you about this latest development.'

'I'd have great confidence in him doing things properly.'

Judge Peters smiled. 'He's got a very good reputation, even if he does sometimes go his own sweet way in the pursuit of justice.'

He held out his hand for the photos, studied them and then looked at Reggie. 'There can be no doubt whatsoever of a relationship.'

'There's also this letter from my brother, saying he was going to marry the mother of his coming child on his next leave. Only he didn't survive.'

'And the date of birth coincides?'

'Yes, exactly.'

'Is the path of your family inheritance specified, for example through legitimate heirs only?'

She shook her head. 'On the contrary, it's deliberately specified that the eldest child of the incumbent is to inherit, male or female, whether legitimate or not. Though if it's a female and she marries the husband must take the name Terryng. The founder of our line was illegitimate himself, you see. And the name is almost extinct except for our branch, I believe.'

'Then I can see no need for hearings or all this fuss. But I will bring in some colleagues before you leave to meet the boy and study the photographs, if you don't mind? And I'll get my head clerk to make a copy of that letter from your brother. You swear to me that this is his handwriting?'

'Yes. There are diaries somewhere in the house written by him. The burglars didn't think to take those.'

'Good.' He rang the bell and gave the letter to the clerk. 'We'll do whatever is necessary to have Reggie recognised as your heir.'

The boy had said very little but had followed every word spoken with painful intensity.

Judge Peters turned to him. 'Are you happy to be recognised as Lady Terryng's nephew?'

'Yes, your honour. But I also want Uncle Finn to be recognised as my adopted uncle, too. He saved me and looked after me after I ran away.'

'Then it seems to me that you're a very lucky lad to have found two people anxious to claim you, so we must be sure to make your Uncle Finn's role in your life official.'

For the first time Reggie smiled more normally.

'No time like the present. I'll round up some witnesses whose probity cannot be doubted. Good thing there are other chambers nearby.' The judge went out.

'What does "probity" mean?' Reggie whispered.

'Honesty,' Finn whispered back.

Judge Peters came back ten minutes later with two gentlemen, one of his own age, the other rather younger, plus a matronly woman. He introduced them as a judge, a lawyer and the senior secretary of a very famous judge. 'I thought it best to have a woman involved as well.'

'I should jolly well think so,' Margot said. 'We're left out of too many things.'

When the formalities were over, and the witnesses had all agreed that Reggie had to be a relative of Lady Terryn's brother, in fact probably his son, the group said goodbye and walked outside. It seemed very appropriate that the sun was shining brightly.

Only Reggie wasn't satisfied. 'Why did they say "probably his son"?'

'Because they're lawyers,' his aunt told him. 'They always hedge their statements with ifs and buts. *I* have no doubt you're Arthur's son.'

'Well, I still think they should have said that.'

Finn intervened. 'Let's go and find somewhere to have a meal.'

Reggie was instantly distracted and let out a little cheer. 'Yes, let's. I'm *dying* of hunger!'

'You'll have to get used to that,' Finn whispered to Margot. 'He's always hungry. Well, he's almost twelve, growing like a weed.'

The next two weeks passed more smoothly than anyone at Heythorpe House had expected, with no attacks or burglaries, or even word of what Buddle was doing. But Finn insisted they still continue to keep a very careful watch for intruders.

Beth didn't trust this uneasy peace and sensed that Finn didn't either, so she made sure the other maids never left an outer door unlocked if no one was close by and made them promise not to discuss Reggie's situation when they went into the village.

She felt guilty that in spite of the worries about Reggie, she was enjoying her own life, learning so much from Carrie and Lady Terryng. Her children were happier too, because they seemed to have acquired an honorary grandmother in Carrie, who soon fairly doted on them.

'I never realised how much she loved children,' Margot said one day as they watched Carrie throwing a ball for Daisy while Felix trailed round the garden after Daniel, to whom he'd taken a strong liking.

The postman appeared on a fine day in July and left his bicycle next to the cars, clumping round to the back door, instead of pushing the letters through the letter slot in the front door. Beth wondered why. She told Dilys to make him a drink of tea and waited to hear his news.

'I came round the back because I've got a letter for you today and none for Mr Carlisle,' he told her cheerfully. 'About time that husband of yours wrote to you. I hope this is good news.'

He handed her the letter and she stared at it in surprise, then frowned. On first sight it looked like Neil's handwriting, which the postman had seen many times in the early days of Neil's absence. But she knew her husband's handwriting better than anyone and something about this address was wrong. She couldn't work out what straight away, it was just . . . wrong.

Maybe the handwriting was neater than usual – oh, yes, that was definitely part of it! – and surely he didn't write his surname with such a big, curly R? No, he definitely didn't. He usually wrote an untidy scribble of an R at the beginning of their surname, after which his handwriting wavered up and down as if a drunken spider had crawled out of an inkwell on to the paper.

The postman was staring at her, so she slipped the envelope into her pocket and thanked him. She wasn't going to open it in the company of other people, in case it was bad news.

'Dilys will soon have the kettle boiling. Do come inside and have a quick cup,' she told the postman automatically.

After one look at her tight smile, he didn't ask about the letter again.

Once he'd left she said, 'I'm going out for a breath of fresh air.'

No one would miss her at this time of day so she went round the house to a wooden bench from which you could look down the valley. It was one of her favourite places to sit.

For some reason, she didn't want to open the letter. She held it in her hands, turning it round and round, doubting it'd be good news. And the more she studied the handwriting, the more certain she was that Neil hadn't written this. Only, if he was too ill to write himself why would anyone have tried to copy his handwriting?

Oh, she was a fool! How could she know anything without seeing what was inside? She opened the envelope carefully and scanned the brief, ill-spelled letter.

Neil had never been a good scholar and hated anything to do with books and writing, but he'd not been stupid. This was so badly written, her first thought was that it only confirmed that the missive wasn't from him.

But the writer used her pet name. Only Neil had ever called her 'Bethiekins'. How had the person known that?

Worst of all, the envelope didn't contain any money. 'Curse you, Neil Rawton! Can't you help at all? Do I have to earn the money for every crust your children eat?'

Her anger flared high as she realised that not only wasn't he writing to help them, he was asking her if she could scrape any money together and send him a postal order. He'd been ill, he said, and was in debt. The landlady's son wouldn't let him leave till he'd paid.

In spite of her resolve to be brave, a tear trickled down her cheek. Neil was going to bring trouble back into her life again, she was sure of it. He knew nothing about her present job, so how could he think she'd have any spare money? How dare he ask her to send even a farthing? Was she to stop feeding his children to find it?

She turned the page round and round in her hands, not knowing what to do, then suddenly covered her eyes with her left hand, willing the tears not to fall, willing herself not to sob aloud.

'You dropped the envelope, Beth.'

The voice startled her so much she dropped the letter too.

Finn bent to pick it up and stood quietly beside her. 'You're crying.'

'Mmm. Sorry. I'll be all right in a minute or two, sir.' She had to keep remembering to call him 'sir' because she always thought of him as just 'Finn'.

'Bad news?'

She nodded, finding it hard to speak without sobbing.

'Tell me.'

She thrust the letter at him. 'From my husband. Read it.'

'Are you sure?'

'Yes. If I trust anyone in this world, it's you, sir.'

'May I join you?' He gestured to the seat.

She nodded and waited as he read the letter.

'I can lend you some money, if that's what's worrying you.'

'It isn't. I wouldn't send him a single penny. He knows the children come first with me. It's not that.'

He waited and when she looked sideways, he had that gentle, caring expression on his face.

'It's not his handwriting,' she blurted out. 'At least, I don't think it is. It looks a bit like the way he writes, but it's not . . . not right.' She spread her hands helplessly, unable to be more specific to someone who'd never seen Neil's hand-writing.

He looked at it again. 'You're sure of that?'

'Yes. Only . . . whoever wrote it called me "Bethiekins".' She could feel herself flushing, it sounded so silly. 'It was his pet name for me. Only he has ever called me that. So I'm puzzled.'

He smoothed out the torn envelope and looked at the postmark. 'It was posted in Adsley. Is that where he was when you last heard from him?'

'No. I don't even know where Adsley is. He was somewhere in Chester working at a church called St Crispin's when he last wrote, but that was months ago. He didn't send me the address. He rarely did. I suppose he thought he'd be moving on in a day or two, as usual.'

She remembered how anxiously she'd waited to hear from him, how often she'd gone hungry so that the kids would have something to eat – until Finn came and helped them.

'He didn't get in touch or send any money for months, and in the end I was so desperate I wrote to him care of the church. I never got a reply, but the letter wasn't returned to sender, either, so he must have received it, don't you think? Or someone else did. I've not heard from him in all the months since, not till this letter.'

'We'll have to see if we can find this Adsley. I think I saw a book of maps of England on the bookshelves. Shall we go and look for it now?'

She stuffed the letter into her pocket. 'Thank you, F— um, sir, but I don't want to trouble you. I'll do that later. I have to get on with my work now. You're not paying me to tend to my own business.'

'I won't mind if you take a little time off. This is an emergency.'

'Not really. Things haven't changed here.' She couldn't stop her voice from growing sharper as she added, 'It's Neil's emergency, not mine.'

Finn wouldn't mind her looking for the atlas now, she knew that, but she would mind very much indeed. She owed him so much and she wasn't going to short-change him in the work she did.

He was still looking dubious, so she added firmly, 'With your permission, I'll look it up in my spare time, sir. I'd better get on with my day now.'

She hurried into the house before he could say anything else, before she could be tempted to let him help. Before she gave in to the temptation to throw herself into his arms and sob out her worries.

But however much the letter had upset her, she didn't feel guilty these days at wishing she would never see Neil again.

If she were rich, she'd get a divorce from her husband. But poor people couldn't afford divorces and fancy lawyers. Most just ran away and started new lives elsewhere under a changed name.

She'd been tempted to do that. Oh, yes. But you needed money even to run away and she had none, well, only the few shillings she'd saved since coming to work here.

Finn watched her go. She always held herself very upright, walked briskly and faced the world with a cool smile. He felt she kept her troubles buttoned firmly inside her. Only someone who had watched her closely, who was starting to know her quite well, would recognise that even the slight frown wrinkling her forehead was an unusual display of emotion for her.

She hated to be beholden to anyone, but in times like these with two small children to support and an absentee husband, she couldn't avoid needing help. And if he could help other people in the village, he could certainly help Beth.

In fact, he wished he could take the burdens off her shoulders completely. He wished it more than he ought to. She was married. He was her employer. He had to keep repeating that to himself because they were reasons for them to stay poles apart. And yet he was starting to care for her, couldn't seem to help himself.

He thought she was attracted to him, too, thought she might have guessed how he felt about her. But she was much more in control of how she looked at him than he was of how he looked at her, so he wasn't quite sure.

Margot had stared at him thoughtfully the other day after he'd been talking to Beth. Mrs Jarratt kept a watchful eye on him whenever he came into the kitchen. Did they guess how he felt? Probably. Women were better than men at that sort of thing.

Never mind that. What would it hurt to do this small thing for Beth?

He went into the house and into the room they called the library, with its one wall of bookcases full of dusty tomes. There had to be an atlas here somewhere, he was sure he'd seen one.

It took him a while to find it, then even longer to find Adsley, which was in very small print, north-west of Chester and out in the country. The village was probably bigger now, because this was a very old atlas.

He put a marker in the page and made a small arrow in pencil in the margin nearest the village. Then he put the atlas on the bare central table, where she'd see it at once, and went to find something to take his mind off Beth and her troubles.

He failed to find anything that would do that, but he kept himself usefully employed at least and out of her way.

Beth managed to keep her curiosity about where her husband was at the back of her mind until late evening. It had been another busy day and none of the maids showed any inclination to stay up late. Even Finn and his guest had rung for a cup of cocoa to send them to sleep and said they were going up to bed soon.

Her children were asleep, so she told the other maids she'd follow them upstairs shortly after she'd chosen a new book to read and went into the room they called the library.

She saw the atlas at once, sitting prominently on the table. It said on the cover that it was a guide to the counties of England. He must have come looking for it to help her. She opened the book at the marker, touched the little arrow he'd pencilled in lightly in the margin and found Adsley nearby.

It was such a small dot and the map told her very little other than the fact that Adsley existed. She didn't think it had a railway station, because none of the black lines went through or even near it, so it must be a small village. Most places were at least near a branch line, but it didn't even have that advantage.

She didn't know which shelf to put the atlas back on and her thoughts were now in turmoil again, so she sat down for a few moments to try to work out what to do.

She'd never be able to sleep. Her mind felt like a fizzy drink that had been shaken up in a bottle so that her thoughts had burst out when she opened the atlas and overwhelmed her in a frothy flood.

Whoever had written the letter had said to send the money care of the post office in the village of Adsley. Send money.

Ha! Even if she'd wanted to help him, she didn't have enough to spare to send any to him. The children were growing fast and would soon need new shoes. She didn't want to be dependent on Finn for everything they wore.

She studied the letter again. No, it wasn't Neil's handwriting. The more she studied it, the more sure she was of that.

But whoever had sent it knew her pet name. Why would he tell someone else that? Who did he know in this Adsley place to share intimate details with?

The door to the library opened and she twisted round to see who it was. Lady Terryng.

She stood up hastily. 'I'm sorry, your ladyship. I was just looking something up. I have Mr Carlisle's permission to borrow the books here.'

'Finn told me you had a problem. He didn't tell me what it was, but I can see you're upset. Would you like to share it with me?'

And so desperate was Beth to ask another woman's opinion about the letter that she fumbled in her pocket, took out the crumpled piece of paper and held it out, quickly explaining her dilemma.

'You seem fairly certain it isn't your husband's handwriting.'

'Yes, I am. Though it's a bit like it, only . . . well, far more neatly written.'

'Then perhaps we should send Finn to this Adsley place to investigate. After all, he was a policeman and I know Sergeant Deemer thinks very highly of his investigatory skills.'

'*I can't ask him to do that!*'

'Well, you can't do it yourself, can you? You have two children and no money to pay for the trip to Chester and beyond.'

'But it'd cost Finn money to go and how would I pay him back?' She heard her voice getting shriller and clapped one hand to her mouth.

'Come and sit down.' Lady Terryng walked across to a brown leather Chesterfield sofa and took a seat, beckoning her over.

Beth hesitated, then went to sit beside her.

'Sometimes we have to accept help from others. You'll be accepting it for your children as well as for yourself. You must realise how important it is to all three of you that you find out the truth. And anyway, you didn't ask Finn to do it. His help was freely offered, only he thought I'd stand more chance of persuading you to accept his offer than he would.'

'I don't want people gossiping about . . . about . . .'

'You don't need to worry about that. You've kept your feelings for him under almost perfect control.'

Beth stared at her aghast. 'I can't have if you've noticed.'

'I've had little to do in the decade since the war other than watch people. I notice more than most. And I've felt it a privilege sometimes to help the people in our village who were in trouble. I'm sure Finn feels the same way. Look how he rescued Reggie.'

She waited, then repeated, 'Let him do this for you, Beth dear. You can't spend the rest of your life in doubt. Your husband seems to have abandoned you and the children. He could be dead, for all you know at the moment.'

'Or more likely, he could have gone off with another woman.' She stared down at her hands, clenched into tight fists. 'He's a man who finds it hard to do without bed play. It'd not be the first time he's betrayed our vows.'

'Oh, my dear! How sad for you!' Margot reached out to hold Beth's hand, and the warmth of it, the caring, motherly look, broke through the barriers Beth usually kept between herself and the world.

A sob escaped her, then another, and before she could stop herself she was weeping bitterly, caught up in the older woman's embrace as the barriers between them crumbled.

When Beth stopped weeping, Margot lent her a handkerchief and said in a matter-of-fact way, 'You needed to weep. Now, you will let Finn help you, won't you?'

She still had to ask, 'If you're sure it's the right thing to do, my lady, if you don't feel I'm taking advantage of his kindness.'

'I'm quite sure. He's the sort of man who welcomes an opportunity to help others. He's had difficult times himself, so he understands how bad things can feel.'

She pushed the sodden handkerchief back into Beth's hand. 'Keep it. I've plenty of others and I doubt you have.'

Beth looked down at it. 'That just about sums it up, doesn't it? I don't even have a proper handkerchief to wipe my tears with, just some old rags.'

'Well, let this be the first of many handkerchiefs you own in your new life.' She stood up and pulled Beth to her feet. 'Go to bed now, my dear. You're white with exhaustion.'

'I thought everyone had already gone to bed.'

'I'd left my book downstairs in the sitting room. I was coming down to find it and instead found Finn, sitting brooding on the window seat at the end of the landing. He knew you were here, but didn't like to interrupt. I, being an interfering sort of person, had no hesitation in poking my nose in.'

Which made Beth smile as she went up the rear set of stairs to the attics.

When he heard someone come upstairs, Finn stopped staring out of the landing window and stood up. It was Margot and she looked thoughtful. 'How is she?'

'Sad. Weary. Worried.'

'Will she let me help her?'

'Yes. I've persuaded her.'

'And you'll stay here to look after Reggie while I'm away?'

'Of course.'

'I'll leave tomorrow, then. Late morning probably. There are some people I want to see before I leave town. I'll drive myself. You never know where a trail will lead and I may have to stay away for a day or two. When I was in the police force, investigating something, I often used to wish I had a motor car and now that I do my task will be easier. If it's going to take longer, I'll phone you.'

'Good. That's settled. Now try to get a good night's sleep.'

He nodded, but he doubted he would. He never slept well when he had something on his mind. Especially something as important as Beth's happiness.

22

Finn went up to see Jonah the following morning, forgetting that it was his friend's day for working at the pawnshop.

'Mrs Willcox is in the brewing room,' the cleaner told him. 'Would you like to see her instead?'

'Yes. Good idea.'

She walked across the yard with him and opened a door, whispering, 'Wipe your feet well. She doesn't like us to tramp dirt in, keeps everything immaculate, she does.' She then raised her voice to a powerful yell. '*Mrs Willcox!* You've got a visitor.'

Leah came to the door, looking flushed and rosy. 'Good morning, Finn. Did you want to see Jonah?'

'I did, but I'm told he's at the shop. I can call in there on my way. I wanted to let you both know that I'll be away for a day or two, but Lady Terryng will be holding the fort at Heythorpe House. With Daniel and Falding there to deal with any trouble, I'm sure Reggie will be safe. But is it all right if I suggest they consult you should any problems arise?'

'Of course. Anything we can do, you have only to say. And I'll tell Ben, too. I'm sure he'll be happy to help and he's still sleeping in the lean-to here.'

'I'll be back before the authorities can arrange another hearing. Judge Peters thought it could be decided informally, but he phoned to let me know that Buddle is kicking up a fuss about it and demanding a proper hearing. Why can't the stupid fellow let the matter drop?'

'You meet people sometimes who hold a grudge to the bitter end,' she said.

'There has to be more to it than simply a grudge against the boy. The judge has asked Sergeant Deemer to look into what Buddle's doing at the orphanage. He won't say exactly what he thinks is wrong but I can tell he's concerned about how the place is being run.'

'We're lucky to have a policeman like him in charge of our valley. Sometimes it feels as though the government has forgotten the more remote villages.'

'Well, considering how they're handling some of the troubles in the rest of the country at the moment, that's not a bad thing. I can understand men's frustration about being out of work for years. And now this government want to cut the benefits and apply a means test that will make them sell nearly everything they possess before they can be given any money. It drives some of them on hunger marches, but if they think they'll make any impression on the government, they're deluding themselves – or being deluded by those who're leading them.'

He stared into space for a minute, then added, 'I can't believe in any of these –*isms*, whether it be communism, socialism or conservatism. They're just vague and generalised theories and ideas. In real life, individual people are very different from one another. We're not flocks of sheep to trot along meekly behind a shepherd and his dogs.'

Finn realised he'd been ranting on about the political situation and gave her a wry smile. 'Sorry, Leah. I do worry about all these men who've been out of work for so long. I met many of them when I was on the road and listened to their stories. They're not out to ruin the country, they just want work that will put bread on the table and clothes on their families' backs, as well as some meaning to their lives. I'm thinking of starting one of those clubs that have been set up here and there, to give them somewhere to go during the day, at least, but till I've sorted out Reggie's future, I don't have the time to look into that.'

'I worry about the situation too. You mention the men, but there are women who need employment as well – widows, spinsters, young lasses just starting out. Perhaps we can work together on your club and include women in it?'

'I'd like that. Jonah too, perhaps.'

She hesitated. 'I think he has enough on his plate. He gets tired quite quickly lately. I'm sure he'd approve of the idea, though.'

'All right. To return to Reggie, I'm not letting him go to live with his aunt so close to Wemsworth and Buddle till his situation is sorted out once and for all. He's safer here, I'm sure.'

'He won't want to go and live there anyway.'

'No, and I won't want to lose him, Leah, believe me. But it's his family home, he has an aunt there and since he'll inherit it one day, it's where he belongs. Don't you agree?'

'Yes. In the meantime her ladyship doesn't seem unhappy to be here. I think she's been lonely. And she doesn't stand on her dignity, thank goodness.'

'She's good company, even if she does bark orders at people. I've never made friends with an older woman before.'

'Well, you two can plan Reggie's future once the problem of Buddle has been sorted out.'

Finn sighed. 'It can't happen too soon for me. I'm wondering if Buddle is afraid of Reggie giving evidence against him. The police are looking for a silver photograph frame Reggie's parents had. There doesn't seem to be any sign of it in the orphanage stores. Deemer got someone on the committee to do an inspection.'

'I bet Buddle got angry at that.'

'Furious. He said he always sold anything of value and put

the money into the orphanage's funds, and there were indeed small amounts of money added to them from time to time. But nothing had been itemised. And there was no amount higher than a shilling or two. A silver frame would be worth more than that, surely. I asked Charlie and he agreed.'

'What a tangle we human beings make of our lives sometimes,' Leah said quietly. Someone called to her from inside the huge shed, and she yelled, '*Coming!* Anyway, Finn, Lady Terryng has only to call on us if she needs help in your absence.'

'Thank you.'

As he walked back down to Heythorpe House, Finn couldn't help wondering about the way Leah talked about her husband. It didn't sound like someone who was in love with him, but someone who was fond of him in a sisterly way. And now he came to think of it, Jonah was always cool and friendly with his wife as well.

When he'd been married to Ivy, Finn hadn't felt at all cool towards her. He'd been in love, wanted to touch her, hold her hand, give her sudden hugs. And she'd been the same with him.

Jonah and Leah didn't touch one another in that way. They were just . . . calm and friendly.

Why was he worrying about his neighbours? He had enough on his plate with Reggie and Beth both needing his help.

Since they didn't have many cars in their new sales yard, or many customers either, Todd was keeping an eye on the pawnshop for Charlie from time to time.

When Finn came and asked to see Jonah, Todd said, 'You just missed him and he won't be back for about an hour. Can I help you?'

'No, thanks. I only wanted to let him know that I'm going

away for a couple of days. I've told his wife, so if you could just mention it as well, I'd be grateful.'

'I'll tell him.'

Since business was slow, Todd went to the front of the shop to watch Finn drive away and stare along the street. He was finding life a little too placid, to tell the truth, but that was only to be expected in the current economic climate. He had enough money saved from his years of working his way round the world to manage on for several years, especially if he continued to live frugally in the tumbledown cottage at the car yard which was rent free in return for doing some maintenance work on the place.

He was making a little money from selling cars every now and then, as well, so his savings might last even longer. When he came back to Lancashire from overseas, he hadn't realised how very depressed the north of England was. And yet, it was home and he still wanted to settle here.

He was concerned about Jonah. He might only have met him recently, but he had really taken to him. Jonah hadn't been looking at all well lately and Todd knew Charlie was worried sick about his brother, even though he was trying to hide it when they were together.

Life was cruel. There Jonah was with a pretty wife, and a very nice woman she was too, and his health had chosen this time to start going downhill again.

Leah was not only attractive but very capable. Todd was going to ask her to show him round her 'fizzy factory', as Charlie jokingly called it. Not many women would start up a business in the best of times, and she seemed to be making money even now by selling mainly to better-off people.

She was a quiet woman, friendly in a restrained way. Todd couldn't abide strident women. If she'd not been married, he'd have tried to get to know her better. He was more than ready to settle down. He smiled. It had taken him over a decade to get the urge to travel out of his system. But he'd seen all the places he wanted to explore out there in the wide world, places he'd read about as an eager lad.

He wasn't sure selling second-hand cars was what he wanted to do with his life, but it'd serve for the time being. He did enjoy fiddling with cars; was a good mechanic. The Army had taught him well. It was one of the practical skills that had helped pay his way round the world.

He held out his hands in front of himself and smiled down at them. Good, practical hands, those. Not pretty and with a couple of scars but they got jobs done.

Jonah didn't queue up at the doctor's like the poorer patients, but went into the surgery by another door at the rear. He didn't usually care how he entered but today he was glad of the extra privacy. Dr Mitchell had once said that better class patients, what few he had, didn't like to mingle with the poorer ones. And since he needed their money, he had to pander to their wishes.

Dr Mitchell examined him, listened to him breathing several times and then told him to put his clothes on again.

Jonah came out from behind the screen and waited for the sentence to be pronounced. When Dr Mitchell began fiddling with some papers, Jonah took the initiative. 'Just tell me, doctor. I know what I'm facing, just not when. I've already lived several years longer than they told me to expect when I left the Army, for which I'm grateful.'

'I can hear further deterioration in the way you breathe, worse than last time I saw you. Do you gasp if you need to exert yourself physically?'

'Yes. But I take my time and try not to get into situations where I need to exert myself too much.'

'What does your wife say?'

'I haven't discussed this with her.'

'Perhaps you should. She must have noticed.'

'I don't want her worrying needlessly. I'd be obliged if you'd say nothing to her or to my brother. I'll tell them when I have to.'

'Whatever you wish. But they've got eyes in their heads, you know. Um, you'd be wise to stay away from people who have colds or influenza this winter. I'm not sure you should go on working at the pawnshop, either. The clients who go there are . . . a very varied crew, many in poor health.'

'I'll do my best to avoid contamination,' Jonah said flippantly.

'Come back again in a month or so. Sooner if you need me.'

Jonah started walking back to the shop, jumping in shock as someone clapped him on the shoulders. 'Oh, Charlie! You startled me.'

'What sent you to the doctor?'

'One of my regular check-ups. You know what doctors are like with people like me, always wanting to keep an eye on us.'

'And what did he say? I can tell it's not good news.'

Jonah hesitated, then remembered what the doctor had said. Of course Charlie had noticed something. Perhaps it was time now to discuss how the family should deal with the inevitable. 'Can we go somewhere quiet? I need to talk to you.'

'Of course. I can get my car and—'

'I'll drive us in mine.' He couldn't face Charlie's erratic driving on top of the bad news. 'Why don't we go and have lunch at that little pub on the edge of the moors? If I remember correctly, they serve very nice cheese there: best Lancashire tasty.'

'I'll phone Marion and let her know I won't be home for lunch.'

'I'll phone Leah as well. We'll just say us two brothers felt like enjoying a good old natter, eh?'

From the sharp way his brother looked at him, he knew he'd judged correctly: he'd not been able to fool Charlie. His brother hadn't made his money by being stupid about people. And it would be good to make sure someone would be there to help Leah if . . . no, *when* the worst happened.

He mustn't fool himself. He'd hoped to spend longer with her, even to see her have his baby and watch it grow into a little child. But lately he felt weary, so very weary.

It was a good thing he'd always kept some distance from his wife, not shown her how much, how very much he loved her.

In the little pub called simply 'Top o' the Moor' the two brothers sat down in the snug, the only customers at this time on such a blustery day.

The landlady brought them freshly baked bread with some of her famous cheese and home-pickled onions.

'Marion will go mad at me for eating these.' Charlie picked up an onion in his fingers, bit half of it off and chomped on it with relish.

He waited for Jonah to start eating and when his brother pushed the plate to one side and bent his head over it, fighting to hide tears, Charlie abandoned any attempt to eat and put his arm round his brother's shoulders, saying simply. 'Whatever I can do, you have only to ask.'

Jonah leaned against him, fighting the unmanly tears and gradually calmed down.

'My lungs are getting worse quite quickly. It was always one of the possibilities. It's the expected long-term development, given the damage. I've actually been lucky, lived far longer than they predicted. Partly due to your help, for which I'm grateful.'

'You've been doing too much lately. I shouldn't have let you work in the shop.'

'I've enjoyed it. I've spent too much time sitting on my own feeling bored.'

'What does Leah say?'

'I haven't told her and I'll keep it from her as long as I can.'

'Is that fair to her?'

'It's how I want it to be. Was it fair for you to force her into marriage with a crock like me?'

'I think so. You needed a wife and she needed help. And anyone can see she's grown fond of you.'

'Yes. But not as a woman is fond of a man she's in love with. I've deliberately discouraged her from growing closer to me, Charlie, for her sake.'

'I've wondered.'

'I've made a will with Mr Lloyd's help, leaving her everything, but I've suggested she ask your advice financially.'

'She'll manage. She's a capable woman. But I'll help her if needed, of course I will. Well, I'm involved in the fizzy business anyway, aren't I?' He began fiddling with the food on his plate, the half-onion lying neglected now.

Jonah had something else he wanted to make clear. 'I hope she'll find someone else to marry one day, someone who can give her the child she longs for. And if she does find someone – don't try to stop her, Charlie. It's what I want most of all for her: a normal life.'

Charlie thumped his fist on his knee. 'How the hell do you manage to face death so calmly?'

'It's been my companion for a long time. During the war and ever since. I've been lucky, lived for over a decade since the war. But the past year with Leah has been the best time of all. You chose well.'

They sat in silence for a few moments, then Jonah squeezed

his brother's hand and picked up his knife. 'Now, let's eat this excellent food.'

But he couldn't force much of it down and even Charlie left some, which wasn't like him.

They didn't say much on the way back. Which wasn't like Charlie, either.

It was a relief to Jonah to have got it off his chest.

He'd be careful, try to last as long as he could, because life was sweet. But inevitably it was a losing battle.

That night he had a longing to hold Leah in his arms, to kiss her soft skin, to love her. She always welcomed his attentions and he wished he had the energy to pleasure her more often.

This time everything seemed much sweeter than usual and things went well. They even fell asleep in each other's arms.

She was up before him, as usual, and looked at him a bit strangely as she served his breakfast, a job she refused to give to any servant.

He was about to suggest they go out for a drive across the moors, just the two of them, next weekend, but he realised that this might lead to them getting too affectionate.

For her sake, he held back the words.

For her sake he ate quickly then left for the shop.

Oh, but it hurt to see the disappointed look on her face! And he had to use his handkerchief to wipe away the tears on the way down the hill.

23

Finn found Adsley easily enough, but as he'd guessed, it had changed a lot since the old map had been drawn, on which it'd looked like a village on its own far out in the countryside. Now, it was more like an outer suburb of Chester.

He went to enquire of the woman in charge of the Post Office whether a man called Neil Rawton picked up his mail from here.

'I can't tell you that, sir.'

'It's an emergency. His wife is looking for him.'

She looked a bit surprised at that, but still insisted she couldn't tell him anything about a customer.

There had been some advantages to being a policeman, he thought as he started to walk out. She'd have told him if he'd been in uniform, he was sure. Then he had an idea and turned round. 'Is there a church called St Crispin's nearby?'

'Not as you'd call nearby, but it's only five miles away,' she allowed.

'Could you please give me directions for getting there by car?'

He had to wait for these till she'd served another customer, but she was very clear in her directions. Not all people were, he'd found.

He drove slowly along the route she'd given him. Comfortable modern houses mostly, a few fields nearby, but not what you'd call open countryside. In fact, it was one of the new 'cottage estates' they were building to house people who'd been cleared out of slums. He'd read about them in the newspapers though he'd never driven through one before.

Mind you, from what he'd heard, the poorer people couldn't afford the rents charged by the local councils and people complained about the lack of shops and amenities, much as they liked having indoor bathrooms and lavatories. He slowed down for a while, interested in what he saw.

He found the church easily, a Catholic church.

Was Beth a Catholic, then? She'd never shown any signs of wanting to find a church and attend mass.

There was no one around to ask about Neil but the church door was open, so he went inside.

An elderly priest was praying at the altar. Finn made sure his footsteps echoed as he walked along the stone-flagged aisle, then he sat down in the front pew to wait.

A few moments later, the man crossed himself, got painfully and stiffly to his feet and looked round. 'I thought I heard someone come in. Can I help you, sir?'

'I hope so. My name's Carlisle and I'm looking for Neil Rawton. I believe he did some work for you a few months ago.'

'Oh, dear! Um, you'd better come into my office. We can be more private there. I'm Father Jerome, by the way.'

'Finn Carlisle.' He took the seat indicated in a cluttered little room with stone walls and a window overlooking the graveyard.

'May I ask why you're looking for him, Mr Carlisle?'

'His wife is the one who's looking for him and since I employ her, I'm helping out. She's still living near Rivenshaw. She received a letter from him recently saying he'd been ill and asking for money.'

Father Jerome stared in shock 'That's not possible. I saw his wife myself yesterday, or rather, his widow, and she lives in this village. And she couldn't have got a letter from him because he died three months ago.'

It was Finn's turn to stare. 'Perhaps we're talking about a different man, though how that can be, I don't know. Mrs Rawton gave me a photograph. Here.' He pulled it out of his inside pocket and passed it to the priest.

'That's the man I know as Neil Rawton and as I said, he died three months ago. I officiated at the funeral, such as it was. One of our poorer parishioners, Mr Rawton.'

'His wife has never visited this part of the country, and she's been working for me for the past few weeks in Lancashire, where she's lived all her life.'

There was silence as each man strove to make sense of this.

'Did he marry recently?' Finn asked after a while.

'Yes. About four months ago. I supervised his conversion to Catholicism, which had to be done rather hastily because the young woman was expecting, then I married them myself.'

'Neil Rawton married the woman *I* know as his wife about five years ago and has two young children by her. They all lived in the village of Ellindale till he lost his job on a nearby farm. When he couldn't find work he went on the tramp. He left almost a year ago. At first he sent her money, then the money and letters stopped.'

'Before we go any further, may I ask your part in this, Mr Carlisle?'

'As I said, I'm Beth's employer and she's working for me as a maid, together with two women who used to live next door to her. All three and Beth's two young children were turned out of their cottages recently. As I'd just inherited an old house and needed staff, I employed them and let the children live in the attics with them.'

He saw the disapproval on the priest's face, so added, 'There is nothing more in our relationship, and most certainly nothing immoral, I assure you. Lady Terryng is staying with me at the moment and she's supervising the servants and looking after the young boy who is my ward. It was she who suggested I find out why Beth received this letter.'

He paused, and when the priest continued to look perplexed, added, 'Beth realised someone was trying to make the handwriting look as if the letter was from her husband. It was asking her for money. She was suspicious because it was a poor imitation of his handwriting. Here. See for yourself.'

The priest's suspicious expression had softened during this explanation. He took the letter Finn was holding out and studied it, then shook his head sadly. 'It must have been a bigamous marriage with Deirdre then.'

'It sounds like it. And you say he's dead? What a mess!'

Father Jerome stood up, looking grim. 'Well, it could only be Deidre who wrote that letter so we'll start with her. She lives nearby. We can go and see her straight away. If she's committed a major sin like that I want to know because . . . well, there's a rumour that she's already found another man. She is, um, a frail vessel, I'm afraid.'

As they set out, he stopped suddenly and indicated a street to the right. 'I think I'll ask her father to come with us. He works as a gardener and his employer will give him an hour off if I ask her. If anyone can get the truth out of Deirdre and pull her into line, it's her father.'

A few minutes later Finn continued through the village with the priest and Patrick Colligan, both of whom were looking furiously angry. Well, he felt angry himself at the way Beth had been treated.

It was a good thing he'd undertaken this task or she'd have believed herself married for years to come. But he didn't let himself think of other outcomes there might be from this new situation. Not yet.

The cottage was small and tumbledown, the garden a mess

of weeds. Patrick led the way in, not bothering to knock. 'Where are you, Deirdre?'

A young and distinctly pregnant woman came in from the back garden, stared at the priest and her father, and turned to flee. But she wasn't quick enough and her father grabbed her by the arm and pulled her back into the house, thrusting his face close to hers. 'Will you never be done shaming us, Deirdre Colligan!'

'My name's Rawton now.'

Father Jerome moved forward. 'No, it isn't.'

Her face lost all its rosy colour and she swayed as if about to faint.

'Don't you go pretending to faint on me,' her father roared, giving her a shake. He dragged her across to the table and dumped her on a chair. 'Do not move an inch! We have questions to ask.'

Father Jerome turned to Finn. 'May I borrow the letter?'

He handed it over and the priest held it in front of her. 'You wrote this, didn't you?'

'I don't know what you mean.'

'Don't lie to us, girl!' her father roared, one big fist raised as if he was about to use it on her.

She shrank away from him and buried her face in her hands, sobbing loudly.

Both her father and the priest began shouting at her, and she wailed even more loudly.

In the end Finn cut through the noise. 'Quiet, everyone!'

They all fell silent and Deirdre hiccupped to a halt, her breath catching in her throat.

As this had been happening a young man had come in. 'I could hear her crying from the street. Leave her alone, you great bully!' he yelled at Patrick Colligan and pushed past them to her side.

To Finn's amazement, she looked up at the newcomer

adoringly. It clearly hadn't taken her long to get over her loss.

'I made her write that letter,' the young man said defiantly. 'She didn't want to but it's only fair that his family pay towards his child.'

'What family?' Finn asked. 'There's only his legal wife and she hasn't got two pennies to rub together because he has two children born in wedlock.'

'He said he had parents still living and a brother as well, not a wife,' Deirdre said, but she was avoiding her father's eyes.

He said angrily, 'I always know when you're lying, girl! You knew he already had a wife, didn't you?'

She shrugged.

'Why did you marry him when you knew it was all a sham?'

'You'd not have let me live with him otherwise, and I wanted to.'

'When this gentleman leaves, you will both come to confession and we'll discuss how you can make amends for your sins, your many sins, Deirdre Colligan,' the priest said sternly. 'We'll deal with this gentleman first, however.'

He turned towards Finn. 'You'll want papers showing that your maid's husband is dead. I'm afraid she'll get nothing else but the documents because he had no goods except what he carried on his back. Deirdre's aunt helped set them up here in the cottage so that they could marry and sorry I am about the two of them deceiving everyone.'

Deirdre was now holding her young man's hand. 'Well, I'm *not* sorry. Neil was fun and I liked being married to him, and John's even nicer *and* he earns more money. You're all a load of miseries, you are, and I won't come to confession again, so there!'

'*What did you say?*'

The young man stepped between her and her father. 'You'll not touch her again, either, Mr Colligan. She'd not have turned to me if you hadn't thumped her once too often.' He looked at the priest. 'I'll marry her, but not till the baby's born. I'm making sure no one mistakes me for its father on the birth certificate. And it'll go to an orphanage after she's got rid of it. I'm not bringing up another man's child. It's hard enough to provide for your own.'

The priest beckoned to the father. 'Come along, Patrick. There's nothing more you can do here at the moment. She's made her bed and she must lie on it.'

'She's no daughter of mine from now on, then.'

Finn suspected the young woman's father was glad to be rid of her in one sense. She was now looking adoringly at her new man again. Even well on in her pregnancy, she was pretty enough to turn anyone's head.

At the church the priest again took Finn into his office, pulled out a death certificate from a tattered file and slid it across the desk. 'I keep some paperwork here, because people can lose them, but this now belongs to the real Mrs Rawton.' He looked Finn in the eyes and added, 'I trust you. You have an honest face, Mr Carlisle.'

'Thank you. What did her husband die of?'

'He got drunk and fell off a wall. He was trying to walk along the top of it for a bet. Stupid way to die, but he wasn't a very clever sort of fellow, was he?'

'Is there anything else I need to do here?'

'I don't think so. I'll deal with removing the record of marriage and informing the authorities so that they can change their records.'

'Then there's nothing more to keep me here. Thank you for your help.'

As he walked out, he decided that it seemed an anti-climax to have things sorted out so easily. He'd expected a lot more trouble dealing with Neil Rawton.

He didn't feel like finding somewhere to stay for the night and decided he had enough time to drive home. He'd be back around midnight.

He filled up the car with petrol and stopped only once, for a meal at a roadside pub where other motor cars were parked.

What worried him was how best to break the news to Beth. How upset would she be?

There was little traffic at this time of night and few people to be seen on the streets. Finn saw occasional glimmers of light across the fields in the smallholdings and farms.

It was nearly one o'clock by the time he got to Rivenshaw, because he hadn't felt like driving fast. All the buildings he passed were dark. Well, most people would have been in bed for two or three hours.

He carried on up the valley, trying to work out how best to break the news to Beth, not only a dead husband but a bigamous one. He racked his brain in vain for a way to soften the news.

There were no lights on in Ellindale village. Or in his house. He parked the car inside the gates and sat easing his shoulders, staring down the slope at the house, which really felt like home now.

When he got out he saw a man moving towards him. He was wondering whether to duck for cover behind the car, but recognised Daniel. 'Everything all right?'

'At the moment, yes, but we had a couple of false alarms about intruders getting into the grounds earlier on – at least, I think they were false alarms. I couldn't sleep so I've been for a stroll round and had a chat to Tom, who's standing guard tonight. We didn't expect you back this late, sir.'

'I didn't expect to be back, but I found what I was looking

for quite easily and decided to drive home. There's nowhere as comfortable as your own bed, is there?'

He was stiff so stretched his arms above his head before moving away from the car. That probably saved his life, because a shot rang out and he felt the pain as a bullet slammed into his arm.

Before he could seek cover, Daniel had knocked him over and rolled him behind the car.

'Where did it hit you, sir?'

'Upper arm . . . just a flesh wound.' It hurt like hell, though.

'Stay there. The shot must have come from somewhere near the entrance. Let Tom check it out.'

From behind the car they could see Tom creeping up along the garden terraces towards the gateway, taking advantage of the cover of various trees and bushes.

But when he got there, he soon called back. 'There's no one here now, but the bushes have been flattened.'

'Don't move. Listen!' Daniel called. 'What can you hear?'

They could all hear footsteps crunching on the gravel of the road. Someone was running down the hill towards the village.

'Shall I go after him?' Tom called.

'Too late to catch him. We need you here. Mr Carlisle's hurt.'

Finn's arm was throbbing with pain and he could feel blood seeping between his fingers. He couldn't help groaning when he moved his arm incautiously.

'You're sure you're all right, sir?'

'My arm's bleeding quite heavily, but I think the bullet passed right through. It's hardly a mortal wound but it hurts.'

Tom called from the road. 'I can't see any signs of anyone else.'

'You stay on watch. I'll get Mr Carlisle to the house.'

Daniel stood up and helped Finn to his feet. 'Best go in

the back way, sir. I haven't got a front-door key. Can you bear to run, do you think? I'd like to get you across the open ground quickly.'

'Not run, no, but I'll move as quickly as I can. Wait a minute! What's that?'

There was the sound of a car engine from the village and it faded into the distance as the vehicle drove down the hill.

'That's a car, not a lorry,' Finn said. 'But there's no way of telling what sort of car.'

Tom called out to them. 'Sorry I couldn't catch him, sir. He must have left as soon as he'd fired the shot.'

'Let's get you into the house quickly, sir,' Daniel said.

'I can move on my own,' Finn said. 'I'd rather no one else touched my arm.' He set off, concentrating on putting one foot in front of the other and ignoring the pain as best he could.

This was not the way he'd expected to come home.

'I wonder why that man was waiting there for me tonight,' he muttered. 'Everyone in the valley seemed to be asleep as I drove through.'

'There was only one way they could have known you were away. Someone from the village must have sent word and they were waiting in case you came back. The moon is more than half full so they'd have been able to see you clearly.'

'Good thing I paused to stretch just then.'

'Yes. Probably saved your life. That wound looks to be about level with your heart. With your permission, I'll cut down those bushes tomorrow. They provide too much cover.'

'Good idea.'

'The noise must have woken somebody,' Daniel said. 'Look!'

There were lights on in the kitchen now, though the curtains remained drawn.

Nearly there, Finn told himself, gritting his teeth as he made it to sag against the wall beside the kitchen door.

Daniel rapped on the door. 'It's me and Mr Carlisle. Let us in.'

The inhabitants of Heythorpe House were not the only ones to be woken in Ellindale that night. Nancy Butler was a light sleeper and was jerked suddenly awake by a sharp single crack of sound.

What was that?

She lay in bed, listening carefully, ready to grab the poker from the side of her bed. She was always afraid of someone breaking into her shop.

She was snuggling down again when she heard running footsteps. She was out of the bed in a trice and went to stand by the window, taking care not to show herself or move the curtain more than she had to.

A man came tearing down the street and as his footsteps rang out, a car started up. It was parked just behind the main street from the sound of it. The car drove out almost immediately, stopped for the man to get in and accelerated down the road towards Birch End. She didn't know much about cars, not enough to recognise what type it was, but she could describe it, she was sure. Not a small car.

The man had been wearing dark clothing, a balaclava helmet and a scarf round his mouth to hide his identity. He'd be even harder to describe.

A few moments later she heard someone creep up the stairs and grabbed the poker but put it down again when she heard Lily's voice.

'Did you see the car, Nancy?'

'Yes. Very clearly.'

'I ran down into the shop in case someone was trying to break in. I saw someone standing in the shadows watching the car leave. I think it was Barry Judson, but I couldn't see him clearly enough to swear to that.'

'Who else could it be if there were people creeping about at night? I wonder what it was all about?' Nancy couldn't hold back a yawn. 'We'll no doubt find out in the morning. Let's go back to bed now.'

'I'm sure I won't be able to sleep.'

'I will. I've been feeling very tired this week, I can't work out why. I usually have lots of energy. Well, I've needed it to run the shop on my own.'

She made a shooing movement with her hands. 'Bed.'

She lay awake for a while, however, because something else had occurred to her this afternoon. She was late with her monthlies, but that could happen to anyone.

Her hand crept to her stomach. But what if . . . It was too early to tell, far too early. But it wasn't too early to hope.

What would Adam say if a miracle had occurred? Would he be as pleased about it as she was?

How long would it be before his divorce came through?

Oh, she was being silly. It was just wishful thinking. She couldn't possibly be expecting, not after only one time of making love with Adam.

24

Finn heard someone inside the house slide the bolts back and there was Beth standing holding the door open.

He could see all the details clearly as if everything was happening more slowly than usual. She was wearing a faded flannel nightdress with a shawl round her shoulders.

Margot was standing further back in the room, wearing a voluminous cotton nightgown embellished with lace and a velvet dressing gown half-fastened over it. She looked very determined as she levelled a gun at the doorway.

But for all her fine clothes, she didn't look as beautiful as Beth did.

'Ah. It really is you.' Margot lowered the gun and ordered, 'Stay back out of their way, Reggie!'

Finn tried to move up the step into the kitchen but stumbled and had to be helped across the threshold by Beth.

'You're hurt!' she exclaimed and immediately everything seemed to speed up as she took over. She guided him to sit at the kitchen table and he was glad of the help because he was feeling more than a little dizzy.

As Beth moved him gently into a position where she could check his injury, she exclaimed, 'Did someone shoot you! Was that the noise I heard?'

'Tried to. They didn't do a good job of it, though. The bullet only winged me.'

'There's a lot of blood. Reggie! Get me some hot water in a clean bowl.'

The lad, who'd been staring in speechless horror, hurried into the scullery.

Once Daniel had shut and locked the kitchen door, Margot put down her gun and came across to peer at Finn's arm.

'That's definitely a gunshot wound. Well, it was that which woke me as well. But I've never had to deal with wounds before.'

'I'll tend to it, your ladyship. I've tended to injuries and it can't be much different.'

For a moment, Beth's hand rested on his and Finn felt comforted, sure she could do what was necessary.

Falding moved into the light. 'Should I go outside and have a look round, my lady, make sure they've gone?'

She looked at Daniel. 'Any chance they're still out there?'

'No. Tom checked that straight away. It seemed to be only one man and he started running towards the village as soon as he'd fired at me. We heard a car drive off soon afterwards, so this must have been carefully planned.'

He joined the group studying Finn's arm. 'How bad is the wound, Beth? He's looking very pale. Do we need to phone Dr Mitchell?'

'What you need to do first is move back and give him space to breathe and me room to mop up the blood.'

Beth turned back to Finn and ordered sharply, 'Sit still and move only as I tell you, sir. Your injury will need cleaning if nothing else. And I'm sorry, but I'm going to have to cut your jacket and shirt sleeves away. They're ruined anyway. Kitchen scissors, someone.'

Mrs Jarratt got them out, gave them a wipe with a tea towel and handed them to her, avoiding looking at the oozing wound.

Beth cut the torn parts of his sleeves away to expose the upper arm. After a careful examination, she said, 'The bullet sliced across the outer side of your upper arm. It's left a long, deep gash and we need to make sure it's clean.'

'And the doctor?' Daniel asked.

'No need to involve him,' Finn insisted, wincing and managing not to groan aloud.

'I think it'd be better to call him out,' Beth said at last. 'He'll have ways of making sure the wound doesn't go septic and he'll have proper bandages. Ah, well done, Reggie. I did need another bowl of water. Put it there and fetch me a clean tea towel.'

'I'm no use here, so I'll go and phone your doctor if you know his number,' her ladyship offered.

Finn gave in to the inevitable. 'There's a list of local numbers on my desk, on the pad near the telephone.'

'Right.' Margot left the room.

He looked up at Beth, her face so close to his as she bent over the wound. Her hair was loose over her shoulders. She looked lovely and— 'Ouch!'

'Sorry, sir, but I have to clean away the threads that are caught in the wound.'

Daniel stepped back. 'Since you're here, Mr Falding, and your mistress has a gun, I'll go out again and keep watch with Tom. They've got away this time, damn them, but we'll be even more careful from now on.'

Her ladyship came back. 'The doctor will be here as soon as he can drive up the hill. Have you any idea who might want to shoot you, Finn?'

'It could be Buddle, I suppose.'

'Then it's my fault,' Reggie exclaimed.

'Nonsense!' her ladyship said at once. 'If someone commits a crime, it's their own fault. No one forces them to do it.'

Reggie was frowning in thought. 'Daniel said the person ran away fast?'

'Very fast,' Daniel agreed.

'Then it can't have been Mr Buddle *or* that Larry, who does things for him. They're both too old and fat to run fast.'

Finn tried to work it out. 'I must admit, I hadn't thought Buddle was the type to commit a murder, and what good would killing me do when it's Reggie he wants to get back at?'

'But who else hates you?' Beth asked. 'You've helped so many people round here.'

Finn could only think of one person. 'Well . . . There is another possibility.'

Everyone fell silent and waited.

'I have a cousin who might have expected to inherit Uncle Oscar's estate, especially as I'd been away for a year or two. I suppose Digby might be trying to get rid of me. I don't know him well enough to say for certain. I'm not even sure I'd recognise him if I met him in the street these days. My parents didn't have much to do with that side of the family.'

'Would Heythorpe House pass to him if you died?'

'No. I can leave it to anyone I want, so I've made a will naming, um, someone else.' He avoided looking at Reggie as he spoke. 'Mr Lloyd keeps the will in his safe, so it should be secure enough there.'

Her ladyship was frowning. 'We seem to have attracted enemies, even out here. I think the war left a lot of people more capable of violence than before, I really do. Not to mention the ones who smuggled guns back to England afterwards, and who knows what happened to all the secret weapons? They certainly haven't been handed in to the authorities. Do you think I'd better send for more of my people to help protect us?'

'We'll ask Sergeant Deemer's advice about that in the morning,' Finn said. 'I'm going to report this incident to him.' He moved his left arm without thinking and sucked in a sharp breath.

Beth took his hand and placed it gently back on the arm of the chair. 'Let me finish washing the rest of the blood off now, sir. And please, try not to wave your arm around.'

Her touch was gentle and she had beautiful hands, roughened with housework, but shapely with long fingers. Again he stared at her and for a moment she looked right back at him. He was very conscious of her as a woman, the way he'd been conscious of Ivy, the way any man would be conscious of a woman he was attracted to.

People would say she was too far below him socially to think about in that way, but now she no longer had a husband so he needn't care about that and— He realised Carrie was staring at them and Margot had said something. 'Sorry. What did you say?'

'Dr Mitchell recommends you stay downstairs and keep that arm still till he's seen it. You should also drink plenty of fluids to make up for the blood loss.'

'Very well.' The moment of connection had passed and Beth was now carrying the bowl to the scullery. He didn't want her to move away, but he didn't want to betray his feelings for her, either. Not yet, at least, and certainly not in front of other people.

'Shall I make us all a drink of cocoa?' Mrs Jarratt said. 'I don't know anything about wounds, but I can soon heat some milk, and cocoa is very soothing. Beth, you should make Mr Carlisle comfier. He could lay his poor arm on a cushion if Reggie will fetch one from the sitting room.'

The boy ran out at once.

Beth hurried back to Finn's side. 'Yes, of course. I should have thought of that. Lean on me, sir, and we'll move you to the armchair.'

'I don't need—'

'We don't want you to stumble and bump your arm. Mr Falding, could you please move that chair closer to the fire?'

She had her arm round Finn before he could protest and though she was inches shorter than him, he could feel how sturdy her body was. He moved slowly because it did indeed hurt to jar that arm.

He didn't want to let go of her to sit in the chair, but of course he had to. Reggie had brought back a cushion, which Beth placed under his arm.

'Are you . . . more comfortable, sir?'

'Yes. Thank you.' He realised Margot and Carrie were watching the two of them and wished they wouldn't.

Mrs Jarratt broke the spell. 'Did you find out what happened to Beth's husband, sir?'

'Yes. But I think I ought to tell her about it privately.'

Beth looked round the kitchen with a wry smile. 'I don't think you'll have found out anything I need to hide from the people here, sir. And perhaps telling me will take your mind off your injury.'

'I'd prefer to tell you privately.'

Margot looked round the room. 'Quite right, Mr Carlisle. When Mrs Jarratt has made the cocoa, the rest of us will leave you and Beth to talk. We'll go into the sitting room.'

'Maids don't usually sit in there,' Mrs Jarratt muttered as she spooned the cocoa into the saucepan of milk and set out the cups.

There was nothing wrong with Margot's hearing. 'It's all right to sit in there when I invite you.'

'Oh, well, I shall enjoy the luxury, then, my lady. Thank you.'

Once the cocoa was ready, Mrs Jarratt gave everyone a cup, then looked at her ladyship in a silent question.

'Come along, everyone.' Margot stopped just outside the kitchen door. 'Where's your daughter, Mrs Jarrett?'

'We left Dilys upstairs to keep an eye on the children. They didn't even wake up, nor did our Gillian. I reckon Dilys will have fallen asleep again. That girl can sleep through a thunderstorm.'

'That's all of us accounted for, then. Let's leave Mr Carlisle to tell Beth what he found out.'

When they were alone Beth folded her arms and stood waiting.

'Do sit down,' Finn said.

'I'd rather stand, sir.'

He didn't argue, just tried to prepare her for what was coming. 'It's not good news, I'm afraid.'

'I never expected any good news, not with Neil involved. What's that fool done now?'

'He's dead, Beth, and has been for three months.'

'Dead!' She clapped both hands across her mouth for a moment and then repeated more softly, 'He's really dead? You're sure of it?'

'Yes. I have the death certificate in my coat pocket and a priest looked at the photo you gave me and confirmed that the dead man was Neil. I hope the certificate didn't get damaged in the attack.' He tried to pull it out from what was left of his jacket but his arm hurt too much. 'Can you get it out of my inside pocket?'

She had gone very still and white, and though she eased the crumpled piece of paper out of his pocket, she made no attempt to spread it out and read it. 'What did he die of?'

'A fall.'

She frowned. 'I don't understand how that could kill him. He was still young and strong.'

'He was apparently trying to walk along the top of a high wall and fell down the steeper side, hitting his head on a rock.'

'Oh. I see. It'd be for a bet. He had a good sense of balance and won money once or twice doing that sort of thing in dangerous places. I went mad at him the last time for taking the risk and he promised not to do it again. He never keeps— I mean, never *kept* his promises. Did someone knock him off the wall?'

'No. I'm afraid he was drunk.'

'Typical! His children could starve but he had to have his beer. I can see from your expression that there's something else. Was there a woman involved? He was a womaniser, given half the chance. I don't know why he ever married me, except it was the only way he could get me into bed.'

She waited for a while, then broke the heavy silence. 'Tell me the rest. I can face what I have to.'

'Well, the full truth is that he made a bigamous marriage four months ago and has left a young woman carrying his child. It was she who wrote the letter to you.'

Beth's eyes sparkled with anger, not tears. 'Oh, damn you, Neil Rawton! I'm glad I'll never see you again. Glad!'

But then she did burst into tears and Finn couldn't leave her standing sobbing on her own, so got up. Putting his good arm round her, he pulled her to sit on the chair arm and lean against him. 'Shh, now. Shh. At least you have the children, Beth.'

Her voice was muffled because she was huddling against him. 'But what am I going to tell them about their father?'

'That he died. Nothing else. You'll still have your job here. I'll make sure you and they don't lack for anything.'

It was a few moments more before she gulped and dabbed her ladyship's handkerchief to her eyes. 'They're the best thing that came from our marriage, those children are, the only good thing. I stopped loving him a long time ago.'

'They're delightful children and—'

They both looked up as they heard a car come up the lane and turn into the parking area.

'That'll be the doctor. And look at me, leaning against you.'

Beth scrubbed her eyes again and blew her nose. 'Thank you for telling me so gently, Finn, and for comforting me. That was kind of you and I needed a bit of comfort.'

'It's easy to be kind to you, Beth. I admire you greatly.'

Her mouth fell open in surprise.

'You're a hard worker, a good mother and pretty—' He broke off as someone answered the front door and Margot's voice boomed across the hall.

'This way, doctor.'

Beth went to fiddle with the cooking range, presumably to provide some reason for having a flushed face.

Finn leaned back and wished the damned doctor had taken longer to get here.

When Dr Mitchell examined his patient, he was shocked to see the gunshot wound. 'You were shot in your own garden? How can this happen in 1931? People played with the guns they'd smuggled home just after the war, and we had some injuries then, but I haven't had one for ages.'

'This person wasn't playing,' Finn said grimly. 'If I'd not stopped to stretch after hours of sitting in the car, he'd have killed me.'

'*On purpose?*'

'No doubt about it.'

'That's incredible.' Dr Mitchell broke off to direct Beth to supply him with a bowl of boiled water, clean cloths and something to put the bloodstained cloths in afterwards, then he set about dealing with the wound.

'You're lucky, Mr Carlisle. It's a long gouge, deeper at the back but the bullet passed through and didn't lodge anywhere. And Beth cleaned it up nicely. I'm going to put a few stitches in this end, where the wound is deeper, and you'll have a scar, no avoiding that, but as long as you keep the wound clean, it should heal quite quickly because you're a healthy chap.'

He turned to Beth. 'I've seen you dealing with other people who've been hurt. I'm going to give you some instructions and trust you to carry them out to the letter.'

'Yes, doctor. I'll do that.'

When the wound had been stitched, Dr Mitchell continued his questioning as he bandaged it. 'I presume the attacker got away?'

'Yes. He was a very fast runner and there was a car waiting for him in the village.'

'More than one person involved then, and the attack carefully planned. Have you alerted Sergeant Deemer?'

'I'll do that in the morning,' Finn said. 'He can do nothing tonight and probably nothing tomorrow either.'

'I suppose not, but he should be made aware of the incident. I don't know what the world is coming to, I really don't. Though this has never been a quiet, peaceful part of England. It's too hard to make a living here. It doesn't breed peaceful, gentle people.'

He stood up. 'Where can I wash my hands?'

Beth showed him into the scullery and found him a clean towel.

When Dr Mitchell came back, he said, 'Come and see me in three days, Mr Carlisle, so that I can check that it's healing properly, unless it looks as if it's infected, in which case come to see me straight away. Get someone else to drive you around for the next week or so, though.'

When the doctor had gone, Falding volunteered to help Mr Carlisle to bed. 'I used to be the batman to her ladyship's son in the army and I helped the other officers sometimes, so I have some experience in helping wounded gentlemen get to bed.'

'Thank you. I must admit I'm feeling rather weary and battered now. I'll be all right in the morning, I'm sure.'

Finn looked across at his group of helpers. 'Thank you for

all you've done tonight, everyone. Do stay in bed longer tomorrow morning. I'm going to.'

When the others went up to bed, Margot put a hand on Beth's arm. 'Do you want to talk about what Finn found out about your husband? I can see you're upset, however you try to hide it, and I'm happy to help you in any way I can.'

'It might be as well for you to know, your ladyship.' Beth explained what Finn had told her.

Margot patted her companion's shoulder as, inevitably, Beth wept again. 'Well! What a villain your husband turned out to be! A bigamous marriage, indeed! You'll be better off without him, far better.'

'Yes. I know. But it still hurts; makes me feel so humiliated.'

'He's the one who should be humiliated, but he's beyond that now. Look, if you're ever in need of help that Mr Carlisle can't supply, don't hesitate to come to me.'

'Thank you.' She was both surprised and touched by this offer.

'Will you be all right now, dear?'

'Yes, your ladyship.'

Only then was Beth allowed to go to bed.

The stairs felt like mountains. Her narrow bed felt cold and unwelcoming, and though she'd vowed a few minutes earlier not to shed any more tears for Neil, she did.

And for herself and her children, too.

She was a widow now, a widow with two small children to raise. That was going to be hard.

Thank heavens for Finn's kindness! And for this job and home he'd given them.

How strong his arms had felt round her tonight. If only . . . She banished that thought quickly, but couldn't help it creeping into her dreams.

25

The older inhabitants of Heythorpe House were feeling anxious the next morning, not to mention tired after their disturbed night. But Beth's children played happily together as usual in the corner of the kitchen, where they had a 'cave' made from a wooden clothes horse covered with a ragged old blanket.

She watched them for a moment or two, drawing strength from the mere sight of them, so young, so innocent and trusting. At only five and three years old they had no real understanding of death and Felix at least couldn't even remember their father. She didn't try to make them understand what had happened.

'Time enough when they grow older and ask about him,' she told the others crisply, trying to make up for her weakness of the previous evening by working even harder than usual.

'Are you going to put on any mourning?' Mrs Jarratt asked.

'No. I don't own any black clothes and I don't have the money to buy them, even if I wanted to, which I don't. Besides, he's been buried for over three months now. It's just . . . an official change of status for me. No real change in my life.'

'You don't seem very upset about losing him.'

'How could I be? I hadn't seen him for more than a year, or even had a postcard from him for over six months. And when he pretended to marry someone else he lost the right to my affection.'

Mrs Jarratt sighed. 'Aye. That were bad of him. He was too charming for his own good, that one.'

Not when you lived with him for a while, Beth thought. Not charming at all when he was in a bad mood. But she didn't say that. What good would it do? Best to forget him now, she reckoned, and get on with her life.

She left the children playing with their toys and went to beat the seats of the chairs in the unused dining room. And if she hit them harder than was necessary and imagined she was thumping Neil each time, who was there to know?

At one point she heard her ladyship in the hall telephoning Sergeant Deemer and alerting him to what had happened.

Shortly afterwards she heard Finn get up and come downstairs. They hadn't dared take him up a cup of tea, because he didn't like them to go into his bedroom before he was dressed.

When she had beaten out the worst of her frustrations on the chairs, she went back into the kitchen and saw Falding shaving Finn in the scullery because of his bad arm. He seemed to feel her eyes on him and turned, giving her a half smile then studying her face, as if trying to work out how she was feeling.

She gave him a quick nod and went across to talk to her children. She really must stop staring at Finn. Though he was a fine sight, so upright and clear-eyed. The bandage on his arm spoke of the attack, though.

What would she and the children have done if he'd been killed?

How would she have coped then?

Sergeant Deemer arrived just before ten o'clock to find Daniel digging up a row of overgrown bushes that must have been growing there untended for a long time, judging by the size of their roots and the difficulty he was having getting them out.

He greeted Deemer with, 'I'm not giving anyone else a hiding place to ambush people from and the sooner Mr Carlisle has a road made to the back of the house, the better. It'll be much safer for him to drive round to the kitchen door and go straight into the house. *And* I'm going to ask Ben up at Spring Cottage what it would take to build a wall to support a road round to the back.'

Deemer was intrigued by this display of loyalty. 'Does Mr Carlisle get a say in this?'

'Aye. But where his safety is concerned, so do we. Us folk in Ellindale owe him a lot and if he won't take more care of himself, we shall have to do it for him.'

'He's given a few villagers jobs.'

'Yes. He's been a godsend round here, especially the way he provides a glass of milk for the children each day. My little nephew is looking better than he has done for ages, and the farmer is happy to be selling his milk so regularly and so close to home. And now Mr Carlisle is talking about giving the kids an apple each twice a week. It's got something called a vitamin in it, fruit has, doctors have discovered, and that's good for folk, he says.'

'Good of him.'

Daniel grinned. 'And no one will have trouble getting kids to eat apples, eh, sergeant?'

Deemer smiled. 'My brothers and I grew up on the old saying: an apple a day keeps the doctor away. My mother might not have known why it worked – these vitamins are a new thing – but she knew it was good for us.'

'It was Dr Mitchell as suggested it to Mr Carlisle. He wants to stop kids getting sick, and Mr Carlisle agreed. And what with the milk and telling them to play out when it's sunny, they say there won't be much chance of our kids getting rickets up here in Ellindale. I thought rickets were just part of childhood, but they're not. A lot depends on what the kids eat. Eh, isn't modern science marvellous to find all that out?'

Daniel realised he was talking too much and gave a shame-faced grin. 'So any road, what with one thing and another, I'm doing my bit to keep Mr Carlisle safe in return.'

'You carry on doing that, lad, and I'll do my part by trying to find out who's coming after him and why. We stopped Sam Griggs a few months ago when that sod tried to set up a protection racket in Rivenshaw and by hell, we'll stop any other villains attacking folk in our valley.'

The two men exchanged nods and got on with their day's work.

Deemer was shown into the sitting room, where Finn had been persuaded to settle on the sofa, with Lady Terryng occupying a comfortable armchair across from him.

Finn smiled a welcome and indicated a chair. 'Please excuse me not standing up to greet you, but once I'd had my break-fast, Beth insisted I have a rest.'

'She's playing the role of nurse now as well as housekeeper, eh?'

Margot answered for him. 'I think Finn hired a treasure there. That young woman has a good head on her shoulders. She asked me to sit with Mr Carlisle and make sure he obeys the doctor's orders, which shows she knows what he's like. He's been twitching to be up and doing, but we don't want him straining that arm.'

Deemer chuckled. 'It'd take a braver man than me to disobey the ladies when they've got their minds set on some-thing, Mr Carlisle. You're well served by everyone here, it seems. I just passed the time of day with Daniel, who's digging up the bushes so that no one else can hide in them and attack you.'

'I blame myself. I should have thought of doing that before.'

'No one is perfect. Now, let's get down to business. Can

you give me every single detail you remember about the attack last night?'

When the incident had been described and further questions answered, Deemer frowned. 'You're right. That was definitely planned in advance, or I'm a Dutchman, and it sounds as if they wanted to kill you. You be careful from now on, lad.'

After some thought, he added, 'I'd not have expected that of Buddle. Theft, yes, cruelty to children, yes, but not outright murder.'

'Have you found out anything more about him?'

'We're getting there gradually. You leave that to us from now on, Finn lad, and concentrate on getting better. We don't want anyone hurting you again, now do we?'

He picked up his cup, drained the last mouthful of tea and stood up.

'I'll leave you to rest.'

'I don't need any more rest. I've only been sitting around,' Finn protested, scowling at Margot.

But when she looked across at him a few minutes later, he was fast asleep.

Lily had been told to watch out for the police car returning through the village and stop it. She did that and took over the shop while Nancy and the sergeant went into the back room for a private talk.

'I don't know if it's any help, sergeant, but we were woken last night by a car starting up in the village and driving off down the hill. Only no one here owns a car, except for Mr Carlisle and Mr Willcox, so we looked out to see what was happening.'

'Ah. Go on.'

'This morning my customers have been telling me that Mr Carlisle was shot last night, in his own garden too, and the thief ran down to the village and left in a car. It has to be the car Lily and I saw.'

'Ah,' he repeated in tones of even greater satisfaction. 'What sort of car was it?'

'What sort? Eh, I don't know enough about cars to tell you that, but it wasn't a big one. It must have been about the size of Mr Carlisle's car, come to think of it, not Charlie Willcox's or Lady Terryng's. Lily did a drawing of it this morning.' Nancy took a piece of paper off the mantelpiece and handed it to him.

He stared at it. 'Bit difficult to tell the make. Could be one of several. Would you recognise it again?'

'I doubt I would, but Lily might. She knows more about cars than I do.'

'Mind if I have a word with her?'

'Not at all. I'll take over in the shop and send her back here. But there's another thing we need to tell you: Barry Judson stood watching the car drive away. We both saw him. He didn't come out of his cottage to do that; he was already outside near where the car was parked.'

The sergeant positively beamed at her. 'That's very useful information indeed, Nancy love. I'll have a word with him before I leave.'

Lily could only back up what Nancy had told the sergeant, and had no idea of the make of car, but he thanked her for her drawing. Then he walked across to the row of cottages where the Judsons lived.

Mrs Judson opened the door, looking so apprehensive the sergeant was immediately suspicious. 'Can I see your husband, please?'

'He's in bed. He doesn't get up till late of a morning unless he has a chance of work.'

'Ask him to get up now, please.'

She looked at him pleadingly, but he pointed a finger to the stairs.

She went up them, muttering, 'It's all right for some. That'll put him in a bad mood for the day, and it's me who'll suffer.'

While she was upstairs having a short, sharp row with her husband, Deemer walked to and fro studying the room. There was a full half loaf on the breadboard, its cut end down, and she'd been drinking a cup of tea, strong tea by the looks of it not the weak stuff you got from reusing tea leaves. That meant there was money coming into the house. And yet the breadwinner didn't have a job.

Judson was his usual uncooperative self. He denied any knowledge of a car parked near his house the previous night and also denied standing outside to watch it leave.

'Several people saw you.'

'Then they were lying, trying to get me in trouble, I 'spect.'

'I don't think they were lying.'

Judson folded his arms and glared at the sergeant. 'I deny being outside and you won't get me to say no different.'

Deemer had seen enough to realise there was something going on, but he decided not to do anything about it straight away. He was a strong believer in giving a villain enough rope and letting him hang himself.

Then, just as they set off, he had a thought and once they were out of sight round a corner, told his driver to stop.

He went into the shop again the back way and told Nancy about Judson denying it and calling folk liars. She grew very indignant, but he held up one hand.

'Doesn't matter. It gave me an idea. It'd waste a lot of police time to try to get anything out of Judson, but if you were to tell some of the men in the village what you saw, maybe they could do something about him. Unofficially as it were. They stick together, the folk up here do. What do you think?'

'You're a cunning man, sergeant.'

'I'll leave it at that for the moment . . . unless anything else is found out, or someone has further information to give me. In which case they'll know where to find me or can phone me at the station.'

'Write your phone number down for me just in case we find anything out. I'll let them use the phone here for free.'

When Mrs Jarratt came in to buy some groceries that afternoon, Nancy asked her to send Daniel down after the shop had closed. She said it openly in front of the other customers.

'Oh? Has something happened?'

Nancy explained what she'd seen the previous night and made sure she spoke loudly enough for three other women waiting to be served to hear every word.

Mrs Jarratt leaned closer and whispered, 'Hasn't he to come secretly, then?'

Nancy leaned even closer to whisper back, 'No. The more who see him the better.'

That whispered exchange would intrigue the other three, she thought, and raised her voice to add, 'I think Barry Judson has been up to something and I think Daniel should know. We don't want anyone hurting Mr Carlisle again, do we?'

'Definitely not. You couldn't work for a nicer man and we servants eat well every day. And he buys all that milk for the children. I'll tell Daniel to come and see you.'

As he watched the sergeant drive away from Heythorpe House in the police car, Daniel decided to go and find out exactly what the sergeant had said to the others.

When Beth refused to tell him, he asked to see Mr Carlisle and when she hesitated, he told her he'd go and find their employer himself if she didn't pass on his request.

Finn came in just as Beth was arguing about it and said,

'Let's go and sit outside, Daniel. I'm going mad doing nothing in that sitting room, though I haven't much to tell you because the sergeant won't tell me anything, either. He's trying to keep me out of mischief.'

Beth gave him a stern look as he moved towards the door.

He grinned at her. 'I promise you I won't do anything but sit on the old bench and chat.'

'Hmm.'

He winked at her as he passed and she blinked in surprise at this familiarity before an answering smile escaped her.

Mrs Jarratt found the two men sitting on the bench as she came hurrying back from the shop along the narrow path that led to the rear of the house. Daniel stood up at once to take her basket.

She looked doubtfully at Finn, then said to Daniel, 'I've got a message from Nancy. She wants you to nip down to see her after the shop closes tonight.'

'I've a good mind to go down now.'

'She was very definite. You're to go *after* the shop shuts.'

'But people will see me whatever time I go.'

'Nancy's an intelligent woman,' Finn said mildly. 'She must have some reason for the request. I could go with you. If I rest all afternoon, this arm should be a lot better by then.'

'She only asked for Daniel,' Mrs Jarratt said doubtfully.

'Let me do as she asks, sir. I'll come and tell you what she wants as soon as I get back.'

Mrs Jarratt escaped into the kitchen, where Beth soon got out of her what was going on.

'I'm going to wait up for Daniel to come back tonight, then,' Beth said in the end.

'I'll wait up with you,' a man's voice said behind her.

She spun round to see Finn standing there. 'Oh, sir! You gave me a shock, creeping in so quietly.'

'I'm following your example and eavesdropping,' he said,

which caused her to blush. 'We'll wait for him together. And when she finds out what's going on, Margot will probably join us.'

'I'll wait in the kitchen and bring him to you.'

'We'll all wait in the kitchen so there's no light showing at the front and it looks as if I've gone to bed early. I'm thinking it might be helpful if certain people believe I'm more badly hurt than I really am.'

Beth sighed. 'It's all such a tangle and I don't want you to go running into any more danger.'

'Don't you? I'm glad you feel like that.'

She flushed and didn't seem to know what to say, which made him feel even more hopeful.

Then Reggie came in and everyone got on with their work. They didn't want the boy going off doing something rash, so the less he was told, the better. He had a tendency to act first and think later, like many lads of his age.

26

That evening Daniel strolled down to the village, whistling cheerfully. But the whistling died away because though he couldn't see anyone, he could sense people watching him from their front windows and see net curtains twitching here and there.

He called on Nancy, who explained what she'd seen and what Sergeant Deemer had said they should do. 'The people in the village can keep an eye on Judson better than anyone, now everyone's sure it was him passing on the information about Mr Carlisle to whoever it was.'

Daniel sat thinking, turning this over in his mind. 'We'll have to plan exactly what to do next. We aren't going to let anyone come and attack our Mr Carlisle again, but we don't want Judson finding out we're on to him and telling those he's working for what Mr Carlisle is doing, not till we're ready to pounce, anyway.'

There was the sound of a car and they both broke off their conversation to listen. When the car pulled in behind Nancy's shop, she went to peep out of the back window and came back slightly flushed. 'It's Mr Harris, um, come for his ginger beer.'

Daniel managed not to smile at this obvious fib as he stood up. 'Enjoy your visitor, Nancy love.' He patted her shoulder and whispered, 'It's about time he sorted out that divorce, don't you think, then you can stop pretending he just comes for ginger beer?'

'It takes time to get a divorce finalised.'

'Well, he's a nice chap, worth waiting for.'

She gave him a little push towards the door. 'Get on with you.'

Then she turned with a happy smile on her face to welcome the man she loved, the man who had made it clear he loved her too.

Daniel walked up the street and decided to have a half pint while he was here.

When he went into the pub, one of his friends stood up and called out, 'He's here. I'll guard the door, as we agreed, and make sure no one overhears us.'

There were murmurs of 'Good lad', and 'Aye, better be careful'.

Daniel looked round in surprise as some of the older men pushed a chair towards him and his father moved out from behind the group.

'We heard you were coming down to see Nancy. Time you told the rest of us what's going on, our Daniel. You're not the only one as cares about Mr Carlisle's safety, you know.'

'I know that, Dad.'

'It's not just the safety of everyone at Heythorpe House I'm thinking about,' his father went on, 'but of us village folk, too. We don't want anyone else thinking they can come here and shoot decent people or they'll be doing it in broad daylight next. If more cars come and park here at night, we've decided to go out and ask them straight out what they're doing. And if they've not got a good reason to be there, a few of us will stand round the car watching.'

There was nodding and a general murmur of agreement from those present and even Daniel was surprised at how determined they sounded. He decided to take a risk, counting on Mr Carlisle supporting him. 'Just a minute, Dad.'

He went across to the landlord who was standing on the outside of the bar, as if to ally himself with what was going on.

'Will you trust Mr Carlisle to pay for a round, Mr Dewey? I haven't got the money with me, but I'm sure he'll agree. It'll make people feel even more linked to him and to one another, you see.'

'If you say he'll pay, I'll trust you. You know him better than we do, though we're getting to know him, aye, and to like what we see. Is he hurt bad?'

'No. But he's pretending to be worse hurt than he is.' Daniel took a deep breath and turned to speak to everyone. 'Nancy wanted to tell me that she saw Judson standing near the car with whoever shot at Mr Carlisle last night. He denies it, but he would, wouldn't he?'

'I saw him out there, too,' someone else said.

Another joined in. 'Yes, so did me an' the wife. Well, you can't help looking out when you hear a car at that time of night, can you?'

'I'd like to push that Judson over the nearest cliff!' one man said vehemently. 'If there's any trouble round here, you can bet he'll be involved.'

'Pushing him over a cliff is tempting but it won't catch the one who's paying him, will it? Whoever that is, he's the one we need to stop,' Daniel said. 'I think we should lay a trap. But Mr Carlisle is the one who's best at working out things like that, so we can't leave him out of the planning, can we?'

'We could work something out ourselves if we had to,' one man said dryly. 'We're not stupid.'

'We don't have to. Any road, he'll want to be involved.'

'What about that ladyship as is staying there with him?' one old man asked. 'She's not from round here. How do we know we can trust her?'

'I think we can,' Daniel said. 'She's very civil to deal with, doesn't put on airs and graces. And after all, she's Reggie's aunt.'

'That's certain, is it?'

'Judge Peters thinks so.'

'Ah well, it must be right, because no one can fool *him*,' one man said bitterly.

The men laughed, not unkindly. 'He saw right through you the one time you were up before him.'

'I were younger then an' stupid. I learned my lesson and I've not done owt like that again. Never mind me, how are we going to do this?'

'We could invite Mr Carlisle down for a drink tomorrow,' Daniel's father suggested. 'Work it out with him.'

'How do we keep Judson out of it?' someone asked. 'He'll smell a rat if we keep him out of here and he sees Mr Carlisle coming in.'

There was silence, then Daniel began thoughtfully, 'How about we do it this way . . .'

But he had to stop when the man on watch called out, 'Judson's coming towards the pub.'

They broke up into their usual groups and by the time Judson came in, two were arguing over a game of draughts, and others were playing darts.

Daniel was sitting with his father, discussing his nephew's better health since the milk had been supplied.

No one talked to Judson or invited him to sit with them, but that was the usual pattern. Only a few labourers from outlying farms ever drank with him.

He stood at the bar sipping his drink, exchanging an occasional remark with Don, and listening.

Why had he never noticed before how hard Judson listened to what folk were saying, Daniel wondered. Was this where he picked up information? How did he pass it on? Probably when he was out and supposed to be looking for odd jobs.

Nancy said Sergeant Deemer had seen food lying around in their house when usually those kids had to beg scraps from the neighbours.

Well, Mr Bloody Judson, you won't be spying on your neighbours for much longer, and I hope you'll end up where you belong: in prison, he thought.

Lily sat in the side room of the shop reading her library book by the light of a table lamp and sipping a glass of Mrs Willcox's delicious ginger beer. This was her reward for staying out of the way when Mr Harris called on her aunt. They made no secret now of wanting to be alone together.

She'd drawn the curtains, not wanting to be on show to people outside and had the table lamp angled towards her book. After she finished her chapter, she put the book down and decided to treat herself to a couple of humbugs, another treat allowed by Nancy as long as she didn't go mad and eat up all the profits. She didn't bother putting the shop light on because she knew her way round the shelves blindfolded by now.

So when a man suddenly appeared right outside the shop, she was startled. He must have been walking very quietly because she hadn't even heard footsteps approaching. He pressed his face against the shop window and she froze, waiting to see what he was doing. Did he intend to break in? If so, she'd scream for help.

He did nothing that she could see, just stared in towards the faint light showing from the parlour at the back, turning his head towards the sitting area where she'd been reading where the light only showed faintly as well.

She didn't think he'd seen her because she was well back in the shadows behind the counter. She didn't move till he took a step backwards and walked on, going in the direction of Heythorpe House or Spring Cottage, or perhaps both.

He was still moving quietly, staying on the softer verge. She didn't hesitate. Strangers who moved round the village like that after dark meant trouble lately. She knocked on the sitting-room door and went straight in.

'We need to phone Mr Carlisle and Mr Willcox at once and warn them. A man's gone up the hill, keeping to the shadows and not making any noise as he walks.'

Nancy and Adam had been kissing but broke apart and Lily immediately picked up the phone and asked to be connected to Mr Carlisle.

After a brief conversation she phoned Spring Cottage as well.

'It's a pity there's no phone at The Shepherd's Rest,' Adam Harris said. 'Let's go and watch for him coming back.'

They all three went into the shop, hiding behind the displays.

'Everyone's keeping an eye on strangers,' Nancy whispered, 'so we won't be the only ones watching him tonight, I'm sure.'

Finn put the phone down and went into the kitchen to fetch Falding. Tom was on duty outside again, but Finn wanted to see what the stranger did, so he and Falding went out by the small door in the laundry and walked round the house the long way, along the side away from the road. That way, any intruder would be unlikely to see them coming.

Sure enough, a man stopped at the entrance to the parking area, hardly visible, just a darker shadow standing very still. You'd not even have noticed him standing there if you hadn't been warned.

Finn and Falding froze and hoped he wouldn't notice them, either, but would continue to watch Tom, who had his back to the entrance.

Tom walked down near the house and disappeared behind

it, on his way to check the back garden and the outhouses.

When the watchman was out of sight, the stranger moved inside the entrance, turning towards the place where the bushes had been the day before as if he knew where to hide. He stopped dead at the sight of bare earth and rocky ground instead of foliage, then glanced quickly round the garden before slipping out on to the lane again and turning back towards the village.

'Good thing Daniel ripped out those bushes,' Finn muttered. 'I'm going up to the gate to see where that fellow goes.'

'I'll come too. Her ladyship lent me her revolver, just in case, so if there's trouble I'll be able to protect you, Mr Carlisle,' Falding whispered. 'I can move quietly when needed.'

'All right.'

They returned a few minutes later and went round to the kitchen the normal way. Tom was just coming down from checking the area behind the outhouses and when they told him what they'd seen, he was mortified not to have noticed the intruder.

'I'll go and check that he really has gone into the village and down towards Rivenshaw,' Tom said at once.

'Take care he doesn't see you.'

'I grew up in Ellindale. I know all the shortcuts through the village. I'll see him come out on the other side if I hurry. If I don't see him, it'll mean he's hiding somewhere else, though there's only one person as would take him in, isn't there?'

'Well? What did you see?' Margot asked the minute Finn and Spalding joined her in the kitchen.

'A chap came into the garden, saw that the bushes were missing so he had nowhere to hide close to the road, and went straight back towards the village. I think he must have been intending to observe us again. I wonder how long he's been doing that for?'

'Or perhaps take another shot at you,' Margot said.

'Well, we'll never know but Tom's gone to check whether he goes straight through the village or stops to chat to anyone.'

Before he could say anything else, Beth intervened. 'Sit down and rest now, Mr Carlisle.'

He did as she told him because now that the excitement was over, he had noticed the throbbing in his arm and how tired he felt.

When Tom came back, he reported that the man had gone through the village without stopping, sticking to the shadows. 'Fat lot of good that'll do him. I weren't the only one watching him.'

'Did you see what he looked like?'

'Scrawny little chap. Couldn't see his face because he had a scarf wrapped round it, but he wasn't bald, must have had dark hair.'

'That can't be Buddle or his assistant,' Falding said at once. 'Reggie's right. They're big men and Buddle is bald on top. Even from where we were standing, I could see the fellow was far too thin for either of them. And I doubt those two will have anyone else involved in their nasty tricks because they don't like to share their money with anyone.'

'What do they do with their money?'

Falding shrugged. 'I don't know exactly, because they don't have much to do with their neighbours, but they do go into Manchester sometimes. Could it be your cousin keeping watch this time, do you think, Mr Carlisle?'

'Possibly. Forewarned is forearmed, whoever it is. Once this arm is better, I'll do some investigating of my own.'

'You're waving your arm around again, Mr Carlisle,' Beth said. 'You've been favouring it as you moved about. It's hurting, isn't it? Try to rest it, stay in the armchair.'

He smiled ruefully. 'I thought I was hiding the discomfort.'

'Not from me, you weren't. Let me just check that it's not bleeding then I'll make us all some cocoa.'

She had slipped off the sleeve of his jacket before he could say anything and unbuttoned his shirt. Her fingers were as light as butterflies on his skin.

He noticed how intently the others were watching and heard them sigh audibly in relief as she confirmed that there was no sign of bleeding. It touched him that they should care.

They were like a family now, he thought, as she pushed his hand away and buttoned the shirt up for him. Shared adversity often brought people closer.

Would Beth let him stay close to her once his arm was better and the crisis was over?

He'd find a way to persuade her, if there was any chance she was interested in him in that way, he swore to himself. And he wasn't going to wait long to do it.

When they all went to bed, Beth lay in her small attic room worrying. Not just about Finn, either. How was she going to make sure her children were safe if intruders kept coming up the valley?

Would things ever settle down in Ellindale again? Not to be like before, never that, but to a more peaceful life.

She thought about the news of Neil's death, as she had several times during the day. She felt guilty at how quickly she was getting used to the feeling of freedom that it gave her.

Freedom for what, though?

Finn was so different from Neil, a man worthy of being loved, one who was kind to everyone he knew. And he was a fine-looking man, too. She didn't think she'd ever get free of caring about *him*.

But women like her didn't marry men who owned big houses. She knew that. They could work for them, though. Work, watch over them, make sure the details of their daily lives flowed smoothly. If she could continue to work for him, at least she could be near him.

That would have to be enough.

Only . . . the way Finn smiled at her sometimes, well, she didn't know what to make of that. It wasn't the smile of an employer. It was the smile of a man who liked a woman.

But he'd never tried to take liberties, never done anything but help her and give her hope, so what did that smile mean?

She fell asleep smiling herself at the thought of him. And dreamed about him. Not for the first time, either.

27

Sergeant Deemer telephoned and apologised for not coming to see them in person. 'Only, I don't want anyone to know I'm planning something, Finn lad.'

'Go on.'

'I want to deal with Lemuel Buddle and his cronies once and for all. We know about Larry Clapton but suspect there are others he calls in sometimes. Trouble is, he's very cunning and the only way I can think of catching him out is to set a trap. I have Judge Peters' permission. I wonder, would you let her ladyship take Reggie to visit the family home and stay overnight? We hope it'll tempt Buddle to try something.'

'That'd put Reggie in danger.'

'I know. But not a lot of danger, because I'll go to the house as soon as it gets dark with one of my men, and we'll stay there till Reggie and her ladyship leave to come back here. They won't be left on their own, I promise you.'

'And if Buddle comes with more than two men?'

'There will be three of us, with Falding, and there are guns in the house. Buddle isn't likely to bring a lot of men, though. He seems to work mainly with Clapton, who has been arrested for violence more than once. But in my book, Buddle's worse than his henchman, because he really enjoys hurting kids, doesn't tackle grown men if he can help it.'

Finn still felt hesitant about agreeing to Reggie going.

'Look, lad, not to put too fine a point on it, I'm afraid of Buddle killing one of the lads in his charge at the orphanage.

He seems to be getting more violent with them the older he becomes.'

Finn gave in. 'Oh, hell! I can't say no to that, not with other children involved. But you'll take care of Reggie, not let him out of your sight for a minute?'

'You have my word on that.'

'Very well. When do you want to do this?'

'Two days from now. That will give them time to hear about the visit casually. I have a man who sometimes does little jobs for me and he'll let the information drop in the right places.'

'And what about the sergeant in charge of that area?'

'I'll inform Taylor what's going on *after* it's all over and done with. I have some worries about him, too. And Finn, while this is going on, there's to be no taking risks with your own life. Don't give that cousin of yours, if that's who it is, the chance of finishing the job he started.'

'I won't.' Finn chuckled suddenly. 'Anyway, if he tries anything outside, he'll have to get past Daniel, and if he comes inside, he'll meet Beth and she's as fierce a watchdog as any I've met.'

'She cares about you.'

'I care about her. But this isn't the time to go courting. Afterwards . . .'

'Afterwards, you can maybe think about your own happiness for a change. You're due for some happiness. Now, tell her ladyship to wait till mid-afternoon to take Reggie to Netherholme, then they'll only be alone there for an hour or two till dusk. And they're to stay inside the house and keep a gun handy.'

'I'll make that very clear, believe me.'

Of course, Reggie was thrilled at the idea of helping lure Buddle to his doom. Her ladyship was less eager, but had to admit Deemer's scheme seemed to be foolproof as far as the boy's safety went, though whether Buddle would fall into the trap was anyone's guess.

Beth and the other maids were informed of what was going to happen and she looked as doubtful as Finn felt.

Afterwards, she caught him on his own in the library. 'I don't like this plan, sir.'

'Nor do I. But whether it succeeds or not, I don't think Reggie will come to any harm or I'd not have agreed to it.'

She still looked dubious. 'I have an uneasy feeling about it. I get these feelings sometimes and . . . well, they usually come true.'

'I get them too. It saved my life more than once when I was a policeman. But how can I refuse when the safety of the other orphans depends on Buddle being trapped and locked away for a good long time? That's why I've agreed to take a small risk with Reggie.'

'I suppose so. As long as it's small.'

But she continued to look worried.

And he continued to feel worried, too.

Reggie was in high spirits on the way to Netherholme and eventually her ladyship spoke to him more sharply than she ever had before.

She regretted her harsh words as soon as they'd been spoken, but one look at his sulky, rebellious expression and she kept the apology to herself. The lad had to learn good manners. Finn was too indulgent with him.

When they got to the big house she tried to mend matters between them and Reggie's scowl lightened a little. However, he grew sulky again when she wouldn't let him go outside unless accompanied by an adult. The trouble was, all the adults were busy just then. She had some important phone calls that really ought not to be further delayed, and even Falding wasn't available just now. He was worried about something that sounded wrong in the car engine and didn't want the vehicle breaking down on the way back.

'But if I just kicked a ball to and fro outside the front door. I'd be perfectly safe,' Reggie protested.

'No, I said. You couldn't do that anyway, because we haven't got a football. All my brothers' childhood toys were packed away when they were killed. We'll get them out again when you come to live here. Look, sit in the library. I'll only be a short time and I'll find you a book to read then join you after I've made my calls.'

Reggie sat down with the book, almost sighing loudly at how boring it looked – who cared about capital cities of the world? Luckily he realised in time that his aunt would take offence at him sighing and call it ungrateful. But it wasn't fair. Here was a big house, with lovely level gardens that were just asking to be played football on, and he had to sit indoors reading a boring old book.

The sunshine outside was too tempting and while she was making her phone calls he went across to the window, turning the key in the lock and letting the sunshine fall on his skin. He'd just go outside the big french doors and stand on the shallow step that ran across outside. She couldn't complain about that, surely? How could it possibly be dangerous?

It had been dull and cloudy the day before and today's sun felt lovely on his face. He couldn't resist taking another step or two away from the house, but walked to and fro parallel with it, not going far away at all.

But he forgot everything when he heard what sounded like a puppy yelping and whimpering pitifully nearby. Maybe the poor thing was caught in a trap. It was certainly hurting badly. He couldn't bear to leave an animal in pain.

Once Reggie had left, Finn tried to occupy himself by going through some more cupboards in the rooms they weren't using, but it was hard with an injured arm and he gave up after less than half an hour, leaving items scattered all over the floor. He went to look for Daniel and found him outside studying the side of the garden nearest the road with Ben.

The thought of being able to drive to the back door got him interested as well and he quickly agreed to let Ben draw up plans for a track that would curve round the wall, going slowly down to the back of the house. It would have to have support walls and proper drainage, but the ground there wasn't solid rock, so it ought not to be too expensive to make a level pathway. A gravel surface would be enough for the few vehicles that would use it.

And a big bonus was that doing the job would provide work for the men from the village. Every bit helped.

When he came back, he went to sit in the room he used as an office. But the warm glow left by the new project soon faded. He scowled at the desk. There were still papers to sort through, because the previous occupants of the house never seemed to have thrown anything away.

Only he couldn't settle, he just couldn't, and with a growl of annoyance he stood up, intending to go back outside.

But Beth was standing at the door with one hand raised to knock.

'Did you want me?'

She sucked in breath as if she didn't know how to start.

'What's wrong?'

'I don't know,' she blurted out. 'I just feel there's something gone badly wrong.' She patted her chest. 'Reggie's in trouble, I know he is. Don't tell me I'm being silly, Finn. I hope you do prove me to be silly but I *beg* you to go and find out for certain that he's all right.'

This was confirmation of his own feelings of apprehension. 'I don't think you're silly. I've been feeling the same thing

and the worries have been getting stronger. It happens sometimes and if I ignore the feeling I regret it.'

He picked up the phone and tried to call Margot, but no
one answered. Surely there were maids even if she was busy?

His feeling that something was wrong grew stronger.
'There's no answer. In a house with several servants. And I
don't think you're being silly, Beth. Or if you are, I'm silly
too.'

She looked up at him and he couldn't resist it a minute
longer. He bent and kissed her cheek.

'This isn't the time, I know, but I've been wanting to do
that. Your skin looks so soft and it's rosy again now you're
eating properly.' He waited but she was staring at him, mouth
open in shock. But she hadn't protested or pulled away, had
she?

'Have I upset you?'

She shook her head. 'No. But you – I – we shouldn't.'

'We couldn't have done anything when we thought you
were married, but what's to stop us now? Once the current
problem is sorted out, I want to court you, Beth, do things
properly; see if we suit. If we do, I would never insult you
by anything less than marriage, I promise you.'

'Oh, Finn.'

When one of her hands fluttered up to touch his cheek
very lightly, he smiled, grabbed the hand and pressed a kiss
on it.

For a moment they smiled foolishly at one another, then
reality took over. 'First things first, I have to find Reggie,
make sure he's safe. I'm going to Netherholme straight away.'

'I'm coming too.'

He stood still for a moment, testing the idea of her coming
and it seemed right. 'Can you leave the children with Mrs
Jarratt and Dilys?'

'Yes, of course.'

'Then we'll do it. Go and get your outdoor things and I'll see Daniel, ask him to get help to protect the house while we're away.'

As he spoke, someone knocked at the front door. He hurried to throw it open.

Leah stood there. 'Sergeant Deemer rang. He'd given his word to the Area Inspector not to contact you, so he telephoned us. He's been taken off the case with Buddle and Taylor, the sergeant in charge of the Wemsworth area, has been put in charge of it. Only Deemer suspects Taylor is hand in glove with Buddle. He said he wasn't telling you what to do, because he promised not to, but he'd not be surprised if you went to Netherholme as quickly as you could and brought Reggie home.'

'We tried to phone Margot and no one is answering, so we were just about to leave anyway.' He gestured to Beth. 'We've both been feeling uneasy, we don't know why. What you've told us makes me think we should get there as quickly as we can.'

He stopped, frowning. 'I think I should take a couple of men from the village with me. Just in case.'

'I'll come too.'

He looked at Leah in amazement.

'I can drive our car there and I have a gun; know how to use it too.'

'We'll leave in ten minutes, then.' He turned to Beth. 'Sort out care for the children and get your coat.'

He went to find Daniel and explained what was going on. 'I'm leaving you in charge of defending this house and Spring Cottage. It doesn't matter how many men you have to hire. Keep everyone here safe. We have one known enemy and one possible other enemy.'

'I'm coming with you, sir, but I'll get some men to take over the defence of the house. I know who to ask. Pick me up in the village.' Daniel didn't wait for an answer, but set off running, yelling over his shoulder as he went, 'And I'll take over the driving from there. We don't want you making your arm worse.'

Finn turned to find Beth behind him, a very determined expression on her face and an object in her hand. 'What's that?'

'A sharpening steel for the smaller kitchen knives. It'll fit in my pocket and won't show. It'll do some damage if I have to hit someone. I hope I don't have to use it, but I won't hesitate if it's necessary.'

'Good thinking.' He led the way outside.

When Leah went home to get her car, she explained quickly to Jonah what was going on.

'I'll supervise the defences at Heythorpe House,' he said. 'Should you?'

'Yes. I intend to use what's left of my life to good purpose. And I did learn to think strategically in the Army. I haven't forgotten that. I'll load your gun quickly while you get ready. Go on. And take Ben with you. He's good in a crisis. I'll phone Charlie and see if he can think of anything else to do.'

Two cars set off down the hill. Daniel was waiting for them in the village with two men. One got into Leah's car, one into Finn's. Daniel took over the driving of the latter and they continued down the hill at a faster than usual speed.

In Rivenshaw, Todd was waiting as they turned into the main square and waved them down. 'Jonah rang Charlie. He's not an experienced fighter, in spite of his war service, but I am. So I'm coming with you. I'll follow you in my own car.'

As the three vehicles drove off, Beth leaned forward from the back seat to speak to Finn, who was sitting in the front next to Daniel. 'Do you think we're making too much of this? Three cars and six men.'

He shook his head. 'No, I don't. I feel . . . anxious, as if something dreadful is about to happen. And if Deemer phoned Jonah to suggest we rescue Reggie, then it must be urgent. He'd not disobey an order lightly.'

'But it won't be Sergeant Deemer we're dealing with now, will it?'

'No. And I'm afraid if this Sergeant Taylor forbids us to get involved, I shall have to disobey him. I *know* Reggie is in danger, I just know it.'

'I feel that way too.'

The man riding with them said, 'You both sound as if you trust your instincts.'

'I do,' they both said at the same time.

'So do I. More than I've trusted some senior officers I've served with. Anyway it's better to be safe and not needed than sorry you did nothing, especially with a child involved.'

'Exactly,' Finn said.

When Margot went to look for Reggie, she found the french windows open and no sign of him. Her heart sank. She called him several times and there was no answer. She walked the length of the house, still calling out.

To her surprise no one came out of the stables to see if they could help her. There were only a couple of horses now, her mare and a placid gelding for the governess cart the servants used to get into the village of Wemsworth. But Falding had his quarters there, with a groom and two of the gardeners. Someone should have heard her.

She found the four men in the room where they ate their meals, three of them slumped across the table in a jumble of empty plates, one of them spread out in an old armchair. At first she thought they were dead, but when she checked them found they were breathing slowly and deeply.

She kept her eyes open in case someone tried to creep up on her, but everything was silent.

She shook the men and Falding, whose plate still had some food left on it, half woke, blinking at her dopily. She saw the bucket of water they kept filled as a fire precaution standing near the door and hurled its contents over them.

Leaving them spluttering and gasping and, she hoped, waking up, she made her way into the house. She locked the french doors behind her and rang for one of the maids.

It didn't take her long to take out and ready the small gun she sometimes carried in her handbag but she also took the time to load a revolver to keep openly in her hand.

There was no sign of a maid coming to answer her summons, so she went to check and found three of them in the servants' dining room, sleeping as soundly as the grooms had been.

She didn't take time to fill a bucket with water but rang the local police station. But there was no answer, so in desperation she rang the Rivenshaw police station, keeping her back to the wall and the revolver in one hand.

'Deemer here.'

'Margot Terryng here. My servants have been drugged and Reggie's missing.'

'*What?*'

'What's more, I can't get an answer from Wemsworth police station.'

'Lock yourself in somewhere till help arrives. I'll try again to phone Sergeant Taylor, but if no one answers, I'll come to you myself.'

'I'm going outside to look for Reggie. He left the house via the library so I'll start there.'

'Lady Terryng, no!'

'Buddle won't dare attack me. And I have a gun.'

As she put the phone down, she heard someone creeping

along the corridor from the kitchen to her sitting room and went to stand behind the door.

The youngest maid peered into the room. 'My lady?' Her voice wobbled.

Margot waited a moment or two but there were no other sounds, so she said softly, 'Shh. Come in and shut the door quickly, Biddy.'

Apart from a little squeak of surprise, the girl managed to keep silent.

'What's happened, my lady? The others are all asleep and I can't wake them. Are they going to die?' Tears began rolling down her cheeks.

'Pull yourself together or you'll be no good to me. Someone's drugged their food and they'll wake up again in a while. How is it you weren't eating with them?'

Biddy flushed. 'I got into trouble with Cook and she told me to go and scrub out the storeroom before I had my meal. I've only just finished.'

'You've been lucky.'

'I don't understand.'

'Someone has kidnapped Reggie. Are you brave enough to help me rescue him?'

Biddy straightened up. 'Yes, I am.'

'I don't suppose you know how to fire a gun?'

'No, my lady, but I could hit someone with a poker, if that would help. I always was a tomboy till I started work here and I'm very strong. That's why I keep getting into trouble. I don't like being shut up indoors.'

'Find any poker you like and come with me. If anyone attacks you or me, hit out good and hard. Don't hold back.'

'I will.' She picked up the poker from the hearth, hefted it and said, 'This one will be fine. It's nice and heavy.'

Margot led the way out.

28

As the dizziness passed, Reggie struggled instinctively against the ropes that bound his hands and feet, but they were tied tightly.

'Stop that!' Someone clouted him over the side of the head and he lay still, recognising the voice. The room was dim but as his eyes grew used to the semi-darkness he knew the man looming over him, knew him all too well.

Buddle. He waited for the familiar fear to paralyse him, but for some reason it didn't. Instead anger filled him. But he wasn't going to show that, so he tried to cringe and look terrified as he'd done when he lived here.

'If you can't remember to obey orders from now on,' Buddle said slowly and clearly, 'I'll have no further use for you and you can stay in here and rot for all I care.'

'Sorry, sir,' he whispered. He didn't even try to look round to find out exactly where he was: he knew that too. In the secret room. He lay and waited for the next order. He'd have to obey it . . . for the time being.

The anger was still there, damped down, but waiting.

'If you make any noise, any noise at all, it'll be the last noise you ever make,' another voice said.

Larry, Reggie thought, a man who could turn violent at the drop of a hat. So he continued to keep quiet.

'We'll leave him here to get used to being back,' Buddle said. 'They'll come looking for him, but they won't find him if he's kept in here. And by the time they come back we'll have a court order giving us custody, because I've persuaded them that he's too dangerous a youth for a woman to handle on her own.'

Larry gave his hoarse chuckle. 'And if anything should happen to her, he'll inherit and we'll still be in charge of him and his money.'

'We fell lucky with this one. Who'd have thought he'd inherit all that?'

Buddle was still talking as if Reggie was too stupid to understand them. He wasn't. And he wasn't going to let them get their hands on his inheritance. What they didn't realise was that now he had friends who would help him. Good friends.

'Better put a gag in his mouth, just in case,' Larry said. 'Lads can get very impulsive till they're taught to obey orders. He's only half-trained and being with that chap up the hill undid a lot of our hard work.'

'Yes, I suppose we'd better gag him. But not too tight. We don't want this one to suffocate.'

Now the terror did jolt back into Reggie. A boy had vanished a few weeks ago, and they'd been told he'd escaped. Had Alan been killed?

He didn't struggle, but let Larry tie a gag in his mouth and then lay back quietly.

Buddle laughed and kicked him in the side. 'I think he's starting to believe we mean what we say.'

When they'd gone, Reggie looked round. He'd been in the secret room before because he'd found it one night when he was searching for a way out. He'd managed to hide and get out again after they'd left. He didn't think they knew he'd been here, that he knew exactly where it was and how to open the secret door.

He should have told Uncle Finn about this room, but once he'd escaped, all he'd wanted to do was forget Wemsworth Orphanage.

There was more stuff in here now than there had been last time. He was lying between piles of boxes, some of them precariously balanced. Had all this been taken from the orphans? No, it couldn't have been. Most of the others had nothing. Where had the stuff come from, then?

He rolled from side to side, looking round carefully. He could knock one or two of the piles of boxes over with his feet, because though they were tied together, he wasn't fastened to anything else, just left lying on the floor. But what good would it do to topple the boxes? He'd still be tied up and the door would still be locked, so they'd come and beat him afterwards for doing it.

Worst of all, he'd still have the gag in his mouth, still feel he was choking. It was hard not to panic. Only the thought of Uncle Finn and Aunt Margot kept him from rolling around like a madman.

He tried to think how to get the ropes off, but it was no good. They were tightly tied and he was helpless.

What were his friends doing now? Were they looking for him? They must be. Surely they'd find him and rescue him, whatever Buddle said.

That stopped his panic. His Aunt Margot would definitely have missed him. She'd probably have called Uncle Finn, or Sergeant Deemer. They'd be on their way, surely they would? Buddle couldn't just take away a boy and no one come after him, cunning as he was.

How could he be ready to call out to them with a gag in his mouth, though? Well, he couldn't. He'd have to find some other way of attracting attention if necessary because this secret room was well hidden. He'd only found how it opened by sheer chance.

He lay back and waited, for what he didn't know. Time seemed to be passing very slowly. At one point he heard voices in the distance, but mostly the world outside was silent.

A couple of tears escaped him, but he gave himself a good telling off for that, and no more followed.

When Deemer left the police station, he didn't go home because that was the first place people might try to contact him. He took the car but not his young constable. He wasn't going to lead a young officer still learning his trade into disobedience and dismissal. No, he had to do this himself. And if he failed, he'd deserve to be dismissed.

He took the car and was surprised when Charlie Willcox ran out of his shop and waved to him to stop.

'Why aren't you at Netherholme searching for the boy?' Charlie demanded. 'Surely someone told you that Reggie was missing?'

'Yes, her ladyship telephoned me. But I've been taken off the case and it's been handed to Sergeant Taylor.'

'Oh, hell! I thought you were on the point of catching that sod out.'

'I was, but someone up the line seems to believe in him and I was ordered to hand the Buddle problem over to the local people. That was before Reggie went missing, though.'

'Well, as it happens, Taylor's wife has just pawned another piece. Good thing you gave me a description of her.'

'Show me.'

'It's inside the shop.'

Deemer pulled the car over to the side of the road, got out and followed Charlie to the back room. The piece of silver that Vi showed him made him close his eyes in sheer relief. It was easily recognisable. This was it. Proof positive.

'I've got to get some men to support me. I can't tackle them on my own.'

Charlie grinned. 'There are several men already on their way there. They're in three cars. If you drive fast, you'll catch up with them. And what's more—'

But he was talking to himself. Deemer was out of the shop and getting into the police car. He set off along the road. He'd go to Netherholme first, he decided, then on to Wemsworth, because he felt pretty certain that's what the others would do. If they left Netherholme and went towards Wemsworth they'd pass one another, because there was only one road.

Hang orders from above. He had proof against Taylor now. He wondered if Taylor even knew what his wife had done? He'd not have sent her into Rivenshaw to pawn the item, or even given it to her.

That gambler brother of hers must be desperate for money once again. He was Taylor's Achilles heel, but an honest man wouldn't have stolen to help him. And Taylor had 'confiscated' a lot of goods.

It'd be a pleasure to arrest his fellow officer. He hated rogue policemen with a passion that almost equalled his loathing of people who bashed children.

Margot and Biddy searched the grounds and found a puppy tied up in a painful manner, whimpering only faintly now.

'Oh, the poor thing!'

Biddy was on her knees untying it before Margot could stop her, so all she could do was hold her revolver at the ready and keep a watch for anyone who might attack them.

'That's how they caught Reggie,' she said grimly when Biddy stood up, cradling the puppy in her arms. 'He came to see what was hurting the poor creature. Look! There are signs of a struggle, flattened bushes and marks in the ground. No, don't move forward. We might be able to see how many men there were.'

They studied the ground.

'Two, I think, my lady, from the footprints.'

'Yes, so do I. Now, run and shut the puppy in a stall in

the stables. Give it some water but never mind tending it. We have to find Reggie so come straight back.'

Margot stood with her back against a tree, listening intently, not intending to be caught out as her nephew must have been.

When she heard footsteps, she could tell there were at least two people and slipped behind the tree. Had the kidnappers come back?

But it was Falding who was with Biddy, weaving slightly as if he was still dizzy, but with hair so wet she guessed he'd doused himself in more cold water to try to wake up.

'You all right?' she asked him.

'Getting better. Biddy says they've taken Master Reggie. I'm sorry I let you down, my lady.'

'How could you have guessed that something had been put in the food – though that means someone here was in with them.'

'One of the gardeners is missing. Patrick, he's called.'

'He must have been paid and then fled.'

'He was wild to emigrate to Canada, so he'll be on his way to Liverpool, I should think.'

'We'll tell the police about him later. I'm going to cut across the fields to Wemsworth Orphanage. No use driving up in a car and advertising our approach, and anyway there's a good shortcut. Better to take them by surprise by going that way. But if you can't keep up, Falding, we'll have to leave you behind and you can do your best to follow us. I don't want to lose any more time. I blame myself for letting Reggie out of my sight.'

He didn't protest at that.

Just then there was the sound of a car drawing up at the house.

'Go and see who it is, Biddy, but don't let them see you. Come back and tell me if you know who it is.'

Of course the maid didn't obey. She shrieked out, 'Mr
Carlisle! It's Mr Carlisle, my lady.'

Margot exchanged long-suffering glances with Falding. 'I
hope she's right, or we're in trouble. No wonder that girl's
always in hot water with Cook or the housekeeper. She can't
obey an order to save her life.'

'She'd make a better outdoor servant than indoor. And
you're going to need a new gardener.'

'Good idea.'

Margot made her way cautiously through the shrubbery,
sighing in relief as she saw Finn standing by a car and two
other vehicles drawn up behind his. Finn tried to make sense
of what Biddy was trying to tell him, but the series of
disjointed phrases was hard to follow. In addition the girl was
waving her arms and a poker about wildly till Leah took the
implement off her.

'Calm down and start again slowly,' Finn said in exasper-
ation.

'There's her ladyship! Let her tell us.' Beth pointed across
the lawn.

Daniel ran across, intending to help her ladyship, but she
directed him to help Falding, who was still clearly dizzy.

'Where's Reggie?' Finn demanded.

'We think Buddle's got him.'

'How the hell did that happen?'

'My fault for leaving him alone in the library. But they
were clever, enticed him outside with an injured puppy.'

His expression was grim. 'Where do you think they'll have
taken him?'

'To the orphanage, only it's a big rambling building built
by the same architect as my house, and it'd be hard to search
every nook and cranny without a small army of helpers. I
think we should hide in the grounds and see where he and
Clapton go.'

'No sign of Sergeant Taylor?'

'No. I phoned the station, but there was no answer, so I phoned Deemer and he said he'd come.'

'He's putting his job at risk.'

'I know. If he loses it, I'll find him another. Never mind that. Reggie's what matters. We can cut across country to the orphanage on foot. It's not far that way, we might be able to see what they're doing.'

Finn considered this, then shook his head. 'I want men and cars stationed nearby as well. We don't want to leave ourselves with no means of pursuing them.'

'Why don't I drive into Wemsworth with Beth in the passenger seat? They'd be less likely to suspect two women of looking for Reggie,' Leah suggested. 'We could hide two men in the back, under blankets.'

Daniel nodded approvingly. 'Good idea. We don't know how many men they'll have.'

'And there's a road that heads south out of Wemsworth. You have to go that way to join other main roads, so a car parked near the junction would see anyone going to and from the orphanage. The road on the north side of the village is little more than a track and leads only to farms and a small hamlet called Little Wem.'

Margot turned to Biddy. 'You're to stay here and try to help the other servants recover. If anyone called Sergeant Deemer comes you can tell him where we are. Repeat his name after me.'

'Sergeant Deemer.'

'You're to tell no one else what we're doing, not even Cook and the housekeeper. You hear me. Do not disobey me in this.'

'No, my lady. Sergeant Deemer. Don't tell anyone else.'

Margot turned with a sigh. Poor Biddy tried so hard, but basically she was a rather simple-minded girl. Perhaps she would make a better outdoor servant, though it wasn't usual to have female gardeners. It'd save a lot of money in broken crockery, that was sure. 'Shall we go, Finn? Who do you want to accompany us on foot, apart from Falding?'

'Daniel and Todd,' he said at once. 'I trust Charlie's new business partner. He has a good brain in his head.'

'Right. Let's go.' She set off through the shrubbery, pointing out the signs of the struggle and the path the kidnappers had taken, then leading them round the edge of a field and over a crude wooden stile.

After a few hundred yards they came to a high wall with pieces of broken glass cemented along the top. 'The orphanage,' she commented. 'Don't worry. I know a way into the grounds. I went everywhere round here as a child.'

When they got to the orphanage itself, however, there was no way of hiding their presence and someone yelled out that there were intruders. So they simply pushed their way in through the front door.

Children walking down the stairs took one look at them and the man who'd come out of a room to one side and fled upstairs again.

The man ducked back into the room as they started moving towards him, shouting, 'Intruders!'

'That's Clapton,' Finn murmured. 'A violent fellow. Watch out for him. Keep your gun hidden, Margot, but use it if you have to.'

Buddle came out of the door and barred their way, glaring at them.

'You're trespassing. Get out of this building or I'll have the police on you.'

'We've already called them,' Margot said. 'Anyway, there's no one at the local police station.'

'Fat lot you know.' He turned round and yelled, 'Clapton!

Call Sergeant Taylor on his personal phone line and report intruders.'

They heard the sound of a phone being picked up.

'Where's Reggie?' she demanded.

'He went off with Carlisle. Not seen him since.'

'You're a liar,' she said.

He folded his arms and leaned against the doorframe. 'You'll not find him here.'

'I'm going to search the ground floor rooms,' Finn said. 'Daniel, you stay with her ladyship and you others come with me.'

Buddle grinned and stayed where he was.

Unfortunately, as Margot had said, it was a rabbit warren of rooms and if someone wanted to hide, they no doubt knew the place better than a newcomer like Finn did.

When he heard a car draw up outside, he hurried back to the hall, asking Todd to stay at a junction of corridors and check whether anyone came and went. 'Yell if you need help.'

Todd nodded.

In the hall Finn found the elusive Sergeant Taylor ordering Margot to leave the premises.

He joined them. 'We'll leave as soon as we get Reggie back, not until.'

'If you don't obey my orders, I shall arrest you. And being *Lady* Terryng won't protect you, madam.'

'I'm going nowhere without my nephew.'

He pulled out a notebook. 'I want all of your names and addresses.'

'You probably know them already,' Margot said scornfully. 'You're just trying to waste time.'

'Why do you insist your nephew is here?'

'I followed the tracks of whoever kidnapped Reggie and they led straight here. The people who made them know nothing about moving round the countryside. They trample plants like a bull in a flower garden, leaving a clear trail.'

Now Buddle was glaring at Taylor and signalling with his eyes to do something about the visitors. But Taylor only glared back.

It seemed they were at an impasse.

We could do with Sergeant Deemer here, Finn thought but there was no sound of other cars pulling up outside.

Leah and Beth stopped the car and strolled round Wemsworth village centre. Not much to see, so they went back to sit in the car, ready to set off at a minute's notice.

A few minutes later, Leah noticed two lads who looked half-starved come out of the village shop carrying a big basket. 'Look, Beth. What's the betting they're from the orphanage.'

'They look as hungry as poor Reggie did at first.'

'Let's offer to buy them a cake. See if we can bribe some information out of them.' She left the car and approached the lads. 'You look hungry. Would you like a nice big currant bun each?'

'We haven't got to talk to anyone,' the taller boy said loudly.

Beth had come up on their other side. She said in a low voice, 'If you wait for us round the corner, just past the last house, we'll bring the buns to you there.'

He licked his lips, exchanged a quick glance with his companion and whispered, 'We can't wait long, missus, and we have to pretend we're not talking to you.' He raised his voice and said loudly, 'We can't talk to you and we have to get back.'

Leah was already on her way into the shop, where she bought some food, pretending it was for a picnic.

Beth stood by the car and quickly explained to the men hiding in the back what they were doing.

The two women walked slowly out of the village centre and round the corner.

The lads were hiding behind some bushes, clearly frightened of what they were doing. They must be ravenous to take this risk.

She held out the paper bag. 'Smell how good they are.' But she didn't let them take a bun, though it hurt her to deny them.

'What do we have to do for it?' one asked.

'Tell us if they brought Reggie back to the orphanage earlier today.'

They exchanged glances and the smaller one said, 'We're not supposed to know what they're doing.'

'I bet you do notice things, though.'

They nodded, eyes on the paper bag.

'Didn't see who it was,' one said, 'but they took him down to the cellar.'

'They allus take people down to the cellar to hit them,' the other added. 'So people outside can't hear the screams.'

He said it so matter-of-factly, her heart ached. 'Thanks. Here you are.' She thrust the bag at them and looked at Leah.

'Let's go. We need to tell the others where to look.'

They got into the car, talking loudly about how good the buns had tasted. As Leah drove off, Beth told the men hiding in the back what they'd found out.

But when they got to the orphanage, they saw a police car parked there, and it wasn't Sergeant Deemer's vehicle.

'You'd better get out now,' Leah said.

The two men did, stretching and grimacing as they eased out their stiffness.

'Do we go in or not?' Beth asked.

'I'll go in. You stay here. You have your children to think of.'

'No, I'm coming.'

'I'll come too,' Daniel said. 'Timmy can stay in the car. Give him the keys in case he has to drive us away quickly.'

The three of them walked into the building without being stopped and then followed the sound of angry shouting.

They found Margot, Falding and Finn confronting Buddle, Clapton and a man in police uniform with a sergeant's stripes.

'Must be Taylor,' Leah murmured. She strode forward to join them trying to look confident, with Beth and Daniel close behind her.

'Who the hell are you?' Buddle asked.

'Friends of ours, come to help,' Margot told him.

'Do it!' Buddle said suddenly to Taylor.

The man hesitated for a moment or two longer, then blew his whistle. Running footsteps heralded the arrival of two police constables, who must have been hiding somewhere.

'You're all under arrest unless you leave the house this minute,' Taylor declared.

'We'll go as soon as you produce Reggie,' Finn said, trying not to wince as one of the men bumped into him.

'He's *not* here.'

Margot opened her mouth to contradict him when another car drew up outside, so she said nothing.

'See who that is,' Taylor ordered the police constable standing nearest the door.

The man went out and they heard him hurry across the hall to the front door.

'Where are they?' asked a voice they all recognised.

29

Finn watched Taylor's face go chalk white. 'That's Deemer!' Buddle snorted. 'And he's been ordered to stay out of this. He's trespassing on your territory and he'll be in trouble with the inspector. You're in charge here, not him.'

Taylor took a deep breath, nodded and straightened up.

Finn shook his head as the others shot him questioning looks as if asking whether to do something. He wanted to wait till Deemer came in. He had a great deal of respect for the Rivenshaw sergeant, while this Taylor fellow seemed to be under Buddle's control.

Deemer strolled in, smiling, all alone.

Damnation! Finn thought. He hasn't brought any men and if ever I've smelled violence in the air, it's here.

'What are you doing here, Deemer?' Taylor demanded. 'You've been told to stay out of this from now on.'

'Have you found the lad?'

'Mr Buddle assures me he's not here.'

'And we traced him and his kidnappers across country to this very building,' Margot said. 'They left very clear tracks.'

'Taylor has made no attempt to search for the boy,' Finn put in.

'I doubt he knows where Reggie is. We need Buddle to tell us that,' Deemer said.

'*Mr* Buddle, if you please,' the owner of that name snapped.

'But I don't please. And I shall get angry if you mess me around.'

'Arrest him too!' Buddle told Taylor. 'He's been told to stay out of this.'

'I can't do that!'

There was a pregnant silence, then Deemer said, 'It looks as if we'll have to do it the hard way, then. Sergeant Edward Taylor, you're under arrest on suspicion of handling stolen goods, and also aiding and abetting *Mr* Lemuel Buddle in kidnapping one lad and ill-treating others.'

The two constables who'd come with Taylor gasped and one took a quick step backwards.

'Don't be ridiculous!' Buddle snapped. 'Sergeant Taylor is a well-respected police officer.'

'Not any longer. And I have proof he's been stealing.'

'You can't have!' Taylor stammered, then realised this might sound incriminating so added hastily, 'Because I haven't done anything wrong.'

'Are you coming quietly or do we need to handcuff you?'

'Coming where?'

'To see Judge Peters, who is waiting to hold a special hearing. You've been under suspicion for some time, you see.'

Taylor suddenly made a run for the door and Finn took great pleasure in tripping him up.

Ben stepped in to help, knowing that Finn's arm was injured. He fitted on the handcuffs Deemer took from his belt and tossed across to them.

'Now, Buddle, where have you hidden the boy?' Deemer asked quietly.

'I don't know what you're talking about. I have many boys here, but not Reginald Barston.'

Leah judged it time to step forward. 'We overheard someone talking in town and apparently he hides his victims in the cellars.'

Deemer smiled, a gentle smile that still somehow looked

triumphant. 'Then some of us will go down and search the cellars. Buddle and Clapton will come with us.'

As the sergeant said that, Finn noticed a lad slipping away from the door, a thin little boy with a big scar on one cheek that looked like a burn scar. Finn made a note of the face but said nothing. First they'd try the cellars. He'd only involve those poor, ill-treated lads as a last resort.

Two hours later, they'd searched every inch of the cellars and found nothing. Buddle refused to help in any way and stood in what seemed to be his favourite pose, with his arms folded across the top of his big belly.

Clapton kept eyeing the police nervously as he stood near Buddle.

'I'm just going up to consult my friend,' Finn said suddenly. He looked up to see the balcony still lined with boys, one of whom was the eavesdropper, who was not quite managing to hide behind a bigger boy.

'Stay where you are, lads. I'm not going to hurt you.' Finn went slowly up the stairs and stood at the top in the centre of the two rows of apprehensive faces. 'If someone wishes to shout out a way of helping us find Reggie, I shan't look at who it is. You see, if we can find Reggie, Mr Buddle will be under arrest and will be taken away from here and won't come back.'

There was a rustle of little movements and some whispering at that, then the thin boy with the scar was pushed forward.

Poor little sod! Finn thought. Talk about a sacrificial victim. He went across to the boy and said quietly, 'Please tell me what you know, what I should do to find Reggie.'

After some long seconds of hesitation someone else shouted out from the back of the crowd, 'Tell him, Natty.'

'Go into the farthest cellar and shout. If he's there, he'll answer you.'

'Where from?'

The lad looked agonised, but again that voice at the back yelled, 'Tell him!'

'There's a secret room. I don't know exactly where it is but some of us know it's there.'

Quite a few boys nodded their heads.

Finn straightened up. 'Stay here, lads, in case I need more help. We have to find Reggie and get Buddle locked away.'

They were clearly terrified but there were a few more nods at the way he ended that sentence and one or two echoed the words, 'Locked away'.

He went back down to the cellars and said, 'I've been told there's a secret room, but they don't know where. They think Reggie's there. If we go into the farthest cellar and shout loudly, maybe Reggie will hear and call out.'

For the first time, Buddle looked shaken, but he still said nothing. Clapton's expression was more fearful, however, so Finn began to hope.

He intended to find Reggie if he had to knock the building down to do so.

Reggie had been in a half-doze, worn out with worrying and trying to find a comfortable position. At first he thought he was dreaming, then he heard it again. Someone was calling his name.

He tried to respond, but hadn't been able to remove the gag and only a gurgle came out.

Despair filled him and he rolled from side to side, but still the gag didn't move.

Then he saw the piles of boxes start to rock and suddenly realised where his only chance of being heard lay. He kicked out with his bound feet at the untidy piles, kicked with all his might then kicked again.

The boxes tottered, hesitated and then began to fall.

Would they make enough noise? It sounded loud to him, but was it loud enough to be heard outside in the cellar?

One of them must have had crockery or glasses in it because it fell on the hard stone floor with a loud crashing sound.

He kicked out again, but nothing else made as much noise.

He could only pray that it had been enough.

The two younger women were standing together at the side of the cellar out of the way of the group of men surrounding her ladyship. Beth called out suddenly, 'That sounded like something breaking. Where did it come from?'

'I heard it too,' Leah agreed. 'You can't mistake that sound. It seemed to come from here.' She pointed to the wall they were standing near, which was covered in wooden panelling like a few other parts of the cellars.

Finn had been watching Buddle as they hunted, and the man's expression had given little away. But when Beth spoke, his face twitched and his mouth half-opened in what looked like surprise.

Were they on to something?

Finn moved across to the wall and began to feel the edges of the panelling, pressing and even thumping bits that looked different, trying to find some way of opening a secret door. It was just the sort of place for a landowner to hide his valuables.

Margot watched for a moment or two then came to join him. 'Let me do that. Unless I'm much mistaken, we have something similar at Netherholme. The two houses were built at the same time and designed by the same architect.'

She studied the wall, then walked along it staring at the floor. She bent and pressed part of the skirting board, but nothing happened.

'Might be at the other end,' she muttered and walked along to bend over and press another panel.

This time there was a muffled grating sound and a section

of the wooden wall began to move backwards. It only moved a few inches but when she pushed it, it behaved as any other door would, swinging inwards.

Finn saw the boy lying on the ground inside. 'Reggie!' He pushed past her ladyship to pick up the lad and cradle him close. 'You're safe, Reggie. We've got you.'

Beth was beside them, untying the gag first, then asking if someone had a knife.

Reggie began sobbing as his mouth was freed, then moaning as circulation returned to his hands and feet.

And all the time, Finn held him in his arms, cuddling him close, sensing that the boy needed that most of all.

Margot joined her to rub Reggie's hands as Beth rubbed his legs and feet. After a few moments, she asked, 'Can you carry him upstairs, Finn?'

'Yes. No.' He scowled down at his wounded arm.

Todd came forward. 'I'll do it.'

'Get him out of the cellar then, into the daylight. And get him something to drink,' Margot ordered.

They left Sergeant Deemer, with the help of the men they'd brought with them from Ellindale, to arrest Buddle. Clayton fought back but the men laughed and held him down while they borrowed a pair of handcuffs from the men who'd come with Sergeant Taylor, but who were now obeying Deemer's instructions.

While Deemer phoned in the news to Judge Peters first and regional headquarters second, Todd and Margot eased Reggie into the car and laid him on the back seat with his head on Finn's lap.

'We'll take him back to Netherholme where we can tend him properly,' Finn said.

Margot wound down her window to invite the sergeant and anyone else who'd helped to join them there. 'Someone needs to look after those boys,' she added.

'I'll organise that,' Todd called. 'I've worked in hotels and know how to organise catering for groups of people. I think what those boys need most of all is food and comfort.'

'Good man!' she called as the car pulled away.

When they stopped at Netherholme, Falding helped Reggie out. He'd have picked the boy up but Reggie insisted he could walk.

Finn kept his good hand on the lad's shoulder, though, because it felt like the right thing to do.

Margot walked towards the front door with them. 'We've got you safe now, Reggie.'

He stopped to say, 'I'm sorry, Aunt Margot. I'd not have gone away from the house, but there was a puppy crying. They'd got it tied up and I couldn't save it. Can you send someone to find it in the bushes near the library?'

'We've already found and freed it, don't worry.'

That seemed to cheer him up enough to lean his head against Finn's shoulder and close his eyes for a moment, then he started walking again.

At the front door he said, 'You won't let them put a nasty person in charge of the boys now, will you?'

'No, we won't,' she promised.

As they took him to sit down, he said suddenly, 'I think they killed Alan.'

Finn got the details of what he'd heard and went to ring Deemer.

When he came back, Reggie had a milky moustache and was tucking into a slice of Cook's fruitcake served by a maid who still looked rather sleepy.

There was a queue of people to use the phone at Netherholme. Leah phoned Spring Cottage to try to tell her husband what had happened. But he was still at Heythorpe House organising the defenders.

'No sign of trouble here,' he said at once when she got through to him.

'Oh, dear. Will Finn still have to worry about his cousin?'

'I'm not sure. One of the chaps says Judson is looking down in the mouth. He went out down the valley this morning and came back in a sour mood. His wife's already sporting a bruise.'

'I wonder why.'

'Some of the men from the village are wondering that, too. They're going to get him drunk tonight at the pub, pretending someone has had a lucky bet on the horses and is celebrating. Only they'll be spiking his drinks. If *I* were a betting man, I'd put money on them finding out exactly what he's been up to.'

'Good. I'll not be back till late. I'm helping Beth and Lady Terryng's cook to sort out some food for these half-starved lads. Sergeant Deeming is going to leave a couple of constables on duty here till a new director can be found for the orphanage.'

'Don't think you'll have a quiet life when you get back. The new batch of ginger beer is ready for your attention, and Peter has got us a few more regular orders. Charlie is coaching him on how to do it.'

'Trust Charlie.'

He could hear her soft little chuckle, a sound he loved. 'So you'll be able to give your full attention to your business from now on. There is still the grand opening of the youth hostel to be got through. Now the mayor is better, Charlie's talking about how to organise it.'

'Ah. I hoped he'd dropped that idea.'

'I'm afraid not.'

She paused and since he didn't speak about himself, she did, just hinting delicately. 'And I can pay more attention to my husband as well. You're all right, Jonah? You haven't overdone things today?'

'I'm perfectly well, thank you. I wasn't really needed here as it turns out. No one came to spy on Finn let alone attack him. I shall enjoy getting our peaceful lives back, though.'

She would too. Sort of. It could get a bit too quiet for her liking, and as her sister grew older, Rosa would have her own friends. But Jonah was so much better living in the fresh moorland air.

Well, he had been up till now. She knew his health was slipping, though he hadn't said a word. She scrubbed her eyes at that thought, took a few deep breaths and went back to work.

She'd deal with Jonah's health when she had to, when he let her.

That evening, when Reggie was fast asleep, Margot accepted a glass of wine from Finn, courtesy of a secret cache left in the cellar by one of his ancestors.

She took a few sips, then gave him a very sad look. 'It was you Reggie wanted, not me.'

Finn said nothing.

'I think it'd be wrong to take him away from you. You'll make a wonderful father.'

He didn't pretend. 'Are you sure?'

'Unfortunately, yes. But I hope you'll share him with me and let him come to stay at Netherholme from time to time.'

'Of course.' He took another sip then said, 'You love children. Have you thought of applying to take charge of the orphanage?'

She paused in surprise, wine glass halfway to her mouth, then set it down on the table with a hand that suddenly felt weak with longing. 'Do you think they'd let me? Won't they want a man?'

'Of course they'll let you.' He grinned. 'What, have a real lady in charge of their orphanage? The trustees will snap your hand off if you offer. And if they haven't got enough funds, you've had experience at fundraising for charities.'

'I think I might like that.'

After a moment or two she said, 'Finn?'

'Mmm?' He was feeling tired, wanting to get to bed.

'When are you going to sort out your own future?'

He woke up fully again at that, asking cautiously, 'What do you mean?'

'That nice girl is madly in love with you, as you are with her. Surely you're not going to let silly ideas of class and status come between you?'

'No. I'm not. But she's not coming back till tomorrow. And I have to catch her at the right moment. She's more conscious of my money than I am.'

'Don't leave it too long.'

'I have to be sure I'm not putting her in danger. Buddle swears blind he's not involved in any plot to kill me and Sergeant Deemer believes him, because Clapton said the same thing, looked genuinely astonished at the idea that they'd waste their time on that when there was money to be made from Reggie.'

'Are the men of the village still planning to tackle Judson?'

'Yes. They're going to get him to confess, then hand him over to Sergeant Deemer.'

'You've done well for this village; won people's loyalty.'

'There are some very nice people living here. They deserve better than to rot on the dole.'

'You'll find a way to help them.' She raised her glass to him and drained it, then said firmly, 'Bed!'

Epilogue

It wasn't till the third evening after Beth's return from the orphanage that Finn saw his way clear. Don from the pub and two men from the village had come to see him that afternoon, behaving very formally for once.

'We got Judson drunk last night and found out that you were right. Someone was paying him for information. He doesn't know who exactly, but he dealt with a man called John apparently.'

'A nice common name, hard to trace. What's the betting the man's called something else?'

'Any road, he got a message the day after that kerfuffle at Wemsworth to say they no longer needed his services. So we think whoever it is might have given up trying to harm you.'

'I hope so. I've been taking a few steps of my own. I got a letter from my lawyer to say that my cousin has accepted my offer of a thousand pounds if he'll emigrate to Canada, only payable in Canada.'

'You gave him money, and him trying to murder you?' Don exclaimed.

'I gave him money as I could afford to get danger off my back. I want to settle here in Ellindale in peace, marry, have children. I've a couple of schemes in mind that will help the village. The ability to do that is well worth a thousand pounds. I'm not a man who hankers after riches.'

'No, but you're one of the kindest chaps I've ever met,'

Don said and offered his hand. 'I wish you well. She's a nice lass.'

'I haven't told her anything yet. Don't give me away.'

The men chuckled. 'You both give yourselves away every time you look at one another.'

They left still smiling.

It had been a fine late summer day with a taste of autumn in the morning air. But the evening was still warm enough for a stroll round the gardens. Finn had a word with Mrs Jarratt and Dilys, asking them to send Beth out to see him on the level patch of ground where he'd had a rough bench installed.

'Oh, and make sure Reggie doesn't interrupt us. Since Margot went home he's hardly left my side.'

They smiled knowingly. 'We'll see he doesn't interrupt you, sir.'

He could feel himself flushing as he went outside.

It wasn't long before Beth joined him. 'Did you want something, sir?'

'Several things. Please sit down, Beth.'

'It's not right for me to sit down with you.'

'Please.' He waited till she'd sat down and went on, 'The second thing I want is for you to stop calling me "sir" or "F-sir".'

She looked at him in puzzlement. 'You're sacking me? What have I done wrong?'

'I'm not sacking you.' He took her hand. 'But I am making a mess of this. Beth, darling, we have feelings for one another, surely you're not going to deny that?'

'But—'

'I love you, Beth. And I think you care about me.'

'But—'

'There are no buts. We're both free, I have a home to offer

you, a life together, I hope. Please, darling, let's get married soon. There's no longer any need to wait, let alone pretend we don't care.'

A smile slowly replaced her frown. 'You sound very determined . . . Finn.'

'I am. Very determined indeed.'

'What will people say?'

He chuckled at that. 'People have been telling me to speak out and marry you for a while now, including all the servants, Leah and her family, Margot, everyone except Reggie. I don't think he notices things like that.'

He waited and she raised his hand to her cheek. 'I can't think of anything more wonderful than to marry you, Finn.'

At which he stopped treading carefully and kissed her with all the love in his heart.

It was a while before they pulled apart.

'So it's agreed,' he said.

'Do you think I'd have kissed you like that if I weren't going to marry you?' She proved her agreement with his plans by kissing him again, even more passionately.

Later, as they stood up, he said, 'You know I'll be happy to be a father to your children.'

'Yes, I know. They love it when you play with them. What's going to happen about Reggie?'

'Margot says he's mine and she won't tear us apart as long as she can borrow him from time to time.'

'He'll be very happy about that. He's been worrying, dreading the idea of leaving you.' She looked towards the house and gasped. 'Just look at that.'

All the servants were standing at the corner watching them fondly, with Reggie in front of them.

He broke ranks to rush across to them. 'Is it true, Uncle Finn? Are you really going to marry Beth?'

'Yes. I'm delighted to say she's accepted me.'

'That's wonderful!' He turned a quick somersault to show his delight.

'Come and give me a kiss, then,' she said.

He flushed and glanced at Finn doubtfully.

'You have to kiss someone who's going to be like a mother to you. Women insist on it.'

'I used to kiss my mother's right cheek.' He moved forward and planted an awkward kiss on Beth's cheek, but she pulled him into her arms and not only kissed him back but gave him a big hug.

When she let go, he stepped back and turned another cartwheel, shouting 'Yippee!' at the top of his voice.

'He's irrepressible,' Finn said.

'Thank goodness. I don't want him losing that exuberance.'

He indicated the waiting group of women. 'We'd better go and accept their congratulations now. They've been very patient.'

So it was hugs and kisses all round, and Finn felt as if the world had settled into a more peaceful rhythm. He had so many plans, but first he wanted to marry Beth, and the sooner the better.

And if his arm hurt a little, he didn't care. But she did. She guided him inside and sat him down in the sitting room. But this time she sat down next to him and took hold of his hand of her own accord.

This is my fashionable great-aunt on my father's side.
Peg quite a gal and she was his favourite relative. She was always very
lively, even in her old age – and dyed her hair bright red when she
was 70, maybe in a protest against declining into old age.
That would be like her.

I couldn't resist using Auntie Peg (again). This is a sketch of her as a
young woman, done by an admirer. We have the original.

I felt we should show something of the other side of my family.
This is my great-grandmother on my mother's side. Ann Wild was the
mother of seven, my granddad being one of the younger ones.
She looks elegant, don't you think? She was quiet and kind in nature.

Don't miss the third book in Anna Jacobs' heart-warming *Ellindale* saga

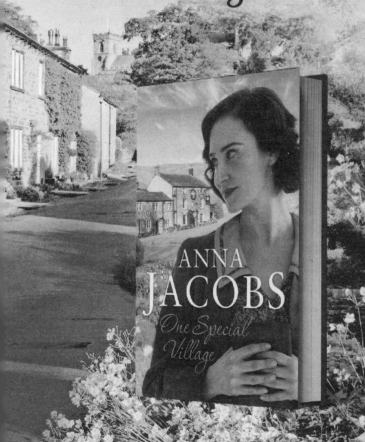

ANNA
JACOBS

One Special Village

Out in ebook September 2018

CONTACT ANNA

Anna is always delighted to hear from readers and can be contacted via the internet.

Anna has her own web page, with details of her books, some behind-the-scenes information that is available nowhere else and the first chapters of her books to try out, as well as a picture gallery.

Anna can be contacted by email at
anna@annajacobs.com

You can also find Anna on Facebook at
www.facebook.com/AnnaJacobsBooks

If you'd like to receive an email newsletter about Anna and her books every month or two, you are cordially invited to join her announcements list. Just email her and ask to be added to the list, or follow the link from her web page.

www.annajacobs.com